Sp



# Space Zero

# The Meld

Author: Rjohn Mills

# Space Zero The Meld

## Title Page

Space Zero The Meld


ISBN: 978-1-257-91527-9

Cover Art: by the Author.

This book is a work of Fiction. The people and places originated in the thoughts and daydreams of the author and any connection to entities in the real world entities is purely coincidental.

First Edition: 2011-August-14 (6th Draft)

ISBN 978-1-257-91527-9
90000
9 781257 915279

# Space Zero The Meld

## Other Books by the Author

Books by Rjohn Mills

*Space Zero* ***The Meld***

***Poems are Forever*** - *Volume One*

## About the author

Rjohn was born as the computer revolution began and took to it like a duck to water. After a short stint in the military the IT industry became his lifelong career. It allowing him to live and work throughout the UK, in many cities across Australia, and inevitably to enjoy the great diversity of peoples found only here in the USA. Travel exposed him to cultures as diverse as the Nepalese Gurkhas, and residents of the world's greatest cities.

Home is where you hang your hat! And RJohn's hats have been at home in far too many places.
His interest in poetry began as a way to keep in touch with friends overseas, more personal than just sending an inter-flora bouquet.
And when word processors arrived, with those wonderful built-in spell checkers, the last obstacle to writing a novel evaporated overnight.

While 'Resting' between contracts the ideas for THE MELD germinated in his fertile mind but being a perfectionist the novel was slow to mature.

It has now 'Come of Age!'

### For the lovers of Poetry

Visit my poetry website at: **www.poemsareforever.com**

There is a link to let you email your views and comments about the poems and/or this novel.

It also has the link to my Novel page on the Lulu website.

# Space Zero The Meld

## The Meld

A billion sentient minds that comprised the Meld prepared for action. They, the incorporeal survivors of a once dominant species basking atop the food chain, holding governance over a thousand far flung galaxies, they through their own arrogance and conceit were struggling to simply stay "alive". Now, as an endangered species, ***they*** were fighting for survival and the battle was slowly turning against them.

As their civilization reached its pinnacle, as they commanded instantaneous travel across the universe and controlled the physical realm down to the lowest quantum level, their egotism pushed too hard. They aimed for the ultimate in evolution. They dared to challenge Death itself. The prize was immortality, freedom from the petty restrictions of a cumbersome physical form, the sharing of group consciousness for all eternity. Temptation beckoned with the promise of eternal peace and harmony. Their leaders pushed for 'The Joining' and eagerly the masses followed.

But there were subversives, dissenters who demanded independent thought.

The Meld remembered them well, a reticent minority craving personal power and wealth, craving status and leadership, craving dominion over their peers. Never would they willingly join the Meld, never would they willingly share their minds in balance and harmony for the good of the many. Not for them an evolving communal whole in which all members could participate, where stronger minds willingly supported those less fortunate.

For the dissidents there was no middle ground.

# Space Zero The Meld

The appointed time arrived. Ten trillion minds supported by the energy of a million stars congregating for the first time inside the super massive black hole at the center of their galaxy. Their minds merged, marinating within the immense energies that would never be exhausted. At last, democratically, they would determine the future of their species.

From the moment voting began every meldling could feel the sway of the communal decision, and it swayed inexorably in favor of ... the permanent joining of minds.

Then suddenly, without warning, disaster!

A billion dissidents attacked with blinding force!

Like a static jolt surging through the Meld the rebel minds screamed "FIRE" and dropped from the flow. But before the communal consciousness could respond, it suffered torturous, agonizing pangs of separation as the million suns went supernova. The saboteurs squandered their very life-force channeling every nova deep into the heart of the Meld. But they underestimated the immensity of their task. Their ethereal discipline untested and weak -- collapsed. Control failures cascaded like an alpine avalanche unleashing the totality of unfocused destruction against a defenseless corporeal universe. The 'would be' martyrs failed miserably, signing their own death warrants and sentencing every living creature across a thousand galaxies to the worst extinction event the universe would ever know.

Barely a billion meldlings survived the pain. Many returned to their bodies only die needlessly in galaxies sterilized and devoid of life. Slowly, still in shock, the survivors clustered together salvaging what little technical and cultural knowledge they could. But too much was missing. The novae annihilated every planet and every databank leaving pitifully little untouched. What had

survived lay strewn among a handful of starships in transit between the galaxies. Now those automated, crewless vessels, devoid of purpose and destiny were for all practical purposes marooned in a dark, lifeless space.
Horrendous as the loss of all galactic life was, it dwarfed in comparison to the Meld's predicament. With their culture annihilated in the blink of an eye, their utopian dreams shattered beyond repair, the meldlings were stranded in a disembodied nightmare. After the vote they should have returned to their bodies to lead rich, full lives until old age was upon them. Only then, as their bodies approached death, would each mind permanently merge with the Meld to spend eternity as an incorporeal lifeform of pure energy. The disaster was catastrophic. Now, prematurely trapped in immortal exile, isolated from the corporeal realm, the Meld was doomed. Without a regular influx of new meldlings to swell their numbers and stimulate their minds stagnation was inevitable. Without interaction with the physical universe their very sentience would cease to have use or meaning. Time would become irrelevant while their minds would atrophy and wither. The Meld would become as insignificant as a photon in a black hole.
They had one hope: symbiosis, co-existence with a physical life form in the newer, healthier galaxies far beyond their own lifeless zone of death. For the incorporeal meldlings locating a host was the easy part and they found many suitable species. But to make contact the Meld needed scarce bio-tech resources that lay stranded in a few surviving starships that would take millennia to transverse the universe. If the precious catalytic bio-mass could survive the arduous journey the Meld's fragile link with the physical realm might be saved and through it control of the Morph Class starship

themselves. Once they made landfall on a living planet the bio-mass could be cultivated and grown, their technology rebuilt, and symbiosis would swiftly follow.
For ten millennia the Meld attempted to merge consciousness with primitive species but with little success. Mammalian thinking habits were too feeble, too inferior for telepathy and the few exceptional individuals who could tolerate contact became outcastes in their own societies. When new ideas clashed with the 'Knowledge of the day' persecution and torture followed, and even without social pressure, enlightening most sentient life forms was almost impossible. They stubbornly refused to see what was staring them in the face - or falling on their heads! It became clear; until a species was ready to accept the challenge of space travel its minds were too tethered by instinct and crude emotion to accept First Contact. But time was on its side.
The Meld would endure and wait.

Five times a new species emerged within the Milky Way and ventured to explore beyond its sun.
Five times the Meld approached.
Five times total failure.
Five times the Meld sanctioned the genus, clearing the way for a new and better life-form to evolve.

Now Humans had reached the optimal stage of evolution.
For the sixth time the Meld prepared for First Contact.
The trap was primed, the lure was set.
Then, like a deadly spider on its web, the Meld watched and waited … … …

A billion sentient minds that comprised the Meld prepared for action!

# Space Zero The Meld

## Space-Zero

Darkon soared upward trading safety for exhilaration. He balanced precariously on the turbulent updrafts ravaging the wastelands of Devestus-7 savoring the sunlit panorama a thousands feet below his wings.

"Below his wings?"

That wasn't right.

Somewhere in the deep recesses of his mind Darkon sensed something was awry; but the thought was elusive, as elusive as the Thouger Moles he would be hunting as the evening daylight faded.

Suddenly a piercing alarm ripped through his mind. His auditory nerves trembled under harsh dissonant abuse as blinding kaleidoscopic colors writhed incongruously across his field of view. Instinctively he recoiled from the onslaught.

Slowly, painfully slowly, the jagged rasping faded, the rainbows began to dissolve. He felt the reassuring pressure of his "G" seat as it adjusted for imminent launch. Virtual Reality collapsed, returning him to full consciousness. The long wait was over.

As the captain of Galactic Lifeship LS48, Darkon Myzelv's career demanded the VR implant. It was crucial for superluminary flight and a blessing during the long hours spent strapped in a starship cockpit awaiting a launch that might happen only once or twice a month. Today, all afternoon, he had co-existed sharing the mind of an exotic bird of prey soaring over its native habitat. But now alarms were ringing and Capt. Myzelv was back in the real world. He was on duty, but more importantly he was ***the*** on-call duty pilot of a lifeboat starship, and someone somewhere was in distress and needed help.

**SOS - MAYDAY - SPACE-ZERO.**

# Space Zero The Meld

Emergency calls had changed little as mankind advanced from the sea, to the sky, and pushed outward into deep-space. Centuries of tradition demanded the highest commitment from the crews of every life-vessel that heard the call. Darkon was such a man. Celebrating his thirtieth birthday later this primary year he was captain of LS48, a four-man interstellar Fast Response Lifeship. He thrived on the excitement, the danger, the challenge to beat the odds and save the fearless men and women who braved the hazards of space so others could enjoy their worlds in peace. He loved his job.

Deep Space Rescue, a subsidiary of Galactic Merchant Insurance (GMI), emerged to combat escalating claims as entrepreneurs pushed the limits of deep space mining. Fiscal loss turned to profit when leading edge safety-surveillance equipment was installing in every registered starship. Rescue was fast becoming a rare event.

**BUT NOW… … …**

**Space-Zero! Space-Zero! Zogar! Zogar!**

The emergency call identified the stricken vessel as the Zogar. "Zogar" was the ships registered name and by convention the callsign for its GMI computer. At a single click or the failure to response at a regular checkpoint it would engaged Emergency-Mode and transmitted the galactic SPACE-ZERO distress call to the nearest GMI Lifepost.

Jana Rook, duty officer at the Sol-Outer station, responded immediately. She interrogated the data stream. The stricken vessel, the Zogar, was a class two heavy ore transporter. It was stranded on the outskirts of the galaxy more than a primary year from its destination.

'Good' she muttered to no one in particular, 'it's one of ours.' Then in a commanding tone,
'LS48. Stand by for launch,'
'LS48. Stand by for launch.'
'Base to LS48' Jana's voice echoed over the intercom. 'Status please'
The lifeship crew, already strapped into their launch seats, waited impatiently.
'LS48 to Base - Captain Myzelv, Ready to Launch'
'Base to LS48 - Stand by to receive data'
'LS48 standing by' he paused watching the monitor as the data loaded, 'Transmission Complete'
'Base to LS48 - Launch when ready, good luck Darkon.'
'LS48 - All lights green - Launch is GO.'
He thumbed the authority sensor. Instantly it confirmed his identity and activated the undocking sequence. The lifeship hummed, magnetic locks released and atomic engines gently nudged the Lifeship out of orbit. Soon they would be in StarThrust shattering Einstein's theoretical limitations on light speed.
StarThrust was new. For centuries portal 'doorways through space' were used to load cargo into low orbit starships and for sub-space communication. But tragedy spawned evolution when a frightened hitch-hiker became sole survivor on a crippled starship. With thrusters destroyed, a dead comms system, and the water supply drained into the vacuum of space his fate was sealed.
Then, while contemplating his imminent demise, he remembered the volatile cargo he'd helped load. Maybe, if he could explode some of it inside the ruptured thruster pod it would send the ship drifting slowly towards the commercial space lanes. If he was lucky, in a couple of decades his remains would get an honorable if somewhat belated burial and bring closure for his family back home.

With nothing else to fill his last hours he used the portals to maneuver cargo into the thruster pod. Ignition though was a problem. He needed at least 2400°C. Then inspiration! A portal could link the thruster pod to the local star. That would be more than enough energy to ignite the payload.

After adjusting the settings he reopened the portal. The cargo erupted but more violently than he expected. Life threatening G-forces were manifest throughout the ship and with inertial damping offline he was slammed backward into the aft bulkhead suffering a concussion that left him drifting in and out of consciousness for several days. Finally, when the fog in his head began to clear, he gazed up to see the stars streaming across the starboard monitor and realized he was still hallucinating. After all, his ship was adrift in space on route its rendezvous with civilization some twenty-years hence. But a day later the stars were racing past even faster. Had the ship been salvaged? Was it even now being tractored to safety? Why hadn't the salvagers resuscitated him? Desperately he scanned surrounding space. There was nothing, navigation was still online but displaying a velocity way above the ships design parameters and it was still climbing. But without thrusters - impossible!

Then Portal Control caught his eye. With no one around to collapse it, it was still active, and having a clear pathway through the thruster pod, the solar wind had been radiating aft of the ship for more than a week. Realization slowly sunk in…. … …. the Solar Wind! That was where thrust was coming from, a steady constant acceleration, and the reason for the dying starships excessive speed. The ship had power! **Eureka!**

If he could recycle what little water remained in his own body, if he could survive just a few more weeks, and if he could make it to the safely of his home planet he'd have a patent every engineer in the Milky Way would envy. He had invented **Portal Thrust**.

One Sol-3 year later, funded by a bottomless pit of royalties, he upped the ante again. Using surplus energy from inside the thruster pods he augmented his Portal Thrust with Gravity Sync. Adding gravity to the equation changed all the rules. While starship speeds remained limited by Einstein's famous equations the Gravity Bubbles that now encased them obeyed a higher authority. Within the G-Bubble, just like at the moment of the Big Bang, the laws of Newtonian Physics are trumped by the Laws of Gravity. To a distant observer, as the G-Bubble breaches the light barrier it ceases to exhibit length. It becomes a flat two-dimensional disk travelling broadside through space at superluminary speed.

He named his second invention: **StarThrust** and it became an overnight success.

It was indispensable for starship travel, the perfect, clean power source for journeying immense galactic distances. The free, unlimited energy tapped from the stars is the lifeblood of the Lifeship fleet. But dangers exist. StarThrust is susceptible to strong gravity wells that make maneuvering within star systems impractical. It forces every lifeship post to reside on the outermost planet of their system. But despite the constraints GMI boasts its lifeships will achieve StarThrust within twelve minutes of launch.

Darkon turned towards Geney smiling as he watched her initiate a micro-portal for a sub-space link to the Zogar. Geney Gound was the comms officer assigned to him when he took command of LS48 and his feelings for her had grown stronger with time. Although four years his junior, she proved more than capable handling the complex algorithms needed for stable portals. He could rely on her to have a comms link up and running within minutes of launch. True to form, as he watched, she turned to him'

'We've made contact with the Zogar. Ray Rongo's the captain. He's dumping the flight data directly to us now, do you want to speak to him?'

Darkon nodded tapping the comms icon on his monitor.

'Hello Ray.'

The rugged face of the prematurely aged space hermit grinned out of the viewer. He was a tall man and ideally suited to the Long Haul life. His full brown beard was balanced by a deep red mop of floating hair and between them like a pair of spinney caterpillars stood two of the bushiest eyebrows ever recorded. He would be well suited the leading roll in the Tri-Di serial:

**'Primitives of AZNEA-2'.**

'Darkon?' He paused, 'Darkon Myzelv?'

'Hello Ray - yes, it's me.'

'You made captain? Last time we met you were chief engineer on the Eve-3/Bounty shuttle.'

'That was my last trip Ray. GMI finally sponsored my pilot training. I've been with them for over four years now. But what's up with you and Zogar? The figures show nothing amiss.'

Ray frowned wearily.

'It's not the ship but I can't explain it on an open channel. Switch to E3 and scramble.'

They switched, and ran through security protocols.

'So, what *is* the problem Ray?'

'It all started,' he began, 'when I entered this poorly charted star system two days ago. The scanners detected an ice chunk in solar orbit, a little unusual I know, but nevertheless I sent a remote probe to collect some virgin $H_2O$. The ship's been recycling water for eighteen months so you can imagine how awful it tastes. It's been heaven drinking fresh water again. Well, following standard procedure I cut power and went into free fall while the ice was collected. Up till then everything was textbook perfect. Zogar produced a plot of the probe's sortie to file in the ship's log and that's when I noticed it: ONE probe trace going out to the ice, and TWO traces coming back. The second was so faint I almost missed it, but when Zogar flagged it with a "UFO" ID it really stood out. The problem is: the object's holding position in the exhaust path of Zogar's main drive so when the engines power up it'll be engulfed. I don't mind exploding the damn thing but not without knowing what it is. It's dangerously close, and if its power cell blows it could take out both me and the Zogar. I'm no expert but it's behaving like an old guard-dog mine from the pre-federation wars.'

'No chance Ray, the war didn't come within ten light years of your sector, and in any case, the power cells were deliberately non-rechargeable so this sort of problem wouldn't happen. But you're right not to risk a start-up. What else do you have?'

'Not much. It occasionally sends a laser burst to the inner third planet. But there's no indication of intelligent life down there just a few class 'M' creatures.'

'Laser, that's rather primitive. Have you located the receiving station planetside?'

'Found nothing, Darkon, I'll run some more scans and have a full analysis by the time you get here but Zogar's only tuned to detect raw materials not modern technology. I'm hoping you guys can pick up something I've missed'

'OK Ray. Our ETA is just over seventeen hours. We enter StarThrust in three minutes so we'll be out of contact till then. LS48 signing off.'
'Zogar out' Ray replied and terminated the link.
Since launching Trudel Stamar, LS48's navigator, had been busy plotting a course to rendezvous with the Zogar. The flight technique was straight forward, once beyond gravity effect of the base and with StarThrust engaged they would accelerate at maximum power to the halfway point then reverse thrust and decelerate at maximum power for the second leg. Only two restrictions applied. They must avoid the gravity wells of all star systems, and other vessels in recognized space lanes. Those factors aside, lifeships have Right of Way throughout the galaxy.
She locked the course into NavCom and began to tie in detours to compensate for time distortion once they broke through the light barrier and went superluminary.

Grinning with amusement she recalled the fears that had beset mankind as he mastered technology and began to race.

1) You cannot drive a horse-less carriage faster than an animal can run.
   The air rushing down your throat that fast will choke you to death,
   THEN SOMEONE INVENTED THE AUTOMOBILE
   - Oops Mr. Ford, You shouldn't be getting rich that way… … …

2) A heavier than air machine can never fly,
   AND THEN ONE DID!

- Oops - Mr. Wright and Mr. Wright, You should have been wrong… …

3) You can never fly faster than the speed of sound, AND THEN SONIC BOOMS BECAME COMMONPLACE!
- Opps Concord - You shouldn't fly that fast with passengers… … …

4) You can never fly as fast as the speed of light, BUT A STAR-FIGHTER PILOT, WHO DIDN'T UNDERSTAND THE RULES, (AND DIDN'T BELIEVE IT WAS IMPOSSIBLE) - DID IT
and promptly got blinded by the spectrum-flash.
- Oops Cordineé - You've broken the rules… … …

5) If you fly faster than light you'll age slower than the people you leave behind, your family and friends will die of old age before you return home a couple of days later.
BUT THEN "THEY" DISCOVERED TIME AND GRAVITY COULD WORK TOGETHER AND AVOID THE DILEMMA!
- Oops Mr. Einstein! We need your help, just a few more calculations…

Admittedly there was some substance to the last fear, but only if you flew at a constant superluminary speed. If you were always accelerating or decelerating and pulling at least two light-gravities, it would take less than nine primary days to transverse the Milky Way while your folks back home would age just sixteen days. Better still, since the pay office remains in the same perspective of the space/time as your family and friends, you get paid credits for the discrepancy... The saying, “Pilots don’t show their age!” had taken on new meaning.

Even today horror stories run rife of crews who disappear in superluminary flight, none more so than the Tri-Di feature films beamed across the spaceways by the mass entertainment media. Their crews arrive decades into the future to save their own descendants from a host of macabre foes both living and mechanical and all by using primitive weapons long forgotten by the future peoples. Good comedy, but very, very unreal.

‘Transition - TEN seconds!’ The warning came from William Forrest, the ship’s engineer. He had been with the Lifeship Fleet for several years but this was his first sortie on LS48, a sudden replacement when a routine medical revealed an unexpected pregnancy for his predecessor. There were still couples who preferred natural conception to the more convenient and controlled genetic selection demanded by the bio-mechanical incubators. It did of course complicate the population controller’s task: unplanned variables in their neat projections, but once in a while a new and useful gene pattern appeared and once tested became available for future parents to choose. The timing was perfect for William. He had been top of the waiting list for a lifeship posting for more than two years, and took a perverse pleasure in replacing his *own wife*. To the rest of the crew it was a bonus. He had been a part of their off duty life for some time since he joined his spouse at the Lifepost. His specialization in StarThrust technology kept him in touch with the latest high-tech developments making him a valuable man aboard any space vessel

# Space Zero The Meld

## Superluminary Flight

**'Three! - Two! - One! - Transition!'** The spectrum-flash struck and the ship went dark. From now on they would be in total blackout until their lifeship dropped to sub-light speed seventeen hours from now. Simultaneously four VR-umbilicals connected activating the crew's man-to-ship interface. Unlike their domestic counterpart, Superluminary-VR is unable to use radio waves and relies on direct electrical connection with implant contacts at the base of the skull. And although human perception is replicated quite well, more subtle detail within ship can be ambiguous or lost. The ship's fixed equipment is displayed accurately but must be augmented with ghost images of moveable items at their last known positions. Control stations on the bridge are displayed best especially when the VR-umbilical is plugged directly into the unit. Their sensors synchronized the image with the physical world even ghosting the crew's hands into the scene. Display icons glow when they are touched and moved and eerie blue/red light shows the position of objects not normally associated with that station. A circular blue glow tinged with pale red is a very important marker. The reddish hue indicates heat.
Access that item … … … and you can finish your mug of steaming coffee before it gets cold!
Trudel leaned back in the nav-seat monitoring the flight path. After twelve hours with only minor corrections to break the monotony she began to feel tired, even though her bio-scan showed she was good for another hour. She waited patiently for Geney to relieve her. Forty minutes later a flashing message superimposed itself on her VR image. Texting had come back into fashion, but without the need for keyboard skills. Taught at school, most

students could mind-generate text as easily as speaking. Their history teachers compare it with watching non-interactive 2-D movies with a system called 'Sub Titles'. The ancient saying, 'A picture paints a thousand words' is true for most situations but an abstract concept is still conveyed more easily by a single word. And in space, there are many abstractions.
"READY TO TAKE OVER" read Geney's text,
"HOW ARE WE DOING?"
"ON COURSE GENEY 2% AHEAD OF SCHEDULE CHECK DARKON IS AWAKE WHEN WE GO SUB-LUMINARY AND CALL ME TOO YOU HAVE CONTROL GOODNIGHT"
"I HAVE CONTROL PLEASANT DREAMS TRUDEL OF ANYONE BUT DARKON HE'S MINE!"
"HE IS?" challenged Trudel, and immediately broke contact before Geney could text a reply.
The frustration driven by the "LINK TERMINATED" signoff began to show on her bio-scan. Quickly she brought her vital functions back to normal. It would be 'inappropriate' to have an unaccountable fluctuation on her medi-chart at the end of the sortie. She wouldn't be able to look Darkon in the face for weeks if she triggered the medical alarms and the diagnosis was: ***Jealousy***.
Geney recalled the day she and Darkon met; and how her emotions ran amuck lacking her normal self-discipline. There had been a glimpse of excitement in his eyes too. It had been there, fleetingly, but in the blink of an eyelid it disappeared. In the two years they served together only once had vulnerability dared trespass there again. They had volunteered for an eco-mission after nine breeding pairs of Heffis birds thought to be extinct were confiscated by federal police during a smuggling crackdown. They were to be released on a sanctuary

planet within a protected system but after contracting a deadly viral infection were quarantined for months while vets fought to save their lives. When the birds were finally declared fit Darkon and Geney were invited to the release ceremony. A year later the chief veterinary sent a video of the first hatchlings, and Darkon's eyes had welled with tears as he watched. He had been unusually quiet for the rest of the day. But by the morning his usual cold repose had returned.

During the early months Geney tried to get close to him. It was not that he rejected her; just that he wouldn't, or couldn't, respond. She yielded to temptation and accessed his history files. Unlike the population in general, he had zero security on his personal data; it was available for anyone in the galaxy to inspect. She did. But if there had been hope of finding a clue to his behavior it would not be from that source. Apart from continuous bursts of delta brainwaves, which appeared consistently in his annual medic-scans, he was a textbook case of health and stability. At one time she considered his being a genetically modified mutant. The experiments had been banned two centuries ago but rumors abound of underground facilities for those who can afford the price. For seven thousand credits you can have any genetic makeup imaginable and no restrictions on staying within HUMAN constraints. However for those who are caught the punishment is server. The minimum penalty for contaminating the gene pool is sterilization, with all parties forfeiting procreation rights. But the innocent victim, the resulting offspring, being a potential but indeterminable genetic risk to the whole of humanity is exiled for life to an isolation satellite. The protective measures may seem cruel and inhuman, until you recall the lenient government of Charter-XIX in Sector G. They allowed mutant humanoids full citizenship rights within jurisdiction of their solar system until a mutant growth gene regressed creating an airborne catalyst. It was genocide for all three viable planets. Fortunately they were distant enough from mainstream population centers for the infection to be contained but within two generations their civilization was dead. Four billion lives was the price they paid for the 'right to life' of one genetically altered mutant.

Her unfounded fears ended after a stag night where his drinks had been laced by the mischievous host. She had found him outside his quarters highly intoxicated and 'arguing' with the security computer to open his access door. The voice activation unit had only a sober voice print on record and refused to recognize him. Despite this he was carrying on a carefully constructed argument attempting to persuade the door to make allowance for his state of inebriation, and to extrapolate from the original voice patterns allowing for the 'SLUR' factor. While this technique might have worked on an office or domestic door, hotels are renowned for using the cheapest models with virtually no AI and this one was no exception. Darkon had not pre-loaded a drunken voice print so the door would remain locked. She persuaded him to return to her unit on the pretext of hot black coffee and he had proven unbelievably talkative. He spoke of a violent childhood, a sadistic, alcoholic mother whose sole interest in him was for support in her old age. To escape her influence he joined the Federation Engineering Corps and after an honorable discharge began civilian life with an Interplanetary Ferry Service. He had had few affairs, none lasting more than a year or two, and when his last relationship collapsed he left the turbulence of the galactic center to take a posting on the mining base of Bounty.

Since then he had been a loner. That night he slept cradled in her arms, curled up before the simulation log fire, snuggling beneath a soft warm rug.
In the morning over breakfast she had teased him about their nocturnal activities. His eyes relaxed focus for several seconds as he delved deeply into his mind. Then he replied simply, 'We both know nothing happened'.
'I wish it had, Oh I wish it had!' The thought screamed through her mind but she held her peace. It was neither the time nor the place to press the issue. When his focus returned he was looking deeply into her eyes, 'thank you Geney.' he added so quietly that she barely caught the words. Then leaning across the table he drew her closer and gently kissed her forehead. He turned and left. She felt an ache deep inside her as the door closed behind him. That ache had stayed with her for many hours.
"HELLO!" texted Darkon, "HOW LONG BEFORE WE CAN SEE AGAIN?"
"YOU'RE AWAKE GOOD TIMING ABOUT TEN MINUTES TO GO WE'RE TWELVE MINUTES AHEAD OF SCHEDULE"
"OK I'LL WAIT FOR TRANSITION BEFORE I GET UP GENEY HOW IS WILLIAM?"
"I'M ALREADY UP" texted the engineer, "YOU KNOW I CAN'T SLEEP IN THIS STATE"
The chatter stopped. Not that texting was hard work, but because they would be talking normally again in a few minutes. Time seeped by.
"TRANSITION IMMINENT"
This time it was the NavCom broadcasting to the crew.

Five seconds later the spectrum-flash struck again.
Sound and vision jumped back as reality replaced simulation, as their senses returned to normal.

'Ready crew - Brunch in five minutes' William's voice echoed through the cabin. Somehow he had been elected cook by a three to one vote. His wife would have some serious explaining to do when he got home. Not that he really minded. On a well maintained ship the engineer was superfluous. After all, in the three years his wife served on LS48 she had never touched a single spanner while on active duty.

After the meal they would get down to the real work: discovering what was hounding the Zogar. They would soon be in contact by conventional comms and their training would once more be put to the test. Meanwhile, they were about to find out if Lynda's boasts of her husband's culinary skills were justified.

Back on board the Zogar Ray Rongo was feeling tense. Eighteen months of solitude and tranquility had passed slowly but the next seventeen hours would take an eternity. It required a special mind set to adapt to months of isolation piloting a long-haul freighter. Now the unexpected interruption - the imminent human contact - brought back the loneliness so carefully buried deep in his mind. In a few hours he would need to be his 'normal' self again. He would need to live and work with the lifeship crew to resolve his ship's dilemma.

Part of him resented the intrusion. He had reached the point where he could mark time and drift easily through the last year of the journey, a year that would complete his target. Even at his premature age he had amassed enough credits to open a charter service near his home world. He could settle down in semi-retirement and comfort operating from any of the hundred tourist centers across the four moons of Steloma-2. Now, after the rescue, it would take weeks to readjust to the timeless state needed

to finish the long haul, and keep his sanity intact. It was a task he did not relish.
'But' he determined, 'HERE is where I am - and HERE is where I must continue from!'
He accepted the inevitable and began adjusting to the new schedule.
On the bright side - Eventually he'd have a great yarn to spin around the local taverns, (and who would notice a few subtle embellishments.) One could never have too many yarns for the cold winter nights when glittering ice and pure white snow coated the great outdoors. He pictured the icy scene: crisp, surreal patterns of refracted light, beauty far beyond the most expensive fractal design. Maybe too, he'd have a trophy, a new alloy fragment from the 'Bomb he had defused'. For two more hours Ray fanaticized the many ways he could share his story to the delight of the young ladies from his home moon: Bumara.
He attended to his routine duties, more to fill in time than from any sense of duty. He knew Rob-3 the general purpose robot, standard equipment on a freighter, would be double checking his work an hour later. In fact, Rob-3 would be checking and rechecking this hour, the next hour, and every hour, on the hour, until the Zogar reached: "The Great Graveyard Fleet in the Void Beyond Far Space". By the time the comms sprang to life he was looking forward to the meeting. LS48 had dropped from superluminary flight and was inviting him to join them for a meal. After a year and a half alone a meal with good company was an offer not to be ignored. Hell! A meal with any company was an offer not to be ignored.

## Alien Artifacts

All too soon the feast was over, and it was on to business. Darkon positioned the lifeship between the freighter and the 'UFO' extending their gravity deflectors, protecting both vessels. The UFO retreated only a few feet, then maintained its relative position. After a few maneuvers it was clear that the UFO's position was based on the mass and center of gravity of its 'target'. And that the target could be either the Freighter or the Freighter and the Lifeship combined. The dance would be amusing were it not for the unknown dangers. Scans of the entity were ineffective. Its outer shell absorbed all energy without reflection, the perfect stealth craft. The only signature it produced was a barely detectable energy trail when it moved and its presence was only visually discernable by the light it blocked from the background stars.
'William!' called Darkon, 'Try the manipulator beam'
'Extending beam now,'
The crew watched as the pale yellow beam played on the object's surface. Almost immediately it began a slow rotation that deflected the beam drenching it with an orange hue.
'Increasing power,' the hue shifted further towards the red side of the spectrum.
'I can't grip it Captain. All the energy's dissipating.
'Test its reaction to physical mass. Use the beam to push it with an empty ballast block. Let's see how it reacts.' William ejected a block from the ship catching it in the beam. He gently positioned the block against the object's surface and pushed.
'The heat signature's increasing,' he responded, 'but no movement.'

# Space Zero The Meld

'Rongo - Use your maneuvering thrusters to move forward 100 feet. Do it slowly though.'
'Moving now - 10 feet'
'20 feet'
**'ALL STOP'** Yelled Darkon. The Object had pushed them aside like a cork in the ocean. It slid past and reasserted its position.
'Get me visual footage of every inch of that vessel. We'll re-assemble at the bridge console in half an hour. I want all the telemetry we've got.
Thirty minutes later saw them all staring in disbelief at the display console. It wasn't the way the UFO had pushed them aside, as easily as a feather blown by the wind, but the sheer efficiency of the operation. It moved in a perfect straight trajectory. They had been forced aside clear of its hull by a mere half inch. It had moved through their deflectors as if they didn't exist. Somehow it maintained deflector integrity by re-routing it around its own hull. That hardly appeared to be the actions of a malevolent design. But what did it want?
Geney broke the silence.
'Putting the technicalities aside for the moment,' she began, 'what can we make of its actions?'
They listed the non-technical issues. There were quite a few.

- The object had positioned itself to 'discourage' the freighter from leaving orbit.
- It is not positively aggressive
- It is actively defensive but not destructive.
- It is signaling to the third planet.
- No response has been observed from the third Planet.
- It appears to have advanced technology.

'Any Speculations?' asked William.
They thought some more.

- It seems it doesn't want the Zogar to break orbit.
- How did the iceberg get into orbit?
- It was too pure to have occurred naturally and how had it remain uncontaminated?
- How did it survive so close to its sun without evaporating?
- Is it bait for a trap?
- Is someone or something trying to communicate with us?

Trudel voiced the question all the crew was thinking.
'If it doesn't wants us breaking orbit, what does it want?'
Rongo suggested an answer, 'If we have the iceberg and the third planet to choose from, it's easier to checkout an iceberg than a whole planet.'
And so the lifeship took a trip to the iceberg. The 'berg was scanned with every conceivable technique. Its orbit and mass confirmed no unexpected buried treasure. It was simply what it seemed to be: 100% pure ice. Nothing else was detected. But when LS48 returned - it too had a UFO in tow. Now both UFOs were signaling to the third planet, and to each other.
'Something put the UFO on our tail,' observed William stating the obvious.
'And it didn't come from the iceberg. That just leaves the planet!'
'And *after* we've reported back to Base, that's what we'll investigate.' Darkon advised the Base of their intentions, just in case it was a trap. A second rescue attempt would not be cost effective - but the star system could be flagged as an 'avoidance zone' protecting future vessels and, more importantly, future profits.
Darkon had a difficult decision. He could take Rongo onto the lifeship and have him remotely pilot the Zogar attempting to leave the star system. The UFO might

survive the propulsion exhaust - or it could detonate and destroy the freighter. But at least the pilot would be safe. A second danger would be that it survived intact, hid its propulsion signature, and followed the Zogar back to inhabited space. Would it would be safer to resolve the situation here where a bad result would do the least damage?

He had to balance the desperate need of the cargo by the frontier planets against the risk of an unknown technology contaminating or destroying their star system. Supplementary to this was the dream of every pilot. Could this be 'First Contact'?

For centuries we were alone in space slowly migrating from Sol-3: Earth, an insignificant star near the extremity of a spiral arm. Insidiously we groped our way towards the more densely clustered stars at the center of the galactic hub, always hoping to find other sentient species, always hoping we were not alone. At the same time fearing a more advanced culture could displace us as easily as the Europeans did the Native Americans, as the British did the Australian Aborigines. It's a Human truth: the strong always displace the weak. But: is that a truth just for ***Human*** life?

He made the choice. They would stay, and investigate. There was really no other option. Mankind could not afford to waste this opportunity. Whoever or whatever intelligence was responsible was not of human origin and sooner or later their paths would cross again. Humanity needed to learn all it could. A six-hour sleep cycle was scheduled and preparations made for planet fall the next day.

At the morning briefing Darkon defined their mission, he was short and precise. 'The primary objective is to locate the receiver for the UFO signals on planet three. Our secondary task is to make contact, if possible, with whatever intelligence is behind it.' That had to be their starting point, it was their only lead they had. The first task proved easier than expected. With the UFO trailing their every move it took less than an hour to locate their target. The closer they came to planet-3 the more frequent the probe signaled and as they entered geo-stationary orbit it took the lead positioning itself at the zenith of the receiver. It latched onto the planetary host with a wide beam laser transceiving on all frequencies between Ultra Violet and Gamma. Clearly it was 'satisfied' with their actions. They scanned the planet but could get no meaningful readings below the topsoil. Some form of shielding appeared to be active. The atmosphere was breathable, a little high on oxygen, and gravity was a comfortable 0.97 standard.

Geney opened a portal to the surface and cautiously Darkon and Trudel stepped through onto the surface of the alien planet. They approached the area illuminated by the probe and were pleasantly surprised to find a circular metallic plate some thirty feet in diameter stretched out under the light. They edged forward, reluctant to walk into the beam. The beam light blinked out. Sounds of mechanical motion strained from deep underground. The metallic surface split open, widening, exposing what appeared to be two human sized seats. As they stepped forward the ground felt soft underfoot despite its unnatural appearance.

Immediately they sat down the seats began to descend, slowly at first then increasing in pace. There was no sensation of falling although they were dropping at great speed. Inertial damping had to be active. After a few minutes they came to rest at the base of a vast cavern. Silently, the opening in the plate above them closed and

turned opaque. Additional ambient lighting engaged. From the floor, two mounds rose and rapidly morphed to form large reclining chairs.
Two holographic images indicated they should move to the new ‘seats’. The crew looked at each other in amusement almost chuckling at the alien introduction. The hologram replayed. Its message was clear. They walked over to the new seats and sat down. This time they felt the chairs contour themselves giving support to their backs and necks. After a tingling sensation - were they being scanned? - lumbar supports extruded from the backrest. Their host, whoever he/she/it might be, was sparing no effort to make its guests comfortable.
In the center of the cavern a new holo-image appeared. It displayed the planet as viewed from space. It was inhabited by a culture with intercontinental surface vehicles, then aircraft appeared, then orbital ships, then larger more complex craft were shown under construction in high orbit. They broke orbit and departed the planetary system.
Occasionally an incoming craft would arrive, receive visits from planetary shuttles and depart again. The planet once deep green and blue took on a dull hue as the atmosphere clouded over. The interstellar visits ceased. Planetary vehicular movement ceased. For several minutes nothing appeared to happen. Slowly, over the southern pole, the arctic ice distorted. It protruded into a spike several miles high, fattened out then expanded to form a frozen glistening sphere over two miles across. Supported by three light beams it detached from the planetary pole and moved into high orbit. Once in orbit two of the beams cut off and the remaining support thinned to a slender shaft of light. The scene shifted. The view point appeared to move away from the planet by

several light years. As they watched the surrounding star movement sped up. The impression was of movement through time over a considerable period. The image highlighted star clusters rotating about distant axis - an illustration of the time scale involved?
The dizzying star chart slowed and the view returned to the planet in close up. Once again it was in bright green and blue. The iceberg was still orbiting like a moon with an occasional light beam springing from the surface to illuminate it.
Now a craft approached the planetary image. A smaller vessel emerged and extracted a sample from the ice. As it departed a UFO materialized to follow it back to the mothership. The craft tried to shake it off without success and finally fired a weapon at the UFO. The UFO absorbed the energy without reaction. After several more attacks the UFO 'dissolved'. When a second vessel attempted to collect more ice it crashed into an invisible barrier surrounding the iceberg. The mothership retaliated firing several volleys into the ice. None penetrated the defensive barrier. But a light beam shot up from the planet and pushed the ship to a higher orbit. Each time the mothership attempted to return it was forced further away. After several attempts the mothership changed tactics. It fired an intense prolonged energy beam at the planet itself. The planet responded. An object that could only be described as a giant reflector materialized above the atmosphere. For several minutes it absorbed the barrage of beams from the ship. Then in an instant of revenge the full, accumulated energy was shot back at the mothership. It vaporized on contact.
Over time other ships visited the iceberg. Those that ignored the UFOs left unhindered. Even those that fired on the UFOs or took the hint when they were forced away

from the planet were allowed to leave in peace. Only two, those that fired upon the planet itself, were destroyed. It seemed that the Zogar and the LS48 were the only visitors to precede cautiously, neither running from the UFO, nor attacking it.

Now the Zogar appeared in the holo-display. They saw their own approach in LS48 and followed its culmination to their present situation. They saw themselves descend to the cavern floor and start watching the introductory hologram. At that point the display dimmed, fading out of existence. It was replaced by a flashing white line that appeared on the floor directly in front of them.

It extended, beyond the earlier presentation area to a brown mottled wall then turned clockwise and ran past several 'windows'. When Darkon stepped onto the line the flashing ceased and another humanoid hologram appeared to illustrate the required action. As the holo-image approached each window an opening morphed to allow it entry. They watched. The procedure was similar to the first demo. A protrusion extended from the floor and the holo-person either sat or lay flat depending on the nature - chair or bed - of the protrusion. For the cubicles however there was one main difference. An image started as a projection just in front of the hologram then drifted to stabilize within the hologram's cranial cavity. It implied the 'image' would be directed straight into the subject's mind. Was this an elaborate form of VR but without the complications of an implant?

Guardedly, Darkon entered the first opening.

As the chair extruded he sat down and awaited initiation. Just as the introduction had shown them the planet's history without using language and translation, this first lesson relied on visual imagery too. Almost at once he was experiencing a bustling community, construction

workers building a vast complex deep within the planet. There was a sense of urgency, a need to hurry, but without danger or agitation. Behind the walls he could perceive the immense machinery that would support the center. Geo-thermal converters tapped the planet's core providing the energy needed to support such an elaborate enterprise. As he watched the cavern was hollowed out and the many cubicles constructed, each of them inter connecting and tapping into the vast knowledge core. He watched as brain patterns from millions of humanoids were copied and routed to the central repository. The significance of the chair or bed became apparent. The chairs were for short study sessions, the beds for long durations. He sensed, without knowing how, that certain sessions would last many days. The secret of the planet crystallized as the cavern fed knowledge directly into his brain. "Education" was two-way. While he received information - the cavern would simultaneously extract his knowledge to add to its store. There could be no secrets.
As the session neared its end, the system had absorbed enough of Darkon's mental patterning to establish common frames of reference. He became aware of the native 'writing' that surrounding him. The patterns on the ceiling began to take on meaning. What appeared to be random scratches in the rough-hewn rock transformed themselves into written words. It was an index of subjects available for study. Whatever culture had devised this library, for clearly that is the nature of this structure, it intended the knowledge to grow and be shared by future civilizations. He watched as a new entry formed; the root entry for the Human Species. It was marked: Current Species: Humans - Status Incomplete.
Darkon realized he understood the meaning. The Library had already implanted that knowledge in his mind.

# Space Zero The Meld

Current Species had incredible significance. The Cavern was offering Humanity the opportunity to be the Library's new caretakers, guardians. For as long as Humans wanted its valuable resources, for as long as even one living human remained within the planet's star system, they and they alone would have total access to the stored knowledge of every species that had gone before. They may never meet the creators of this incredible library, but its knowledge base was theirs for the taking.

But before the first session ended one last dramatic message impinged upon his mind. It was a warning. The cavern forbade examination its own structure. It issued a stern warning against tampering with the advanced technology that would share its knowledge with them. The cavern's workings were sacrosanct, the forbidden tree in the Garden of Eden. The military would certainly be against such a restriction but it was a condition the scientific community could easily live with. And since the planet was uninhabited when they arrived Darkon, under inter-planetary law, could claim it on behalf of GMI as Civilian Territory. Any military options would be pre-empted.

He rejoined Trudel in the main cavern as a new holo-image appeared. They found themselves looking into their own lifeship's bridge and could hear Geney attempting to contact them by radio.

'They're trying to call us.' Trudel exclaimed.

She was obviously heard. 'Is that you Trudel?' Geney replied excitedly. 'We've been out of touch for nearly an hour, ever since you disappeared from the surface. What's your status?'

'Yes! Yes!' Trudel cried with relief, and realized she wasn't using her suit radio.

Their personnel comms were purring white noise, but they could hear their crew mate as clearly as if they were standing next to her on the bridge. While Trudel updated the orbiting crew, trying to explaining the unbelievable happenings deep below the surface, Darkon studied their immediate surroundings.

He stepped into the descent zone looking up at the closed ceiling. It opened and the seat-unit began the ascent. He turned back urgently calling to Trudel to rejoin him, but as he looked down towards her the 'elevator' reversed and returned to the cavern floor. The mechanism it seemed was sensitive to his line of sight. Look up and you go up or look down and go down. Instinctive controls of this nature of implied an advanced, perceptive culture, and it was a culture that could analyze and replicate a visiting ship's comms after what must be millennia without maintenance. But where were the creators of this technology. Did they want to make contact? This whole environment was clearly designed to communicate with them. What other surprises could they expect? When they returned to the ship it was not a surprise to find the two UFOs were gone.

Agreeing a name for the star system was simplicity itself. Ancient Earth history told of a Great Library at Alexandria - reputedly the greatest source of knowledge to the primitive world until it was destroyed by the stupidity of a barbarian race. Being the third planet from the sun, the planet would be known as: **Alexandria-3.**

To prevent the military pre-empting their claim to the planet they needed to set up a ground based operations center. That was a simple matter. Like all lifeships LS48 was designed for extended duty in deep space. It was self-sufficient, could house a four-person crew for at least three months and had a specially designed, detachable control module for use in space or planet-side. The following day LS48 delivered the module to Alexandria-3 locating it walking distance from the Library Entrance. With their base camp established Darkon's next task was to contact GMI headquarters. They needed the company's specialists to join them as soon as possible without alerting less scrupulous elements within the federation. He sent a carefully worded message.

For the first time in the history of Galactic Merchant Insurance Ltd. it received a priority one alert - without a Danger Rating. Only a handful of the most senior directors would recognize the significance of that omission. And that handful responded faster than a stock broker making a trade! In less than three earth days fifteen percent of GMI's gross worth was converted to pure energy to literally pour the galaxy's top scientists and support engineers onto a solitary planet in the middle of, well, nowhere!

## Repository of Knowledge

Jeff Discman was the first to arrive; he would head the team investigating the Library. His first priority was to establish a link between the cavern and the outside world. It would be foolhardy to rely on the library's own comms even though the arrangement appeared, on the surface at least, to be benevolent. A simple misunderstanding co uld leave them trapped and isolated from the surface, an unnerving thought. Since the ceiling plate at the planet's surface was translucent three sets of laser transceivers established wideband links and a backup magnetic unit provided emergency voice comms. Next, plans for an administrative center were drawn up as a first step to developing Alexandria as the most advanced Learning Center in the Milky Way. The library's resources were going to be fully utilized.

But before colonization could begin - raw materials were required. This proved less of a problem than it might have been. Sitting in solar orbit just beyond Alexandria-5 was the Zogar with all the resources they would need for the next decade.

Geney arranged a conference with the authorities of Targonia Colony, 'Journey's End' for the Zogar's Ore. They were expecting a significant penalty for calling out the lifeship services but they were in for a pleasant surprise. Darkon had already broached the matter with his GMI bosses and had wide leeway to negotiate.

Before long an arrangement was reached with both parties feeling they were walking away with the best part of the deal. For GMI's part they were already entitled to entitle 20% ownership of the Zogar and 10% of future profits. It took little persuasion for the colonies to except a flat 20% of the current cargo as full settlement. They were a little less happy when Darkon insisted on keeping Ray Rongo. He was the senior of the two man exploration team who had spent two years prospecting this sector of space; his knowledge of the area would be invaluable. But when GMI offered to fly a replacement pilot to the Zogar at no cost to them and to do it within three days they finally agreed. GMI would be sending a second lifeship with considerable support services to Alexandria-3 anyway and a detour to Targonia to collect the pilot would be a minor inconvenience. It would also justify sending a second lifeship into the rescue zone and keep the news agencies from becoming too curious. All they needed to know at this stage is was that a planet potentially suitable for habitation had been found. Long before they realized the truth - GMI would be firmly in control of the real discovery.

With the base camp construction under way, Jeff and Darkon went to investigate the cavern in more detail. Jeff experienced the holo-introduction then together they sampled several of the 'lessons'. Newcomers, especially the construct workers, were encouraged to try the study sessions during their free time and give admin some feedback. Too much was unknown about the system's efficiency, and virtually nothing of the side effects of interacting with it.

Then one afternoon Mark Quison burst into the Chief Administrators office interrupting the important weekly meeting.

'We've got a problem!' he yelled 'We won't be able to sell the knowledge.'

Mark was GMI's Science specialist. He had arrived earlier that day and was returning from his first visit to the Library. Mark was in his mid 40's and had been with the company for most of his career. He was an unusual character, both an "Ideas" man and equally capable of turning his ideas into reality. Those traits had shot him past more senior managers until on his fortieth birthday he had been promoted to lead the Research and Development department for the Lifeship Project, the most prestigious branch of GMI.

'Go on,' urged Darkon, his curiosity aroused, 'Where's the difficulty?'

'We can't patent the new technologies.'

'We've got to give the information away for free. If the Library senses we're not sharing the knowledge it's going to cut us off!' He had taken only a few sessions in a chair, but had chosen the responsibilities of Library custodianship.

'And there's more!' He continued, 'It doesn't know about Portals.'

'There's a gap in its knowledge regarding anything beyond simple gravity manipulation.'

'Apparently, we're the first culture to master it.'

'We've been "requested",' and he emphasized the word "requested", 'to supply it with all data we have on the subject. And it wants a linkup to our ship's network to see what else we may have that it doesn't know about.'

Darkon was becoming concerned. Was the Library genuinely interested in their new knowledge? Or was it a trick to learn about an enemy before attacking? After all, they had only the Libraries version of its historic past.' He pondered, 'Was there any way to interrogate the Library? He threw it out to the meeting:

'Has anyone asked the Library a question or are we all just passively absorbing everything?'

'I never thought to try when I was down there,' he added, confessing.

Nobody responded.

'No one's mentioned having a conversation with it - did we all assumed it was just instruction and suction?'
Still no response,
'If it's capable of draining knowledge from us it may well be fully interactive. We need to find out, and soon.'
The meeting adjourned with Mark and Darkon being assigned to investigate immediately.
Although it was becoming second nature to use the 'ramp', avoiding the temptation to look around, which disrupted the descant, took a little more discipline. They were meeting Jeff at the refreshment area where a mobile kitchen and bathrooms had been installed. The Cavern initially tolerated the intrusion, but a few hours after construction, the floor "drifted" them away from the descent shaft to a new location. With an undulating movement, like a rippling wave ambling towards the shore, the portable units had been ushered sideways to where the Cavern considered an appropriate place. Protrusions grew from the floor tapping into the plumbing and energy supply giving the kitchen and washrooms endless supplies of fresh water and maintaining their power cells at full capacity.
As they approached Jeff's table, two chairs morphed from the floor anticipating their need. Mere days and the Cavern was already adapting to Human customs and habits.
'No,' Jeff confirmed, 'I haven't asked the Library about any of its systems. It never occurred to me to do so.'
Over coffee, they discussed and framed the questions they needed answering and within the hour they were ready to approach the Library in a new manner.

## Morph Introductions

They chose a free cubical and waited for the chairs to extrude. They were not disappointed. But no sooner had the chairs encompassed them than the cubical changed. A circular table formed in the center of the room and the chairs, with their occupants still seated, slid around it leaving space for a fourth person. A new extrusion arose from the floor. It took on humanoid form in the same mottled brown tones as the walls, its surface semi reflective like a highly polished rock. As they watched it morphed to assumed facial features and became animated. Gargling sounds emitted from the area of its mouth and slowly its utterances became intelligible.

'Welcome to the Library.'

were its first words.

'This unit is created to interact and speak with your species. It is an extension of the Library.'

'It will adapt to any alternative or additional requirements you may choose.'

'You may request additional units as you require them. You have questions.'

'This unit will,'

it paused, sensing discomfort from the human guests,

'I will' it continued 'answer any of your questions that do not endanger the safety of the Library or the planetary system.'

'What about the safety of your creators?' asked Jeff?

'My creators, the Meld, no longer exist in what you would call time and space.'

'They have evolved beyond your understanding and can not return. They created this Library to assist other developing sentient life to reach their level of evolution.'

'Are you part of this complex - or can you exist independent of the Library?' the question came from Mark. He could imagine many uses for this - whatever it is - at an advanced training center in a more centralized area.

'I and all units like me are by design an integral part of this Library'

'We are dependent on the Cavern for our physical form and must remain within it.'

'What if we help you to go outside?' asked Jeff.

'Outside the cavern we would decompose. That is our design.'

'Can we take knowledge away from here other than in our minds?'

'Bring your machines, with you. When you study we will transfer knowledge into your devices.'

'Can you send it directly to our orbiting Ships?'

'We will only work with devices within the Library. Those devices may themselves transmit to your orbiting ships. Choice and control is yours.'

'Tell us about the restrictions on selling the knowledge.'

'The data, knowledge originating from the Library must be shared freely by your species. You may not profit from it. You may recover only the cost of extracting and disseminating the knowledge. If you attempt to profit from this knowledge the Library will cease to function for your species and you will be removed from this planetary system.'

'Knowledge extrapolated and enhanced by the input you share with the Library will not be restricted.'

'Can you give us an example?'

'The hybrid device using your Gravity science and the Library's Teleportation science is not restricted. Designs you receive from the Library using only Teleportation Science must be shared freely'

'Are there any other species currently using the Library?'

'No. Since the Library was created there has only ever been a single sentient species in what you refer to as this Galaxy.'

'How long may we remain the custodians?'

'You may remain until you endanger the Library, until you attempt to profit from our knowledge, until you evolve to join the Meld or until you choose to leave.'

'How many other species joined the Meld?'

'None have yet joined. All the preceding custodian species have become extinct.'

'Are you sure? Could they just have moved away?'

'Knowledge is power. No Species has abandoned the Library once they

experienced its power. The Meld would inform us of such a happening.'
'I assume we can colonize the planet to develop the infrastructure for our,' Jeff hunted for the right word, 'Our students?'
'The Library will permit limited colonization and will protect itself from degradation, pollution and overpopulation.'
'How should we address you and your,' he paused, 'Clones?'
'The nearest word in your language is Android. You may ask for an Android to be generated anywhere within the Cavern except the access shaft. The units will void when no longer required.'
With that the unit sank quietly into the floor blending into the surface as though it had never existed, voiding before their eyes. They realized they were out of questions. Then it dawned on them; the android had realized the same thing, but had realized it before they did.
GMI's investment had already sliced deeply into fiscal profits, more deeply than the combined ventures of the past twelve years. Developing the Library was a gamble, true, but one they could not afford to ignore. Even the limited technology they had seen so far could bring immeasurable profit once reverse engineering discovered the science behind it.
Darkon and Jeff were out on a limb. Head Office would abide by their decision and give them full support, but if their judgment proved wrong they might never work in federation space again. Not because they'd be on every blacklisted across the known Universe, but because there

might be no human race left to employ them. After First Contact, new knowledge might advance mankind beyond their wildest dreams or release devastation throughout the inhabited stardom.

Apparently the Library would not or could not access their ship and its systems unless they gave it permission. That was a point in its favor. But who's to say it would not lock onto their ship and interrogate it anyway should they attempt to break orbit. If they withheld their Gravity technology until they were more 'comfortable' with the Library, would it be any more than a token gesture. If the Meld operates on a longer time scale than mankind and is prepared to wait years before invading - is a hundred or even a thousand years an acceptable delay until they acquire our knowledge? How powerful are they really? If they are so far advanced that we stand no chance against them the decision becomes irrelevant, and simpler to make. They talked for more than an hour wrestling with the decision. Could the Library's integrity be tested?

'We need another Android, please'. Jeff made the request and new android morphed from the floor, or was it the original one returning? It did not matter.

'Library! We need more information.' he demanded.

'How do we know this isn't a trap for the human race'?

We can not give proof.' replied the Library.

It continued, reassuringly,

'To answer you: We have the power to destroy all life in your galaxy within a single rotation of this planet.'

And elaborated,

'Just as you have the technology to destroy a single planet with only a pre-industrial culture you do not do so, even though you have the power.'

'The planet's primitives could not prevent you from invading or annihilating them but they live without fear.'

Darkon and Jeff finally understood. If the Library had enough advanced technology to be of use to mankind, that same technology could destroy them. It was the proverbial Double Edged Sword. A laser knife is used by both the surgeon and the assassin alike. Without the new sciences they were already at the mercy of the Library. If they choose to learn, they would have an option to resist. But is the Library really that far advanced.

'Can you show us your power - safely?' asked Darkon, 'A couple of demonstrations.'

The android shimmered for a few seconds as the Library responded to a request outside of its design parameters. Although they did not realize it at that moment, Time within the cavern was frozen - the Library shifted away from normal space/time to communicate with the Meld. When it returned and the shimmering stopped thirty-three alarms activated simultaneously. Every calendar/clock that had been brought into the Cavern was triggered to critical alarm mode.

'We're out of sync with LS48's chronometry.' Jeff was startled, 'We've gained over seven seconds.'

'To be accurate,' responded the android,

'your chronometers have been displaced for, and are ahead by, 7.324 of your seconds. That is the time period we spent in voided-space resolving your question.'

'We regret we are not permitted to

`demonstrate our power. It would compromise the Library's security.'`

Darkon contacted the ship before resetting the timepieces. They had indeed experienced a temporal shift, just as the android had stated. The ship's chronometers maintained integrity by reference to the local star and its planets. And the planets were precisely where they should be.

So, the Library could not, or would not, demonstrate its powers. But it already had. What greater proof of its powers could they ask for than a seven-second shift through time? Jeff made a mental note: the Library was surprisingly myopic regarding time.

Outside the cubicles most of the GMI staff was huddled around tables in the canteen speculating upon the alarms. Jeff hurriedly explained to an amazed audience and watched their respect for the library visibly grow. As scientists, they realized they had experienced something far beyond the reach of their own technology. And this was tangible evidence that did not require specialized knowledge to understand.

The choice: to proceed, or not to proceed, no longer existed. They could only go forward. For better or worse Pandora's Box had been opened -- and if the technology were not harnessed for the benefit of mankind it would inevitably be monopolized to its detriment.

Darkon and Jeff settled down for an evening meal before returning to Base Camp. It would take a long time to prepare for the arrival of humanity's hungriest minds.

The first successful joint venture was the hybrid Teleportal. It merged the Library's teleport expertise with Human portal technology and was completed in time for the center's grand opening. Transmitting the teleport stream through a portal dramatically increased the range without an increase in energy cost. The library's limit for

human teleport was about sixty thousand miles. The hybrid portal increased that distance to over thirteen light years, a very useful increase. It was ‘a marriage made in heaven’. As word of the success spread the center was inundated with requests from specialists in all fields clambering for study time.
Alexandria-3’s spaceport, such as it was, comprised a single room in the Admin block. Mark equipped it with twenty four new Tele-Portal units. Visitors using the system to transfer down from orbit would experience first hand the success to be gained working with the Library. It was a better advertisement for the Knowledge Center than all the publicity GMI was paying for.
When the day of the grand opening arrived the Alexandria Knowledge Center could accommodate a modest two thousand students, four hundred staff, and further six hundred service personnel. The limit was imposed by the Library. In orbit were several cruiser class starships that ferried in students from every corner of the galaxy. Their carefully selected crews would be amongst the first to absorb the new star map knowledge that would be disseminated to every culture in the federation. They were supplemented by a handful of private vessels run by the more successful corporations. The two Federal Police units remained in orbit, primarily because the Library would not permitted planet-fall by armed vehicles or personnel. When one of the craft ignoring the prohibition had dropped from orbit attempting a landing the Library had simply extended a beam and pushed it back. No objection was made a few hours later when the officers ported down to visit the site without their ship, or their weapons.

## Lost Time

The opening ceremony was conducted by Doctor Brian M. Millfrad the managing director of GMI for more than twenty Earth Years. It would be a simple service, but first he introduced an unexpected ritual.

'Before we begin,' he pausing, waiting until he got their full attention, 'I have a pleasant announcement from Federal Headquarters on Earth.'

'The Federation has formally acknowledged Alexandria-3, as an independent star system, to be Neutral Territory - Communal Property with its resources freely available to all lawful citizens.' He turned and nodded towards the Library entrance and added with a sly grin, 'Subject, of course, to the Library's own powers of veto!'

When the laughter died down he turned back to the audience. 'Jeff Discman - Please come forward.'

The Project Controller hesitated. He looked around, puzzled for a moment, and then slightly perplexed stepped up to the podium. The M.D. opened a small case to withdraw a 'Sash of Office' which he held high for all to see. A gasp rose from the gathered throng, most of them familiar with the symbols of officialdom. Observing the ritual, Dr. Millfrad lowered the Sash holding it out waist high in front of Jeff.

'On behalf of the Federation I bestow upon you the title: **Governor of Alexandria and its Planetary System**. May you serve the People and our Democracy with honor.'

Jeff dropped to one knee amid a roar of applause as the Sash of Office was draped upon him.

He gave the formal reply, 'Sir, I will Serve with Honor and Pleasure.'

'And now the bad news Jeff,' he continued in a somewhat quieter voice. 'Your military status is reactivated with a promotion fitting your new office. You're back in the service. Congratulations Commander-General Discman.'

They shook hands. Commander Discman stepped back and saluted, did a smart about face and proudly saluted the audience. Readjusting the sash he stepped from the stage amid roars of applause.

The main ceremony began. A short speech by the MD introduced the Library Center Complex. The Chief of Security gave a presentation which included the planetary defense system, and finally an introduction to a mechanized mockup of the androids they would encounter inside. The perfunctory red ribbon was cut and the MD proudly led the way into the Cavern.

While the now familiar introductory holograph played, several androids morphed into existence instructing the various groups in their mother tongues. After the tour, drinks lasted long into the evening as the visitors enjoyed their last night before the serious studies began.

Most of the students chose to live planetside but the select few, in their own orbiting luxury, inevitably forged an elitist class separation. It was upsetting for 'the few' that the Library was indifferent to all forms of rank and status. The most esteemed professor, a company president, a Federal Government high official - all had to wait in turn with the humblest student. The morphing androids selected the visitors in the order they were expected impervious to both bribery and flattery. All were equal in the eyes of the Library.

Post study debriefing during the first few months was intense. This was partly to ensure the safety and free distribution of the knowledge and partly to better understand the Library's nature. It soon became clear the Library had not been completely open with them. Infiltrators from the military, who of course had been anticipated, highlighted the mixed results. Not surprisingly data on weaponry was withheld. But so was all information related to cutting edge technology in any military direction. Search and surveillance knowledge was available but stealth technology to gain it was classified as "UNNECESSARY" and withheld. Bioengineering for crop production was available but pesticide research was "UNACCEPTABLE USE".

The vegetarians were pleased when Animal Husbandry was classified as "UNACCEPTABLE USE", and the Animal Rights movement applauded when cattle for milking, sheep for wool were both classed as "UNNECESSARY".

In fairness to the Library, after declining the initial requests it frequently offered technological alternatives to provide similar products. Not only were all humanoids deemed equal in the sight of the Library, but apparently so also were many other forms of animal life. In short - we would gain much - but in return we were to be directed in our technological advance. If we continued to use the Library, Mankind would no longer be in control of its own destiny.

In a disturbing display of arrogance several member planets posted military vessels in high orbit around the Alexandria-3. Each sub-culture was fearful that another would make arrangements with the Library and gain economic control of the federation. Although tolerant of their presence, the Library maintained military starships at a higher orbit than those of the student's crafts and at first the militias were content to monitor the data streams between the planet and visiting ships. As time passed they ported down small groups to study and investigate the center. Each time they probed further into the defenses and limitations the Library had imposed.

Over the weeks it became clear that there were weaknesses to be exploited. Explosives could not be transported from orbit. But if the constituent chemicals were independently brought down the explosives could be reconstituted planet side without detection. Similarly component parts of low-tech weapons could be re-assembled without difficulty. Subtle interrogation of the ancient warfare tools showed that the Library had difficulty distinguishing between weapons and tools. It used context to differentiate and could be misled by human deception. Shown a farmer near a tree stump with explosives, it treated the dynamite as a tool. But a soldier with an identical package was interpreted as carrying a bomb.

Paranoia grew; increasing military supplies were smuggled down and stored near the Library. It was only a mater of time before suspicion and fear reached dangerous levels. The first incident emerged as a group from Heggardy-2 lead by geologist Harry Marson began mapping the territory to the northwest of the Library. They stumbled upon a labyrinth of caverns loaded with armaments and called security for backup. When it arrived, less than forty minuets, later both the Heggardy-2 group and the alleged arsenal had disappeared. At their location, only a series of caved in ditches were visible. From orbit several starships scanned for the missing personnel but no sign of the group could be found, so when diplomatic approaches failed, accusations bounced between the militias. The only indication of trouble had been the abrupt termination of the backup call and the simultaneously loss of telemetry from the personnel and

their equipment. The telemetry showed the mapping party entering the caves, conducting a search and initiating the call for backup. Then all went blank. Heat sources showed fifteen traces leading up to the site, then nothing. No trace of humanoid bio-matter showed to a depth of five hundred meters. No sign of hostility or weapon activity, not even the tell tale signature of a site to site teleport. Rumors spread that whoever had done this was using new technology gleaned from the Library. The more irrational rumor mongers declared the Library had formed a secret alliance with one of the federation planets and was assisting them to dominance. Maintaining neutrality the Library declined to comment on the incident.
Then on the 32nd day the Mapping Party, in a highly agitated state, reappeared at the outer gate of the Library compound. They needed a few days hospitalization before debriefing could begin but all fifteen members recounted a similar story:
When the arms cache was discovered Harry called the security center, for backup. But as soon as the word armament was mentioned they experienced what in any other place would have been an earthquake. A sucking sound grew louder like a giant vacuum pump springing to life. It came from behind the cache store. Before their eyes, the weaponry dissolved, disappearing into thin air. Their surroundings became transparent and as they watched the cave roof collapse burying them alive. But the soil had no weight, no pressure, it caused no pain and somehow they were still breathing despite being surrounded by translucent soil. Some feared they were dead, others still felt alive. For two days they remained buried, unable to move or speak, and watching the rescuers search frantically for any trace of their bodies.

The least fortunate of the group was Sonia Wright. Being nearest to the cave entrance she was terrorized for hours as the ground around her torso was excavated, the diggers passing straight through her body. The rescuers could neither see nor hear her. So severely traumatized was she that it would take months of specialist care for her to come to terms with still being alive.

They watched through the glass like soil as their rescuers departed. Then time contracted. In what for them was little more than a day, they watched thirty cycles of sunset and sunrise before they returned to normal time. As the ordeal neared its end they began to hear natural sounds: the whisper of the wind, chirping of insects, and the taste the sweet aroma of fresh grass. Like ghosts they rose slowly and steadily through the topsoil till even their feet emerged just clear of the ground. Then came the jolt. It shot through their bodies as if they had missed a stair and stepped down heavily onto the one below. Some stamped their feet on the grass if in disbelief, half expecting to slide below the surface again. Other started hugging and feeling each other, crying with relief that they were flesh and blood again. But were they alive, or dead?

With their communicators inoperative, they had to walk several miles to reach the Library. Apprehensively they approached the spaceport office until the receptionist turned to greet them with a cheerful,

'Hello! What can I do for you?'

'You can see us?' cried Harry.

'Of course I can.'

'What time is it? What day is it? Never mind! Get Jeff Discman down here straight away and have Jan Fong bring her emergency medical team ASAP. We all need immediate medical treatment for dehydration and Galaxy knows what else!'

None of their ID keys registered. This was no surprise since after 30 days they had been classified: “Missing Presumed Dead”.

The security officer refused to believe their story. To him it was a joke in very bad taste being played by the spaceport staff. After all, his staff had spent all of the past month trying to locate the survivors with absolutely no success. How could they suddenly turn up again? But they had! Fifteen identities to be reinstated with the same “Unknown” Explanation Code would trigger warnings all over the personnel system. He would have a lot of explaining to do to his superiors if he ever found an explanation that made any sense.

Jeff arrived at the spaceport and was struggling to comprehend the eyewitness accounts. Three days beard growth on the faces of every male in the team contradicted the 32-days they had been missing and lent plausibility to their incredible claim. But first, full medicals: validation of their DNA and checks for residual damage to their bodies and minds. After debriefing, while the survivors recuperated, he led a committee to interrogate the Library, to get its version of what had happened, and to find the reason it failed to keep them informed. He felt the stirrings of suspicion he’d carefully held at bay since the Library opened

He reviewed the situation.

The Library had free access to all their weapons technology but withheld data on energy weapons from prior civilizations.

It supplied them with medical, agricultural, and technical research but withheld all bio data on alien life forms including higher primates and the earlier guardians.

It denied knowledge of gravity technology but appeared adept at time manipulation - fields that were inseparably interwoven.

Jeff speculated upon areas of research that were being blocked, upon avenues of exploration they were encouraged to drop.

The list was significant: Weaponry, Animal Intelligence, Human Genetic Engineering, and Space Exploration beyond their own Milky Way galaxy.

Could they trust the Library when it claimed there were no intelligent life forms in other galaxies or indeed within their own? The Library was feeding them sufficient new knowledge to allow extensive development within their own systems, but in doing so their natural curiosity to explore further into the universe was being curtailed. It was becoming more difficult with funds being funneled in favor of more profitable short term ventures.

He began to assemble a committee from the original discovery crews where trustworthiness was above suspicion. Mark Quison his Chief Scientist, Jan Fong from medical, Trudel Stamar and Geney Gourd both experts in the gravity applications, and finally William Forrest and Darkon Myzelv experienced space engineers. Their first meeting was off planet on the GMI star-cruiser hopefully far enough away from Library's sensors. They had one immediate problem to overcome. During Study sessions their minds and thoughts would be accessible to the Library and any plans would be unveiled. Whoever they sent to interrogate the Library could not know the real reason and that fact alone excluded everyone on the committee. It took several hours of hard discussion before they agreed a plan of operation. To placate the Library they needed a historian with a genuine interest in the earlier Custodian species. That person could investigate the extinctions on the pretext of allowing us, the Humans, to avoid making the same mistakes. It didn't take long to find a suitable candidate. With an endless stream of applicants vying for personal access to the Library, the difficulty was choosing amongst many eminently qualified academics. Their final selection was based on enthusiasm, and a slight naivety that would prevent discovery of the truth behind their facade.

They chose a university lecturer: Sheila Fayamore, who has spent several years researching interactions following "first" contact. Although these First Contacts were between Humans they were between the Space Faring culture and Sub-cultures that had become separated and isolated from the mainstream population. Her studies included re-assimilation of the two races: Qwadray-2 and Qwadray-3 that had previously opted for isolation outside the federation. Sheila jumped at the chance of an early visit to Alexandria-3 in return for including studies of the Guardian species in her research. And a generous fiscal bonus was icing on the cake! They arranged for her to work under Harry Marson knowing he'd be unable to avoid discussing his unusual experience. No one could have foreseen his sudden demise three months later or the disturbing results of the post mortem. He suffered a total neurological collapse exhibiting the same symptoms as VR addicts who spent all their waking life plugged in to the systems. But whereas addicts collapsed only after two or more years of abuse, and the disorder progressed only slowly, Harry had appeared normal and rational until days before his death. He complained of confused and sluggish thinking one morning then after work he checked into the medical center. By evening he was in a coma and died three days later without regaining consciousness. At the time it caused concern even though he had spent far less time studying in the inner chambers than many of the full time academics. The records showed several of the elderly professors, perhaps fearing their time in this life was running out, were cramming all their waking hours into intense study intent on completing their projects and getting their names forever embossed in the history of human achievement - before they themselves expired. But seven months later, with all but one survivor from the ordeal dead, concern turned to trepidation.

The sole survivor was Sonia Wright. She never fully recovered from 'The Ordeal', partly because of the trauma from the mechanical diggers during the rescue attempt, and partly because she couldn't, or wouldn't, accept she was still alive. Shortly after debriefing, refusing to stay on the planet, she was transferred to the GMI Institute on SOL-3 where intensive testing could find no trace of neural dysfunction. Her only medical disorder: she had been rendered sterile many years earlier following a meteor strike at an orbital station. She suffered extreme radiation poisoning and treatments to save her life had left her barren.

## Problems Shared

When Sheila began to investigate the prior guardian extinctions progress was slow. The Library refused to provide specific information regarding the cause of their demise, claiming none of the Guardians ever made the data available. Apparently as the decline progressed the cultures began spending less and less time at Alexandria-3 and eventually ceased their visits altogether. The Meld would later inform the Library each time a Guardian Species became extinct. Sheila decided to switch to a different tact and view each Guardian approach to the Library as a standard First Contact encounter with a significantly more advanced alien species. She could compare each culture's social and economic progress before and after contact allowing for the intrusion of new technologies but this time with the unusual absence any of physical contact with the dominant species.

Months of hard work began to pay off and gradually a pattern emerged. Our Human approach followed a similar pattern, only more rapidly. The reason was obvious: we had a unique advantage. Having already evolved portal-technology we were able to develop an infrastructure on Alexandria-3 more rapidly than the Library was accustomed.

The history of prior Guardians, like our own, showed a demographic surge during the century preceding First Contact. With the consequent explosion of resources and manpower exploration and planetary colonization became feasible. Accelerated by population pressure within the inner star systems migration towards the outer limits became inevitable and inexorably led to discovery of the Library.

# Space Zero The Meld

Colonization of the Milky Way, in every case was similar. The species were all air breathing humanoids. They all, from the visual images from the Library archives, could have passed among the space farers in our culture without drawing more than the usual casual acknowledgement. Their general appearance varied in shape and size by little more that our current sub-species and the medical archives showed similar internal organ arrangements with documented diseases comparable to our own. This might explain how easily the Library had been able to assist our own medical developments.

She began to daydream and speculate! Had the first Guardians Species populated the galaxy and become not quite extinct but reduced to isolated primitive non-technological levels? Had just one of those cultures struggled up the evolutionary ladder once more and, after millennia of lost time, venture again into the far reaches of space to become the second Guardian Species? Had this catastrophic process been repeated innumerable times until now we Humans become the latest link in the chain? Was history doomed to be repeated in an endless spiral until the universe collapses in on itself before the next Big Bang? It would certainly explain why most sub-species in the Federation interbreed without difficulty and why the gnomes for our cultures had such consistency.

'Wow! I've been working too hard!' she exclaimed and added in silent thought,

'Yes, and I've started talking to myself as well!'

But the thoughts wouldn't leave her mind. She couldn't shake them off. They stuck to her like burned flesh with the tenacity of an irritating song that after one hearing repeats itself for days before fading into oblivion, only to reappear a week later with the same persistence.

'Just like new Guardians appear on a grander time scale,'

she censored the thought. It was paranoid and it was getting too great a grip on her mind.
But three days later the thoughts were still with her and she knew of only two solutions.
Get Drunk, and let alcohol dissipate the chains of thought by disrupting her neural pathways for a several hours, or
Talk it out with close friends until so many more avenues of probability emerged that none were dominant.
(And maybe augmented it with a little of the first option.)
But none of her close friends were within a hundred light years, and Harry was out of question. She called Jan at medical saying she needed to talk. They agreed to meet at the spaceport social center for a meal that evening. But when Sheila elaborated, disclosing the ideas racing through her mind Jan realized the meeting could be useful to the committee and suggested a foursome with Jeff and Darkon. After months working more or less alone Sheila needed very little coaxing to agree.
Later that day, while struggling with her choose of evening attire, she realized just how much she was looking forward to the dinner and it had nothing to do with her original need. Until now she had only socialized with a few fellow students from the Library cafe. But she knew who the two committee men were and more importantly that they were both single - gossip in a campus this small was ‘all encompassing’ - it created difficulties. Should she dress casual but elegant, formal with a few luxury accessories, or go all out to make an impression that every bachelor would remember? She called back on the pretext of checking if their companions had agreed to join them and was delighted to learn Jan was ‘Going for the Kill’ too. She had decided on a green/brown silken bodysuit streaked with thin crimson threads running from head to toe and trimmed with

yellow pastel fur, (simulated of course,) in strategic places. Her outfit would be topped off, or more accurately ***toed off***, with scaled shoes of incandescent deep rust red that shimmer tantalizing in the glow of a setting sun. They would complement her flaming red hair as it stretched halfway to the ground. 'I can do better than that!' Sheila muttered, talking to herself again without realizing it. She looked at her naked body in the wardrobe reflector, and had the projector overlay images of her wardrobe-choices. Her own bodysuits were dramatic enough under normal circumstances; sleek and revealing they would accentuate her natural curves without the need for enhancement. But today she wanted more than a fantastic look. She wanted to project more of herself than just a sensuous body. She had a mind as important to her as looks and that was how she would impression tonight's target. She corrected herself: tonight's *guest*. Was she becoming too predatory as the years passed? It didn't matter. Not at the moment. She had only an hour left to get ready and the wardrobe was rejecting too many combinations. She felt like a schoolgirl on here first date and imagined herself back at class in her old school uniform. Bold contrasting colors, standard skirt, blouse, jacket and hat. Thank goodness those days were past. But she liked the image, it just needed to be brought up to date.
Silk was obviously the "in" fabric this evening. Out came a long sleeved blouse in flaming red and pink the colors blending easily with her complexion. Deep red pleated pantaloons followed to envelop her shapely legs. Shoe-socks grounded with soft dark soles that slowly faded in tone and texture as they crept up her calves becoming silken drapes as they reached her thighs. She alone would know where they finished and that would be her secret, leastwise for tonight. The reflector image was coming to

life, but something was still missing. What was it? She rotated slowly watching the image replicate her movements.

**'View: Reverse!'** she snapped. The image spun a full half circle to better display the rear of her costume. There was the problem. It was still too bland.

**'Give the back of the blouse vertical flutes - fourteen of them - GO.'** The wardrobe complied.

**'Start the flutes an inch lower - GO.'** It obeyed.

**'Rotate flutes - left clockwise, right anti-clockwise, five twists - GO.'** It adapted again.

**'Interleaf bronze and gold fluffed threads along the flutes - GO.'**

**'Two more twists - GO.'** It was beginning to look more alluring.

**'Left and right flutes separately, tie at vertical mid-point.'**

**'Use half inch wide matching bronze strip, tie horizontal bows one point five inch wide - GO.'** much better!

**'View: 12 second Rotation!'** Sheila watched as the reflector slowly rotated her image - she felt good, she was pleased. Two rotations later, as it returned to the rear view she called out,

**'View: Normal!'**

and the Reflector returned to standard mirror mode.

**'Reshow - Last Garment - GO.'**

**'Darken pantaloon red by fifteen percent - GO.'**

**'Slow walk - Far Left to Near Right - Twenty Paces - GO.'** She watched the image move closer and smiled.

**'Darken another Five Percent - GO.'**

That was perfect. Color, texture, movement, they all felt comfortable.

**'OK Wardrobe: LOCK design and BUILD NOW'**

**'AUTHORITY: Sheila Fayamore - CODE: PRIMROSE-THREE - GO.'**
***"Voiceprint Valid - Authority accepted."*** The wardrobe confirmed the transaction, and started humming as its internals began to create the new garments.
Meanwhile bathing and makeup were the order of the day. The clothing would be ready long before Sheila was out of the cleansing cubical, so she could enjoy the luxury of a sonic/aquatic shower for a few more minutes before sliding into the silken garments. As usual the vestments fitted like familiar gloves caressing her every movement. She wondered how many spiders had spent their entire lives weaving luxury garments for imperial courts in the centuries before technology could out perform them. Do spiders still exist or have they outlived their usefulness fading into the quagmire of creatures destroyed by man. She had no way to know that spider silk was a course fiber compared to the ultra fine membranes that covered her body, membranes that would respond to pressure and heat in ways no spider could have understood. Micro tendrils continuously adjusting to the stress of her every movement to balance the pressure across every inch of her body and doing so at precisely the level she preferred with warmth or cooling responsive to her voice.
She crossed the walkway leading to the spaceport center, the cool evening air playing across her neck. It felt good to be alive and young in the eternal summer of Alexandria-3. She recalled its topography: no planetary tilt to generate seasons, an almost perfectly circular orbit, the only divergence: the occasional heat wave when sunspot activity ran high.
As she entered the restaurant Jan crossed the vast vestibule to greet her. They eyed each other closely

examining every facet of each other's dress with an attention to detail no mere man could match. In the few seconds it took to cross the marble tiled floor the assessment was complete. Each came away feeling she had a slight edge and would stand out just enough to make the difference. Their victims, the men, had already arrived. They were seated at a window table enjoying the panorama of undulating grassy plains wafting in a light breeze stretching out to meet the ragged mountains on the far horizon. The moonless sky was clear. Starlight would arrive shortly but for now they enjoyed the setting sun as it glistened across the distant snow covered peaks. The ladies arrived punctually; Jan's timing had been perfect. As they approached, the last rays of sunlight caught her incandescent shoes with the expected results. A smile crept across Jeff's face relishing the spectacular display. His gaze moved slowly upward until their eyes met, eyes that had squandered time savoring the many delightful views en route. She'd obviously put more effort into this meeting than he'd expected. Did she have an ulterior motive? He hoped so. Fortunately, the men had both changed into civilian clothes before the meeting, more out of habit than expectation. They were dressed in casual one piece tunics, close fitting and comfortable. Not ideal considering the way their dinner partners were attired, but quite in place for the business dinner to which they had been invited. He glanced at his colleague who appeared equally pleased with the minor change of plan. 'Why not mix business with pleasure,' he thought suspecting the same idea was running through Darkon's mind. The latter's grin suggested it was.

Jan made the introductions, pleased that Sheila appeared happy to be monopolized by Darkon which left Jeff free to attend to her. They ordered drinks and turned to the menu. After the waiter-bot received its instruction and retired out of earshot they turned to business. Sheila explained her deliberations regarding the prior cultures' ascent and descent, her daydreaming, and the idea she couldn't shake: of a cycle that was repeating itself over a gigantic time scale. She half expected hefty rebuttal, or at the very least an alternate argument or two from these veteran spacers. But none were offered. Instead they were following her line of thought and speculating on the validity of the idea. It was almost as though they were expecting it, though nothing could be further from the truth. True, they had been expecting some kind of similarity between the cultures, something to uncover a deeper involvement with the Library. There were just too many discrepancies between the Library's versions of history and their own knowledge of how advanced cultures expand. When a major branch on a tree is ripped off in a storm, the rest of the tree continues to grow sometimes for centuries. Even an interplanetary war couldn't collapse a whole civilization when so many diverse sub cultures were not only against warfare but had sufficient distance between themselves and the centers of conflict to avoid being dragged into the fray? Library records showed no wars during the periods of destabilization and yet every culture disintegrated within a few centuries of discovering the Library. It was an ominous warning in which only the Library and the cultural extinctions were common factors. And there was the other glaring contradiction: the Library had shown the iceberg orbiting Alexandria-3, but Ray Rongo had encountered it in solar orbit.

Office talk stopped when the waiter-rob returned with their dishes and during the meal conversation switched to more social topics. This was a time to enjoy each others

company, to learn individual histories, and swap yarns from their experiences in space; business could await the end of the meal, there was still plenty of time, ***or so they thought!***
A few weeks later they met again, this time with the full committee. There was more to discus. The Library was slowly giving up its secrets to the gentle probing of Sheila's mind. She still believed any influence the Library held in the cultural demise was purely incidental, not malevolent and Darkon encouraged that belief, leastwise for now. He needed the Library to trust her and was beginning to hope she trusted him too. A consistent theme with all the Guardians cultures was a slowdown of population growth once they encountered the Library. That growth would eventually turn negative and spread like wildfire through the spiral arms of the galaxy. There was no detail on the cause of the scourge only rampant speculation from the news media. At first it appeared as only a minor blip in statistical surveys from the rim. Then slowly it migrated down the spiral arm to the galactic center before rocketing outward along the remaining spirals. Within a century the entire galaxy was showing signs of population decrease, slow at first but with each generation the demographic curve became more pronounced on its fatal, downward slide. By midway through the third century the birth of a humanoid child was a rare event, both natural pregnancies and artificial wombs failed to gestate with any success. At this stage the Library, unable to provide helpful assistance, was gradually abandoned. It monitored the reducing comms traffic throughout the galaxy until silence ensued.
Searching the final logs showed that once the danger was recognized both professionals and students concentrated on the sterility problem. But records gave little practical

detail of their research. There was plenty of data on unsuccessful tests, but no appreciable leads to identify the causes or indicate new avenues of research. Surely at least one Guardian would have found a way to diagnose the affected patients even if they were unable to treat them. Something was niggling at the back of Darkon's mind. One piece of the puzzle was missing, the kingpin that would snap the picture into focus. Jan pushed it into place.
'Sonia's release medical from Sol-3 Central arrived this morning. They've cleared her for normal duties but she won't be coming back. She's asked for a transferred to the terraforming unit close to the hub; that's about as far from here as she can get.
I don't blame her, with all her old team dead and that month of terror, no wonder she doesn't want to come back.'
'Fate hasn't been any too kind to her either,' she continued,
'With radiation killing any chance she had for children, and Galaxy knows what long term side effects will turn up from the ordeal - I wouldn't want to be in her shoes.'
'She's barren?' interrupted Jeff, 'Are you sure?'
'Yes, of course. That's why we didn't have to run the usual pregnancy tests before firing her over the teleport to Sol-3. It was just as well; our testing equipment was on the blink for several days. But of course you men never think of all the extra hassle we women have to go through each time we port.'
'OK! OK!' cried the two men in unison,
'We get your point,' Jeff added, 'We're always taking you lovely ladies for granted, ignoring your needs!'
'Do the restrictions apply to our older portals or just the hybrid teleports?' Darkon asked somewhat surprised.

'Yes, of course. It makes administration simpler,' Jan told him. 'That way we have one protocol regardless of the system we're using. The auto-routings don't need to check each pathway individually. It was cleared by Admin Central after we installed the upgrades.'
'Why wasn't I informed?'
'Need to know basis perhaps?' she was feeling more confident now, 'Why? Were you planning to have a sex change in the near future Darkon?'
The group erupted into laughter, drowning out his reply.
'That must mean there've been no pregnant arrivals planetside and presumably no pregnant departures either?'
'That's right! I guarantee you: if anyone gets pregnant down here they stay down here until the baby's born or transferred to an incubator.'
'What about new pregnancies while on planet, there's presumably lots of fraternizing this far from home.'
The ladies glanced at each other, and smiled knowingly
'We'd spot them,' exclaimed Jan, 'its standard procedure to run pregnancy checks on every bio-scan.'
'What are you getting at Darkon?' Jeff could sense something was gelling in his mind.
'We're the only Guardians that didn't bring fetuses to the planet, right? Our own safety rules prevented us even though we didn't realize it. Remember when the Library moved the cafe and connected its own water supply, no one bothered to check it out, we just assume it was safe. We trusted the Library but now it's got the perfect delivery system if it wants to infect us. Everyone in the center uses it, almost daily.
'Precisely *what* are you getting at Darkon? Are you blaming the Library?' Jeff was persistent.'
'It's the only common factor, Jeff. Picture the scenario. The Library waits till we establish a permanent base here.

It expects a few pregnant women will arrive as students, or conceive while they're here. Unknowingly we thwart it by keeping pregnancies off the planet. None of the students intend getting pregnant while they're here because they'll be stuck for the duration, before they can port home. It's only members of the permanent staff who'll be on station long enough to go full term, and they rarely go to use the study center because its heavily booked. So what happened when the Library realized that? It needed an alternative way to get access to the unborn babies.
On the flimsiest of excuses: the sighting of an arms cache that no one has ever confirmed, that might just have been a deliberate hallucination, it abducts fifteen staffers including the two pregnant women and puts them in a Limbo. It had a full month to develop a pathogen, test it on the babies and manipulate the genes of everyone in the group. When it was ready it released them but because the women knew they were pregnant they wouldn't port home until after the babies were born. Effectively their pregnancies quarantined them to the planet. When they got sick Health Services put the whole group into isolation at the spaceport center. The Library couldn't have anticipated that, it would expect them to leave and be on their way to hospitals on their home planets long before their condition became terminal. If they'd left earlier they'd have taken the contaminated fetuses with them and already be out there contaminating the gene pool.'
'But why concentrate on the pregnancies Darkon?' Sheila was not convinced. 'Surely the sheer size of an adult's body would make it easier to hide the pathogens?'
'Yes, but no culture's going to subject their fetuses and newborns to that level of intensive scanning, the risk to their DNA is much too high. Just look at the stats for mothers that get caught smuggling contraband in their babies' diapers.'

Jeff interrupted, ‘By the way, Jan, what happened to the bodies from the ordeal?’
‘They’re safe for the moment,’ she replied, ‘they’re in the morgue’s stasis pods. The specialists scheduled a pickup for later this month; they don’t seem to trust our quarantine and want to collect them in person.’

## Truth and Suspicion

'I still don't get it Darkon.' Jeff was unconvinced. 'The two women were barely here long enough to get pregnant; how could it have happened so quickly especially with all the contraception that's available?'
'That's the easy part!' this was home ground to Sheila, her specialty was: Individual Psychology, 'You remember both women knew they were pregnant. I'm wondered how they knew so quickly. Then it hit me! Does anyone know the cost of sperm donors these days, especially if you want to select for intelligence and longevity?'
'It's more than I can afford on my salary.' Jan volunteered, 'I'd need at least three more promotions to be in that pay bracket. I looked into it, out of curiosity, a few years ago. The intelligence genes carry a high premium, but nothing like the cost for longevity. Anyone with hot genes in both those categories can retire on the proceeds.'
Sheila smiled, 'So you spend a fortune - or do it the old fashioned way!' she pauses to let the words sink in. 'Do you realize, ninety percent of the professors here have IQs above 180 and at least half of them are doing research just to fill in their retirement? They all passed a strict medical before porting here so they're in almost perfect condition. If a young woman is comfortable seducing a healthy old man with a brilliant mind she'll be hard pressed to find a more suitable campus to make her choice. The best genes in the galaxy; and they're all free of charge. And I'll bet two or three of the senior professors felt they got the best part of the deal. No commitment, no child maintenance without a prior written agreement, and a few nights of pleasure they thought they'd never see again. An excellent trade as long as their wives don't find out!'

'So,' continued Darkon, 'the Library finds two ideal subjects, plucks them out of the space-time continuum and infects them. But because they knew they were pregnant they stayed on Alexandria-3 and it proved fatal.'

'What are your ideas on how the disease spreads?' Jan was not convinced.

'If my guess is right it'll probably classify as a venereal disease, with men as the carriers and women becoming the sterile victims. With enough promiscuity it'll only take a few generations to infect every star system in our galaxy, a few more generations to spread across all of the planets, and a few more before every woman in the species become infertile. Maybe a handful of isolated planets will survive but without support from federation supply ships it's only a matter of time before they deteriorate into pre-industrial cultures.'

'So far that's speculation, with only circumstantial evidence to support it. Where's your proof?' Sheila was pleased Darkon had developed upon her ideas, but she was too good a scientist to accept an idea just because she wanted it to be true.

'You'll get all the proof you want from the autopsies,'
Darkon continued.

'Those corpses mustn't be allowed to leave the planet the risk is far too high.'

'And now you know where we're heading Sheila, you can't go back into the Library. If you interface again it will know we're on to it. You'll have to get an assistant, someone you can rely on but don't let her in on the details. We need more data from the Library so see what she can get on nano machines and nano bioforms, and anything else you think could change DNA from inside the body.'

Jeff took back control of the meeting.

'We've got to find a way to shut it down when the post mortems confirm the threat. We'll probably need some form of engineering solution and that's a job for your department Mark.'
Then he threw in an unexpected tidbit.
'After inspecting re-runs of the introduction I don't think it's as all powerful as it claims to be.'
'What! Surely there's enough proof. Look at the way it destroyed the hostile visitors, and the ease at which it keeps military ships in a high orbit, It's got plenty of power?' Trudel herself had been in a military craft when it was forced away from the planet.
'It had so much power our inertial stabilizers overloaded by 120% just keeping us from becoming mush on the cabin walls. I still have nightmares about it.'
'I don't think it actually pushed you anywhere.' Was Jeff teasing her? 'It simply doesn't have the power.'
Five sets of eyes swung to meet his. He was grinning, like a cat that had just swallowed the pet goldfish.
'It didn't need to push you any where, you went their all by yourself!'
'What! We pulled at least 50G when it forced us away and we were only using docking thrusters. The main drive wasn't even online.'
'It's the centripetal force gambit, Trudel.' You've got medals for if from your track and field days. You set a new distance record for the Ball-and-Chain Swing at college, didn't you? Remember when you let go of the chain, the ball flies off at a tangent. Now, what if we replace the chain by gravity? Cut the gravity for a split second and then allow it back under very fine control. You'll shoot to a higher orbit until you reach a new equilibrium. The Library was simply using your orbital velocity as a power source. The visual beam's probably

just for effect, to make it look like the energy came from the planet, to make us think it has unlimited power.'

'And as far as destructive power goes, it had to absorb the alien weapons fire for several minutes before sending back a single destructive burst. If it has the raw power to throw ships around space why didn't it tractor the Zogar to a geostationary orbit above the Library? That would be a lot easier than the cat and mouse game it played with us using the probes. There are still a lot of things that don't add up.'

'If we do get proof the Library's dangerous, how are we going to evacuate the planet without the Library putting us all in Limbo? We know it can reach at least nine miles beyond the study center.' Mark was clearly concerned that he, and others, might be trapped for eternity if the planet retaliated. It was a very real threat, one that had unnerving implications. Everyone at the table was uneasy. They knew no one could be allowed to leave Alexandria-3 if they even suspected infection. And they couldn't warn the Federation, there would be no way to stop the news leaking out into comms traffic where the Library was eavesdropping. They were on their own. There was nowhere they could turn for help. On that sour note the meeting broke up. Trudel, Geney and Mark ported up to the GMI-1 where they had equipment to examine the planet in more detail. They would begin in the morning.

Darkon and Sheila stayed for desert, the chocolate delight, before moving to the dance hall to unwind and finish their drinks. It would be the last evening they would relax for a long time. The holiday atmosphere had drawn many couples from the restaurant onto the floor and quite a few were worse for wear after too much alcohol. When the tempo changed to a slow rhythm the floor quickly became packed, leaving little room to do more than undulate in time with the music. Darkon was happy with the slower pace. So when Sheila's head nudged gently into his neck he pulled her closer enjoying the subtle perfume, and her soothing warmth. Completely sober, he felt the moment burning itself deeply into his memory. He would remember it for an eternity. When music paused, she made no move to leave the floor. They stood together hand in hand, both wanting the same thing, both waiting for the music to start again, both wanting the rhythm to be slow. They were looking deeply into each others eyes, both happy. When the music began he gently caressed her neck, finger tips sliding softly over the silkiness of her skin, light movements barely touching, teasing her with the promise of tenderness to come. He felt her relax, snuggling close again, the tensions of the meeting melting away. He stroked her cheeks, followed the curve of her ears, savoring every exquisite sensation. A quiet moan slipped from her lips as he guided them towards his. They kissed. Gently, slowly, like twin airlocks meshing for the first time, each making sure their fit would be perfect. It was. And when their lips parted there was no need for words. Each knew how the other felt and each knew this was more than just a passing flirtation. They were oblivious to the crowds milling around them. If they were ever to be pulled into Limbo, let it be together like this. The music continued late into the night but they hardly heard it. They followed their own rhythm, the rhythm of movement, the rhythm of sensuality, the rhythm of love. Their drinks grew lonely at their table, forgotten and unneeded.

They left long before the last dance, and in the porch light of Sheila's apartment they kissed, passionately, like

adolescents on a first date. Then as he turned to leave she clung on to his hand, refusing to let him go.
'Darkon,' Sheila was hesitant, 'don't leave me alone tonight. I want to be with ***you***.' Her eyes were sparkling in the starlight, tears of happiness welling from the dark green depths. How could anyone refuse? She went inside, quickly packed an overnight bag and set her wardrobe for external access. She wanted a full choice of clothes in the morning without having to return home. Ten minutes later they arrived at Darkon's quarters. Thirty minutes later privacy screens engaged throughout the apartment with their Comms reset for emergency calls only.

**'Beeeeeeeeep! Beep!'**
**'Beeeeeeeeep! Beep!'**
**'Beeeeeeeeep! Beep!'**
**'Beeeeeeeeep! Beep!'**
**'Beeeeee-CLUNK!'** A heavy hand lashed out at the time-panel atop Darkon's bed. The giant hand was loosely attached to a sluggish body straining to stay asleep. 'Ten more minutes, *PLEASE!*'
'Make that *THIRTY*!' a quieter voice, to his right, countermanded the plea. Memories of the previous night to come flooding back, dragging him through the fog of sleeplessness back into the real world.
'Hello? What's ***your*** name?' he joked, a smile playing across his unshaven face.
'You'd ***better*** know my name,' she responded, throwing a playful punch to his lower jaw.
'Steady Sheila!' he cautioned, 'I'm very fragile before breakfast.'
He pulled a ragged face, 'How hungry are you?'

'Very', she replied, 'For some reason I'm really tired this morning. Maybe I did too long a workout last night? What do ***you*** think?' It was her turn to tease.
'I think we both did!'
He cued the house monitor, **'Kitchen: Two full breakfasts, Juice, Cereal, Toast, Cheese and Tomato Omelette, Hot Chocolate - HOLD.'**
He paused looking back to her, 'Anything else you'd like?'
She shook her head, dark tussled hair rippling over her shoulders.
**'Kitchen: SERVE in Fifteen Minutes - GO.'**
***"Confirmed: Breakfast in Fifteen Minutes."***
That would give them plenty of time to cleanse and dress, and time for Darkon to check his mail.
**'Comms: Normal! - Display Incoming - GO.'** The wall lit up displaying the new mail, a few personals from his family, a dozen or more junk mail flagged for deletion, and one from Mark on the Control ship. He opened the latter. It was brief and cryptic. Up in orbit they must have been working throughout the night and they were not going to let the cat out of the bag informing the Library.
It was marked

**URGENT**

To Jeff, Darkon,
Remember the Bounty/Eve-3 shuttle runs. We may have a new use for those old ships that tie in with out earlier discussions. Clean out the mothballs and we'll have what we want. No need for excuses, we have some ready made. Come up and join us as soon as you are free.
Mark Q.
Darkon thought back to his days with the old shuttle fleet. They were obsolete crafts, their technology more than a century out of date: simple nuclear motors, barely enough

power and speed to reach escape velocity, and only designed to hop between planet and moon. What use could they be here? Alexandria-3 has no real moons and the iceberg was in solar orbit, too far for the shuttles to reach. He knew Mark and his team would be eager to fill in the details.

Meanwhile, the sonic/aquatic shower was waiting, and this morning he really needed it. Passing the bedroom door he could hear Sheila's muffled voice conducting a heated debate with his wardrobe. How can women take so much time dressing he wondered, we (the men) never rely on a wardrobe's opinion no matter how sophisticated it's programming. Surely it's quicker to picture it in your mind then grab what you want. 30-seconds! That's it! Finished!!!

His father had warned him of moments like this. He bit his tongue, as he ducked into the shower. Steaming hot jets waved up and down massaged his body, sending irritating sensations through his nervous system.

**'SHOWER: RESET TO OWNER STANDARD - GO.'**

The cubical complied resetting to his personal preferences, 'Yes Dad,' he though, 'and they want the toilet seat put down too!' The spray dropped to a refreshing 75°F, pressure doubling until he could feet the water stinging into his muscles. The sonics kicked in dislodging every particle of clinging debris from his body. After two minutes the flow cut to gravity feed at a humble 55°F, closing his pores in the cooler water. Then as the water cut off the remaining moisture evaporated in a blast of ultra dry air, immediately followed by hiss of aerosols as his skin was infused with replacement oils and today's choice aroma, randomly selected.

He stepped from the shower pleased to find the wardrobe was free. No fiddle-fuddling about, he grabbed an office standard one-piece with embedded shoes - dark blue or grey, he didn't notice and more to the point he didn't care. After all it was just for the office. He slid into the clothes, paused while they adjusted to his body and was ready to start the day.

Sheila was already in the kitchen when he entered. She had waited for him to arrive before starting her meal. A nice touch he thought, very considerate. They ate breakfast in silence, happy glances bouncing across the table like two fire flies courting in the cool night air. They were holding hands as they finished their drinks, unwilling to end the closeness of the night before. But work calls! Darkon would be busy for most of the day and didn't know how long he would be detained in GMI-1, the orbiting Control ship. Together they walked to the spaceport center then a quick hug before parting; Sheila going to the Admin block and Darkon heading for the teleport center.

He flashed his GMI badge as he passed through security. Nodding to the duty guard he inquired, 'Which door for GMI-1 today?'

'Extreme right sir. It opens every 5-minuites if anyone's waiting.'

'Thanks.' He cast a look over his shoulder to the offices where Sheila would be working, 'And thank you too,' he whispered.

## A Promise of Hope

On cue, his end of the teleport opened. He walked forward, handprinting at the security grill. His ID badge bleeped as it was successfully scanned and the grill dissolved. He glanced through the newly opened portal to the center of the ship suspended many miles above and walked through. He heard the familiar "pop" as the portal, now clear of any non-gaseous mass, collapsed behind him. Mark rushed forward to greet him hardly able to contain the excitement bubbling through the whole crew.

***'Port Closed - Security Level RED.'***

The ship advised its status to anyone who cared to know.

'Great!' exclaimed Mark, 'Jeff's already onboard, and William close docked LS48 last night at the starboard airlock. Have we got some good news for you!'

Then before Darkon had time to catch his breath,

'There's been a leak. The shit's hit the fan! News of Sonia's ordeal and the fourteen dead staffers has gone viral on every newswire across the galaxy. It seems someone at the Sol-3 hospital sold the information to the local media and it's escalated out of control. Pressure groups for the top thousand Universities are lobbying Federal Parliament already, demanding better protection for their students at Alexandria.-3'

'Someone's calculated that, in an emergency, with all the teleports working it'll take at least two hours to evacuate the planet. They must have included a full staff compliment, even the positions we haven't filled yet, to get that figure.

'So what're you all excited about? You called it GOOD news!'

'You haven't heard the ***good*** part yet! Some idiot demanded that we treat the planet like a starship - and fit it with Escape-Pods - and those dumb federation politicians jumped all over the idea. It got tri-partisan support in record time and just before the night sitting ended it was transmitted for Presidential Approval. By all accounts he likes the idea too, anything to keep the flow of new technology coming to enhance his image as the **Father of the New Age**. That, by the way, is his slogan for next year's election.

'But Mark, Escape-Pods won't ever get off the planet - you'd need booster rockets even to reach low orbit!'

'And that,' Jeff interrupted, 'is where your old job comes into the picture, Darkon! I got a call from the Graveyard Fleet last Night.'

The Graveyard was a planetless star around which GMI "parked" its retired lifeships. Over time it had become the dumping ground for all obsolete space craft in the cluster. The caretakers take a 50% commission on all sales and for that they handle all the legal niceties and documentation. It had become a dumping ground for hundreds of companies when their fleets were updated. And one of those companies ran the shuttle fleet where Darkon worked early in his career.

'They have all twenty of the retired nuclear fleet that were put onto mothballs, professionally preserved and still in perfect working condition. Nobody's going to buy shuttles when they can get interplanetary jumpships for the same price. The caretakers proposed donating them as a tax write off and GMI not surprisingly is all for it. Tractoring them here behind a Lifeship, is nothing compared to the cost of decommissioning. They're all rigged for passenger service and we have an engineer/pilot right here who's familiar with the equipment and can train the new crews - don't we Darkon!'

'Hold on, Jeff,' he wasn't going to have that role thrown in his lap without a fight. 'Their engines alone take 20-man-hours servicing after each flight, that's not cost effective in anyone's book! It'll take months to fit them out for long term standby duty.'
'Yes,' William interjected, 'but, we will only be using them TWICE!'
'Once to evacuate the planet …' he paused,
'and once to land them empty, and Blow the dammed planet to a billion pieces!'
'How does it sound to you NOW ... ... .... Ha! Ha! Ha!' his raucous laughter echoed throughout the ship.
'But the Library won't let you land ships with munitions aboard; it'll punch them into high orbit the moment you try to send them down.'
'context… … …Context… … …CONTEXT!' shouted William, leaning forward with a grin stretching from ear to ear across his face. 'I can see those cogs whirring in your head Darkon!' he was enjoying taunting his friend.
'When is a bomb NOT a bomb, my sluggish friend?'
He watched, waiting for the answer to strike Darkon like a fly swat crushing a Maeconian Flea. It struck! And the same grin wrapped itself around another face.
Slowly Darkon mouthed the words, almost afraid put his voice behind them,
'When the bomb is the Engine … all twenty of them!' then in a louder voice,
'Sneaky, young William. You are ***sneaky***!'
He did some quick mental arithmetic,
'Fourteen would be enough for a planet this size if they blow together, that gives us over forty percent overkill, a forty percent safety factor. You think you can set it up, no electronics, no comms, and no kamikaze?'

'I've got some ideas in my head. It'll take me a few days to work out the details without using the computers and more time in the workshop to build a prototype mechanism. It has to be a mechanical trigger that can't be remotely cancelled once we initiate it. Then we can get a workshop crew to build the subassemblies. They won't even know what they're working on. I'll assemble them in orbit and they can be fitted when you and I do the inspections before we send the old kites down to the planet. I can build in a mechanical isolation switch to protect us until we're ready.'
'OK William, Get back to Jeff and me when you have something definite, and good luck! We'll see you in a day or too.
And remember. **NO OPEN COMMS TALK;** not even between ourselves**.'**
Three days later the Hazmat team arrived to examine the corpses. Their Chief Coroner was Julian McNess, head of GMI's Interplanetary Medicine for the last three years. His department was responsible for cataloguing all emerging diseases following colonization of new planets. Invariably there would be pathogens for which treatment was urgently needed and over the decades GMI's record, though not perfect, had been eminently successful. There were only two cases of total failure where promising "M" class worlds had to be branded "Off Limits" to Humanity, with indigenous fauna and flora symbiotically dependant upon micro-organisms deadly to Mankind. With GMI's reputation preceding them, McNess was confident the current problem would soon be resolved under the meticulous scrutiny of his dedicated team.
By the time the Hospital Ship arrived in orbit he was up to speed on the Library's history, its affect on the residents of Alexandria-3, testimonies from the fifteen staffers

following the Ordeal, and Sonia's full medical records. He was ready to call it a night. His team would start the post mortems early the following morning so, allowing for a few inevitable surprises, he expected to be on his way back home within the week, with another mystery filed under the heading "Solved by McNess!". Even in Virtual Reality his folder was already bulging at the seams. But nature abhors a braggart and the surprise that awaited him the following day would literally be 'Out of this World'.
The early morning saw Tom McFarland, the medi-team's intern, heading across campus to the morgue. This was his most important assignment since joining GMI fresh from college a year earlier. He was determined to make this a text book example of how to prepare bodies for post mortem, and in the process get a few brownie points from McNess. Julian had selected him for this high profile project from a shortlist of more experienced applicants specifically because of his attention to detail and impeccable penchant for procedure. He would not let him down.
Manual labor first! He cleaned and disinfected the tables. The doctors would be arriving within the hour to begin the examinations and he knew each of their personal preferences and quirks by heart. Their equipment was sterilized, laid out, and covered ready for work to begin. Three sets of ceiling mounted monitors were primed to record every movement occurring on the tables below. All that remained was allocation of the best preserved corpses for initial examination. The female body would be easier to select with only two specimens. One had died in her quarters and had lain undiscovered for forty hours the other, hospitalized and in intensive care, had entered stasis within minutes of being declared dead. He chose the

latter and moved the stasis unit to table-one ready for Julian to unlock. The first male to die: Harry Marson would be an ideal subject for Dr. Masters. With several thousand autopsies to his credit, Paul would easily recognize any unusual characteristics. Harry's corpse-box went on table-two. Judy Farmer however, with a background in forensics, would be comfortable digging into a body that was somewhat more decomposed. From the records he selected an appropriate cadaver: Pod thirteen. While moving it to table-three a subtle odor wafted from the unit.

'Funny,' he thought, 'these stasis pods are supposed to be air tight.'

As soon as the transporter had disengaged and retracting back to its wall recess Tom inspected the stasis pod for leaks.

**'LIGHTS - Table Three - Full - NOW.'** The room responded bathing the table in intense light: full visible spectrum, plus ultra violet. Side wall illumination increased to improve lateral visibility. The pungent aroma was more pronounced now, and it was definitely coming from the pod.

The outer doors of the Medical Center activated as the doctors arrived.

'Doctor McNess?' he called through the intercom.

'Good morning Tom.' replied Julian. 'Have you had time to rustle up a pot of coffee yet?'

'Two pots ready and waiting in the office, I'll join you in a couple of minutes. I'm almost finished here.'

When Tom joined them for his second coffee the doctors were already reviewing their charts. He mentioned the leaking pod and called tech. support to book a servicing.

'Is the Bio-Hazard Failsafe engaged, Tom?' Julian was looking around for the security monitor.

'Switched it on as soon as I came in this morning. There's a status panel over the pressure lock going into the mortuary, and it feeds into the admin general alarm system. Everything checks out OK, apart from the smell on table-3.'

'Table-3? So I get the smelly one ***again***?' Judy joked, 'I'll get started then, if you've got nothing else for me Julian?'

'Nothing. Go ahead Judy; we'll be through in a few minutes.' The men relaxed to finish their drinks in comfort. They were pleased to have a few minutes without needing to watch their language in front of a "sensitive" female. She was an excellent doctor but a woman from the old school. One who not only expecting equal rights, which she clearly deserved and already received in full, but also the privileges and perks of chivalry from that long dead system whereby females contributed little and in turn demanded everything their mates could afford.

'If we get this cleared up in eight days, we've been promised a bonus on top of hazard pay. So let's get to it!' They finished their drinks and Tom led them to their waiting "guests".

'Is that the display?' McNess was pointing to a flashing icon above the 'airlock' doors.'

'Yes doctor, but it shouldn't be flashing! It was steady when I left fifteen minutes ago. Don't say the something else is broke. This place is falling apart.'

They stepped towards the door and almost bumped into it. 'That's odd they open automatically.' Tom stepped back and retried. No effect.

**'DOORS: OPEN!'** he demanded. The doors remained firmly closed.

**He** clarified the command,

**'MORTUARY: OPEN DOORS - NOW!'**

Still, the doors refused to obey.
He shouted through the door, 'Judy, can you let us in please, the doors are playing up again.' 'JUDY - CAN YOU HEAR ME? Let us in, the doors aren't working.' There was no reply.
'There's a viewing window round the corner.' Tom was getting annoyed by now. Everything was piling up to ruin his work and if Julian remembered today, it would be for all the wrong reasons: smells, jammed doors, surely nothing else could go wrong today!
That, in a few seconds, would turn out to be the biggest understatement of his life.
They rounded the corner and FROZE. An unimaginable scene confronted them. Hardened medics familiar with the realities of life and death stared, transfixed at the phantasmagoria playing out before them. Beyond the glass, streaming from what was left of the corpse, a sickly mustard ooze had spilled out over the table. It flowed down onto the floor and was pulsing as it crossed towards Judy's inert body. It moved unlike any fluid they had ever seen, like an amoeba encircling its prey. Her head and upper torso were quickly engulfed. Before their horrified eyes the protuberance that had once been her head collapsed into the sludge, before they could react, the collapse flowed along the length of her body reducing it to nothingness. Judy was dead. The ooze undulated with purpose towards the door. With the others, Julian heard the words drag themselves from his still frozen mouth, not knowing how he had summoned the strength to utter them:

**'MORGUE: TOTAL STERILIZATION,'**
**'ALL SYSTEMS - ENGAGE!'**

# The Ooze

The tears in his eyes screamed in abject helplessness as he issued the irrevocable command. His mind reeled. It reeled back to that fateful day fourteen years earlier, back to the most agonizing moment in his military career, to the day he slammed shut an emergency hatch to save the lives of four hundred soldiers and in doing so sentenced twenty young recruits to an agonizing death by suffocation. Twenty young lives cut short; his own brother among them. He swore he would sooner die than make the same judgment again. But he just had! Part of him, the rational part, knew Judy was beyond hope. But the feeling part, the part that made him Human, that part cried out in pain, cried out sharing the agony Judy and his brother had both suffered.

The window darkened as shields engaged. Behind them he could sense the enormous heat building up, the chamber flooding with deadly radiation, searing heat, toxic gas. When the radiation stopped an emergency portal opened in the center of the morgue, the other in airless space dangerously close to the local sun. Through the insulation he could feel the vibrations as vacuum strained to suck the vicious menace to a fiery death. The window cleared while the portal was still open allowing them to inspect the damage; but the ooze far from gone. It was still alive it was still struggling despite the lack of air and pressure. It was straining to reach the door, straining to escape, and gradually making progress. But it couldn't be allowed to reach the airlock, it couldn't be allowed to reach them!

'Tom stay here, monitor its distance to the door, Paul follow me!' Julian yelled instructions as he rushed to the office, 'Get Darkon on the comm. Get me the coordinates of the nearest black hole, hurry!'

As he dropped into the control desk he prayed he could remember his portal training.

'Have you got those coordinates yet?'

'Not yet he's accessing the data now,'

Julian pulled up the security system isolating portal-controls his mind straining to recall memories unused for years.

'We've got the Black. Darkon's downloading its position now.

'Got it! Refocusing Portal-1 now!' He reopened the portal facing the black-hole positioning it close to the event horizon.

'Tom! Any changes yet?'

'Not yet... Wait something's happening ... ... ...'

'the whole damn room is imploding ... ... ...'

'the goo's still moving to the door ... ... ...'

McNess adjusted the business ends of the portal, slowly widening their apertures, exposing the morgue to more of the black hole.

'It's slowing down ... ... ... stopping'

Tom was getting excited,

'It's losing its grip... ... ... It's being dragged backwards'

'NO! ... ... ... It's still gripping the floor, its not being pulled into the hole ... ... ... '

'Can you lower it? ... ... ... Lower the portal this end - about three feet? ... ... ... '

'That's it ... Keep going ... Down ... Down ... Down ... Down ... ... ...'

'Nearly there ... Nearly ... HOLD IT! ... That's it! ... It's being pulled in... ...'

'80% ... ... ... ... 50% ... ... ... 30 ... ... 20 ... ... 10 ... Almost gone ... ... ... that's it!'

'That's it! It's gone! ... ... ... IT'S ALL GONE! ... ... ... You've done it!'
Julian kept the portal open a few moments longer despite urgent cries emanating from Tom as the morgue doors fought desperately to retain their integrity. With stresses far exceeding any design parameters, they threatened to buckle at any time under the perilous pressure differential and immense gravitational pull. Inside, anything that was not an integral part of the room's structure was pulling apart. Body cubicles burst open spewing their stasis pods across the room only to be tugged through the portal by the enormous power of the black hole.
Integrity alarms blasted their message throughout the spaceport. For precious seconds he stared at the CANCEL button as it blinked indifferently in front of him. He knew that unless all traces of the contamination were evacuated from the morgue no one on the planet would survive. With trepidation he pressed the cancel-icon collapsing the portal. The noise subsided. Tom, still trembling, entered the office slumping down in a seat next to Julian and Paul. All three were drenched in a sticky sweat that had nothing to do with the office temperature.
Tom grabbed the half empty coffee flask and unceremoniously downed its remaining contents in a series of frenzied gulps. Noone would be getting a bonus this trip. Jeff, followed by a dozen security guards, rushed into the office. They'd seen the buckled walls of the morgue as they arrived. Leaning over the console he turned down the screaming alarms, everyone would be aware by now there was an emergency in progress.
'Judy's gone! That dammed Library of yours just absorbed her out of existence! That dammed monster it just....It just....' Julian's tortured face showed the anguish he was fighting to control. Doctor Fong burst into

the room leading the emergency medical team. She was in time to administer a mild sedative to McNess before he lapsed into shock, he needed to explain what he could while the memories were still fresh in his mind. Slowly he told of the last few minutes, the evacuation, and the black hole. Then relieved, he drifted into a black hole of his own, as he willingly surrendered to unconsciousness.

'We may have it on record.' All heads turned towards Tom, 'The monitors were on standby when Judy started. They should have seen everything.' He looked around uncomfortable at being the center of attention.

'I'll make a backup copy first,' he explained fumbling with the master controls, 'its procedure.'

'Look!' he added apologetically. 'Here it comes.'

The recording snapped on as Judy leaned over the table inspecting the equipment. She sniffed the air, her nose clearly reacting to an unpleasant odor.

'Tom was right,' she spoke into the monitor, 'the pod is leaking, but it isn't the normal body decay, it may be a cooling fluid from the stasis unit itself. It's stinging my nasal cavity, tastes like a very weak alkaline.'

**'Morgue: Table-3'**

**'Air Extraction 50% - Allocate to Bin-3a - GO.'**

'That's better, opening the pod now.' The bin was heard hissing open and the body on its support base rolled forward onto the autopsy table. She nudged the pod's control panel and it auto-retract folding itself to minimal size. Judy moved it temporarily to the side of the room, scrawled 'Inspect before re-use' on its surface, and slapped a warning sticker over the controls.

She returned to the body and began. 'No Riga Mortise. The body appears intact but has begun decomposition. There's another odor. This one must be coming from the body, but I don't recognize it.' She took a sensor off the tray and ran it over the length of the body. 'Let's see if the database can find a match.' She replaced the unit and turned back to the corpse. 'The abdominal skin is taut.' She applied light fingertip pressure to the stomach area. 'It feels like an inflated balloon, not skin. I'm making an incision.' Reaching out, she selected the appropriate scalpel, 'Cutting laterally from the sternum.' For the first inch the skin separated around the blade's edge then suddenly split open down to the pelvic bone revealing a mustard/grey mass inside. The shapeless mass bubbled and burst spraying a fine mist in all directions. Judy gasped and stepped backward before slumping to the floor motionless. The monitors focused in on the remaining movement the churning action within the body cavity. The mass seemed to be digesting the corpse. It flowed out through the perforated skin, spread across the table, accumulating at the side nearest the doctors collapsed form. After pausing for only a few seconds, it spread out like a swarm of army ants on migration. Finding a table leg it oozed downward until it reached the floor then headed directly towards Judy's head. Once it made contact pincers stretched out, 'tendrils' racing around both sides of her body till they met at her extremity of her feet. Then like a paint book coloring an outlined shape the mass thickened and slowly enveloping her from head to toe. This was the point when the doctors arrived at the observation window. Everyone in the room watched in silence as the mass dissolved its way down her body increasing its own volume as it digested her. Only when the deadly task was complete did it rest, but only for a few seconds. Then with deliberation the mass now approaching three hundred pounds started oozing towards the door only fifteen feet away. The replay cut off as the

emergency sterilization kicked in, blinding the sensors and scrambling the transmissions with radiation.
They ran computer analysis on the captured gas in Bin-3a. It confirmed what was suspected. Cooling fluid from the Stasis Pod had leaked. With defective refrigeration the pod had warmed up, the fluid became gaseous at room temperature. Had failure of the stasis pod led to the disaster, or was it just coincidental. And what of the second gas Judy detected. The computer analysis revealed nothing unusual. In addition to normal proportions of nitrogen and oxygen found in ambient air the sample was comprised of carbon, hydrogen, sulfur, and a few rare elements in unrecognized proportions. So far there was nothing to raise the alarms. Jeff had copies of the monitor data transmitted to GMI-1 for relay to head office. The experts on Sol-3 would want to be kept in the loop. Whatever the cause it was clear that a serious problem was developing on Alexandria-3. Could the Library be eliminated as a conspirator, or would the Humans have to face an awful truth?
For the next few days the morgue remained sealed and new external monitors were installed to watch for any re-mergence of the ooze. The committee, which would soon include Julian McNess, retired to GMI-1 to continue their investigations. Tom, the only eye witness to the whole episode, was asked to join them. For the remainder of the day and well into the night, they attempted analysis of the entity. Many questions needed answers. Was the ooze natural, mechanical, bio-mechanical? Was it alive and sentient? Was it intelligent or acting on blind instinct?
Could it be killed by anything less than a black hole?
Had the black hole indeed killed it or merely pulled it into eternal exile.

By the early hours of the morning they were exhausted. Every facet of the ooze that had been recorded was enlarged and examined. It appeared shapeless, without structure at the highest magnification. Down to 1/100,000 of an inch resolution it appeared only as a fluid apparently held together by a force similar to surface tension. Clearly it had purpose. Its movement from one corpse to another exhibited deliberate behavior. It had ignored the inorganic material of the table and the floor, but absorbed clothing around the bodies. They reviewed its digestion of the first corpse zooming in on the peripheral view of the table, examining the residues. Small particles of clothing or personal effects had been missed - or at least rejected. Maybe that was a clue, was there some substance the ooze disliked? It was too late to tell what the residue had been, it was long gone into the gravity well of the black hole, but it hinted at a weakness in the slime's metabolism. There was at least one compound the ooze could not stomach. They had got almost nowhere, barely the wiser for their hours of toil; they couldn't determine if the ooze was a pulpy substance or if they'd just seen the outer skin of a more powerful organism.

As the monitor replay approached its conclusion for the tenth time Ray RONGO entered with more jugs of coffee. He heard McNess give the order to sterilize the mortuary area, and looked over to the view screen.

'That's odd,' he commented in his usual carefree manner, 'I'd have thought an order like that would need a security check.'

'No! Not in the morgue Roy', it was Tom, pedantic as usual, 'It got our voice prints and security clearances as soon as we arrived. Dr McNess downloaded them before we ported down.'

'Not even a conformation request?'

'Not for that one. Leastwise, not unless there's someone still inside, and still alive of course. It's got an immediate execute rating, just like a bio-warfare lab. There's no time to double check in an emergency, it's better to rebuild a room than kill off everyone on the station.'
'So how does the room know someone's inside and if they're still breathing?'
'There're plenty of motion detectors all over the place, including the body drawers. And then of course there's the remote ECGs tuned to human brainwaves, just in case we make a mistake and someone isn't really dead when we put them away, and a few more detectors scattered across the ceiling with a clear view of everyone inside. Yet another expense courtesy of Federal regulations.'
'Quite impressive, we've nothing as extensive at the Rim just a few automatic drawers and plastic tables. We can't even keep the rodents out in the hot season. You can imagine what the families say about that.'
Darkon had been following the conversation, 'Are the ECGs running all the time - the ones in the drawers I mean, are they logged?'
Tom thought for a moment, 'I'm not sure, it'll only take a few minutes to find out. Do you want me to check?'
'Yes, if you can, pull records for all the pods please… and you might as well grab the ceiling ones too.' It was worth a quick viewing, they had nothing to lose.
A few minuets later Tom had the fourteen scans neatly laid out on the wall screen along with matching sound and thermal traces. He called Darkon over to inspect them and had the computer scroll through the traces looking for any unusual activity. Initial traces showed the bodies cooling down as the stasis pods did their work. All traces low lined until two days before the post mortems. Only one abnormality occurred. Pod thirteen emitted a quiet wine

for about ten hours, then as the temperature rose the ECG detected weak beta wave activity. It was far too low to trigger the alarms, barely noticeable on the traces, but easily detected digitally by the computer. It reached a peak in less than a day then tapered off within a few minutes to almost zero again.

'Switch in the ceiling traces. And throw up the clock.'

Tom added them to the screen. At six fifteen activity started again.

'That's me. It was my job to prepare the bodies.'

When pod thirteen was pulled from the drawer the ceiling ECGs showed the same weak beta waves activity again, still below significant levels, but they were increasing slowly. By 07:55 hours they had been stable for almost fifteen minutes. The recordings indicated Tom leaving the room, then ten minutes later a second set of traces arose, 'That'll be Judy arriving.' They synchronized the Monitor screen to the traces, seven minutes layer, the beta levels rose as Judy opened the Stasis Pod. They continued rising steadily until the incision on the corpse abdomen and reached a level just below the alarm trigger point. By the time the ooze attacked Judy's body it was stabilized at the higher level and stayed that way until the sterilization began. At that point it shot off the scale. The trace remained at maximum until the end.

Before turning in for the night, Darkon put a call through to the Admin Center advising the staff to monitor for beta frequencies within the shell of the morgue. It might be the only way to detect the danger. They were only too happy to comply, and without asking for permission installed Beta Wave detectors all over the Admin Complex.

## Mini-Portal Tool or Weapon

Back in the Control Center on GMI-1 Jeff and Darkon considered the problems another attack posed. If the Ooze reappeared, they must be prepared for it. The first time they had been lucky with the danger arising in the protected area of the morgue. Had the ooze escaped confinement many more lives would have been lost. They called in Geney and William to join the brainstorm. Both were qualified in portal-technology, Geney an expert in portal-usage, and William in engineering.

At first they bounced around ideas for fixed location safety holes similar to the vacuum system installed in the morgue. An add-on for that: automatic switching to a black hole gravity extractor as needed. Mobile scanning units to 'float' round the complex and link to extractors if the ooze was spotted. Weapons of various kinds were suggested, defensive and aggressive. Could voice-activated barriers be used to block or destroy the target? And as a last resort personal teleports to permit a rapid escape.

Aggressive weapons could have their energy turned against them and in any case the Library would probably not allow them on the planet. Personal teleports would require too much energy and be too bulky. Barriers, no one knew what materials or energy force would work on the ooze. Fixed location extractors seemed to offer the best hope for success, but it's unlikely they would be in the right place at the right time, and if the Library can sense them, the ooze, can avoid them. One idea put forward was to set up a central Porting Control Station. In an emergency anyone could call in and have the business end of a portal opened at their location. Plausible except

for the difficulty Tom and Julian had working together and they were already familiar with the equipment.
'What if they don't have to talk?' William speculated. 'Remember the federation wars. We'd spot our targets with particle beams, upload rough co-ordinates, and the gunner's locked in on the targets without knowing exactly where they were. Can we do something like that?'
'You bet we can,' it was Tom interrupting, 'hang on a minute I've got something in the kiddy box on HS03.' Tom disappeared down the corridor, through the airlock and into the Hospital Ship. A few minutes later he reappeared grinning sheepishly holding something behind his back. Everyone looked at him in curiosity. Without warning he drew a pistol, pointed straight at Geney Gourd, and fired point blank. Whoosh! A micro hole opened up inches in front of her chest and what looked like the discharge from a narrow-angle particle-beam struck her just above the heart. Feeling the impact, she clasped the "wound" in disbelief, a red sticky fluid trickling through her hand dribbling down to the floor.
She stared incredulously at her hand, gazing transfixed into the bloody mess. Then as she watched the "blood" evaporated before her eyes. She stared at Tom, mouth gaping wide open while everyone else was staring at her, watching the red smudge on her tunic vaporize to reveal - nothing?
'Its "kiddy powder"!' laughed Tom. 'It sublimes at body temperature. But watch the micro-hole.' He flicked a slide on the pistol grip with his thumb changing the setting to Flashlight mode, then squeezed and held down the trigger. From the micro-hole a light beam shone out. 'Watch!' He swung his arm pointing at each of the crew in turn. The micro-hole followed the pistol maintaining a position

exactly three feet in front the gun in precisely the direction it was pointing.
'And now,' he placed his other hand against the top of the barrel and applied pressure. The micro-hole shot forward moving away from the gun.
'The harder you press the greater the distance, logarithmic scale of course.'
'What ***is*** it?'
Jeff was getting interested. He wanted more details.
'It's a prototype. My brother designed it for the military but they rejected the system because the base unit isn't portable enough for use in the field.
They told him: "Go sell it to a toy company".
'How's it work? How powerful is it?' asked Darkon, taking the bait.
It's basically a micro-portal based walky-talky. Here's setting one.' he flipped the thumb slide to the top notch, and raised the pistol grip to his face like a microphone.

'Alexandria-3 to Sol-Outer GMI Lifeship Base - Jana Rook please.
A few seconds later Jana's voice came across loud and clear,
'Sol-Outer Jana Rook.'
'Hi Jana, Tom McFarland, Can you send the data my brother forwarded please.'
'OK, wait out … … … Transmitting … … … … … Transmission Complete'
'Did you get it OK Tom? Did it work?'
Tom looked at the icons displayed on the pistol grip, he seemed satisfied,
'It looks OK Jana, thanks; I'll send a full report by the end of the day. Thank you, Alexandia-3 Out.'
'Bye Tom, Sol-Outer out.'

‘What’s that all about?’ Jeff wanted a bit more seriousness and the meeting was getting much too casual for his liking. ‘What did she send you?’ he demanded.

Tom removed a data pack from inside the pistol grip and plugged it into their desktop consol. Pulling the new data he displayed an index of available sources.

‘It’s a list of direct supply points that have portal access. The “gun” can uses up to six of them at a time and you select one with this slider on the pistol grip.’ He showed how easily it switched settings. ‘Just squeeze the trigger to open the delivery portal, and squeeze harder to increase the aperture size. Then press the top of the barrel to move the portal further away from you.

‘Without supplier details it defaults to use six chambers in Base Unit that’s in the Hospital Ship hold.’

‘Setting 1 is for the comms link and 2-to-6 for the 5 pressurized compartments in the base-unit. At the moment they’re filled with the usual kiddy things:

2-Flashlight mode … …

3-Water … …

4-Suction ... …

5-Funny Powder … …

‘Basically, it’s an intuitive remote control for portals. The power’s in the base unit, all the gun does is point to where you want the local portal to open.’

‘How do the gun and the Base Unit communicate?’ it was William’s turn to show some interest.

‘Normally while it’s in your hand a conventional comms link opens but if there’s no local network it initiates micro-portal comms. The military demanded we incorporate voice or palm print identification.’

‘And the military doesn’t want it?’ again Ray was surprised.

'You haven't seen the Base Unit yet - one-hundred-seventy pounds unloaded - it'd take both of us to lift it when it's full! The team just couldn't get the weight down to the eighty-five pounds the military needed, that's as much as a soldier's expected to carry. They tried using a remote base but it was too easy to jam, the old inverse square rule, so beyond about one-fifty miles it gets unreliable. That just wasn't enough for them. They tried using power shields instead of pressure plates to keep the weight down but the energy signature was visible all over the battlefield.'

'Does GMI know you're carrying that much dead weight half way across the galaxy?' Jeff was surprised that untested equipment was adding to the transport budget.

'They were the ones who suggested bringing it, for field trials. They're all in favor especially if it stops people crowding the ship comms panel. If we have spare time they want us to run some trials after the PMs are finished. And,' he added tentatively, 'port the bodies directly to Sol-3, if you kicked up a fuss. But I guess that's a moot point now.'

'What GMI likes most,' interrupted Dr. McNess, 'is it can draw power from the base unit and recharge all our portable equipment. There's no need to carry a dozen different power packs when we port down to a planet or a disabled starship. That's a lot of weigh we save. And of course if we run into danger it can pack a hefty punch as a side arm.

Jeff exerted his authority. 'How many units have you brought?'

'GMI purchased all fifty of the trial units but Graham, that's my brother's name; he threw in the five early prototypes that only have four settings. The base unit can

handle 64 inputs, either from the guns or a standard comms feeds, of course weapon systems get priority.'
'I assume the Library already knows about them?'
'Unlikely, you know how paranoid the military is. Their tests were done covertly and the design department computers don't talk to anything in the outside world. Graham only told me about the system a few months ago while we were on holiday. That was just after the military turned him down. When I suggested GMI he jumped at the chance. He hasn't contacted anyone else yet, he figured GMI's the only private company that can afford to fund further research.'
'Where are the manuals?' It was William, wanting the usual seven levels of documentation.
'Apart from manufacture, we don't need any. The gun was designed to be used by "canon fodder", the front line soldiers that do all the dirty, dangerous work, guys that need a weapon that works instinctively. It took less than ten minutes to train three battalions for the field tests. All they wanted to know was what the six settings did and their platoon leaders' only concerns were: how to use them, what was the IA if it malfunctioned, and how to make them self destructed. That's setting six, it opens a hole directly below the gun for five seconds so it can be dropped or be thrown through. That was O.K. for them just enough time to stop the enemy getting hold of it.'
'Yes Tom, but what about configuring the six settings.'
'Oh right, William. You program the Base Unit from its own control panel, or over a link. It uses the same user-friendly program that's here. Just select the source location and drag it to one of the six slots shown here on the right, or you can set the co-ordinates manually the same way you do for your lifeship's thruster drive. The gun selects the source it wants so when you squeeze the

trigger it syncs to the Base Unit which then opens the portals and continues monitoring the gun moving the delivery portal as needed.'

'Who pays for the consumables?' Jeff was always hot on expenses.

'Standard account protocols, you can pre-load some defaults then set any of the guns to override with their own account.'

'What's your brother's salary? Never mind we can discuss that with him later.'

They continued talking for several hours. Tom had memorized the main results from the military trials and apart from the 150 mile limitation for the portable Base Unit the system had proved highly effective. Matter and energy transmission was accurate and a hand weapon that could use both had played havoc with the opponent's defense shields.

William installed the Base Unit safely in GMI-1 just as the Library rotated into morning sunlight. The committee agreed to four trial settings to be used against the Ooze.

| | |
|---|---|
| Setting 1, | Voice channel, and combined flashlight function, |
| Setting 2, | Open at the upper atmosphere allowing the debris to burn up on re-entry, |
| Setting 3, | Open at the sun irradiating the target area & gravitating matter into the solar furnace, |
| Setting 4, | Open near the local black-hole; they dared not test this option and hoped it was not needed. |

With all the options being passive, using negative pressure and gravity, they were optimistic that the Library would allow them to use the devices on the planet. With two spare settings they kept the sixth for

Disposal/Retrieval as the military done and assigned a drinking water supply at #5. They could change the settings latter as needs arose.
They marked the gun-like devises as inconspicuously as possible:

| | |
|---|---|
| Setting 1, | Comms-Light |
| Setting 2, | Re-Enter |
| Setting 3, | Starlight |
| Setting 4, | Blackout |
| Setting 5, | Water |
| Setting 6, | Return |

The five early prototypes only used the first four settings.
Early next day Jeff and Darkon were ready to port down to Alexandria-3 carrying the new devices. To misdirect the Library they both initiated comms calls from the 'guns' and were deep in conversation when the portals opened. Jeff was first to step through, he turned flashing a relieved look back to the ship, and carried on talking with Julian at the Admin hospital. So far: so good. Darkon with the smaller 4-setting unit didn't have to feign genuine conversation. He was unabashedly distracting Sheila from her duties to arranging a second date later that evening. If the Library had objected to the weapon and had zapped him out of existence, he would hardly have noticed. Fortunately, it did not.
After a week of forced separation Darkon was feeling low, like a little boy who had received a giant box of chocolates for New Years Day and forgot where he hid them. But it was more than that. He couldn't remember when he'd last felt this happy, he wasn't really sure if he had ever felt this way before. When he thought of her, he ached to feel her arms around him, to feel her touch, her warmth… … …
'Oh! Hell!'… … … he missed ***everything*** about her.

'Hello, are you still there? Hello! Hello!' He snapped back to sanity, it was Sheila's voice echoing through the comms.

'Yes, yes, just got a bit distracted. So you're on for this evening! Great!' it was not like Darkon to get flustered.

'Shall we meet in the restaurant?' Sheila was asking.

'Wait... ... ... I'll be visiting the office later today we can arrange things then, OK?'

She agreed and closed the link.

He was uncomfortable. Emotions should not be that distracting. He had learned in his early life to keep them under strict control; they should stay out of the way until they were needed. Their place was at social events, at the bar, at home and only then if he was with an attractive young woman. They certainly shouldn't be breaking through during his daily routine. That was too disconcerting.

'Damn it!' Before they'd discovered the Library he had everything under control. All this inconsistency was getting to him. It was bringing up emotions that long ago had been organized, filed, and put in their appropriate place behind bolted doors.

So why did he feel angry. A moment ago he was full of spring fever, not that he didn't want to be, but now he was felling upset and annoyed. He focused his mind allowing the feelings to subsided, all the feelings, including the good ones. He monitored his body as it stabilized.

Blood pressure: 110 over 80, pulse 68, respiration 9 per minute.

Much better, with his mind and body under control Darkon was ready for the tasks ahead. He had lost sight of Jeff but knew he was heading for the hospital where Julian was about to check out. He joined them both in reception, and was pleased to find Julian more composed after a much needed rest. Together they inspected the Admin Center to check the readings on the Beta monitors. So far there was no active sign of another infiltration by the ooze. The Morgue, or what was left of it, was still under lock and key until radiation levels dropped. It would be another 48 hours before it would be safe to enter without protective clothing.

They were anxious to test the new portal guns at orbital distance from the Base Unit. The term was becoming cumbersome so they agreed an easier name: stargun. The starguns had already checked out for the comms link. They borrowed a room in the Admin center with washing facilities. Jeff stood back four feet from the preparation area. Selected 5-Water, and squeezed the trigger, water was discharged successfully accumulating in the basin. He practiced with the stargun until he was comfortable with the way it handled. 'Tom was right,' he said casually, 'it needs hardly any training. Your turn Darkon, try the vacuum.'

Darkon selected: 3-Starlight, 'Don't want to advertise to local Gods just yet.' He moved across the room and opened the hole at its minimum size. There was a slight hissing as the micro-hole began to 'suck' and around the aperture the air began to glow as the superheated molecules became incandescent. It was difficult in the ambient light to focus on the small hole but as the aperture size was increased the heat haze surrounding it became obvious. Pressing the top of the stargun moved the haze closer to the basin and it proved easy to direct the suction to a point directly above the water which was promptly pulled into the orifice and ported out into space for dispersal. He released the trigger and applied the safety.

'It's very comfortable and not the slightest feedback pressure. Tom's brother did a good job.'
'Here Julian,' Jeff passed him the standard model, 'Have a try. Safety's on.'
Within minutes, he too was impressed with the ease of use, and asked tentatively, 'Did you anticipate any problems using the device down here?'
'We were expecting it to be recognized as a tool. After all, the chef uses a variety of knives that could be interpreted as weapons, and we refrained from using belt or shoulder holsters to avoid implying it was a weapon. Now we know it works we need to issue the … … …,'
he paused,
'the tools?... ... … to the important staff members.'
Again, he chose the words carefully; avoiding the term "security guards" just in case the Library was eavesdropping.
'I'll join you in the ship later, Jeff.' Darkon pocketed his stargun and turned to leave. 'There're a couple of items I need to have investigated at the Library. See you later Julian.'

## Emerging Patterns

When Darkon entered the office Sheila was busy analyzing the latest data on earlier guardians. She smiled as he leaned across the desk and gently placed a kiss on her forehead.

‘That’s quite enough,’ she whispered, ‘in public!’

He changed the subject, ‘Have you found anything new?’

‘Wendy, she’s my replacement, she’s in the Library now. We’re still trying to get medical details from the final centuries. But everything we try just runs into a silica wall. How did you get on upstairs?’ she asked, using the common euphemism for an orbiting starship.

‘I heard about the ooze. Galaxy! It makes my blood run cold just to think about it. Did she suffer?’

‘I don’t think so. I doubt she even realized what was happening. From the monitors, it looks like she passed out as soon as the vapor hit.’

He returned to the matter in hand, ‘Have you planned anything else for Wendy at the Library?’

‘Nothing specific, but we have her booked for a few hours later this afternoon, why?’

‘Good. Have her look at the ooze on the Morgue replays first. Then see if she can get anything on it from the Library. It may have been developed by one of the earlier Guardians and somehow escaped contaminating the local area. The group could have been exposed during the Ordeal. And ask her to carry this detector when she goes down.’ He handed her a palmtop sampling unit. ‘It’s just to monitor the EMFs during a session. None of Harry’s group spent much time in the study zones so there may be some protection the students get from the Library, something that staffers missed out on. But I’m not very hopeful it’ll come up with anything. Anything else?’

There was. Sheila enlarged a graph on the wall display. 'This is from demographics covering the five centuries following First Contact. That's the longest any species survived. I've aligned the individual graphs to intersect when the Libraries opened for general access.'

'You can see the curves are similar for all the Guardians: a steady growth rate around contact time and continued to increase for about fifty years then the rate of increase starts to drop off. The rest you know. Whatever happens appears to begin almost immediately, and to have a noticeable galactic effect in such a short time span it must be highly infectious, but without symptoms.'

'The library's given us very little on the nano technology you asked about, mechanical or bio-tech and what they do have only starts with the fifth Guardians. That suggests the technology wasn't around during the first four extinctions. It may only be coincidence, but it was the fifth Guardians that survived the longest.'

'What did you get on genetics?' If, as the committee still suspected, that was the mode of attack Darkon didn't expect the Library would volunteer help in that area either. 'Have any of the Guardians shown expertise in genetic engineering?'

'Each time we try to question the Library it insists development in that direction is too dangerous.' Sheila had tried to get information herself, several times, 'It implies that to follow the path would cause irreparably damage to the gene pool and could lead to extinction the same way it had for our predecessors. Could we have misjudged it? Is it really on our side?'

'I'd like to think so. But every other species is extinct, and we may already be beyond "the point of no return".'

A cold shudder ran down his spine, 'If we're wrong I

doubt the Library will hold it against us, but if it is malevolent we have to act soon or it'll be too late.'

Wendy returned from her study center session very excited, it had been more productive than usual. The Library had made unexpected revelations.

'I asked for additional demographics during the extinctions to see if other creatures were infected. I wanted to know what other life forms were undergoing a population decline. In every case it's the same. Only the dominant species suffers. Even their closely related higher primates were safe, healthy, and breeding successfully.'

'That's what we suspected.' Darkon was hoping for something new. 'Did that lead anywhere?'

'By itself - No, but I output the genetics for the surviving primates and ran a match against the next Guardians. In every case the new species has a better than 99.4% genomes match with one of the prior culture's primates. There's very little doubt, each Guardian is a direct descendant from an earlier non-dominant primate.'

Darkon began speculating, 'It's as if something extinguishes each culture just when they're ready to expand beyond the Milky Way. That's animal husbandry on a colossal scale! That "Something" allows them to develop, acquires all their technology, kills them off, then waits for a new culture to develop with something new to exploit. If that's true, the Milky Way may only be one of countless galaxies being farmed that way. How do we fight something that organized?' Once again a cold shudder ran down Darkon's spine, only this time it didn't go away.

By the time they met for dinner Wendy had been debriefed after her second visit to the Library. Sheila was eager to discuss the latest news with Darkon but, even as they sat down to order, the exhaustion from the tensions of the previous week showed on their faces. Everyone in the complex was in the same worn out state, the regular staffers being hardest hit. Senior management was exempt the two year contract clause and had the freedom to leave but GMI had guaranteed study time in the Library as an inducement to recruit volunteers for this remote posting. They were realists and realizing employees with as little as a year's Library "training" could become marketable commodities had written severe penalties for anyone who broke their contract. So, despite the increasing dangers, few of the staff could afford to abandon the job or request a transfer.

'Tom called just before I left. He's arranging "training sessions" upstairs tomorrow. I'm booked with the mid afternoon group.' She looked at Darkon expecting an explanation.'

'Some new safety devices, they'll be issuing them soon, I'll be helping Tom with the training.'

'And he said to tell you, "they've changed setting six to a standard portal into the control ship, and removed the timer." He said you'd know what that meant.' Then she added, 'Oh, and to emphasize there's no longer a timer.'

'Thanks, we'll explain it all in training tomorrow. It'll make sense when you see the new kit. How did Wendy's session go?'

'It seems the ooze has been spotted before!' Sheila's opening comment riveted Darkon's attention. 'There were several references to it in the history from the Fifth Guardians.'

'Did they say what it was, or how to kill the damned thing?'

'No. All Wendy could find were hints about it from personal logs of exploration ships. The only official documents classify the reports as myth and superstition.

There are no records of it ever being captured, and nothing better than a few second hand reports over the comms. Seems, anyone who found one barely had time to report it before disappearing.'

'How widespread were then sightings.'

'The reports are somewhat vague, but they mainly come from this end of the spiral arm, nothing from close to the central hub. And here's Wendy's recorder.' She handed him the palmtop monitor.

He took it and scanned the summary. 'Wow!' He was caught off guard unable to hide the surprise in his voice. 'This wasn't what I was looking for.' For a few more minutes he studied the recording keeping his dinner guest in suspense. 'When the chairs and tables morph they generate similar beta waves to the ooze … … … same thing with the androids.'

'Does that mean the Library Created it?'

'Not necessarily,' Darkon was considering all the possibilities, 'It could just be a side effect of the same process. If the Library uses bio-matter as raw material for morphing, it makes sense there'd be similar EMFs when the ooze converted human tissue to make more of its ugly body.'

'But nothing natural can work that fast, there must be something more to it.' Sheila's mind was working overtime, 'Is that why you asked about nano technology Darkon? Do you think we're fighting a nano-weapon? Or a nano-modified life form?'

'It's beginning to look that way. Nano-probes would account for how the sludge could hold on to the floor so tightly when the black hole was tugging at it.'

'Ah! Here's food!'

They settled down to enjoy the meal.

Talking about the ooze had not disturbed Darkon's appetite but Sheila was clearly having a problem pushing it out of her mind, especially with a large, dark-brown legume staring her in the face. She pushed it to the side of her plate, 'I know its not going to eat me, but wouldn't be able to keep it down today!' she eyed it uneasily.
Suddenly Darkon's fork struck out, stabbing, severely wounding the offending vegetable. Then after wrestling it closer to him lethal, fearless teeth slashed deeply into its tender flesh, again and again they struck shredding all life from its tattered form. Never again would it dare to endanger a Human Life. As his vicious tongue purged the final remains of the legume from his blackened lips Sheila burst into irrepressible laughter. Fingering the stargun in his pocket Darkon wondered: should he instead have sentenced it to the oblivion of space? Within his mind an army of legumes appeared. He held them prisoner, watching in turn as each suffered the fate reserved for all aggressive, mushy vegetables in that gigantic void above the sky. A legume exploding into the vacuum of space is not a pretty sight.
All too soon the meal was over and two tired people were happy for the first time in days. Even the senseless assassination of the legume had been forgiven. With an hour of sunlight remaining they sauntered lazily across the campus grounds and outward into the grasslands beyond. The air was warm and sweet reminiscent of tropical nights back home on Sol-3 with a cool refreshing breeze blowing in from the south-east. Only the twittering of insects indigenous to the planet and the churning of a distant waterfall disturbed the silence. They wandered along the narrow banks of a rippling stream, content for the moment to be free from the intensity of modern life. Here there were no comms to bleep, no AI systems

persistently checking and double checking every aspect their lives for the next ten decades, not even the incessant hum from a thousand techno devices intent on stimulating their auditory senses 24/7. Here while it lasted it was peaceful and quiet. They sat gazing at the slowly drifting water as it flowed on its endless pilgrimage to the unseen ocean beyond the horizon. The dying rays of daylight kissed snow capped peaks atop distant mountains, sending living shadows racing across the grasslands to meet them. As the air chilled, they turned away from the setting sun allowing its last lingering rays of warmth to caress their backs. Twilight was drawing to a close as they reached the perimeter walls. They were pleased just to be with each other and when they reached Sheila's quarters there was no question where Darkon would be spending the night. This time they showered together, sharing, enjoying the massaging streams of fragrant water while sonics cleansed away the pollens and dust from their rare venture into the primitive, natural world. As the shower cut off he leaned over to whisper in her ear, 'I'm not on duty until tomorrow afternoon, and,' he gently nibbled her earlobe, 'and, I know you aren't either.' Clean and fresh they slid between silken sheets to renew the passion still simmering from their first night of pleasure.

Next morning Sheila was the first to wake with sunlight streaming through the bedroom windows. She was pleased with her choice of apartment sited as it was on the outer wall of the complex. True, "a room with a view" cost quite a few extra credits but there was little to compare to the sensuous feelings when sunbeams stream through translucent drapes flooding the room with blinding light. The eyes may take longer to adjust to such intensity but it is more than compensated by the '***alive***' sensations surging through the body. A few minutes later

Darkon awoke to the sight of a beautiful woman stretching left and right before the open window, her limber body straining as she performed morning calisthenics.

'This is the way to wake up ***every day***!' he yawned, feigning sleepiness.

She turned seductively beckoning him to join her. Never one to refuse a challenge, he dove from beneath the sheets, rolled across the floor and in a smooth effortless motion unfolding into a handstand against the wall then for a "coup de grace" pumped thirty vertical press-ups before collapsing in a heap in front of her. 'I've got to get into better shape!' he joked; I think I need the "Kiss of Life".'

'Too late!' She chided as she kneeled down beside his prone form, 'You used up all your rations last night!

'Then I'd better give some back,' he retorted springing for her like a savanna wildcat. But she was too well trained. Pivoting quickly she ducked beneath his outstretched arms. Spinning full circle she dropped her whole weight soundly onto his back. Laughing he went sprawling full length, air bursting from his lungs as he hit the floor. She allowed him roll onto his back then firmly pinning him to the ground she helped herself to a generous portion of the rations he'd promised to return. When their playfulness finished, he stood up and turned to face her. 'Careful Sheila.' respectfully he gave her a small bow, 'your black belt's showing.'

She smiled appreciating the gesture. He'd recognized her skill and wasn't too embarrassed to acknowledging it. Perhaps this was another hobby they could indulge together. Grabbing a robe she headed for the kitchen. This wasn't a full workday so there was ample time to prepare the breakfast herself. She was free until the late

afternoon's training session and Darkon wasn't expected to show until then either. Shower time could wait until later. And she thought mischievously, another smile breaking through, "why shower ***twice*** before lunch."
Darkon was clearly enjoying the hand cooked meal. Unlike many spacers who habituate to the fluid rations that supply nourishment with neither texture nor flavor, he was savoring each bite. 'These aren't synthesized flavors, they're far too complex. Did you bring them with you?' He knew the weight restrictions by memory. The only reason he'd been allowed luxuries was his status as the Lifeship Captain. It had been a hard choice deciding which items to take aboard LS48. He'd settled for a few souvenirs from earlier travels, items that could never be replaced that would trigger enjoyable memories from his past in ways no Tri-Di image could. Real artifacts have an essence of their own that copies just cannot capture. This meal, so lovingly prepared, would seal itself forever among the memories of their first days together.
'Yes,' she opened a draw to show him the portable hydroponics unit, 'I used my full allowance for these. Most of the herbs come from my home planet. Sanson, that's, Professor Dirth, checked them against the local fauna and he's allowing me to grow them under control conditions. He helped find the best local soils since I can't use fertilizer. Most of them are doing quite well, but the garlic, that's a specialty from Sol-3, doesn't want to germinate. Maybe it was damaged in transit or just doesn't like this planet.' She paused, realizing she was running away with her answer. 'I get a bit too enthusiastic when it comes to cooking.'
'You're certainly enjoying it, and I really like the final results.' He licked his lips to illustrate the point, and this

time it wasn't to dispose of a legume. He toted up the score so far… … …

- Intelligence,
- Beautiful,
- Healthy, fit and combat trained,
- Great dancer,
- Enjoys cooking,
- And she knows how to make her man happy.

He wondered what her singing was like.
Not that it mattered, he liked listening to her voice and it didn't need to be very good to improve on his. If it came to a duet she would be the one getting the worst part of the deal.
He began to realize his roaming days might be coming to a close and could almost hear William and Lynda arguing whether or not he would succumb to Sheila's charms before the end of her two-year contract. Lynda would be wagering on an early engagement, and he was beginning to think she had the better chance of winning.
'Hello! Darkon! Hello there!' Sheila's soothing voice once again snapped him back to the present. 'Where were you? You seemed planets away. Are you all right?' she was clearly concerned.
He smiled reassuringly, 'Yes I'm OK. You don't know how long it has been since I felt this Happy. I was just daydreaming.'
'About anyone I know?' she enquired, thinking *"It had better be me."*
'Oh! Just someone I've been missing for a few days. Someone I keep thinking about when I'm supposed to be working. Come here!' He opened his arms invitingly. Slowly, coyly she sauntered round to his side of the table and gently perched on his lap. He was stroking her neck

as they shared a hot chocolate when the comms shattered the moment. They both grimaced.

The comms identified Wendy as the caller.

'What is it Wendy!' Snapped Sheila, annoyed to lose her precious morning off.

'I'm sorry to call you today Sheila, but I've just got back from the Library. There's something you need to see. I think it's urgent, I'm sure it is. And I don't know how to handle it. I'd go through official channels but I don't want to put it on the computers until you see it first. Remember you asked me to notice anything on nano-tech. Well, I came across it by chance and it's … … … you've got to come and see what's turned up. Please Sheila, it's really bad.'

'Calm down Wendy, it's all right.' Wendy was clearly panicking, 'Can you bring what you've got over here or is there too much?'

'There's a lot of it, but I can get Tom to help me carry it if that's all right?'

'Tom?'

'Tom McFarland,' she sounded uncomfortable, 'we were going to meet for a late breakfast. He got delayed so I spent an extra hour going through the printouts. That's when I came across it. When he got here and saw what I'm working on and said it could be linked to the morgue problems and to get in touch with my supervisor immediately. That's you!'

'OK Bring it all over and we'll look at it together then decide what to do. Have you told anyone else yet?'

'No just Tom, shall I leave a message for the rest of the team?'

'Not yet Wendy, we can decide that later, after we've all looked at it. I'm at the southwest corner of Living

Quarters, the ground floor. See you in half an hour. That'll give me time to finish breakfast.'

And she thought, time to dress and get Darkon looking like he's just arrived.

Without pausing for breath she called out:

**'DOMESTICS: Rapid Clean with Fresh Aroma - All Rooms - NOW!'**

Remembering Sheila had linked their wardrobes the previous week Darkon requested one of his office standard one-piece suits. He dumped yesterday's clothes and was slipping into the new uniform when Sheila rushed back to the bedroom, nearly giving him a heart attack.

She snapped,

**'WARDROBE: Office Formal wear - NOW!'**

This was impressive she could act quickly when the situation warranted it. He fought hard to resist his instincts as she flung her robe in to the recycle bin, pranced naked across to the sonics/shower for a thirty-second emergency cleanse and almost jumped into her formal attire. The house-bots were busy cleaning the apartment and removing all signs of the morning's romantic activities. Their final touch: a hissing spray of fresh pine and herbs to permeated every room.

## Webs of Deceit

Within minutes the comms announced the arrival of Wendy and Tom. And when they entered it was clear there was more than one romantic couple in the apartment. Sheila wondered if Wendy's discovery was an attempt to impress Tom with her detective skills. She had achieved remarkable results from her limited time in the Library.

Unable to get meaningful answers from extinction queries she changed her approach. Switching to developments in automatic breeding chambers, the artificial wombs, she found a wealth of ancillary data. It covered a period both before and after the fifth Guardians realized their population was declining. With a greater segregation between technologies than other cultures they had failed to connect nano technology with their infertility problem. The Library, in turn, also failed to suppress the information. But the theories the fifth Guardians evolved would cast a different complexion on the committee's first impressions.

Wendy unearthed inconsistencies in their nano research. They had used nanos for centuries before discovering the Library but many within their culture feared the microscopic machines. They worried that, like robots, they could become sentient, take over the galaxy and enslave them. The scientific community appreciated their irrational fears and understanding their own sentient nature went to great lengths to appease the small but vocal minority. Wherever nanomite treatments were administered the patients were monitored to ensure the nanos did not begin to reproduce. Daily scans checked to ensure their self-destruction after the pre-determined time span.

# Space Zero The Meld

Within three decades of using the Library, populations closest to the Alexandria-3 showed inexplicable variations in their female medi-scans. Regularly up to thirty percent more decomposed nano material was detected than had been administered as medication. Even females who received no treatment showed an abundance of nano residue. And while the males did not present with the first problem virtually all post mortems showed minute but measurable decomposition debris.

A second problem that was recorded but not considered significant was an increasing failure rate of the Guardians own nanomites predominantly those for regulating the auto immune system. While the failure rate remained within acceptable limits it had more than tripled from consistently low levels of the previous seven centuries. No serious research had been conducted against the data with the only investigations coming from a group of undergraduates who had teamed together for a shared thesis. After their research had been ridiculed by academia they were branded Anti-Nano-Activists and accused of spreading socially disruptive rumors. However their investigations were fully documented and still on record.

Wendy handed out translations and summaries from the thesis. Not all their conclusions were fully supported, but the results of their investigation clearly foretold the disaster that would soon follow. In chronological order they outlined the chain of events.

They had traced the source of nano debris in the male population using their own male members as source material. Knowing they were free of medical nanos but discovering they too were affected by the surplus nano debris they had used university's tech labs to biopsy most organs and body fluids. They discovered an

undocumented nanomite in the male seminal fluid that was apparently inert. It maintained a population level of approximately sixteen thousand units. Whenever quantities were drained, surgically or otherwise, the count stabilized within hours.
During heavy exercise or following an adrenaline surge up to half the nanos migrated to the skin surface where they would self destructed within a few hours. But the presence in seminal fluid suggested a sexual connection so the group had switched their investigation to the effect the nanomites would have on women. The nanos seemed unable to survive more than four days within a female host. They did not reproduce but had a deadly effect on the host's reproductive system. Those that entered via the skin immediately migrated to the bloodstream, into the uterus, and entered the fallopian tubes. When an ovum was encountered the first sixteen nanos entered the cell and appeared to attack the nucleus for several hours before migrated back to the skin surface to self-destruct. The residue of the nanomites continued on to the ovaries and attacked the ripening eggs. After several hours they too returned to the surface of the skin to self-destruct. It became clear the nanos were designed to infiltrate female bodies, gradually destroy their reproductive cells, and self-destruct before the damage was detected. Clearly sexual activity was the prime route hence the male host site being the seminal vesicles. Even in the event of non sexual activity skin to skin contact would ensure that virgins too would have their germ cells destroyed eliminating them as potential sources of viable eggs for the artificial incubators.
The slow pace of cell destruction and the time scale of the attack had counted against the thesis when it was originally submitted. None of the academic

establishments would accept that the existence of the nanomites after several failed attempts to reproduce the results at their five main universities near the Central Hub. At the time, without a connection to the Library, the significance of a thesis arising from an outpost university at the Spiral Rim was ignored. The committee would not make the same mistake.

Disappointed at the rejection of their thesis several of the undergraduates spent another year in a vain attempt to gain incontrovertible proof. As sponsorship for their project dried up they published very little of their later research, but within their files was a strange entry. A fellow student had spent several months with her new husband at the Library. He was an established academic in the field of pure mathematics, and their sponsor allowed both husband and wife to attend study sessions. Their time at on Alexandria-3 was not entirely spent in study for when they returned a year later she was heavily pregnant with their first son. The child died six months later when their flyer suffered a lightning strike and crashed. The medical students had offered to prepare his body for the funeral and save the parents the expense of a professional mortician. They needed an excuse to use the University equipment so the parents gave permission for non-intrusive body scans for the thesis. The results were most disturbing.

Bone marrow throughout the boy's small body was contaminated by dormant nanomites. The structures were so densely packed that at only four months old they accounted for six percent of his body weight. When samples were extracted and tests run using male organ donor bodies the nanomites were found to activate when introduced into the bone marrow of matured males. Once active many of them migrated to the seminal vesicles and established a stable population. The remainder gradually migrated to the skin of the hands and face but these did not self-destruct. For a period of several weeks a steady stream on nanos maintained dense populations at the three locations until the marrow samples were depleted.

The group's final summary was brief - barely two hundred and fifty words:

We believe that the fetus became infected with dormant nanomites from an unknown source. The contaminants remained dormant until introduced to mature male bodies, a process that may occur naturally during puberty, at which time the primary nanomites become active. Some remained within then body relocating to the seminal vesicles and become reproductive establishing a stable population at about sixteen thousand units. The remainder, over a period of time, migrated to the interpersonal contact areas: the hands and face, where they can be transmitted to new hosts contagiously.

It appears that on contact with a male host they establish a stable population in the seminal vesicles of the new host. Ejaculation during intercourse will transfer significant nanos to the female host where they appear to seek and destroy ovum in the fallopian tubes and the ovaries. In the female host these nanomites after successfully sterilization self-destruct by the fourth day eliminating any detectable connection to the damaged egg cells. Since the damage is irreparable and female ovum quantity is a finite non-renewable resource then over an extended period the sexually active females will become sterile. Non-sexual contagion operating with a slower infection rate will also destroy the ovum supply of sexually inactive females decreasing the viability of artificial incubation using donor eggs.

Finally: This is a new pathogen. That implies the source of contamination most probably originates on a recently colonized planet. The planet of the New Library should be considered as a possible source for this contamination.
Incoming legal documents were filed shortly afterwards. Their officialdom implied that their reference to the Library was a serious matter and that legal action was being considered against both the authors and the university.
'As you can see,' Wendy rounded of the presentation, 'the authorities didn't want the research to continue. And we all know the final results for Guardians number Five.'
All four: Sheila, Wendy, Darkon and Tom, looked at each other for several minutes weighing the implication of the thesis. If it was true, the danger was more serious than they had imagined. To date no pregnancies had left Alexandria-3 but that may only be the Libraries ***preferred*** method of delivery.
Darkon broke the silence, 'Where there any details on how to recognize the nanomites Wendy? Do we know what we should be looking for?'
'Nothing… … … sorry… … …that's all the files on the students work. I can look for more later on today,' volunteered Wendy, 'I've another session scheduled this afternoon.'
'That's good,' Sheila didn't want Wendy realizing the Library was their enemy, 'just search through the University's data. It might just be some students getting over enthusiastic on their project. And check the dates of the publications. Make sure they don't coincide with any of the culture's hoax celebrations. You know, like "All Fools Day" on Sol-3. Remember the joke that ran out of control several years ago. Some prankster released

"proof" that portals had triggered temporal distortions that were converging on the central hub.
'You think it isn't true then?' Wendy was beginning to feel guilty about interrupting her boss on her morning off.
'If it is we should be able to find supporting data in the university files. Otherwise, we'll just write it off as a case of group paranoia just like the $5^{th}$G did.'
Seeing her disappointment Tom started towards her, but Sheila intercepted him. 'While you're here Tom can you help me with my hydroponics unit, it's not keeping the humidity high enough - it'll only take a few minutes.' She took his arm almost dragging him into the storage area, 'And Darkon, get Wendy another drink she's been looking at her empty glass far too long! Be a good host.'
Sheila closed the door behind them and pulled out the hydroponics tray. Before Tom could comment that there was no humidifier she put a finger across his lips and whispered 'Keep quiet, I'll explain.' Manually activating a cleaning drone she sent it noisily scurrying around the room close to the door to drown out their conversation.
'What's going on Sheila?' Tom was upset, 'Wendy was so pleased when she found the thesis and you made her feel like an idiot for believing it so easily. And Darkon, he barely acknowledged it had any real meaning. The poor girl's feeling lousy. And from reading between the lines these past few days you were expecting something like this. I'm not going to let you steal all the credit for yourselves?' He was very angry.
'Listen Tom!' she looked him straight in the eyes, 'We need Wendy to go back into the Library and dig around for a lot more information. If she realizes how desperate we are the Library will sense it, and could keep it from us. Our only hope is for Wendy to think it's an empty lead and keep on digging not expecting to find any real results.

If anything comes up she'll be expecting us to reject that too so she won't get overly exited about it and tip our hand. If she even suspects how vital her job is we won't be able to send her into the Library again. Why do you think Darkon and I haven't been near the place since the committee was formed?'

Tom was taken aback. 'Is it that serious?' he asked dumbfounded.

'If not worse! Unless we identify those nanos everybody on this planet and everyone in orbit could be deemed expendable. We'll all be isolated to protect Humanity from the same fate as the other Guardians. Every one of them died off within fifteen generations of finding the Library.'

'So now you know! And you're going to have to live with it like the rest of the committee, just like Wendy will in a few days time. For galaxy's sake - let her have what little time's left before she has to face the truth.'

'But that means none of us can ever go back home, we'll be quarantined on some remote planet for the rest of our lives?' Tom was beginning to realize, it was slowly sinking in. 'The militia ships, they won't go along with that, they won't take it lying down, they'll fight for their freedom - you know that.'

'And,' Wendy added, 'if they escape they'll spread the infection all the way back to their home worlds!' Looking into his eyes again and saw the fear he was trying hard to control. 'Now you realize why I had to be so cavalier with Wendy. We need her to be out of the loop for at least a few more days. Then we have a chance to get some answers. Now stay here. I've got to send Wendy back to the library before it's too late. And you're in no shape to talk to her right now.'

'Where's Tom?' asked Wendy as Sheila returned alone to the lounge.

'He'll be back later, he needs some special parts that Sanson's got in his place, He said he'll comm. you later, he had to rush to catch Prof. Dirth before leaves for the hospital.'

'Darkon, you'll walk Wendy back to the office won't you? I'll tidy up all this paperwork and take it in with me later.'

Taking the hint, Darkon ushered her to the door.

As they walked across the campus Wendy began talking. 'She's not normally like that; usually she makes the time to be friendly. That's why I like working for her.' She too was feeling a little uncomfortable.

'It's the deadlines.' Darkon lied, 'After the "Ordeal" GMI's put so much extra Admin work on her, and now with this morgue trouble she's under a lot of pressure from the Hub Uni. Group.' 'Have you heard their latest demands?'

'The grapevine's saying we've got to have an Emergency Evacuation Plan, a plan to get us off the planet a lot faster than the Library elevator. Is it true?'

He spotted an opportunity and grabbed it. In an hour's time the Library would be downloading everything he was telling her.

'Can't I keep anything secret around here?' he jested, and then explained, 'The federation insists we set up some high speed evacuation procedure. They're sending us twenty orbital shuttles to surround the Library ready to lift off at a moment's notice.'

'But it takes ten minutes to get a dozen people up from the Library Complex to the surface, how will that help when the "elevator" is the biggest bottleneck?'

'We're toying with using our own portals.' He was getting into his stride. 'We put dozens of them in the library with their other ends opening straight into the shuttle cabins. In an emergency, we can link the portals in Living Quarters and the Offices as well so when the sirens blow, if they ever do, everyone rushes to their nearest portal and ports directly onto their shuttle. As each ship fills up, it jumps into a high orbit and its feeder portals switch to another shuttle with some spare seats. The only delay we expect is getting all the patients out of the hospital and collecting a few drunken stragglers from Living Quarters.

'And when it's all over you just reverse the process?'

'Not quite.' He let a disturbed grin sweep over his face. 'Did I mention the twenty shuttles came from the Graveyard? They've been in mothballs for a very, very long time.' He paused to let it sink in. 'Take off's safe enough even with a full load. The danger's at re-entry. If anything goes wrong then the ships could be too sluggish to respond especially if they're still fully loaded.'

'We're thinking of moving the passengers to the larger Militia ships first and then sending the shuttles back empty, one at a time. The military has more than enough portals to send everyone back planetside after the shuttles land safely. If there's a crash we'll have one hell of a mess to clean up, but as long as we keep everyone in orbit, they'll all be safe.'

'How long is that going to take? And how many practice drill until you get it right? I'm only going to be around for another seventeen months.' Her sarcasm was showing.

'Once we get organized we'll only need one or two full practices. I can't see GMI funding twenty launches every week just to keep the "Professors" happy.'

'Is that what the training sessions are all about this afternoon?'

She was a very inquisitive woman. Darkon understood why Sheila chose her to continue the research. 'Partly, we've picked the twenty pilots and backups, and we're also going to be training the security staff to use remote controlled portals.' This time he didn't need to lie. He just kept quiet about ***which*** remote function he was thinking.

'Don't worry too much about those last results,' he tried to sound nonchalant, 'there're always dead ends before you strike the mother load.' They reached the Admin complex. 'I'll see you around sometime.' He smiled as she headed into the Admin Offices and was relieved that, as she reached the door, she turned and smiled back, giving a gentle wave.

"How soon he wondered before the Library sucked that information out of her head?" As long as she believed what he'd told her she was in no danger and since it was true, as far as it went, it would withstand any scrutiny from the Library. He suspected it would be monitoring GMI's transmissions as the shuttles were tractored to their new home but with GMI unaware of the real intentions there was no risk of any leaks.

## To Catch a Shuttle

Although arrival of the shuttles was imminent, the militia was still unaware of the role it would play once the Library threat was proved. The captains involved with its destruction would eventually have to face federal justice. How they emerged, whether as heroes or the villains, would depending upon how the courts interpreted the facts. And to date those facts were few and far between. The nano replication method, if confirmed, would show a belligerent intent and that would go a long way to justify their actions, but there was still no way to identify the infected patients and prove the danger was real.
Tomorrow Darkon was hoping for news on two fronts; from Wendy for the nano data, and from William on the trigger mechanisms for the shuttles. Time was running short, and they still had next to nothing on the ooze, how it had occurred, or what it was. With two hours before the training sessions begin, he had time to check progress at the morgue. For the first time in days there was good news. Radiation levels had dropped quicker than expected and a team was already onsite doing the preliminary investigation. Their first task was to search for any surviving trace of the ooze. Courtesy of the orbiting military they had access to the most powerful portable sensors in the galaxy, leastwise the most powerful ones not on the official secrets list. With the loaned equipment the floor area where the ooze had been attached was examined down to the molecular level. The computer was analyzing the readings and it would be several minutes before any results would be available.
Darkon felt tired with the pressures of the last week once again bearing down on him. Thinking back over the last twenty-four hours, he was grateful for the few hours'

respite he had shared with Sheila and realized how much he was relying on her strength and support and the incentive she gave him to stay ahead in the battle with the Library. Feeling the need for a hot drink he headed for the Café-Bar at the social center and was pleased to see Tom enjoying a meal. He grabbed a mug and a large jug of steaming coffee and went over to join him. 'How much did she tell you Tom?'

'Sheila?' he asked, Darkon nodded, 'She told me what we're up against and how much we need to keep Wendy in the dark for now.' Looking around he asked, 'It's safe to talk? I didn't realize the morgue was just the tip of the iceberg.'

'As long as you're not on a live comms link we should be OK. I don't think the Library uses acoustic monitors, it's probably to too high tech for such simple ideas.' He topped up his mug, 'You seem to be getting close to Wendy?'

'Yes. She's great fun to be with but we're not getting serious.' Then he added, 'Not like you and Sheila!'

'Is it that obvious already?' Darkon had not expected the news to leak out so quickly. 'What gave the secret away?'

'That was easy,' Tom sniggered, 'You just have to watch Trudel and Geney scowling every time they see you with her. What's been going on in that Lifeship of yours to make them so jealous?' he paused, 'Maybe I should change my job and get in on some of those fringe benefits.'

'You'll have plenty of benefits without needing to retrain especially if Wendy's an example of how you operate. How long have you been planetside? A week and she's missing you already.' He grinned, 'I doubt you're quite as innocent as you look!' He downed the remaining coffee

and stood up. ‘The morgue scans should be ready by now, care to take a look at them with me?’
‘Why not,’ Tom replied, ‘it can’t be any worse than watching the real thing.’
Ten minutes later they were looking through the results. After eliminating the floor structure only a few compounds were left. They were all the same form, microscopic clusters of a laminated ferrous/silicate amalgam, interlaced with copper/gold strands either three or five molecules thick. The sensor had ascertained the mechanism. Paired strands, one thick one thin, linked to each amalgam platelet and controlled it by switching the static charge. There were nine charge levels each representing a different degree of flexing.
Tom recognized its function at once. ‘Do you realize what we’re looking at Darkon?’ then without waiting for a reply, ‘It’s a mechanical muscle! GMI’s been working on that for fifty years, but the prototypes are heavy on power and give out too much heat.’
‘Are they strong enough to resist the massive gravity pull?’ Darkon was unfamiliar with nano-tech, ‘They look flimsy?’
‘For a ferrous/silicate amalgam? It’s got an exceptionally high tensile strength and look how the “limbs” are curled around the floor molecules. It could hardly be more secure if it was part of the floor itself. I’ll bet we only succeeded because its control unit was in the main body of the ooze and when that was pulled off it simply didn’t have the time to regenerate. Galaxy! We really were lucky! That scares me.’
Darkon discussed the results with the senior investigator and came back carrying a pocket datastore. ‘I’ve got the results.’ he told Tom, ‘It’s time to get back to the ship.

We can go over for them with the committee after the training sessions. Are you ready?'
'I'm ready whenever you are - looks like it's going to be another long day.'
The training went well. Most of the staff were familiar with hand lasers and found the starguns just as easy to handle. The need to treat them as tools rather than weapons was emphasized continuously but it was made clear that if the ooze reappeared they must act immediately and act with deadly force. The new Setting-6 was explained in more detail. Once the trigger was squeezed a static Human-sized portal would open exactly three feet in front of the stargun but would not be tied to the guns movement like the other settings. The one-way portal would connect to an emergency Hazmat ward on the hospital ship: HS03, and was only to be used as a last resort to escape from immediate danger or if they came into contact with the ooze and needed emergency isolation. They were warned against misusing it. It might already be occupied or contaminated and once inside they could find themselves in a long and dangerous quarantine.
After training with the starguns, pilots selected for shuttle duties were given an introductory lesson by Darkon using a mockup of the cockpit control station. Although the ships would be on auto-pilot they needed to know the manual overrides in case of a malfunction. The mockup was fitted with William's auxiliary controls which, after reaching orbit and disembarking their passengers, would switch the shuttle into "Autopilot Return" Mode.
As far as they were concerned all the switch did was disable the portal and activate the autopilot for a remote decent and landing back at the Library Complex. They did not know it would also switch the nuclear engine's failsafe shutdown into reverse mode. When the failsafe

triggered, the lead rods would be ported out of the reaction chamber causing an instant chain reaction. All that kept the failsafe in safety and held the explosion at bay was an electronic “Dead Man’s Handle” in the form of an encoded signal pulsed from GMI-1. If that signal stopped or was jammed in any way twenty neutron engines would simultaneously achieve critical mass. Their unleashed energy would return the planet to the basic elements from which it was forged countless eons ago. In the process the molten core would vaporize the Library into oblivion. Leastwise that was the theory.

Before returned planetside the forty trainee pilots were issued starguns with the remainder going to the committee which included Tom. Three of the prototypes were assigned to the GMI ship’s Captains leaving just two in reserve as spares. With the formalities over the committee settled down for dinner. The evening’s work would start soon and there was a lot to discus. Meanwhile, for the next hour William’s cooking skills would once again be on parade again. “And this time,” Darkon thought, “I’ll be comparing them to Sheila’s dishes.”

An hour later the meal was finished and the tables cleared for the meeting.

**<u>They had 6 main points.</u>**

- Arrival of the Shuttles and their Retrofitting for Auto-Landing,
- Evacuation Training Procedures,
- Hardware Infrastructure for the Evacuation Portals,
- Networking the Portal Routing,
- Post Evacuation Return Procedures,
- Shuttle Re-Entry Crash Procedures.

**and 4 unofficial ones.**

- The 5th Guardians Thesis,
- Nano Structures from the Morgue Disaster,
- Library Destruction Requirements
- Militia Captains Need-to-Know Requirements.

The first five points were covered quickly but the Re-Entry Procedures needed more deliberation. A shuttle crash with a nuclear engine explosion would totally destroy the Education Complex. They could attempt to port a stricken shuttle back into High Orbit but, though theoretically possible, to open a portal large enough for a complete ship the energy drain would be immense. Fortunately William's military service included using linked mega-portals so he was familiar with heavy vehicles recovery. Starships in comparison are lightweight and it is only their size and shape that make the task difficult.

The militia already had mega-portal capability and GMI's craft could easily be upgraded. With seven militia and three GMI ships in orbit they had ample resources for a shuttle recovery so long as they were returned to the planet one at a time. And with the federal government mandating the shuttle evacuation, cooperation from the military was guaranteed.

William visualized the layout: a central hexagonal portal with six more linked edge-to-edge forming an almost circular mega-portal. It could easily expand to accommodate a shuttle and port it into high orbit. From there any of the GMI ships could tractor it to a heliocentric trailing orbit. William was delegated as liaison between GMI and the militia and tasked to arranging at least two simulations before the first shuttle attempted to land.

With the meeting officially over, all comms to the room were terminated and the all important secret session began.

Sheila opened with the Fifth Guardian thesis on the Nano Sterilization emphasizing the stealthy nature of the dormant infant-host phase. This was followed by a showing of the Morgue disaster, and rounded off with Tom's description of the nanomite pseudo-muscle structure. He admitted this was an area of technology where the Library had the upper hand. Jeff summarized the available options if and when the Library's involved was confirmed.

Of immediate concern was how the militia would react when they learned the Library was going to be eliminated. Their cooperation was critical for shuttle safety since a premature detonation would alert the Library and could prevent the remaining ships from landing.

The floor was opened to questions and suggestions. Ideas were bounced regarding anti-nano measures but without a specific target little preventative action could be considered.

Bringing pregnancies to the planet to obtain sample nanomites ran in to ethical problems. The mother's couldn't be aware of their complicity or the Library would know it, but to use them without their knowledge was not only illegal but ran the risk of a rebellious mother absconding with an infected fetus or child.

Challenging the Library directly would have similar problems. It could hold the students hostage, or change its method of infecting the population, developing an entirely new nanomite strain with totally unknown properties. That was a risk they dare not take. It could trigger the worse case scenario demanding destruction of the Library

while the planet was still occupied, with the whole student body and faculty being deemed expendable.
After several hours they were back with the original proposal: Run an evacuation and detonate the shuttles before anyone returned to the planet.
Non-Launch trials could test the procedures until they were reliable after which there would be one full scale evacuation. After that they would be on standby awaiting proof that the Library was safe or hostile.

They prioritized their procedures:

- Establish a network of portals to connect the Library and Admin-Center to the Evacuation Shuttles,
- Prime the Shuttles for Self Destruct,
- Determine the Library's Intent,
- Find a method to detect the Nanomites,

Over the next few days twenty short range portals were installed in the Library Complex. They were live-tested using receivers onboard the shuttles. Then another twenty units were distributed throughout the Admin Complex. Monitors were adjusted to transmit live telemetry to the displays on GMI-1. Only two people knew an isolating connection from the monitors fed duplicate data to the stand-alone computer on the GMI-1's bridge. The Library could not sabotage what it did not know about.
After the Shuttle fleet arrived William and Darkon were kept busy retrofitting the detonation units and completing the pilots training. When the 'end of the week' came, the militia was ready to test the linked mega-portal array. As the fleet maneuvered to battle formation just outside the planet's gravity well William sat at the control station aboard GMI-1. He waited patiently to take command of the fleet's portal controls. One by one primary and

secondary systems were released to his station. Two green indicators showed transfer complete for each of the seven militia starships and the backup LS48 and HS03 units. On the bridge Jeff transferred GMI-1's control giving William the final two greens. He activated his VR headset interface, he was ready.

For the first test Darkon would pilot the shuttle himself. He checked in ready to begin the first run. The shuttle would freefall from orbit at re-entry speed passing between the battle formation and the planet. William's task was to establish the mega-portal ahead of the shuttle then "catch" and port it to safe location. If all went well it would exit down orbit from the formation with a velocity differential equivalent to re-entry speed. Immediately GMI-1 would lock on with gravity-tractors, stabilize its gyrations, and bring it to a relative standstill hopefully still close to the militia battle formation.

There was one small catch. William had to wait for the shuttle's Space-Zero call before responding. He would be totally dependant on computer-tracking during the 'fly by' and for automated mega-portal activation but he would not know until the last moment what had triggered the emergency. Then, he had a twenty five seconds window to affect a "rescue". The difficulty was matching the mega-portal to the target gyrations and that depended on his VR interface.

He gave the command:

'Portal Control to Shuttle-05,'

'Initiate Fly Past when Ready.'

'Shuttle-05 to Portal Control ... Starting Run Now.'

There was a long pause … … … … … … … … … … then:

'Re-entry speed Achieved.'

William monitored the shuttle.

The time passed by slowly.

Suddenly, Darkon threw the shuttle into a 2D spin and hit the "Panic" icon. The distress call went out!

***Space-Zero! Space-Zero!***
***A3 Shuttle-05! A3 Shuttle-05!***

The emergency call identified the stricken vessel as an Alexandria-3 Orbital Shuttle. "A3 Shuttle-05" was the ships registered name and by convention … … …

William's mind jumped in to action capturing the coordinates several seconds ahead of the spinning craft. He initiated the first portal. The next six auto-activated meshing seamlessly around the first: six hexagons encircling a seventh. Three seconds had passed and the shuttle was less than two seconds away. His thoughts drove the VR link, rotating the mega-portal to synchronize with the ship's gyrating less than half a second away, time for fine tuning. He maintained the portal advance keeping it just ahead of the shuttle until the ship's extremities aligned perfectly. The instant they matched he froze the advance and watched the shuttle race through. It emerged perfectly on target just aft of the battle formation. As the mega-portal collapsed GMI-1's gravity-tractors fanned out ensnaring the spinning shuttle, absorbing its momentum and stabilizing rotation. In less than a minute they had it under control and synchronized to the fleet's orbital speed.

'Shuttle-05 to Portal Control: Request Permission to Power Down'

'Portal Control to Shuttle-05, we have you in Tractor Hold. Cut Thrusters Now'

'Shuttle-05 - Thrusters Offline - You have Control'

With the test complete portal control was handed back to the militia ships and finally, mentally exhausted, William disengaged the VR interface. He was pleased. The test had passed without incident, but it would take at least four hours to run through the logs to confirm all safety concerns had been met. Tomorrow, the next day at the latest, they would rerun the test and this time someone else would be at the controls.

Earlier three of the best pilots had been chosen and put through Mega-Portal training, one of them would be sitting in the hot chair for run number two.

When William called his wife Lynda, before the next work cycle, he would have today's success story to talk about and after all the secrecy during the last few months he looked forward to speaking freely again. But right now he had telemetry to study and then a good night's sleep.

Three days later, the second test proved successful. Four shuttles were cleared for planetfall with Jeff and Darkon piloting the first remote landing to establish re-entry parameters. Next came three fully automatic landings and after another week of intensive post-flight servicing before the remainder of the fleet were cleared to land. By then GMI had recruited six of the original Eve-3/Bounty engineers to join the team on Alexandria-3. Generous bonuses had tempted them out of retirement.

By the end of the second week whole fleet was planetside and together the new ground crews took little time giving the remaining shuttles a clean bill of health. They stood fully serviced, parked like sentinels around the Library entrance. Each was retro-fitted with the new short range portal and linked to central control.

Notice was posted to the faculty and students alike advising of the first Stage-1 Evacuation Test.

It was set for mid morning the following day.

## Silence is Golden

It was a hectic week and Darkon finally had a few hours free time. Eagerly he arranged a date with Sheila that evening. He had neglected her cryptic messages all day and suspected there was news from the Library. So when he arrived at the social center it was no surprised to see her at the bar sharing drinks with Tom and Wendy but they looked very worried. With barely a word spoken Tom led the group to the teleport and insisted Darkon authorize porting directly into his Lifeship.

As soon as they were onboard he killed the power to the onboard teleport. 'That's against regulations,' Darkon started to say then realized something was seriously wrong.

Sheila whispered into his ear 'Take the comms offline. Please hurry we may not have much time.'

Puzzled he opened a service panel and withdrew a control board stowing it in its protective casing. 'OK. We're isolated, apart from the airlock intercom.'

Tom went over and closed the lock door. He attached a mechanical device and flicked its switch. An irritating babbling noise emanated from it. 'It's just white-sound,' Tom advised, 'it'll only last about an hour. Where can we play this on a isolated device?' He passed Darkon a datastore.

'Through here.' He led them to the office area of LS48 and dropped the data into a portable player. A view of the hospital reception area was displayed on the screen.

Tom adjusted the viewer to show a close up of a middle aged woman. He cued image recognition software. One second later the name "Sonia Wright" jumped onto the screen.

'She's been back on Sol-3 for months now. The committee's been watching her progress. How old is that data?'

'Quite old, but have a look at the date.' Tom brought up the time/date display.

Darkon looked at it, 'No that can't be right. Someone's made a mistake.'

'That's before she left isn't it.' Wendy was confused. 'So what's wrong?'

'I imagine you've heard about "The Ordeal"?' Darkon pointed to the month on the display. 'All fifteen of them were trapped in some kind of temporal distortion. In our timeline they were in Limbo for thirty days including almost all of that month. She couldn't possibly have been in the hospital that day … … … for that matter she couldn't have been anywhere that day.'

'I've validated the recording,' Sheila was confident of that fact, 'We've spoken to the people in front and behind her, unofficially of course. Seven of them were regular patients and three of them were students who only went to the hospital or Admin office that one day. We've confirmed their dates with the hospital records. The recording ***is*** genuine.'

It was Darkon's turn to feel uncomfortable. His mind raced through the possibilities. The tape could have been tampered with, but who would have a reason to change it. It could be a failure of the image software, but he remembered Sonia himself and there was noone who looked remotely like her on the base or in the HR files. And in any case, this recording was long before the Library came under suspicion.

A distressing thought crossed his mind. When the recording was made everyone who knew Sonia believed she'd been buried at the cave-in. Only the Library knew she was still alive but incommunicado. Could it have cloned or morphed her and if so why? But it claims morphs cannot exist outside the Library Complex so if that is a lie, what else is it lying about? They could all be in serious trouble.

'If morphs can leave the Library, was the ooze morphed too?' Darkon broached his fears to the group. 'If it was, was it meant to go on a killing spree or did something go drastically wrong - did something in the morgue scramble its "brains"?'

'Wendy's got an idea on that. Tell him what you found, go on, we're on your side more than you realize.' Then to Darkon, 'She thinks we won't believe her, again.'

It took a little encouragement to get Wendy talking. Her investigation had been thorough and she had made two breakthroughs. 'When Tom showed me the nano results I looked up the Fifth Guardian work on ferrous/silicates. They had to abandon it. The research was successful under control conditions but they couldn't replicate it the real world. Their static controls were disrupted by Electro Magnetic fields and since like us their development was based on electrical energy they simply had too much existing technology that, to use your own very descriptive words, "scrambled" it. Their highway comms simply drowned out the sensitive controls signals.'

'What was the problem?'

'The controls got disrupted by their roadway autopilot systems.' Wendy explained, 'Their road sensors used radio frequencies and ultra high frequency acoustics to talk to the street traffic, it worked very efficiently. But when the nanos neared any traffic their controls bent berserk and if they got too close to an acoustic transceiver they "died". It seems the shatter frequency for their ferrous/silicate was a harmonic of their main transceiver carrier wave.'

'I don't suppose you know what frequency they used, do you?' Darkon knew it was a long shot.

'2.7 Mega per Euvol'

Darkon looked puzzled, 'What's that in our notation Wendy?'

'That's where I hit a silica wall. I couldn't get any sense out of the Library when I asked for a translation, and you'd told me not to push if I felt too much resistance didn't you Sheila'.

'That's right!'

'We didn't want the library to know we were suspicious.' She turned to Darkon,

'I think she "needs to know".'

'She "needs to know", **now!**'

'Yes,' he agreed, 'you've done all you can at the Library Wendy and it probably isn't safe for you to go back. Can you bring her into the loop Sheila? Tom and I have some extra work to do.'

He led Tom to the flight deck.

'How quickly could the starguns be adapted for ultra sonics, assuming of course we can find out the right frequency?'

Tom thought it through for a few minutes. 'It should be straight forward. We can use the base unit to generate ultrasound and tie into the stargun settings so whatever you aim at will be targeted automatically. The users won't notice anything's changed.'

'How long will it take? Things are starting to move too quickly here.'

'I can do the preliminary work this evening. There's no special kit needed. I can even rig some remotes to set the frequency once we know what it is.'

'No!' shouted Darkon abruptly, then he elaborated. 'No remotes Tom. The library knows our comms protocol and we can't afford to have it throw us a virus. The Control Ship's always manned so it can be adjusted manually whenever we're ready. By the way, where did you get your engineering training? It's an interesting mix: guns and medicine.'

'That was Graham's influence.' Tom explained 'He hooked me on technology while I was still in school. But Mom and Dad wanted me to study medicine like they had and keep it in the family, so I ended up majoring in both subjects just to keep everyone happy.'

'That's a heavy workload. You can't have had much time for socializing.'

'I always found studying easy, but you're right, I did put in a lot more hours than most people. Maybe that's why I've enjoying spending time with Wendy.' He smiled, 'Normally I'm not that quick off the mark. It usually takes me ages to get to know someone, but we get on so well. We've rarely missed a meal together since our first date. I just enjoy being with her.'

Darkon was pleased for them. There were going to be difficult decisions to make in the coming weeks and close friendships would be very important.

'Can we get access to any of the morgue samples, the nano fragments?' Tom had a hunch, 'I could try to find the shatter frequency by old fashioned "Trial and Error". If we put a portable lab in one of the escape pods there'll be no way for the Library to "hear" the tests and we can easily calculate the probable frequencies. You could have the results before you go to bed tonight.' Tom was an eternal optimist.

'We've the best six platelets under round the clock surveillance next door, in GMI-1. I may be able to get

half of them for testing but Jeff will want to know exactly what you're going to be doing. They're the only real evidence we have.'
Darkon went to the Control Ship to updated Jeff on the latest revelations. Not surprisingly he was disturbed that the Library's androids could impersonate humans and might not be confined to the Study Center. A heated discussion ended with two of the platelets being made available for testing. Now they were up against the clock. Darkon and Tom were prepared to work through the night if necessary and the others would only be in the way.
As captain of LS48, he offered the ladies the hospitality of the ship's sleeping quarters and promptly apologizing for the cramped conditions. They could use the starboard bunks, and the port ones would be available for the men as and when, as the women phrased it, "they finished playing with their toys". All four were somewhat pleased that for one night at least they would not be sleeping so close to the Library.
Two and a half hours after local midnight Jeff was summoned from his slumbers by "the boys with the toys". And their toys were working. It had taken four hours to find the shatter frequency for the first platelet but, once they had, it only took a few minutes to select a suitable harmonic. They tuned an acoustic generator now installed in the base unit. Tom set the stargun at - 2-Re-Enter - aimed and squeezed the trigger to activate the micro-portal. The ultrasound was inaudible but they could hear a gentle hiss as air was sucked imperceptibly from the cabin. The platelet began to shimmer as it vibrated sympathetically with the ultrasound. Then after less than a third of a second it shattered spraying microscopic, powdery fragments over the inner surface of the containment jar. When Tom tapped the jar to settle its

contents the particles were drawn instantly to the magnetic tip of his screwdriver. In this fine powder form a simple magnetic field would be enough to contain the particles.

They showed Jeff the replay. 'It looks like you've gained us a reprieve Tom.' He was pleased with the work. 'Put the residues back under surveillance and we'll examine them again in the morning. You've both done a good job. Now get some sleep. You know we've got a full day tomorrow.' He turned to leave. 'Goodnight Darkon, night Tom. And thank you!'

Five minutes later they were in their bunks, too tired to use the sonic cleansers. That could wait until morning. Six minutes later, a "Space Zero" alarm couldn't have woken them.

The next morning, all too soon, the chronometers reached Zero-Nine-Hundred hours. One hour to go before the mass exodus would begin. Jael Reece wondered how much confusion there would be. She would find out soon enough! As Head of Security at the only Base on Alexandria-3, she was expected to perform the impossible. Almost three thousand people needed to be ready to blast-off in less than twenty minutes. Six seconds per person per portal would take fifteen minutes. That meant five minutes from alarm to entry portal then exit portal to shuttle seat. A militia unit could easily achieve that, but these were civilians. She would be pleased if the first exercise was complete by midday and there would be ample room for improvement on the second run. Her schedule was still clear, so, if she took a coffee break now it wouldn't matter if the evacuation overran her lunch break.

Forty-five minutes later Jael was back at her station checking the systems were online and active. She was

only doing it to keep calm while she waited for the test to start. The system would warn her, and everybody else, if the slightest error had occurred. But it was her only habit, and no one would dare suggest to her that it was merely a displacement activity.
Up in orbit committee members were busy rechecking the control and monitoring networks. They had already logged the equipments initial status and the teleport center was ready to switch to Evacuation Mode. Jeff personally checked the shuttle pilots and was waiting for replies from the last two. A few minutes later he checked them off as ready then leaned back in his recliner to watch the countdown. The tension in the starships was intense.
A dozen sets of eyes were glued to the monitors.
The countdown progressed:
'five… … four… … three… … two… … one … … ZERO!'
Jeff inserted his key and switched the override:
It flipped from "LIVE LAUNCH" to
"TEST Mode NON-LAUNCH"
When "Test Mode Confirmation" started flashing he raised the safety cover and depressed the "Emergency Evacuate" button for the required three seconds. The system acknowledged his request, circling itself with a red flashing halo as a hundred evacuation sirens throughout the center simultaneously roared into life.
Five seconds later the control panel lit up as automated systems went online and locked in.
Panels monitoring pilot status followed suit, twenty amber lights for the pilots, and another twenty for the co-pilots. As each of the twenty crews logged in, another shuttle commenced its pre-start procedures.

- Life support: ON.
- Navigation: ON.
- Entry Portals: ON.
- Automated Portal Control: ON.
- Emergency Shutdown Switched: Manual Only.
- Nuclear Drive: On Standby.
- Thruster Safety: On and Locked.

Each shuttle primed itself and went into standby mode awaiting only an authorizing palm or voice print to initiate Liftoff. When the full complement of one-hundred-fifty passengers and two-pilot crew was onboard not even the Control Center could veto a Launch for the first 18 shuttles. For the remaining ships, there were safeguards. Once all personnel were accounted for and determined to be onboard the ships they would be advised for immediate liftoff. The pilots had three minutes to react, then, ready or not, the Autopilot would commandeer control and initiated the launch itself.

However, today, since the system-test override was selected BEFORE the evacuation alarm was raised then when the pilots command LIFTOFF they and their passengers will be advised:

"THIS HAS BEEN A TEST - Please await disembarkation instructions."

A few minuets later their portals would reopen in one-way transmit mode to allow them egress back to the Teleport Center.

Jeff at the primary control station was watching progress. The auto routing was running smoothly. All pilots had been ported to their correct ships, and several of the shuttles were loading at or above the target speed of 10 passengers per minute. But he was getting queries over the comms. Only half the teleports in the Library were being fully used. Those near the café area were being ignored as the students insisted on using the units surrounding the Ascent Shaft. Was it herd instinct or were people more comfortable queuing where they could see their normal exit.

Fortunately, one security guard was up to the challenge. He called for android assistance and when it morphed he instructed it to move the unused portals closer to the exit. The android told him to position himself where the units were required. Then, to the amazement of the students, the floor repeated the trick it had done with the original café modules. Ten fully functioning portal units glided behind the guard like a troupe of obedient chickens trailing their mother hen. When he turned to thank the android it melted back into the floor amid laughter and applause from the student throng. With the portals relocated, to where human nature demanded, they became fully utilized and the passenger boarding rate improved significantly.

An orange light began flashing on the main monitor panel; the first shuttle was ready for simulated launch. Within seconds it would change to a steady glow for a pilot authorized liftoff, or in three minutes a rapid flicker if the autopilot took over. It turned steady.

Another flashing orange, then another, each in turn went to a steady glow. In the following minutes another fifteen began flashing, with thirteen turning steady. Shuttles 05 and 15 did not. "That's good" Jeff thought. Those two pilots had been instructed to wait out the pre-launch cycle and allow the autopilots to take over. Another orange flashed and went steady, then another.

Indicator 05 burst into rapid pulses as the autopilot kicked in for launch, seconds later number 15 followed suit.

'Seventeen launches - three to go.' Jeff shouted as he looked at the un-launched passenger counts.

| | | |
|---|---|---|
| **Shuttle #18** | | **067** |
| **#19** | | **125** |
| **#20** | | **117** |
| **Passengers** | **Un-launched** | **309** |
| | **Launched** | **2584** |
| | **Shuttle Total** | **2893** |
| **STATUS:** | **Planet Total** | **2895** |
| | **Loading Incomplete:** | **-2** |

Two passengers were not yet on board. They would be the emergency wardens checking for stragglers.
The Un-launched Passengers Count incremented to 310.

'One to go!'

Another minute passed. Jeff manually released the two Shuttles with the higher passenger loads. Numbers #19 and #20 simulated launch. He monitored their 'Liftoff'. Two more steady orange lights appeared. That left only Shuttle #18, he watched the count.

| | | |
|---|---|---|
| **Shuttle #18** | | **068** |
| **Passengers** | **Un-launched** | **068** |
| | **Launched** | **2826** |
| | **Shuttle Total** | **2894** |
| **STATUS:** | **Planet Total** | **2895** |
| | **Loading Incomplete:** | **-1** |

Jeff wondered what had happened to the last warden. He pulled up Shuttle #18's onboard portal monitor. It was looking through the portal, through the hospital reception area and into a ward. The reason for the delay was clear. One patient was trapped under some overturned

equipment. The image was not clear at that distance, but the warden and a nurse were struggling to lift the heavy appliance while someone else was pulling the patient clear. Then he was free. They helped him onto a stretcher then came rushing towards the camera and the last open portal. As soon as they were clear the portal collapsed and automatic launch control authorized Liftoff.
Twenty five seconds later the last shuttle simulated Launch.
"There's always something to sort out!" thought Jeff, but all-in-all the test seemed to have gone well.

He turned to the monitor to reset the system and Cancel the TEST status.

| | | |
|---|---|---|
| **Passengers** | **Un-launched** | **0** |
| | **Launched** | **2898** |
| | **Shuttle Total** | **2898** |
| **STATUS:** | **Planet Total** | **2895** |
| | **Loading Incomplete:** | **+3** |

He did a double take. **Incomplete: +3**.

"Incompetent!" He thought,
"Someone's doing sloppy job programming."
The message should be more meaningful for a positive count.
**Then it hit him.**
They'd loaded more people into the shuttles than had been down on the planet!

## More is Too Many

That couldn't be right. Probably just a programming error, but it needed to be sorted out before they used the shuttles as bombs. No one wanted detonation while anyone was still planetside.
Jeff opened comms to the shuttle fleet pilots.
'Evacuation Control to all Pilots.'
'Evacuation Control to all Pilots.'
'Make a visual count of all unused seating capacity and report in over the comm. please. I say again: Make a visual count of all unused seating capacity.'
Another ten minutes and the counts had been reported in.
'Evacuation Control to all Pilots.'
'The test is complete.'
'You are cleared to disembark.'
'Thank you for your patience.'
'You are cleared to disembark.'
Then remembering his trips on the Eve-3/Bounty flights Jeff flipped open the comms link for an extra message:
'We thank you for flying "Alexandria Luxury Shuttles" and look forward to serving you again on your next flight. Please take the opportunity during your stay on our wonderful planet to visit the galaxy famous "Repository of Learning". Tour guides are available on request. Have a Nice Day. Thank You.'
Jeff scheduled the committee for an informal meeting later that day to discus areas of further investigation and the main debriefing with the security department for the following day. He delegated Mark to search for the program bug that caused the passenger count discrepancy. With his experience he should have no trouble with a simple tallying error.

Later that day the bombshell burst. All the programs and hardware proved flawless. But how could they all be error free? If there was a tallying error one of the counters must be incorrect.

But Mark had been thorough. He'd inspected the monitoring logs for the transmitter side of the portals, and cross referenced the linkups to the shuttles receivers. Everyone who ported to the ships had arrived successfully and as every engineer knows while it is possible to lose something (or someone) in transit it's impossible to get more out of a system than you put in. So how could the system teleport 2895 people successfully and end up with three extra people at the other end?

They did the math. The service crews had physically checked the shuttles to make sure they all had the full complement of 150 passenger and 2 crew seats. There were exactly 3040 seats available on the shuttles and the pilots had counted 142 empty ones. It was simple arithmetic and it was driving the software engineers crazy. Darkon threw down the gauntlet quoting an adage from computing folk law:

**If every thing is set up correctly,**
**and everything is working correctly,**
**but you still get the wrong results,**
**then:**
**ONE or MORE of your ASSUMPTIONS is WRONG!**

Slowly he looked around the room,

'So what are we assuming that "Just ain't so"?'

For an hour they brainstormed the problem getting nowhere until a Jael in frustration suggested:

'Perhaps we've got stowaways,'

**'Let's dump them out the Airlock!'**

Her comments cut through the tension, sending some of the committee members into reeling with laughter.

When the rumpus died down they began to speculate how stowaways could get into the shuttles. There was nowhere in the cabin area for anyone to hide. Even the seats were designed to limit carry-on luggage and the pilots being first onboard could have spotted stowaways anywhere in the cabin area or the flight deck. The logs confirmed the pilot seats were first to be occupied.

Eventually a flaw in the design was found. As the evacuee ports into the ship the portal counter increments, but until the passenger finds a seat and leans back to activate the safety restraint the onboard seat counter isn't incremented. During that time the seat and portal counters are out of sync so standard procedure is to use the higher value expecting it to come from the portal count. The Control Station then displays that value as the number of passengers who ported into the ship.

In reality the number represents either the number who ported in OR the number seated and the latter would include any stowaways. Any passengers gaining access without using the official portals would undermine the count and, although their method of boarding was unknown, once aboard they would go undetected.

Since everybody leaving the shuttles had been scanned, Mark ran image recognition to cross reference the HR databases. When the run finished they would know who the extraneous passengers were and if the militia had hacking into the portal system for some clandestine purpose their operatives would easily be identified.

The committee adjourned for a short break while the programs ran. When they returned the output would be ready. Darkon took the opportunity to enjoy a mug of steaming hot coffee and joined Sheila with her cup of iced tea. He mused how drinks at both extremes of temperature could have the same refreshing effect. Little did he realize how alert they would need to be for the shock that was about to hit them.

When he returned Tom and Julian were staring at the display in disbelief. They beckoned him over. The three on-screen images looked familiar but he could not remember where he had seen them before. The names too sounded familiar: Harry Marson, Tony Struthers, and Christine Skinner.

'Have you pulled their files?' Darkon queried. 'How soon can we question them?

'I don't need to. I already know who they are,' Julian was fidgeting, 'or more accurately who they ***were!*** That one,' he pointed at the older male, 'That one is Harry Marson. Paul was scheduled to do his post mortem two weeks ago. All three of your stowaways were in the morgue when it was destroyed.' He looked back at Darkon. 'Do you still want to interrogate them? How good's your ESP?'

By the time the meeting resumed it was clear the Library ***was*** involved and the earlier recording of Judy Farmer was genuine. But what disturbed them most, far more than the Morphs ability to leave the Library Complex, was their talent as doppelgangers to infiltrate the entire base posing as humans.

When the rest of committee returned they adjourned to LS48, undocked from the control ship and activated a full security lockout. This meeting could not be recorded, and any electronic media must be considered unsafe. Future communication would have to be by word of mouth.

It was time to involve the militia and do so at the highest but safest level. Communication with the Federal Government was precarious at best so the starship commanders would be taking full responsibility for any moves against the Library. Hopefully normal military paranoia against civilian and governmental interference would work in the committee's favor, as would the more aggressive, confrontational attitudes intrinsic to the military mind.

Two tasks lay ahead: adapt the Evacuation procedure in light of the morph intrusions and liaise with the militia to develop strategies for a first strike. The official report blamed computer errors which during evacuation could leave students or staff stranded on-planet. After "correcting" the software another test would be staged and this ideally suited the committee's purposes. The Library was free to check their 'conclusions' and with the data files already showing a discrepancy in the passenger count their story would hold up.

The next test would be conducted under more controlled conditions and this time the Library would be on trial. They could not risk a direct confrontation so total secrecy would be imposed until they initiated a pre-emptive strike.

During the days that followed Jeff and Darkon visited each of the Militia Captains on the pretext, spoken over the radio-waves, of discussing the evacuation problems and arranging personnel allocations for the second stage testing. The Library was lead to believe they were discussing the relocation of personnel from the 20 Shuttle Escape Pods into long range escape vessels which were predominantly the militia and Admin starships. The true reason was to establish non-electronic communication and arrange protocols for the next phase of testing. The commanders readily understood the genocide threat to the human race and the danger inherent from morphing androids impersonating the Admin staff. Any form of fifth column intrusion was totally unacceptable to their military mindset.

Meanwhile Mark, Tom and William were working on ways to isolate and eliminate any morph that successfully infiltrated the escape shuttles. It was taken for granted there would be more intrusions on the second test and they would need to resolve the threat without alerting the Library. Their initially thoughts were to delay action until the Shuttles reached orbit then saturate the Pods with intense ultra sonics shattering the silica platelets. It would be crude but effective. However, if the Library was in continuous contact with the morphs and detected their destruction it could inhibit the shuttles return to the planet. They needed to isolate the morphs and hold them incommunicado until the shuttles had done their work destroying the Library's nerve center. But if the morphs were capable of independent action they would need to be immobilized directly.

Without knowing how the Library communicated with them it was impossible to block or jam their signals. That only left deception so if they could re-route the morphs to an alternative ship without raising suspicion they could destroy them later at a time of their own choosing. They brainstormed ways to intercept the morphs during portal transit. Hi-Tech methods could alert the Library but once again the ever practical Ray Rongo came to their aid. While discussing the problems during lunch he asked how they would be transporting the evacuees to the starships.

'It's quite simple,' Mark had explained, 'we photo identify each person and selectively route them to the appropriate ship. Each Shuttle will be handling its own passengers and crew.'

'So what happens when a passenger isn't on the transfer list?' Ray asked, 'Won't we have a dangerous situation if a morph goes ballistic on the shuttle?'

He began thinking aloud.

'What if we treat them like Public Transport Passengers at the Inter-Galactic Transit Hub on Sol-3? I worked that station in the service depot for years!'

He went on to explain. 'We've twenty portals on the Hospital Ship HS03 haven't we? So we set half of them to receive, and half to transmit. When a shuttle passenger ports in they simply choose the destination portal and walk through. We can label them just like a conventional transit terminal. The passengers do the choosing themselves. If any ship becomes full the passengers get ported to the most suitable of the ships remaining. For Administration purposes they'll expected to photo-identified and entered into the ship's database. So anyone not recognized, namely the morphs, can easily be shunted to an isolation ward on HS03 without raising any suspicion.'

'We can program the ward-bot to tell them their bio-scan results were unintelligible so they're being isolated for the duration of the test. It can recommend they report to the medical center for a more thorough checkup when they return planetside.'

'It's not public knowledge, is it?' William interrupted looking somewhat surprised, 'Does everyone know the isolation wards have Level-Nine bio-protection?' A sly grin was spreading slowly across his face. 'Did you know that, Ray? Did you know we can jettison an Iso-ward and port it straight into a black hole in less than four seconds?'

'That's better than I'd hoped,' Ray replied.

'It's much more reliable than the sonics. I was worried the morphs might react quickly enough to disable them.'

'You've really got the knack of cutting things down to size Ray. Who was your mentor back home?'

'That was Old Man Milleski. Do you remember his favorite catch phrase, **STAW** & **STAC!**?'
They both quoted the old master in unison… … …

"**S**imple **T**hings **A**lways **W**ork!

**&**

**S**imple **T**hings **A**re **C**heap!"

They broke out laughing. It made even more sense here in deep space especially when expensive failure costs lives.
The next two weeks dragged drag by as preparations were made for the second test. Visual portal scans were sent directly to the computer archive on Alexandra-3 where the Library had access. They were making it easy for their nemesis to monitor the recordings in a place where it could easily cover up its own interference. The Library would think it was still in control, but what it wouldn't know was the same signals were being passively tapped and fed to a free standing computer with absolutely no A.I. That device would mechanically switch portal destinations to reroute the Morphs. And with only primitive electrical switching there was no way the Library could override the process.
The Library would be satisfied the Humans considered Alexandria-3 a safe location for their vital data and comms chatter from GMI was on their side. Head Office, impatient for news of a successful evacuation, was pushing hard for an early second test. They themselves were under pressure for a press release in time for an upcoming election. Reluctantly Jeff gave them a date knowing they would be far from pleased when they discovered the truth.
The beginning of the second week brought another shock. A new student, Lan Davmont, had crushed his hand while over-exerting himself showing off in front of several young ladies in the Gym. The Medi-Center ran a routine

amputation and limb-regeneration to repair the damage. Lan however was worried. The weights he claimed were well within his safe working limit and insisted he should have handled them with ease. But, not willing to forfeit time on his Library schedule for a full examination he had insisted they used his severed hand for diagnosis.

'After all,' he explained, 'that's the part of me that stopped working properly!'

When the results reached Tom's station he immediately ported the severed hand to an Isolation Unit onboard the Hospital ship and summoned an emergency committee meeting.

An hour later all the Group-B committee members were in an isolation pod onboard HS03 receiving the devastating news. Jeff led the meeting and started with two simple demonstrations. He vaporized the first joint of the index finger, except that after all the vaporized gasses were evacuated, the monitors showed Point Zero-Three grams of solid matter still remaining. The matter, invisible to the naked eye was analyzed as 99.8% ferrous-silicate-A011. 'And that,' explained Jeff, 'is the designation we gave to the residue from mass of ooze in the morgue. It's clear we've all been exposed to contamination.'

Cold shivers ran through the group. He paused a few minutes for the full implication to sink in. If they were contaminated, they might all be put incommunicado for life, sterilized and imprisoned in an off-planet isolation unit never to see a natural sunrise again, never to feel the breeze blowing through their hair on a hot summer's day. Worse still, galaxy forbid, in the light of the Charter-XIX disaster they could be deemed too great a risk for isolation and under Galactic Emergency Protocols be declared a "Level Nine" Biohazard and humanly executed.

Jeff waited till their faces showed the reality had sunk in. 'There is one ray of hope.' Jeff placed a second isolation jar on the table. 'This is from the middle finger of the patient and it's been on life support since amputation.' He scanned the container. It registered Point Zero-Two grams of ferrous-silicate-A011. He drew his stargun.

'I'm using seting-2: for the Ultra Sonics.'

He squeezed the trigger keeping the portal just outside the jar boundary and started counting.

'And....1, and...2, and...3, and...4, and...5, and...6, and...7, and...8, and...9 and...10!'

'There! That should be more than enough overkill.'

He scanned the container again, and this time there was no signature for the amalgam. 'Watch what happens this time!' He placed a focusing magnet on the side of the jar and activated the vaporizer. A few seconds later a barely visible cloud of matter particles began to accumulate at the focus point.

'These molecules appear to be inert unless we catalyze them with active nanomites. In their present state we can filter them out during normal site to site porting. It's still in the experimental stage, so the medics and the engineers will be working very closely for the next day or two. We need a full scale solution available for the evacuation on Friday. I don't need to remind you that this is on a "Need to Know" basis, we daren't have any leaks to the Library.'

He watched their reactions carefully before adding,

'I want you all to spend Thursday night here onboard; we can't risk any unforeseen accidents to any of you that might upset the schedule.'

'To keep "it" happy,' the "IT" of course was the Library, 'I've scheduled a dinner party for 1900 hours. Make sure you're all here promptly.'

## First Strike

The day and hour for the second test arrived.
Once more a dozen sets of eyes were glued to their monitors. The countdown progressed:
'five...... four...... three...... two...... one ...... ZERO!'
Jeff inserted his key and left it at **"LIVE LAUNCH".**
When "Live Mode confirmation" started flashing he raised the safety cover and depressed the "Emergency Evacuate" button for the required three seconds. This time the icon itself began flashing as the sirens screamed into life. He monitored the procedure closely, and this time with an extra set of twenty mechanical counters atop his control consol.
As the minutes progressed each shuttle took its turn to nudge free of the planet's gravity and join a holding pattern in high orbit. When the last craft joined them Jeff compared the portal counts to the mechanical counters. Again there were three more escapees than there had been humans on the planet, but this time they knew which shuttles were hiding them.
Jael Reece's voice broke the silence and echoed through the shuttle and starship PA systems.
'Only THREE of the Shuttles made the target on time! We'll be re-running the test again in another ten days.' It was a coded message. It informed the committee members there were three morphs onboard that they would need to deal with carefully.
'The next stage - transfer to the militia ships - will begin in five minutes. To keep the lines flowing, please make sure you know which transfer portal you will be using at the interchange before you leave your shuttle.'
'Lunch will be served onboard the militia ships while we return the fleet to the Library. Once they've landed and

been cleared for flight you'll be free to port back to your studies.'
William double checked the portal routing system on the transfer ship for the tenth time. His anxiety was beginning to show.
'Attention all evacuees! Attention all evacuees!'
Jael's voice came back online,
'You may begin disembarkation and transfer to you destinations ships now. You may begin disembarkation immediately. Your shuttle pilots can help with any difficulties and there's additional staff at the transfer station to assist there. You are reminded; lunch will be served onboard your transfer ship. Thank you.'
The transfer began. Twenty orderly queues formed inside the shuttles and the heart of HS03 became as busy as a transit station in the rush hour. The only discernable difference was the total lack of anything but hand baggage. Darkon foresaw a massive class action claim for lost possessions and research material in the very near future. But that was a minor concern at the moment as filtration and re-routing of the three clones became his prime concern.
The first hit came almost immediately. Clearly the doppelgangers intended boarding the starships early so they would have time to morph into the furniture and fittings before the alarms (if any) were raised. The first morph had been number five in its queue. William heard the electro-mechanical switch activate and was already at the viewer when the morph was ported to the isolation chamber. He recognized the image from the 'Ordeal' files as the deceased Christine Skinner. When the chamber played the pre-recorded message to advise an inconclusive bio-scan the morph froze for an instant. Had William been monitoring the shuttles containing the

remaining two morphs, he would have observed two passengers freeze at exactly the same moment. Each eased out from the queue, surreptitiously moved to the back of the passenger compartment and morphed into the rear cabin walls.

Apparently the Library, believing it had all the time in the world to pursue its course, did not perceive a single unexpected 'capture' as significant problem. Normally a morph is easy to hide and they could readily be reabsorbed once the shuttles returned planetside. And in any case, even if the morphs bio-matter was a total loss, every primate species so far had imported extensive raw material in the form of foods and drink which they carelessly discarded. There was always a surplus after each guardian species had been eliminated. In the worse case scenario, the Library knew it could contact the Meld and replenishment could be delivered from another galaxy. Time was on their side even if the "time" was measured in millions of years. This Primate species seemed as gullible as the others. They used Gravity Control for more than a thousand years but were still using primitive Mass Movement for travel.

This time however the species was proving unusually challenging. Their innate attitude to safety had circumvented the Library's initial contamination. But that same paranoia could be used against them. After all their males were contaminated it would simulate a geological catastrophe releasing toxins into the atmosphere. That would force an evacuation and immobilizing their teleporters would prevent their returning planet-side. Even if it took a thousand years the ships would eventually tire of waiting and return the infect to their home planets. Another few centuries and: "Goodbye Humans!" It was all just a matter of time, and time was on

the side of the Library. With casual indifference it watched the Humans play out their puny safety game.
Now they were completing the second stage: transfer to the long range starships. As each crew checked in to report their shuttle's disembarkation was complete it was cleared for the re-entry queue. A last minute visual cabin check and the crew exited the shuttle themselves. A careful observer would have noticed each co-pilot flip the arming switch to "Landing mode" AKA "Live Bomb mode" before porting. In reality the co-pilots believed they were simply deactivating the portals to prevent the shuttles being misused for contraband. Ten seconds after the circuits tripped no one and nothing could be ported back inside.
As the last crew cleared the transit station Jael Reece's voice echoed through the starships.
'Evacuation is complete. I repeat: Evacuation is complete.' Then in a sterner voice,
'Only ONE Transfer matched expectations: Most of you will need to move more quickly next time. Enjoy your lunch. We estimate two hours before you can return to the Library. Most ships have viewing areas where those of you who wish to can watch the Shuttles returning to Alexandria-3.'
She turned to William as she cut the intercom,
'What happened to the other two morphs Willie?'
'I don't know. The best bet is they're still on the shuttles. I hope they don't inspect the modifications in any detail. Still we'll know soon enough.'
'What mods are they?' she asked.
'Sorry I can't give you that information yet Jael; I'll explain later, I'm needed for the Re-entry phase.'
When he ported across to GMI-I Jeff and Darkon were already waiting. William reached the Shuttle Recovery

station. 'Ready to go folks!' he chirped. 'Are we transmitting the failsafe at full strength?'

'Yes!' was Jeff's curt reply, 'We started transmitting when the emergency alarms rang. The signals are tied to both the main alarm circuits and two backup transmitters. They're fully synchronized.'

They settled down and checked telemetry for all twenty shuttles in the fleet. Only two irregularities occurred: an additional ninety-five kilograms on shuttles 13 and 17.

'Are they the ones we're expecting?' Jeff queried.

'An exact Match' Tom answered.

'That will allow us to land them in sequence and avoid any suspicion. We need at least fourteen shuttles to detonate together, the first fifteen if we assume the morph is able to sabotage the trigger on its own shuttle.

'Let's get the first one down, and see how the reception committee reacts.'

Jeff contacted the militia and within minutes the fleet was in trailing heliocentric orbit behind Alexandria-3 while the shuttles dropped to geostationary orbit in the planet's solar shadow.

Settling in at the control station, William received portal control from the militia and GMI ships. He linked into the first Shuttle's Auto pilot and initiated the reentry sequence. Visually and on sensor screens they watched the process unfold. Seven minutes later Shuttle-1 nestled onto its launch pad adjacent the Library entrance and cut propulsion. 'A clean landing' Jeff was relieved. He kept the comm. channel open so it would not seem strange when he did the same for the morph ships.

'The monitors can show us if anything untoward happens after landing. And we may find out where the morph is hiding.'

'Starting Reentry Two,' another shuttle dropped out of orbit and began the descent.
A few minutes later… … …
'Another clean return - starting Reentry three'
'Reentry-four'
… … …
'Starting Reentry thirteen' this was the first Morph ship. They were ready for anything. After seven tense minutes Shuttle-13 was safely landed. They watched the monitor closely. Nothing happened at first but when the ships engines went offline a humanoid shape morphed from the far cabin wall and began inspecting the interior of the ship. At first it paid attention to the Porter unit - blending with the assembly and flowing over every nook and cranny.
'Starting Reentry fourteen' they needed at least another two shuttles on surface before the Library became suspicious. During this decent the morph on Shuttle-13 extracted and examined the self-destruct control board from the porter control panel. It merged its hand into the circuit for several seconds then replaced it into the porter. The telemetry from the ship changed. 'Jeff!' William shouted, 'The porter is active again. That damned morph has switched it on, and switched the bomb OFF! But it'll still self ignite when the others blow, just a few microseconds later.'
The morph did not appear to attach much significance to its action and simply merged into the porter unit.
While it descended they turned to Shuttle-17's monitor just in time to see the morph emerge from the wall and merge with its own porter. A few seconds later a cry from William confirmed, 'Shuttle-17's porter is also back online.'

Jeff was monitoring all known transmission frequencies without success. 'They must be communicating, but don't ask me how! Maybe they're not using an electro magnetic medium.'

Shuttle 15 landed. From now on they were safe. They had reached the minimum level.

Shuttle sixteen landed AOK and reentry for the second morph shuttle was initiated. What would happen once the Shuttle landed and the library had its morphs back intact?

… … …

Shuttle 17 landed.

They watched closely. Both morphs emerged from the porter units and activated a site-to-site transport. 'They're somewhere inside the Library.' William commented, 'But the coordinates are meters below our access level.'

An alarm triggered, 'They've detected our failsafe signal. They're jamming it for a kilometer around the Library.'

'Maybe they don't have the concept of a dead man's handle; of a negative, failsafe device! How long before they detonate?' Jeff demanded urgently.

'Less than 30 seconds,' William replied.

Darkon took charge of the situation switching to full PA on all linked ships.

**'SPACE ZERO! … … … SPACE ZERO!'**

'Brace for Impact - Brace for Impact'

'This is not a Drill - This is not a Drill!'

'All ships trim for Full Battle Alert.'

'All civilians remain at your current location and brace for impact.'

'All Captains - Revert to Battle Plan Beta - Orbital Shuttles are Active.'

'Ten Seconds Captain', William was attending to the fine details, 'plus or minus Zero Point Two-Five.'

From his consol he entered the Fleet override password and keyed a command.
‘All deflector shields at max power and integrated!’
‘Three……. Two …… One …… **Brace! Brace! Brace!**
Every visible star disappeared from view; nothing was discernible beyond the twilight of the flotilla shields.

## The Nightmare Begins

The deflectors responded to the intense surge of gamma radiation from the suicide of the nuclear engines. Far below them the area that had once been the Library began to erupt. Unimaginable energy from seventeen ground and one air-born detonation had begun its deadly work. Were they not protected by their ships' shields they would have seen the eighteen plumes merge into a single mushroom cloud as the cascading reaction evolved and now only seconds later they would unknowingly be absorbing fatal doses of deadly alpha and beta radiation which was bombarding their area of space.

Instead it was the flotilla's turn to glow. A fiery haze surrounded the gravity deflectors as they rerouted the radiation and contamination that was spewing from the dying planet. Simultaneously a thundering hiss erupted from the center of each ship as sonic emitters activated at the morph platelets shatter frequency. The emitters maintained their deadly work for a full minute before canceling and while passengers and crew might be feeling somewhat strange as their autoimmune systems began to attack the atomized platelets within their bodies, the death sentence hanging over their heads received a reprieve.

Once the deflectors turned from opaque to clear, all eyes were on the glued to the planet. They should have been staring at the scatterings of the molten core from a body stripped of its continental plates but instead there were staring into the hollow of an immense ruptured sphere almost six thousand kilometers across. It was clearly an artificial structure.

'The jamming signal has stopped,' interrupted William,' we still have shuttles nineteen and twenty active. What do you want to do with them Jeff.'

As he spoke a light beam shot out from the crippled planet and began to “push” the nearest shuttle towards the armada. The beam flickered and collapsed after only a few seconds. Moments later it tried again, only to repeat the failure in much less time.

‘We have to hit them again while they’re weak.’ Jeff said solemnly, ‘Send the last two in. Can you set them to detonate close to the source of that beam?’

‘Not easily with their autopilots, but we could port them using the matrix.’

‘Do it! We may have only a few minutes before they recover.’ He watched the portals materialize, one just outside the planetary sphere.

‘Here we go.’ Both shuttles began their descent. In tandem formation they headed for the closer portal. Twenty-seven seconds before they entered the failsafe signal was cut. Two and a half seconds before entry William relocated the exit portals to where the beam had originated. As they watched a plume, smaller this time, erupted within the artifact. A secondary eruption followed with infinitely more energy than any shuttle engine. The remaining planetary shell visibly shuddered then broke apart like an eggshell shattering in free fall. For a few moments its integrity appeared to stabilize as it struggled to reform. Then in a cascade of plasma discharge the fragments lost cohesion releasing another torrent of radiation to swamp the ships. The fleet deflectors held.

They could see movement beneath the fragments. It was difficult to discern a shape but its extended across almost twelve degrees of arc. At first it appeared as an energy ball of immense size. It moved, glowing, pulsing like a giant heart. Each beat radiated enormous energy in the infrared spectrum. Initially the output was pure infra red, but then the sensors detected Beta waves implying what was left of the Library was morphing and taking control of the remnants of its physical environment.

The specter began to contract but its energy level was still rising. The nebulous form started to take on a more defined shape. Clearly spherical, the surface was becoming solid and their sensors were picking up reflections from a dense metal surface. Simultaneously there was a surge in Beta activity. When the surge leveled off the object could be seen deep within the zone moving slowly and erratically. It was slightly larger than a shuttle when it began to circumnavigate the inside of the shattered shell. As they watched it continued to reshape. A triad of protrusions extended across a common plane. They expanded, glowing, pear shaped formations that flattened and merging to form a circular disk, a giant halo surrounding a central sphere. The halo grew casting shimmering reflections of every spectral hue from the radioactive residue of the dying planet. The halo was feeding on the radiation and its structure was stabilizing.

'It's getting stronger,' Jeff exclaimed, 'what do we have in the militia arsenals?'

'NO!' yelled Darkon, 'We can't use energy weapons.' He was recalling the Library's initial introduction. 'Remember! It uses your own energy against you, and we won't have the element of surprise this time to get close enough to overload it.'

'We can't wait much longer it's getting too powerful. Look at it. It's almost doubled in size during the last ten minutes. We have to separate it from the energy in what's left of the planet.'

'William, can you use the mega-portal to drag it into the local sun?'

'Not the way that halo's soaking up everything it looks at. I'm guessing it would love to feed on the solar furnace.

We'd have a better luck dousing it with a bucket of cold water.'

'You can make it a lot colder than that!' It was Ray joining the discussion. He'd been quietly watching the action since the shuttles attack began.

'Colder!' It was Jeff's turn to be puzzled, 'We don't ***have*** any anti-matter weapons. They were the Library's first restrictions.'

'Use your own idea Jeff. Use that porter matrix, but reverse the polarity, set it up like a mirror and bounce the solar energy back into the sun or to whatever else that thing tries to soak up! Look at the monitors. That halo is only catching energy that comes in perpendicular to its surface. We can use twin portal matrices, one each side of the halo, to deflect any energy before it reaches their ship.'

'We can do better than that if we keep the portals linked!' Trudel was thinking even further ahead, 'We can set it up so anything inbound bypasses the ship completely. We'll keep that saucer thing in a total "Zero Energy" zone.'

'I can keep the matrices locked around it up to Point Three Light speed.' As usual William was confident of his skills, 'above that and we risk slicing junks off their ship if it tries to break out.'

'I'll authorize *that* risk - with pleasure.'

As Jeff spoke, the stress in his voice was easy to hear.

There were no dissenting voices.

'Get it isolated,' he ordered, 'Do it now.'

As William initiated the first mega-portal Trudel settled into the adjacent control station and began manipulating the second. Within minutes they had the gravity shields rotating about the saucer as it twisted and turned in an attempt to reposition to face any source of energy.

'Its input's been reduced to barely Point Zero Two percent and it seems to have stopped growing. Have you got any readings on it mass change rate Trudel?'

'No, but I'm showing a slight energy buildup inside the sphere section. It's weak but it is a rising positive.'

'Keep monitoring,' Jeff advised, 'and let me know the moment anything changes.'

Once the halo stopped sucking energy, the shimmering gave way to a dull gray tone and it was obvious why the term saucer had been used to describe it. Early human history had many references to air-born sightings of similar shaped objects. UFO's they had been called: Unidentified Flying Objects. After space flight began they faded into folk law, but one multi media entertainment company still offered a spectacular finders fee for anyone who could deliver the genuine article to the home planet, Sol-3. For the first time that prize was at risk.

'She's increasing her speed and moving away from the planet. She knows she can't recharge herself here.'

Within minutes the Saucer had edged away from the devastated wasteland and was heading outward, away from the solar system. Slowly, picking up speed, it strained to outmaneuver portals that were depriving it of energy and life. William and Trudel hung on until almost half light speed before it broke free of their constraints.

Once free it tapped the feeble starlight and accelerated to near Sol-1 attempting to escape the militia's pursuit. It was impervious to the fleet's artillery with both energy and gravity beams losing most of their force at near light velocities.

'William, Can you throw up en entry portal directly in front of the ship?' demanded Jeff.

'Of course I can.' he replied, 'But at this speed we can't hope to match the ships vector exactly - we could end up splitting the ship in half!'
'That's exactly what I want! Can you do it?'
'OK. Where do you want to redirect the chunk we break off?'
'Put it on a reverse vector two light minutes ahead of the target. You'll have just enough time to collapse the portals before the secondary impact. I'd like to see their faces when they realize what is going to happen.'
'Portals in position, impact in 5 seconds',
'3… … … 2 … … … 1… … … Contact'
'Portal-1 has collapsed on impact'
'Portal-2 is ejecting the debris. Almost forty eight mass units have been turned to the reciprocal vector. I'm collapsing the second portal… … … **now!'**
'Impact 23 seconds'
The impact of any matter at near light speed creates unbelievable energy. 48 mass units striking 460 mass units at light speed using the $E = MC^2$ principal can equate to almost the full energy output of a dwarf star in collapse. They monitored the collision hoping with blind faith that the aliens would be unable to change their vectors.

**'BELAY THAT LAST ORDER!'**
**'BELAY THAT LAST ORDER!'**

Jeff had suddenly turned white and was ***singing*** the order,
'Re-Vector the missile section directly into the emergency black hole.' he continued in a deep operatic voice
'Do it quickly! Your lives depend on it! Do it quickly!'
Despite the strangeness of the order two sets of hands flashed over their control consoles, one pair routing the

output matrix inside the event horizon, the other regenerating the catching matrix seconds before impact.
'All pilots,'
he continued singing visibly struggling to contain his fear.

**'SPACE-ZERO! - SPACE-ZERO!'**

**'Re-engage Battle Plan Beta!'**

**'Re-engage Battle Plan Beta!'**

A Space-Zero order would never be disobeyed by any sane person even if it made no sense, and this order was no exception. Again the deadly hiss as ultras sonics showered every millimeter of the ship with their penetrating vibrations. Jeff stumbled to the consol and focused a magnetic confinement beam in the center of the cabin. In the swirling air incandescent particles began to gather. When the concentration became a thick cloudy mist he drew his stargun at level-4: the Black Hole setting, and ported the contamination out of the ship.
**'Now'** he demanded in his normal voice**,**
'Morph Isolation Ward, Standard Level Nine Bio-Hazard Termination.'
'Execute Immediate!'
The crew complied, ejecting the pod and what remained of the third morph into the limbo of the same inescapable gravity well. They turned to Jeff demanding an explanation. Why had he ordered such an abrupt reversal? He looked terrible, soaked in sweat, panting and shaking violently, like man who had just witnessed his own death.
'How?' Darkon demanded pointing to the now vanquished platelet cloud, 'We destroyed the platelets more than an hour ago. Where did these come from?'
Jeff had almost recovered. He answered quietly. 'We never tested the system, not on a fully formed Morph, just on a few sterile pathogens.' He paused clearly in pain, 'And we know surviving platelets can reconstitute

themselves given time. I don't think we killed the morph on our first attempt. Whatever survived somehow made its way to the ventilation system and was able to contaminate the whole ship, and that includes us. Whenever I tried to give the order to jettison the pod my mind went blank. Worse still, I should never have given an order to force a collision of that magnitude. We all knew the saucer was capable of sucking in immense quantities of raw energy.'

'It dawned on me - something was influencing my thoughts. I tried to fight it but it had too strong a hold. Then I remembered how they teach autistic children to communicate using the other side of their brain, the side we normal people use when we sing. I realized if I could sing out the orders quickly enough there was a chance that the platelets wouldn't be able to jump the Corpus Colossus quickly enough to regain control. But I needed you to react like the trained spacers you are without challenging the order, before their mind control had time to stop me again. Thank the galaxy you did.'

Back on the saucer the Meld, or to be more precise the subset of the Meld consciousness that administered the Library, was running its own 'post mortem.' It had felt the Human called Jeff planning his escape from their control, but it had been unable to take action against him in time. They Library Mind had all the time in the universe on their side, but time was now becoming their greatest enemy. Their group consciousness was powerful but it had been living and thinking on such immense time scales for so many millennia that it could no longer think and react in the Human time frame. Now, as a result, it had lost a major portion of its bio-mass.

On the saucer fragment, trapped within the gravity field of the black hole, a thousand minds were working furiously

to minimize the loss. They morphed enough platelets to adjust the gravity thrusters but the more power they sunk into the grav-engines the faster they accelerated into the depths of the black hole. They had little time to spare. Even now they were passing the theoretical event horizon and once past that threshold not even light radiation could escape. Despite being the weakest of the four forces this gravity was too strong to fight. Then a single mind jumped outside the box!
"We don't have to fight it," it thought. The rest of the local Meld was listening, "Let it fight US!" Now the out of step mind had the attention of the Meld both within and without the black hole.
"We cannot fight its massive gravity so let us invert our own gravimetric polarity."
"Let the hole eject us out of its own accord."
It was a simple solution. They were going into the Hole because of their positive Gravity. If they could flip their thrusters to generate negative G's, anti-gravity, the black hole itself would spit them out like sour grapes from a connoisseur's palette. All they needed to do was maintain an overall negative value across the whole ship. Rapidly the minds reconfigured their single grav-thruster and morphed the ship's interior as a protective spherical shell to surround their bio-matter. Infinitesimally their acceleration began to slow, but their momentum was still high and gravity was beginning to affect the ship's integrity. They had done all they could, the idea had worked but was it too late to save the saucer? As the minds abandoned ship the whole Meld experienced their disappointment. They had returned but without the bio-matter from their section of the saucer. It felt the dilution as the remaining bio-structure was shared. It was the Libraries turn to shudder. For the first time since the post

nova suicides the Meld had suffered a major loss. Replenishment, even if possible, could not reach them in anywhere near a reasonable time frame. The Library Mind tried to think quickly. It vaguely remembered how easy rapid thinking use to be then realized, during the last several million years, such speed had come to lose both significance and meaning. There had always been eons of time to react. The waiting between guardianships was so drawn out and uneventful that thinking quickly was no longer an advantage. On the contrary, it frequently led to boredom and depression.
An uncomfortable idea germinated within its stream of thought. Could the dissidents have been right after all? Were their predictions true? Would Group Consciousness destroy the very commonality the majority had sought so long to achieve? It paused contemplating the notion before sharing the awesome idea with the rest of the Meld. For the first time in eons powerful emotions surged through the complexity of the great consciousness. For the first time in eons it began to segregate into opposing trains of thought. Consciousness no longer remained singular and united. It hurt! Doubt had been sown into carefully organized thoughts. Already, minor decisions needed validation against an undulating value system. And that system was straining at the seams as both extremities re-evaluated their every belief. With trepidation the Library-Minds withdrew from the Meld, returned to their physical home in the carcass of the Saucer fleeing the Milky Way.
The instant they returned, without warning, violent shock waves struck every ship in the armada. But in space there is no medium through which shock waves can travel!
While the Library Minds recognized the phenomenon, it would be a long time before the humans realized what had

happened. The event was not a disruption of space, but of space/time. It always happened when the Library-Mind returned after a lengthy joining with the Meld.

While joined a temporal equilibrium forms but as they separate threads of gravity/time emerged straining to retain the status quo. As time and distance increase the threads stretch, straining across the space-time continuum extending to breaking point. Eventually, like a polar inductor's flux, they collapse releasing immense temporal energy. Just like a tsunami focusing in the shallows surrounding an island the collapsing temporal flow increases in amplitude as it approaches the gravity wells of each ship. But without the protective mass of a sun or even a gas giant to absorb the energy the starships suffered the full force of the temporal gravnami.

## Nature Invented Weapons

With inertial damping designed for gravity and acceleration it gave scant protection against the temporal shocks. Damage reports came flooding in and casualties among the passengers were high. Fortunately, though many had suffered server trauma, no one had died.
The fleet withdrew to what it hoped was a safe distance. It monitored the saucer on long-range scanners while the Hospital Ship, HS03, prepared for an influx of severely injured patients. It was fully equipped and able to accommodate more than a hundred and forty patients. With three specialist ship surgeons and a score of medical staff from the Alexandria-3 Center it was better staffed than most planetary hospitals on the Rim. Those with lesser injuries were treated as out patients before returning to the militia ships. As an added bonus patients who ported to the hospital ship served as guinea pigs to evaluated the new nanomite filters
Despite the pressing need to pursue the enemy saucer and prevent it tapping new energy sources, the hospital ship would be fully committed with the wounded for several days and that would impose a severe limit on the flotilla's resources. Starships FS-S3M-122 and FS-S3F-14 from the Mid. and Far sectors of Spiral-3 were assigned to escort and defend it and act as an extended out patient wards. They were chosen because of their registration in the local Orion Arm of the Milky Way; the spiral arm where both Alexandria-3 and the Home Planet Sol-3: (Earth) were located. This gave Jeff, acting as Commander-General, the authority to commandeer the ships at his discretion and this in turn encouraged the militia to co-operate; not that any encouraged was needed, both captains realized the seriousness of the situation.

Besides, the local militia had excellent relationships with GMI since most governments subcontracted their deep space recovery missions to the company. Those relationships would now be put to the test.

As Commander in Chief Jeff proclaimed martial law and with the fate of the Human race at stake the time had arrived to release their hard won knowledge to the widest possible audience. The Library might have the power to destroy the flotilla, but before that happened they would give the rest of humanity a fighting chance. Data streams were prepared disclosing the events and discoveries leading up to their Pre-emptive Nuclear Strike. All data regarding the morphs, the nanomite platelets, their ultra sonic destruction frequencies, and the purging of nanomite debris from the Human host bodies, all the data so carefully accumulated in secret was now encoded on datastores and distributed to the militia captains. Every available ship was scheduled to transmit on cue across all frequencies.

At a predetermined time a thousand micro-portals opened, every ship transmitting full strength to every sector of the Milky Way. The data was broadcast to governments on every inhabited planet and to every vessel in federation space. Ignoring the most sacred of Federal Protocols GMI-1 transmitted on every known emergency channel. The first broadcast took less than one tenth of a second and was followed by more detailed reports to each governing body in the galaxy. In less than two minutes the full data stream had been broadcast a hundred times.

With the information released to the entirety of the human race, there was no way the Library or the Meld would be able to suppress the knowledge. At this very moment the data was being loaded and backed up on every A. I. database known to man.

William, who had prepared the data cubes, was lost in a daydream. He visualized the billions of children busy at work building their own sonic disrupters to shatter any morph or platelet that dared threaten them and their families. It was ironic that before any government had time to plan their strategies the humblest citizens: the Pre-Uni students; would be hard at work making the first defense shield for the Human race with an enthusiasm shared only by children. He knew that before the night was over millions of effective, though not necessarily efficient, disrupters would be resonating within countless homes throughout the Milky Way. The Library might not be vanquished yet but for the first time a Guardian species would be able to fight back.

Almost a day had passed since the first shockwave. There were several more shocks of varying intensity each several hours apart and only the increased distance from the Saucer offered any protection. At their current displacement the Inertial Dampers were coping and no new casualties had been reported. But whatever weapon the Library was using there was clearly no defense against it and if the attack was repeated at close quarters they would be helpless. Their aggressors had seen the success of their first volley and had repeated the assault several times, but only at an ineffective distance. The lengthy time delay between shots could be accredited to slow recharge rates, or limited energy reserves, but their failure to optimize their attacking range was inexplicable.

The committee was perplexed. They knew the Library was intent on genocide; it had an ideal weapon but was not pressing home its attack. Instead it allowed them to escape when it could have destroyed the whole armada in a matter of minutes. No warnings would have been sent and the Library would be free to infect the crews on every rescue ship that came to investigate the sudden disappearance of Alexandria-3. It had been one move away from “check-mate”. Why had the attack stopped? It simply did not make sense.

Several light years away the saucer finished regenerating. It had repaired the earlier damage and although it was smaller now it had full structural integrity and increased power reserves. After being bisected it had slowed to a halt and made no move to either escape or attack; instead, it remained motionless but alert. If they were facing a normal enemy the humans would suspect a trap. But the Library was not human and unbeknown to the armada it was facing an ethical dilemma of its own; a quandary far more complex than the human’s own unresolved deliberations on fetal rights to life.

Earlier during Human history the Meld intervened many times with the emerging species. It was instrumental in the Ten Great Laws they held sacred; laws that were molded around the Meld’s own; laws evolved over millions of years.

It was their fifth directive: Do Not Kill; that now paralyzed their thoughts. When the Meld made their communal decision to find a life form symbiotically compatible with their minds, a life form in which they could cohabit in harmony there had been no sentient life in the universe. They assisted the first primates as they dragged themselves from the depths of caves to evolve and populate three star systems. However when the population growth reached the minimum level for symbiotic balance the Primate minds had evolved sufficiently to reject any offer from the Meld. Their resistance was too strong and the Meld realized a more suitable life form would not evolve while the current primates were still dominant. They had to be purged. The problem was: their own morality forbad such action and while they struggled for a resolution the first Primate species spread like a malignant disease throughout the Milky Way.

They infected almost every inhabitable planet, destroyed eco-systems so severely it would take tens of thousands of years to rejuvenate. The Meld's culture had always lived in harmony with their worlds going to great lengths to repairing any damage no matter how minor, but not so this species. It was indifferent to its abuse and destruction. A parasite protects its host, but this parasite had no respect even for its own long-term survival. It was arrogant, irrational; it believed there would always be new worlds to infest. It was dangerous to the point of insanity. As the Primate colonization expanded to the limits of their galaxy they grew more destructive and greedy with each star system they conquered.

When they emerged from the caves their home planet was teeming with life but now they coexisted there with less than a thousand species. Tens of thousands of life bearing planets had been mined, stripped bare of water, stripped of all their minerals and carbon based compounds then left to deteriorate allowing only simple micro-organisms to survive. The Meld felt the need for this diseased species to be purged from the galaxy. But how could they do it when their own moral code forbad them from taking a single life much less the lives of two hundred billion sentient, though stupid, creatures.

When all hope seemed lost the Primates supplied their own solution. To curb their mounting population explosion they decreed all children of physically impaired parents were to be sterilized at birth. The population's reaction was immediate. The decree was challenged and overthrown in almost every legal system throughout the galaxy but the Meld found the concept totally acceptable. Preventing conception was better than murder; it was akin to the Primates' own methods of birth control. They could commit genocide without destroying a single life. It might take a thousand or more years, but time was on their side and after all what were a few centuries measured against the time it would take waiting for another species to evolve.

Their next task - establish a ***modus operandi.*** Another thousand years passed before they evolved the concept of the Library but with the galaxy so overcrowded it had to be located on a viable planet far away from the central hub. During the following centuries they accumulated bio matter needed to generate the platelets and transported it to the chosen planet. Nano-technology, developed long before their own culture was destroyed, could easily be controlled by the Meld's disembodied minds. The sole drawback: the platelets were constrained by the laws of physics. While the Meld minds could manipulate physical matter they had to follow natural law so for an efficient galaxy wide delivery system they would need the primates to act as their own agents of death.

Finally the Primates took the bait. Their greed for new knowledge drew the best minds from across the galaxy; male and female primates visited the Library from all three arms of the Milky-Way. At first no pregnancies arrived so the library gave them teleport technology to remove the risk of miscarriages from the high "G" forces needed to reach escape velocity. It finally worked. Fifteen years later the first mothers returned home with their infected fetuses. Another fifteen and the maturing children reached puberty. Members of the Meld aligned themselves to the infected children controlling the platelets and managing the 'disease'. With ever improving control the females could be sterilized successfully and incriminating platelets eliminated from their bodies avoiding detection. It also allowed better monitoring of the male carriers making for a more selective transfer of the 'infection'.

The fifteen-year 'incubation' period was ideal. It was impossible for the primates to trace the source of their contamination back to the Library. Within one generation the process reached "The point of No Return". Seven generations later the culture was in every meaningful sense already dead. But by then the Library was deserted, and a billion Meld-minds were scattered across the galaxy engaged single-mindedly in a "Search and Destroy" action for the lingering residue of viable ovaries.

The task had become almost addictive. For the first time since the mass novas the Meld had a common purpose. It had a task that must be done. It had a reason to exist, a communal action that brought the Meld into unison for the first time in its history. It possessed a single feeling, a single desire. It was a single being. That oneness that would sustain it through five cycles of hope and disappointment as Species after Species evolved to become the Guardians and to share the same vicious fate. When the Library allowed itself to be discovered the Primates' fate was sealed. Leastwise it had always been that way until now. But this new race: this primitive Human species was different. It had dared to change the rules. For the first time the Meld supremacy was being challenged. Worse still, that challenge was stirring up suppressed thoughts and feelings buried deep in the meldling minds. Some openly questioned their right to eliminate an entire species. Some sectors were comfortable with the earlier decision while others experienced unimaginable guilt from their complicity vanquishing five sentient species. Each faction believed it was acting in the best interests of the Meld. It was a civil war: schizophrenia on the grandest scale ever conceived and it threatened cohesion of the Meld. The minds could barely achieve consensus on the simplest decision. They were becoming immobilized in thought and action. Each time the Library Mind rejoined the Meld attempting to resolve the issues the growing turmoil proved too severe, it had to retreat from the chaos.

The Humans, believing the disturbance to the time-space compendium was controlled weapons fire were justifiably afraid of the enormous power the Library had suddenly acquired. In truth the Library *could* instantly destroy the armada. It need only direct its returning minds into the heart of each starship. Shock waves generated with such magnitude would rip the fabric of time and space destroying every living creature within miles of the epicenter. Nothing living could survive. They had learned to approach their own Saucer with great care to avoid destroying the vital bio-matter. Nevertheless, even though its continued existence was at stake the Library could not sanction deliberately taking a single sentient life.

But the minds within the Library had grown accustomed to thinking independently. Although considerably weakened, while they remained isolated they could maintain their sanity and achieve crystal-clear consensus. That consensus' gave top priority to the safekeeping of their priceless bio-matter without which it they would be severely handicapped.

Suddenly the Saucer began to accelerate. 'She's moving.' Trudel was on station her shift had hardly begun when the sensors screamed an alarm, 'But barely making half-Light speed. Where's all the energy she's been throwing at us for the last three days?'

'Ray!' she called. He was the duty pilot, 'Lock on the Saucer and follow it before it gets out of range, and get the flotilla mobile. We need every one of their porters in the matrix if we're any hope of stopping them!' Ray initiated the pursuit, and alerted the militia, in that order. Then he settled down anticipating an exhausting shift.

Minutes later Jeff and William were at their control station establishing the portal matrices. At first they positioned the pair parallel to the saucer's disk attempting to suffocate its lust for power but it was clear the saucer had adequate reserves. 'Let's try turning them round,' Jeff suggested. 'Lets make them burn up their reserves just to keeping on a curved line - You catch them, I'll redirect.'

Seconds later Williams' matrix swept in front of the enemy craft like a butterfly net trapping its prey. The saucer was "caught" and immediately emerged from Jeff's matrix on a divergent trajectory. He had related with at an eight-five degree offset. For less than a second the Saucer continued on the new trajectory before abruptly returning to its predetermined course. He called to Trudel who was closely monitoring the ships status, 'How much energy did we lose that time?'

'We didn't!' she replied, 'At this speed we've a surplus from the Thrust Portals. If it keeps below Light speed you can keep this up indefinitely.'

'OK! Let's see how it reacts when we repeat the trick.' They did. They repeated it several times and each time the Saucer returned to the same vector apparently ignoring the intrusion.

By now Darkon was monitoring the auxiliary sensor arrays. 'We're getting some small Beta readings Jeff; every time it recovers vector. What do you make of that?'

'Could it be morphing to create the energy it needs to change its trajectory? If we're detecting radiation this far out it must be expending a lot of power. Do we have any readings on its total power level?'

'Not yet.'

'Try some different deflections Jeff, I'll see if there's any difference in the Beta output'.

'OK Darkon.'

'William! Start playing "Catch" again.'

Mark joined them as the cat and mouse game ran on for over an hour. Slowly a pattern took shape. 'I've just about got a working picture.' It was Darkon and he sounded very pleased. 'It's not just the angle - It seems to need more energy turning towards the Central Hub and less turning away. Moreover, it's almost doubled when you forced it off the galactic plane. There's still some inconsistency so there's got to be at least one more factor we're not seeing.'

'And on top of that,' Trudel interjected, 'since you started playing with it, the ships lost almost Point Zero Three percent of its mass.'

'If it's converting its mass to energy do you realize what that means?' Mark challenged the crew for an interpretation. 'If it's sacrificing its mass to escape it can't have all that surplus power we've been worrying about!'

'If that's the case we'll keep to the same tactics for a while and see what develops.' Then after a few moments thought Jeff added, 'Trudel, have a look at the duty roster. Get our six best portal experts down here right away, they'll be running shifts: two hours on - four hours off, for twenty-four hours. After that I'll re-evaluate the situation. I'll check in with Control before turning in this evening.'

'In the meantime,' he turned to Darkon, 'you're not due on duty for three hours Captain. Either: go back to bed or put some damned clothes on; this isn't a pajama party!'

## Space Zero The Meld

The game resumed and for the next half day the three shifts of portal controllers became fluent managing their disruptive scheme. It was clear that the Saucer would not escape unless it changed tactics. The Saucer obviously came to the same conclusion. With almost half a percent of its mass depleted it decelerated, once again coming to a halt. The armada took up a defensive position at what they hoped was a safe distance. For more than an hour they remained motionless in a stand off position.

## Hit and Run

Sheila and Darkon were busy in the Lifeship galley preparing a mouth-watering meal for their guests. During the past two months Dr. Fong and the chief Administrator Lance Denman had become a matched pair, and the young couple had surreptitiously commandeered the Lifeship's smaller starboard cabin. Now after a grueling eighteen-hour shift on the Hospital Ship they were sleeping soundly. Only Lance's snoring disturbing the peace reverberated gently through the cabin door.

'Thank the Galaxy that's the only noise they're making.' Sheila joked casting a contemplative eye towards their room, 'Young love can be quite noisy at times.' then turning to Darkon with a mischievous grin stretching from ear to ear, 'I'll bet you were far from quiet at Lance's age!' They started to laugh.

But their laughter was cut short. A barrage of shock waves struck the ship with awesome power. Their lifeship was tossed around as easily as an escape pod in a magnetic storm. Alarms thundered throughout their vessel and everything that was not anchored down hurtled across the cabins at neck-break speed. Fortunately they were in a ***Lifeship***, the only spacecraft design that demands everything be firmly secured at all times and secured by automatic systems. Even Sheila and Darkon sitting at the dinning table were suddenly immobilized as seat restraints gently but firmly secured their torso and lower limbs. They were glad they had been seated. The tables and work surfaces triggered defensive grav-fields to secure everything in place. Crockery, eating utensils, even people were all treated alike. The only uncontrollable substance was their liquid drinks. Water and wine cascaded around the room like a cocktail in a mixing jug.

When the shaking subsided they were wet and severely bruised but free of seriously injury

Jan and Lance however were not that lucky. They were still attached to their sleeping harness, and each other, when the terrifying screech of explosive decompression ripped through their cabin; the outer hull was breached. They had no time to react before their lives, their hopes, their newfound dreams were heartlessly wrenched away. For the briefest of moments two agonizing screams merged with the deadly cacophony as their bodies, still entwined, were torturously extruded through the shredded cabin wall. They were dead before the cold emptiness of space could claim them, before their remains succumbed to the vacuum of space. Their blood boiled entombing them in a surreal aura of crimson mist. Moments later even that was gone leaving nothing to salvage for a respectable funeral.

In the galley-dinner Sheila and Darkon were helpless, still trapped in their chairs. The cabin monitor automatically routed to the outboard scanners at the location of the hull breach forcing them to witness the unfolding scenario. Even though there was nothing they could do, in their hearts they felt an overwhelming guilt. The 'Guilt of the Survivor', the guilt known only, shared only, by those who have endured similar devastating tragedies watching those close to them perish while they alone had the audacity to survive.

**THUD! THUD! THUD!**

The noise was unfamiliar to Sheila's ears, but was the sound dreaded by every seasoned spacer. Triggered by vacuum pressure the cabin failsafe had activated sending three powerful bolts shooting home, securely sealing the room, and sentence everyone inside to certain death. It was a cruel necessity of life in space. It had to be done to protect the ship and the ship's fragile Life-Support system. Sheila with tears in her eyes stared at Darkon from across the table as the torturous egress of their friends kept replaying in her mind. She strained across the table to reach Darkon's hand. Both of them were unashamedly shaking. There was no need for words. Minutes passed as they sat in silence waiting for the chair's safety locks to unlatch.

In space mistakes cost lives but this was no mistake. The Library, or however much of it remained, was hiding in the saucer. The Library had caused the disaster. Of that Darkon was sure and he would hold it accountable. He vowed the Library would pay dearly for taking the lives of his friends. It was a vow he would keep.

The armada was at full alert by the time the shock waves subsided and LS48's seat restraints unlatched. Darkon rushed to the control cockpit to access the damage. The hull breach was the only catastrophic failure. They suffered a temporary loss of navigation, a malfunction of several internal scanners, and an eight percent loss of air reserves. That was well within limits unless all four oxygen-scrubbers went offline. He activated the repair-bots to seal the hull fracture knowing from experience it would be several hours before his ship would be ready for pursuit.

He called in a damage report and learned his was the only ship affected with the epicenter a mere hundred meters forward off his starboard bow.

'What in Galaxy's name hit us?' he asked Jeff when the comms finally came back online.

'We know they've got something, but what commands that much force?'

'Still no answers I'm afraid, Darkon. We picked up a large amount of telemetry this time but none of us can

make sense of it - and the computers are throwing it back at us: ***Insufficient Data.***' I've got Mark working on it. If anyone can make sense of it he can.' He felt a minor tremor. 'What was that?'
'I felt something too!' they both scanned the immediate area. It was the hospital ship's turn to be the center of activity. She gyrated wildly in all three planes. But this time the flotilla was ready. From several ships grav-manipulators extended. Their beams spread out evenly, encasing the SH03 within a tell tale yellow glow. Gradually the hue turned orange-red as energy levels increased countering the momentum from the crippled ship. Slowly stability was restored. The beams held fast, remaining steady until a shaken McNess hailed to confirm he had regained control of his ship; but he was hailing on an unusual frequency.
'That's because I'm using a spacesuit transmitter, 'he told them. 'All the onboard comms are going haywire - we've barely got internals online.'
Then to Jeff, 'Can you lend us an emergency comms pack and port it over 'til we can get back up and running?'
'It'll be with you in five minutes.' he turned and gave the orders to have the unit dispatched. 'Do you need any techs to help with repairs?'
Before Julian could answer another shudder reached the fleet. A third ship was under attack. 'They've hit **US** now'. It was Jeff. GMI-1 was under attack.
'This is Ray Rongo; give me a minute on the air Jeff.' Then to the rest of the fleet,
'Pay attention all you military types out there. Those last three volleys were exactly nine minutes fifty-three seconds apart. That's too close for coincidence. I'm betting that's how long it takes to re-charge. I'll sound an

alarm 5 seconds before the next one's due.'
'Back to you Julian, what's the damage?'
He began his report but was only half was half way through when Ray's alarm buzzed. True to Ray's prediction five seconds later another blast hit and the first of the Battle Cruisers felt the impact of the new weapon. In the two hours that followed every ship was targeted and suffered minor damage but while all the fleet was render unserviceable only one more life was lost.
That occurred when the Battle Cruiser: FS-S1F-84 dispatched a flyer to attack the saucer. Admittedly it was a long shot and despite the anticipated result Lieutenant Wagler had willingly volunteered for the sortie. He engaged, if the attack could have been called engagement, he engaged the enemy at close quarters with a barrage of gravity and disrupter beams. Diverting all the power from his StarThrust he poured maximum energy into the saucer without any noticeable affect. At first the saucer ignored him; it lay like a basking crocodile soaking up the morning sun. Then after less than thirty seconds the saucer glowed brightly and for a split second sent a pinpoint energy beam piercing through flier. As soon as it had pierced the small ship the beam expanded into a cone engulfing the full width of the ship hiding it from sight. When the beam collapsed nothing was left. No ship, No debris, Nothing.
It proved beyond doubt that conventional weapons were as ineffective against the saucer as bows and arrows against an armored tank.
With the fleet disabled the Saucer began to move again. Slowly it edged away from the pack still moving at less than light speed. The armada monitored its retreat for as long as possible, later they would rely on tracking the miniscule energy trace left behind and hope there would

be no cosmic storms to dissipate the trail. Its movement was strange. First it headed to the nearest star staying long enough to absorb its fill of solar energy. Then it went superluminary and hopped from star to star on a course heading outward along the Orion arm. It took two days before the armada was repaired and battle worthy again but by then the saucer had escaped beyond sensor range.

News of the couple's gruesome death overran the armada grapevine. While the younger students were noticeably disturbed, this being their first exposure to real danger, the older students and the professors were more tolerant. Some, with military training, were better prepared for the emergency. A few were thrilled at the opportunity and eagerly re-enlisted 'For the Duration'. They were proud to literally be on the front line of the new venture. Most, however, only wanted to escape from the danger zone. It was a complex logistics problem but not insoluble. During the next few days dozens of GMI Life ships raced across the spaceways to populate an escape route portal-linking the battlefield and the nearest colony at Troydom-4. Almost a hundred nodes were established both to shunt the faculty and students to the safety of the planet and to bring in portable shelters and provisions to keep them safe until the arrival of passenger liners.

Three thousand temporary residents would be a heavy strain on the colony's resources, but after the visitors departure it was cost effective for GMI to leave their emergency accommodation behind rather than shipping it back for storage. Troydom-4 would end up with a healthy injection of capital wealth: eight hundred fully functioning homes, a significantly asset to favorably tilt their balance of payments over the next two years.

The Colony announced its readiness and within hours the evacuation was underway. First the library's Admin staff ported through to set up the Administrative system and allocated accommodation. When the remaining faculty and student body arrived they found fresh clothes, fresh food, and good night's rest awaiting them. For many it was the first night of normal sleep in several days, but for others the vision of Alexandria-3's last minutes would be their nightmare for years to come.

Back in the armada, free at last from constraints imposed by a civilian presence, the senior staff met to discus new stratagem. They planned a more aggressive approach without the risks from well meaning but untrained civilians. Militia from the Perseus spiral arm had already located "illegal" anti-matter weapons the Library had banned. Not surprisingly the Space Service's paranoia that other governments would retain the technology convinced them to mothball thirty percent of their arsenal before publicly decommissioning their official stockpiles.

No one knew why the Library had banned specific weapons but it was highly probable the ban targeted armaments against which it had no defense. Many leading mathematicians insisted their computations proved energy fields ineffective against anti-matter.

Taking advantage of the GMI portal network before it was dismantled the armada replenished its supplies. If the hunt continued beyond the spiral arms this battle fleet would not be thwarted by a lack of provisions. Acquiring the forbidden armaments was more difficult. They had to assume the Saucer and the Meld were monitoring their comms so normal contact was out of the question. The alternative however, old-fashioned face-to-face contact, would mean shooting one-man capsules through portals. The cost was high but several senior officers would be needed to liaise with the unofficial armory stores. They could not rely on open comms channels to back them up and would need to organize a reliable delivery system to port the Anti-matter missiles at a moments notice. There would be no room for error.

Time was passing slowly. The full armament allocation was scheduled for upgrade. A proportion of the torpedoes would be modified for anti-matter delivery while others, using standard warheads, would be retrofitted with mass detection homing systems and triple point heavy duty grappling restraints. In short they could home in on the densest structures within the target, attach themselves to allow sonic resonation to disrupt the saucers repair capability and only then detonate their warheads.

Meanwhile the ships were undergoing repair but with each lost hour the Saucer edged further into the uncharted extremities of the Milky Way. It was almost ten Sol-3 days before the armada could return to the hunt. Every ship had its long-range sensors tuned to search for the faintest energy signature the Saucer might leave. Though the trail was intermittent it was far from cold and they were making good their pursuit. The increasing strength from their prey's stardrive signature confirming they were closing in and for more than three days their greater speed slowly reduced the gap but on the fourth day - nothing. The trail stopped dead.

With the GMI ships as an anchor point the better armed militia fanned out in a standard 3-D search formation. Had the Saucer doubled back on its trajectory? Was it hiding behind one of the local star clusters? Was it using an alternative drive to jump the immeasurable gulf between galaxies?

Jeff summoned the committee to discuss options and was joined by the militia captains in holograph mode. Twice they extended the search zone in an attempt to find any trace or abnormality that even a hinted of an alien influence. Twice their results were fruitless.

In a final last-ditch attempt they agreed to follow the Saucer's projected flight path while remaining in the extending search pattern. If the alien ship was trying to lose them by cutting engines and cruising in Free Fall there was a slight chance they could detect a power surge when the stardrive restarted. Without thrusters the craft's path had to be a relatively smooth curve through space following gravity gradients and it could not waste too much time before restarting. They allowed themselves two days. By then the variables influencing free flight would become too unpredictable and the armada simply did not have the resources to continue an effective search. They would have to admit defeat.

## Morse on Offer

Towards the end of the second day Darkon had just finished his shift. He was enjoying a late night meal before retiring when the strangest of calls came through.
'Darkon.' it was Geney, she'd replaced him on LH48's comms less than an half an hour earlier. 'Darkon, I'm sorry to disturb your dinner, but I have Captain Vaslar demanding to speak to you, personally.'
'OK Geney, Tell him I'll call back in an hour - it's the first break I've had in twelve hours.'
'He's not going to wait Darkon; he said to tell you "It's an Emergency Call and you're the only Lifeboat in the sector".'
'What! He's calling us a Life***boat***! He's been watching too many Tri-Di history films.'
'He's been in the fleet for over thirty years Darkon. He knows what he's asking for but he's ready to abandon his ship and port directly into your quarters if you don't take his call - and we all know what that would do to his career.'
'Damn it! Did he say what it's about?'
'He won't discus it with anyone but you and he wants permission to send over his chief comms officer.'
'This is getting weirder by the minute.' He looked longingly at his dinner, 'OK' he said grudgingly, resigning himself to the situation, 'Put him through.'
The starship captain wasted no time getting to the point.
'Thank you Captain Myzelv! This is Megan Vaslar of the FS-S3M-122.' The stress in the Battle Station Commander voice was evident.
'OK Megan,' he responded impatiently 'I don't like talking business while I'm having dinner especially not on

a Life ***SHIP!*** - Why didn't you call Jeff Discman directly, he's the one in charge?'
'I don't think this call's directed at him Captain, and the term "Lifeboat" that's exactly my point. We've picked up an "S O S", an ancient planet-side emergency call for "Lifeboat" assistance; and before you ask I did executed **Battle Plan Beta** before calling you just in case our ship had been infiltrated. My comms officer: Ensign Joanah Quahn, he's been monitoring the "S O S message" for half an hour and he says it's directed specifically to your call sign. It's coming through on a standard emergency frequency'.
'We're monitoring all those channels ourselves - and we're not picked up anything or I'd be the first to know it. If it's on an open channel what makes him think we missed it?'
'Apparently it's not in computer protocols - he referred to it as: "HUMAN READABLE **MORSE CODE".'**
Darkon paused for a few seconds, the term sounded familiar but he could not recall where he'd heard it before. Then impatiently he returned to Captain Vaslar, 'What's so urgent about this message? Ours are the only ships this far from the hub. We passed the last outpost days ago.'
'Apparently this Morse code is a series of bleeps that decode into letters and numbers. They use it to spell out words. It's very slow, very low tech. but it's coming through on our most advanced hyperspace comms link. It reads:
"**S O S**" followed by a one second pause,
"**S O S**" another pause,
"**BASE ONE TO HUMAN LIFEBOAT LS48**" another pause
"**FIFTH GUARDIANS NEED HELP**" another pause,

**"CRITICAL YOU REPLY SAME FREQUENCY SAME PROTOCOL".'**
'That's the message and its being transmitted continuously with 17 second breaks between repetitions.'
'So where's it's coming from, have you located the origin yet?'
'No, that's another inconsistency, none of our tracking systems can get a fix, and it's as if it's coming from a thousand places at the same time.'
'How am I'm supposed to answer it if we don't know where to respond or where to look for them? We don't have any, what did you call it, "*norse*" code translators?'
'***Morse*** code, Captain. That's why I've got Ensign Quahn standing by; he's had experience with the system. I can port him over? - He say's there is no special equipment needed, just a trained hand and ear and he'll be able to explain it better to your comms officer in person. If the call's genuine we can't afford to pass it up.'
Darkon thought carefully for a few moments, 'I'll get back within fifteen minutes.' He terminated the call to consider the situation without pressure from the military. The Saucer already knew their whereabouts so they had nothing to lose by responding. He called Jeff to advise him of the situation. With the "S O S" being an emergency call, it was clearly the Lifeship's duty to respond but they both considered it prudent to have a Starship Cruiser on standby in case a trap unfolded. Arrangements were made to port over ensign Quahn and within minutes he was eagerly explaining the incongruous signal.
'Apart from its arrival on a hyperspace link,' Joanah elaborated, 'it's basically a primitive signal. Before aviation became commonplace it was the standard

signaling protocol for ocean going vessels. They used it with encryption during the nation-v-nation wars, and at close quarters they flashed narrow focused light beams to send the signals between ships so the enemy wouldn't eavesdrop on radio comms.'

'How come you know it so well and how could you recognize what was coming through?' Geney Gourd's curiosity was almost matched the ensign's enthusiasm.

'That was my grandfather's doing, he was Professor of History at the Cambridge-Oxford Euroversity on Sol-3. He was so fascinated with ancient communications that when we went on holidays he would teach me the old techniques so he had someone to practice with. There was semaphore: messages you send using two-short flags, Morse code: we used simple flashlights to signal across the river Thames, and a Whistling Code they used in the Netherlands to "shout" messages across the mountainous.'

'But how did you notice this one was audible code?'

'Oh that!' he smiled rather sheepishly, 'I often pump the comms through speakers when I'm alone on duty. Apart from being a pleasant background warble I can often recognize a message type from the way it sounds. There're subtle differences between text data, film sequences, and compressed speech. They're quite distinctive and it helps keep me alert guessing what type of data I'll have when the transmissions stop.'

'It was several minutes before I realized this one was repeating but that unique sequence, the "S O S":' he imitated it with glee,

# Space Zero The Meld

**Beep Beep Beep**
**Beeeeep Beeeeep Beeeeep**
**Beep Beep Beep'**

'It stands out like a nova in front of a black hole. After it came up for the fourth time well, that was just too much of a coincidence. I listened carefully and started to decode it. You can imagine my surprise when it translated in fluent Federation-Speak. I haven't played with the code for years, not since grandpa died, and it took a few repetitions before I got the full message.'

'And that's when you called us?' she prompted.

'Galaxy No!' at first I thought it was my shipmates on S3F-14 playing a joke. They're always ribbing me about Grandpa and his strange habits so I scanned to see where they were sending it from. That's when I realized it was coming from, well, - everywhere. Believe me, none of us would squander all that energy on a joke, the Commander would throw us out the airlock for being so wasteful. I must have checked and rechecked it a dozen times before daring to call it in. I mean, if you've got the tech to generate a hyperspace carrier, why use such primitive encoding?'

'Are you certain of your translation? I mean, there's no chance it's just a freak abnormality?' Secretly Jeff was hoped it was not.

'No doubt at all Sir. The signal's too perfect. The bleeps, actually they're called: dots and dashed, they're pure tones - no harmonics - no distortion and they're tuned to exactly 10000 Hz. There's no way that would occur naturally; not that level of precision. Whoever's behind this must know about our time scales and hearing physiology.'

Jeff was seriously considering a reply. 'If we want to return a message, how long would it take to set it up - what special equipment do we need?'
'I can send one manually right away, Sir. I can send a short message from any of the comms panels by hand but I'd only be about 98 percent accurate. If you want the full 100 percent I can put a Morse Translator into your VR texting interface so anyone can send it; but that will take about an hour.'
Jeff and Darkon spent a few minutes in private discussion. They wanted to reply but they didn't want to commit to a course of action just yet. Finally Darkon stood up. 'Joanah,' he addressed the young officer quite casually.
'Yes Sir!' the ensign jumped to attention.
'Relax Joanah; we're quite informal on Lifeships.' He led him to a comms unit. 'Is there any special way to talk using this system?'
'Yes Sir! Its best if you just use brief, short sentences Sir.'
'Ok, but just call me Darkon. Save the formalities for when your own officers are around.'
'Thank you Sir … … … I mean Darkon,' he was not used to such casualness with senior officers.
Darkon thought deeply for a few minutes then asked,
'Can you send this? "Your message received and translated, request under consideration. Question 1: Why this protocol? Question 2: What proof of your claim?"'
'Yes Si...' he paused, 'Yes Darkon, do you want me to send it right away?'
He thought for a moment, 'How long before we can expect a reply?'
'They seem to have very advanced comms, but without knowing where they are I can't even make a guess. Their signals were very strong though if that's any help. They could be using sub-space portals.'

'Geney,' Darkon called to his own specialist.
'**One**: have comms trap everything using this Morse code and get it rerouted into an isolated secure store.'
'**Two**: Get Joanah cleared to access it and our ships comms.'
'**Three**: See how he transmits the message then help him to set up the SL-VR interface while we're waiting for a reply.'
'**And finally:** get this all documented in case anyone else gets sucked into space.'
'Meantime, I've got a cold dinner waiting - you'll find me in the galley.'
He turned to Jeff,
'This is going to be a long night.'
'We might as well plan our next move over a meal.'
As he was leaving he called to the ensign.
'If you haven't eaten yet, Joanah, have Geney bring you to the galley when you're finished. You might as well wait for the reply in comfort while you explain the interface to us.'
Back at last to his dinner. Darkon reprocessed the remnants of the last meal, selected a large jug of coffee and slumped down for the belated feast.
'Help yourself Jeff; you know your way around this galley as well as I do!'
'I'll just have a cold drink. I finished a hearty meal an hour before this fracas got started.' He helped himself to a chilled pineapple juice and found a comfortable chair across the room from Darkon. 'What do you make of it, genuine? Or is it another of the Library's tricks?'
Darkon was in no hurry to reply, after an hour's wait the food tasted really good. He let the juices soak slowly into his mouth savoring their every flavor and as his teeth chewed on the meats his mind chewed on a multitude of

explanations for the strange signal. He swallowed noisily. 'If it's on the level, we can really use an ally right now. Didn't Wendy discover the fifth guardians had done a lot of research on nanomites?'
They continued talking for several minutes until Geney interrupted them with news of the returning Morse code message. 'It's quite short and Joanah's given me the decoding sequence. I can pull him off the interface if you want to give this priority, or I can start the translation myself.'
Jeff took the initiative, 'Let him get on with the automation. We'll make up any lost time as soon as he gets it working. Are you comfortable handling the message?'
'Yes Jeff. There're less than fifty codes in the table and any mistakes will show up immediately. How urgently do you need it?'
This was Darkon's home ground; they were asking for Lifeship assistance. 'If they really are the fifth Guardians they've been waiting hundreds of thousands of years already, another couple of hours will be just another star in the sky to them. If they're not, we have no reason to rush into an ambush. We'll reassess the situation in an hour or two when Joanah's finished, or when you've got something definite to give us. What's the latest from the militia's search?'
'There's been nothing since their last routine check-in, Darkon. The telemetry's still negative.'
'O.K. Geney I'll leave it in your capable hands. You know where we are if anything comes in.' He finished the coffee and drew another jug of the steaming brew. It was regrettable that caffeine had been outlawed. He could use a stimulant to keep him alert for what was going to be yet another long night.

Less than an hour later when the intercom buzzed, they were both asleep in the galley loungers. Geney had finished translating and posted the message on their monitor. As he read it Darkon downed the last of the now cold coffee, shuddered at its bitter taste, and shook himself awake. An hour was far too short for a full sleep cycle and he felt the inevitable heaviness that comes from wakening in the middle of a deep REM dream. In his line of work it was a familiar feeling, and he steeled himself to face the next few hours before his body was fully recovered. A yawning Jeff joined him at the master consol and together they digested the message.

WE ARE THE LAST OF CUANTA THE FIFTH GUARDIANS. WE RISK DISCOVERY BY TRANSMITTING AND HOPE THE LIBRARY WILL NOT RECOGNIZE THIS PRIMITIVE PROTOCOL. WE SURVIVED IN SUSPENDED ANIMATION SINCE THE LIBRARY GENOCIDE BUT OUR LIFE SUPPORT IS FAILING AND WE NEED HELP. WE HAVE OBSERVED YOUR SPECIES FOR SIX HUNDRED SOL-3 YEARS AND MONITORED YOUR COMMUNICATION ON THE NANOMITE ATTACK. WE HAVE USEFUL KNOWLEDGE OF THE LIBRARY AND OFFER INFORMATION AND TECHNOLOGY. WE ADVISE, THE ATTACK ON YOUR FLEET USED TEMPORAL SHOCK WAVES. WE OFFER ALLIANCE AGAINST THE MUTUAL ENEMY OF OUR TWO SPECIES. WE HAVE COMMON ANCESTRY. TRANSMISSIONS HAVE DRAINED OUR ENERGY. WE OFFER TO TRANSPORT TWO EMISSARIES TO YOUR LOCATION. YOU MUST RETRIEVE THEIR LIFE PODS. IF YOU REPLY NEGATIVE WE WILL NOT

RISK CONTACT AGAIN. WE AWAIT YOUR ANSWER. END TRANSMISSION.

Darkon and Jeff had a serious decision to make. They could not risk transmitting details to the federation for fear of the Library intercepting the signal but by accepting the offer their on behalf they would be committing to a full restoration of the Cuanta civilization. As with any first contact, a lot could be gained by both sides although in this case it would be difficult to evaluate the package they were being offered. They would have to take it on trust.

Once again, they had little choice. At the very least they would learn more of Library's strategy and tactics and that would be to their advantage. The current situation had proved their own resources inadequate as they tried to track the Saucer and, even if it was located they were still defenseless against its temporal shock attacks. The Cuanta had survived almost total annihilation so they must have some useful technology at their disposal. Jeff recalled an earlier discussion. 'Don't we already have someone with "First Contact" experience on the committee? Wasn't that one of the reasons we recruited Sheila?'

'I'll wake her,' Darkon said quietly, knowing she would be very unhappy to lose a nights sleep but this was priority and he was certain she would be more displeased if someone else beat her to "First Contact".

'It's up and working Sir's.' Joanah and Geney entered the ship's galley. The ensign turned to Jeff, 'If you're ready I can talk you through the protocols now sir.'

The Commander-General stepped to the consol and selected a SL-VR headset,

'No need to plug it in below light speed' he commented as he mentally activated the link.

'Select "Format Morse" sir,'

'then select the "Hold before Send" option,'
'then text a test message Sir.'
'Done' Jeff confirmed.
'Now select "Send to Galley Intercom" and select "Send"'
'O.K. - Done'
The galley speakers burst into life:
**Beep Beep Beep Beep**
**Beep**
**Beep Beeeeep Beep Beep**
**Beep Beeeeep Beep Beep**
**Beeeeep Beeeeep Beeeeep**
**Beep Beeeeep Beeeeep Beeeeep**
**Beeeeep Beeeeep Beeeeep**
**Beep Beeeeep**
**Beeeeep Beep**
**Beep Beeeeep**
**Beep Beep Beep Beep**
**Beeeeep Beeeeep Beep Beeeeep**
**Beep Beep Beeeeep**
**Beep Beeeeep**
**Beep Beep Beep Beep**
**Beeeeep Beep**
**Beep Beeeeep Beep Beeeeep Beep Beeeeep**
The ensign spelled out the signal as it emerged,
**"H E L L O J O A N A H Q U A H N full-stop"**
'Hello Joanah Quahn.' he recited the translated phrase.
'And you remembered how I spell my name, thank you! I've made the interface as user friendly as possible so anyone can use it.'
'So much for transmitting, but how do we translate their messages?'

'I've added the Morse translator to the standard receiver protocols. They'll recognize it automatically and translate to whatever mode you're using at the time. They'll output the Morse code in background mode, audible or texted, and superimpose the translation as the foreground pattern. Listen.'

He whistled the "S-O-S" loudly in the galley.

'I see it,' exclaimed Jeff in surprise as he monitored the text through the SL-VR interface'

`'... --- ... (S O S) .... . .-.. .--. (H E L P)'`

'The texting will add the interpretation at the end of each letter group, that's normally after each word.'

He turned to address the ship.

**'Galley Auto Translation Mode Include Language MORSE. GO'**

***'Command Accepted'* replied the Galley.**

'Commander, please try the texting again'.

**He obliged, but this time the galley speakers interspersed words into the streaming bleeps.**

**Beep Beep Beep Beep**
**Beep**
**Beep Beeeeep Beep Beep**
**Beep Beeeeep Beep Beep**
**Beeeeep Beeeeep Beeeeep**
**HELLO**

**Beep Beeeeep Beeeeep Beeeeep**
**Beeeeep Beeeeep Beeeeep**
**Beep Beeeeep**
**Beeeeep Beep**
**Beep Beeeeep**
**Beep Beep Beep Beep**
**JOANAH**

**Beeeeep Beeeeep Beep Beeeeep**
**Beep Beep Beeeeep**
**Beep Beeeeep**
**Beeeeep Beep**
**Beep Beeeeep**
**Beep Beeeeep**
**QUAHN**

'And that completes the lessons for today Sir!' Joanah smiled broadly, he was obviously delighted with his evening's work.

Sheila and Darkon returned just in time to catch the tail end of the demonstration. 'That sounds interesting. Who's the beeping nuisance around here?'

'Quahn's done a good job on the interface Darkon; he's earned his supper today.' then turning to the youngster, 'Help yourself to a good meal young man, you *have* earned it. If you need any help with the galley systems ask Geney, she knows them better than anyone else on the ship.'

He turned to her, 'Can you find him some quarters? He'll need to be on hand for a few days until we get some modern comms up and running'

'We've still got the forward cabin.' Geney answered, 'It hasn't been allocated yet. The techs re-certified it late this afternoon.' she glanced at Joanah watching his reaction. By now everyone in the fleet would know what transpired in that room only a few days earlier.

Quahn nodded. 'That's fine with me,' he answered, 'As long as their ghosts don't snore I'll sleep like a baby.'
'You can plan on being here at least a week ensign.' Jeff added, 'And Geney, have Megan's ship port over whatever he needs from his quarters. Now let's all adjourn to the bridge we need to draft our reply. You'll need all your skills on this one Sheila.'
'And,' she smiled at Darkon, 'if I'm going to be any use to you I need a little more information than, "Wake up, get dressed, we've got a First Contact!"'
Darkon turned to and Joanah grinned,
'That's more that someone else around here had to work on!'
The ensign grinned back.

# First Encounter

The captain's room on a lifeship bridge is a very cramped area, barely enough space for the four-person crew and filled with every conceivable gadget and gizmo that can assist in a crisis. But, it is designed to be the ships primarily faraday cage. It can be switched to total communication blackout mode. Once the mechanical isolation circuits were tripped nothing would leak out and only the bridge could send a one-way message into the room. Jeff engaged the system and brought Sheila up to date. 'Now, 'he stated very seriously, 'we have to decide if they're telling the truth, if we dare trust them, and whether or not they're a greater danger to us than the Library. I'm open to suggestions.'

'What do we know for certain, and what do we need to take on trust for the time being?' Sheila wanted the facts before beginning any speculation, no matter how few they may be.

'To start with,' Darkon began, 'they *claim* to be the Fifth Guardians. So far we've only their word for that, but in all fairness, I've examined our data for this sector of space and there's no references to any settlements this far out. The one we passed a few days back is only sixty years old and they don't have the resources for exploration outside their own star system. I spoke with their senior governor an hour ago. They had no record of signals from this sector until we arrived and they hadn't picked up any unusual comms on the hyperspace link we're using. I think we can safely assume either they are who they claim to be: the Fifth Guardians, or they're connected to the Library and the Meld and it's a carefully laid trap.'

'They're claiming knowledge of the Meld, 'Jeff took his turn, 'but again, even if that's true, it doesn't help decide which side they're on and we have no way to validate any evidence they might give us. If they've been monitoring us for several centuries, just like the Library, they'll know how to be deceptive. This isn't going to be a normal first contact.'

'It never is.' Sheila brought reality back to the situation. 'The main difference this time is the minority culture that has the greater knowledge. Usually the dominant group initiates first contact after they've been the watchers for many years. They may have evolved since the Library destroyed their culture, but clearly they've been unable to re-establish themselves - if they are genuine - we can assume their need for help is greater than ours. After all, we survived the first assault and it seems we're the first species to do that. Their hiding may be as much to protect themselves from us as it is to stay free of the Library.'

'Put yourselves in their position. If we're strong enough to be a successful ally then we could be a greater risk to them than the Library. They lack numbers so their main contribution will be their knowledge of the enemy. If we turn out to be aggressive, and they've see how we handled ourselves during the pre-federation wars, they'd be right to worry about out intentions. Once we know where their planet is, we've ample resources to destroy their whole life support system and rape their data banks for every grain of knowledge they've so painfully acquired. On the other hand our hospital ship has the best equipment this side of the galaxy and if the aliens are willing to be examined we can tell within hours if they genuinely have common ancestry with us.'

Clearly there was insufficient information to make any valid decision. They would need further input and that could only be achieved by accepting the offer of the two emissaries. However, they would make it absolutely clear:

if they weren't convinced the aliens were being truthful they would be considered prisoners of war and treated accordingly.

A Morse signal was drafted and transmitted. They waited impatiently for a reply.

It took less than a minute to arrive. It was simple. "Advise when ready."

All four ships were put on standby in staggered pyramid formation with each vessel at the limits of manipulator beam range. Four sets of portal generators were brought online and all sensors activated. The Aliens had not released details of their delivery but it was clear recovery was totally in the hands of the alliance ships.

When they were ready Joanah was given the order to transmit manually.

**Beep Beep Beep**

**Beep**

**Beeeeep Beep**

**Beeeeep Beep Beep**

'"SEND" transmitted Sir!'

Within seconds a zone close to the center of the pyramid formation began to glow. Immediately gravity deflectors from all four starships responded. They powered to full strength; each ship was ready for a surprise attack but the energy level within the glow remained safely at a low level. For several seconds all attention was on the portal as in tandem formation two golden life pods slowly emerged. The instant the second pod cleared the glowing orifice it blinked out like a spent volcano. The two pods were left stationary and shimmering in the reflected haze of the deflectors.

Mark Quison aboard GMI-1 was the first to respond. 'There's a low level heat signature coming from each unit. I'm going for retrieval - activate Battle Plan Beta

NOW!' All ships responded and the familiar sonics flooded them from every available acoustic outlet. If it was a trick they would exact a heavy price. Twin manipulator beams played out from the lead ship to grip the first pod. They met no resistance easily adhering to the noble metal - or was it a camellia alloy? The first pod was eased into the launch bay and safely imprisoned within powerful gravity shields. Again the manipulator beams foraged outward and connect with their second target. Slowly they reeled it in bringing it to rest incarcerated alongside its partner. While the bay doors remained open giant clamps locked onto the extremities of each pod radiating them with high-energy sonic waves for a full three minutes. If the aliens were damaged that would be unfortunate - but if this was a trick the library platelets were not gaining ingress to this ship and remaining intact.

With their task complete the clamps lowered the life pods to floor level and the outer hull doors slid shut. Air pumped into the chamber to restore a normal atmosphere making the sonics louder and more unpleasant. Two medics, without face shields, stepped forward to show the occupants of the pods that the air was safe to breathe and to make an initial, visual inspection. 'I can't see any release mechanisms or "instructions" for opening. The controls must be on the inside. We'll have to wait till their ambassadors are ready to come out.'

'This one's turning translucent.' the first medic uttered, 'I can make out a humanoid inside!'

'This one is too!' confirmed the second. As they watched, the pod casings began to melt from their upper surface. The structures flowing like dissolving ice cubes to form a gelatinous yellow fluid on the floor revealing two humanoid creatures dressed in bright red full-length tunics. The most striking features were huge jet-black eyes set deeply in heads almost twice the size of the humans. In stature they were shorter at about sixty-five inches with their torso and limbs comparable to primates including powerful hands with elongated fingers and opposable thumbs. Like humans the male, for their tunics were not designed to conceal body structure, had a clearly defined musculature that almost rippled as he moved and turned. The female with small but distinctive breasts exhibited a similar but less pronounced muscle development. Their silver-grey, satin smooth skin appeared devoid of hair and the female showed a distinguishing maroon head patch where they would normally expected hair to grow.

The creatures stepped clear of their pod residues. Their movements were smooth and flowing. Their limbs were almost human in appearance, but the larger heads turned more slowly than normal and their necks were sturdier structures than in Humans. In the Central Hub they would be noticeable as a new culture but uninformed citizens would not suspect their ancestry was so far removed from the Human genome.

They turned to shine a yellow light onto the remaining yellow mass. Instantly the puddles reshaped into a meter high cube and solidified. The crimson “Guests” laid their two hand devices on the top of the block which immediately absorbed them into its substance. They stepped towards to the medics; then in perfect Galactic Speak with a Central Hub accent, the taller alien spoke.

‘Our pods have self-destructed to protect the Cuanta in the event that this meeting fails. The control devices have self destructed for the same reason. If you need to examine us before we converse we are ready. But first,’ he carefully removed a flat sheet from his tunic, ‘this document is written in your language. It has the location and vector of the Library ship, the one you refer to as the "Saucer". We offer this data as,' he paused searching for the best words, 'as "a sign of good faith". It was accurate when we arrived at your location. It documents methods you may use to track the Saucer.' He laid the document on the floor and stepped back.

'Our name for the aliens who control the Library is: Acodea.'

Jeff came through on the launch bay comms. 'Get a copy of that document to the militia immediately, but warn them to take maximum precautions. Leave the cube for the techies, and bring the emissaries to the porter station. They'll be debriefed on the Hospital Ship.'

McNess took the controls to port the aliens into the hospital's isolation ward. From the safety of the receiver ship he initiated filtered transports. The first alien had minimal contamination which was easily isolated and quarantined on the initial pass; a relatively clean transmission. The second was another story. It was extensively contaminated with nanomite debris and it took several scrubbings before successful elimination. A greater surprise came a few minutes later when the platelet residue was examined. The particles were a third of the size they had expected and they were not the regular crystal shapes the sonic shattering normally produce. These platelets had been destroyed a long time ago by a different but equally ruthlessly technique. He would be asking the aliens for an explanation as soon as their medical inspections were complete.

The Chief Coroner entered the ward to greet the aliens. 'My name is Julian McNess, welcome to my hospital ship. You will be staying here for a few hours while we complete our quarantine and safety checks.'

The taller alien spoke again in fluent Galactic, 'I am Zholtair. This is my partner Verrringah.'
He went on to explain. 'We volunteered for this mission because we are expendable. Our hibernation station is designed to support a minimal staff so when hiberpods malfunction those of us who survive emergency resuscitation must fend for ourselves on the outside: on the planet's surface. Anything less would be unfair to those still hibernating and jeopardize the repopulation program.'
'Unfortunately a hundred and thirty thousand years ago intense volcanic activity destabilized the planet's atmosphere and destroyed our ozone layer. It never recovered. Life on the outside is short with a life expectancy of about six years. There are only thirty of us so you can see there is little choice in partners. Not that it matters much, all the females in the group are sterile and any offspring would die before reaching childhood.'
'Does the sterilization result from the nanomite attacks?" Julian asked. 'I assume you are familiar with the Library's skill in that area.'
'Yes! We are from the university that developed the thesis. Once the population decline was confirmed we knew the Library was the source of contamination but we clashed with too many vested interests. Nearly everyone in hibernation was trying to escape before the 'disease' reached us but we let a few late comers into the colony and they were infected. Most of our females were sterilized long before we perfected the anti-nano technology. That is what destroyed our platelets. However we have only two thousand pre-puberty females who went into hibernation before the platelets activated but we dare not retrieve them until we can destroy their platelets during de-hibernation. We don't know why but when

their bodies are in stasis the nanomites remain inactive. As soon as someone is revived, as soon as they come out of stasis, the Library nanos overrun their bodies before our units have a chance to immobilize them. If we had developed the sonics technique you perfected we could have protected all our fertile females instead of just the immature ones.'
'But if you know our technology, you already have the solution. So what's stopping you now?'
'We lack the energy! We don't have the power reserves to develop a viable porter system. We'd need to disconnect more than half our population to run a single teleport filter similar to the one you just used. When the hibernation started we put our chance for survival at only twelve percent. That's why when the units fail so many of us are willing to accept just a few years of life on the outside. We knew the chance of success was very low when we started.'
'We watched your culture develop and hoped you would reach us before you found the Library. When you did not we expected your species to follow us into near extinction, but you achieved the impossible. By pooling resources we may both survive.'
'You'll be meeting Jeff Discman soon.' Julian interrupted. 'He's the one to talk to about an alliance.' He looked toward the female, 'Is Verrringah always this quiet?'
'Not normally but it's her first trip into space. She was born on our home planet after the platelets struck so her parents put her in stasis a year before puberty. Then they demanded I take her to Atnera, that's what we call our planet. ***Her passage*** was their price for sponsoring our university for three escape ships. Her life was just beginning when everything went on hold and now

because we've no ozone layer she's had face the six year death sentence. She's finding these new developments overwhelming.'

Rather tactlessly Julian asked, 'Then why is she here?'

'There are thirty of us on the outside. We are a small but balanced group: three males and three females from each hibernation unit. When ours failed, as a pre-puberty female she received the anti-nano treatment but it was unsuccessful. The platelets destroyed all her ovaries before they were neutralized and she has been the only pre-puberty resuscitation we have made. My original partner and a younger male in our pod failed to resuscitate. Since the others pod survivors were already linked we became partnered by default. Being the last pod failure she's had no opportunity to re-partner with a younger male.'

'We were at the Hyber-Center for our regular medical checks when your ships came into comms range. We were visiting and shared the excitement. It was intense and there were several agonizing days not knowing if you would break off the pursuit and retreat before the Saucer moved beyond sensor range so we could try to contact you. When your reply came Verrringah overheard them argue over whom to send if you accepted their offer. None of the Administrators wanted to risk their ultra safe lives in case you weren't convinced we are also the Library's victims. They were afraid of being executed or marooned off-planet - we know you cannot afford to take risks with the Library. For them, inside the safe zone, they can expect to live at least two hundred years; they had much to lose.'

'For us, we had very little to lose and much to gain. After five years on the outside the effects of exposure to ultraviolet radiation was beginning to show. If we stay on

Atnera we'll be lucky to survive until the next harvest. Only last season we watched our four older pod mates endure their last months withering away with malnutrition. They were too weak to work and barely able to feed themselves. For us as outsiders, being away from Atnera's sun, we can expect a few extra years of life even if we become your "prisoners of war," and if it gives the Cuanta a chance for survival that is a bonus. In the words of our Administrator, "You have a greater incentive to make the meeting successful than any of us."'

Julian had been listening carefully as the alien rambled on. Not only his ears but also the ears of the ship's A. I. were monitoring every statement. Any contradictions would be identified and carefully scrutinized during the formal interrogation. He noted the relaxed posture of the creatures and their easy conversation but deferred judgment on that issued until he could study their medical data. He did not have to wait long.

Tom and Paul entered the ward with the preliminary results, and offered them to Julian. He declined. 'Lets start without any secrets,' he announced, 'let our visitors know what we've learned.'

The two aliens moved closer together, an almost human gesture, and for the first time their faces looked strained. A lot would depend on how much trust was engendered by these revelations. Paul outlined the results, 'Apart from the platelet debris that's already been filtered out and damage from ultra violet radiation all their body organs are relatively healthy. They also appear with only minor variations to be consistent with Human physiology. There is nothing to indicate they are not normal biological entities' He glanced at the female then turned to Julian. 'We scanned their reproductive system to determine the extent of the damage. There's extensive mechanical

damage to the ovaries and less than zero point one percent have any chance for incubation. However we identified one ovary that's ripening and almost ready for release. Its DNA appears intact although without a base genome we can't map for irregularities.
Verrringah spoke for the first time. She looked directly at Paul and her words came slowly, 'Are you saying I can breed?'
'Yes' an excited Tom intervened, 'You won't have many opportunities, and you'll need regular screening to detect an ovum release but if you port out any viable eggs for artificial fertilization and incubation you'd increase the chances to almost a certainty.'
Verrringah began talking rapidly to her partner in their own language while the medical team waited patiently. Zholtair paused and briefly apologized for the interruption then gave his full attention back to his agitated partner. It was a full ten minutes before the alien female regained her composure. She thanked Paul for the news then turned again to her partner.
'Ask!' he advised her quietly, 'they can only say "No".'
She spoke directly to Paul. 'This is not part of our assignment.' she stated, 'It is not authorized by our Administrators. They could not have foreseen the results of your tests. They may even demand we withdraw the request.' She hesitated again.
Paul waited but the female was having difficulty with her words. If she were Human he would have thought "emotional difficulty".
'If you have a question we have no taboos against guests asking for anything. We may need to restrict our reply for various reasons, but you welcome to ask.'
'Ask them Verrringah!' Zholtair encouraged her again.
Paul's intuition prepared him for her next words'

'You said I have an egg that is almost ready for release.' She was under extreme strain, 'Can you protect it now? Can you save this one it in case I never get another chance, so it can be fertilized later when I'm ready to breed? And what will I have to do to repay you.'

'Cost! You're asking what it will cost!' Paul was taken aback, 'Humans don't pay for medical services. We wouldn't expect you to either.' He spoke to Tom, 'Do we have the facilities onboard?'

'Yes, we can set up a "Freezer" quite easily. From the look of the scans it will be at least a day and a half before the egg is released and then we'll have about three days to port it into a stasis or cryogenic chamber.'

Paul turned to the aliens. 'We'll need your government's approval Verrringah, but apart from that, we can have your egg in protected stasis within the next few days. It will be ready for you or anyone else you authorize to use and if you need to use an artificial incubator we can arrange that too. Consider this our "sign of good faith".'

Before she could answer, the Cuanta female did a very Human thing. She broke down and began to cry uncontrollably. Zholtair went to her tenderly cradling her head against his chest. He turned to the Humans 'Please continue,' he requested, 'she will recover in a few minutes. In times of stress we Cuanta occasionally succumb to our primitive reactions. I assure you at this moment Verrringah is experiencing happiness not sorrow.'

Paul continued his report at a more leisurely pace. He was finally feeling relaxed with the aliens. 'Both of you have suffered irreparable tissue damage from the solar radiation but that's only a superficial problem. We can treat the melanoma and the scar tissue can be cosmetically reconstructed. If you're diligent, avoiding strong sunlight and extreme weather that can aggravate the condition, your life expectancy will be close to your norm. Your bodies have been weakened and they'll react badly if you neglect them so you need to be more meticulous than normal about regular medical checks. On the positive side, there's been negligible DNA/RNA degradation from the Hibernation. Its less than you'd suffer from a severe childhood illness.'

He turned to Julian, 'Genetically we're almost as close to this species as we are to the primates on Sol-3. If the rest of their species confirm their genome I can formally declare them from the same ancestry. But to guarantee legal status we need at least a thousand authenticated "live" scans.'

Zholtair was concerned, 'That would mean resuscitation and with the Hibernation units designed for only one cycle we would need to relocate to another more suitable planet.'

'If we defeat the Library I'm sure that will be the least of our challenges and if we fail,' Sheila shuddered, 'I doubt any of us will be worrying about habitable worlds.'

## What Atnera Knows

The comms signaled an urgent incoming call. Julian responded. 'I'll take it on the bridge,' he said, leaving the informal gathering. The news was good. Following the Cuanta's projection the armada had successfully located the Saucer. Once again they were tracking their enemy but this time without interference. They had gained an ally but their current priority was to keep a low profile until the knowledge and resources of their two species could be optimized and a viable plan of attack developed. The ambassadors' presence removed any lingering doubt as to the Library's deadly intent and while it might be possible to co-exist with the Meld, a vanquanda will never become a domesticated pet. With five successful genocides and a sixth attempt in progress no species would be safe. In less than a thousand years even the most carefully documented warnings would fade into folklore and their species would be vulnerable to another insidious attack. To the Library a thousand years was just a blink of their "eye" and yet in the natural world a time disparity of that magnitude usually gives the smaller entity the advantage of speed. These and a trillion more thoughts were racing through his mind as Julian returned to the ward. 'Do you need food and fluid?' he asked the aliens, 'We will be meeting the Commander in an hour, and it may be a long wait before we can take a refreshment break.'

'I am ready to feed, replied Zholtair, 'and I suspect Verrringah will appreciate sampling your foods.'

'Yes,' she replied, 'we grow very limited crops on Atnera. Our historic records show the great diversity available before the collapse but we are unsuccessful growing any but the basic cereals and root crops. I am eager to taste your cuisine and enjoy exciting new flavors.'

They adjourned to the hospital canteen. Two hours later, after their most satisfying meal since hibernation, two satiated aliens were ready for the most important meeting of their lives. Upon their shoulders would rest the final hopes of the Cuanta, and the last chance to revive thousands of souls frozen in the eternal limbo of the long sleep.

Jeff was waiting when they ported to the command ship. He led them to the wardroom and introduced the committee. The meeting began with all cards exposed; neither side could afford to waste time with petty face saving games. For their part the Cuanta admitted the loss of a viable atmosphere had crippled any plans they had for revival; the planet could no longer support their recovery. The humans confessed they were powerless against the Library's latest weaponry and were at a loss as to how use their own anti matter arsenal to do significant damage to the Meld. Put simply the Humans knew virtually nothing about their enemy.

The admissions made a powerful starting point for discussion. The humans had more than sufficient resources to resuscitate and relocate the entire Cuanta population and to protect the viability of their females. The Cuanta had knowledge gained during the centuries they were under attack and had millennia of research and speculation awaiting further investigation. Jeff's diplomatic skills were almost unnecessary. GMI's primary business: Interstellar Recovery, kept him up to date with the latest details of new and habitable planets most of which were readily available for colonization. He had stats on at least a score of worlds within easy reach of their current location stored on the ship's databank. So when he projected the star chart above the table and zoomed in to show several suitable planets in more detail the emissaries were visibly delighted. When he added GMI's promise that regardless of the outcome of the war the company would guarantee relocation to a planet of the Cuanta's choice and assist them to re-colonize the alliance was sealed. On their part the aliens were willing to share information they had accumulated on the Meld along with any data the military could use.

Of course, the final decision would need to be ratified by the Cuanta Administrators. Ensign Quahn was called to the bridge and a low energy Morse signal transmitted towards the co-ordinates Zholtair supplied. Within seconds the dim energy glow returned midway between the ships and for several minutes a Morse code dialogue bounced between GMI-1 and the Cuanta Hibernation planet. Arrangements were made for a more formal interchange. Not surprisingly the Cuanta wanted the same opportunity to examine the Humans to ensure for themselves that they were not Library Morphs. They requested, or more accurately demanded, reciprocation for the two emissaries who voluntarily had risked their lives for first contact. These Human emissaries would be free to inspect the Cuanta base in more detail so they wanted one to be a technician, and the other to be familiar with federation politics. When Jeff requested a third person, Sheila Fayamore, as his First Contact specialist they readily agreed but were more reticent when he offered to add a portal generator. For the first visit they wanted only the human life forms - NO technology. Their restricted energy supply made the process slow. First they sent an unmanned probe through the orifice. It was a single high tech tool. Zholtair used it to restructure itself and the residue of the original two pods into a single

four-humanoid capsule. Then he and the three humans entered the pod and sealed it from the inside. Verrringah watched as her partner and the strangers were eased through the orifice. Once again as soon as the manipulator beams withdrew the glow blinked out. Alone for the first time in her short life she was isolated from everyone and everything she had ever known. She was amongst hundreds of strange and intimidating creatures that she had known for only a few hours. Struggling to control her irrational fear of the unknown her hand strayed to the belt pouch at her waist fingering the comforting coldness of the micro freezer Zholtair had given her before leaving. It contained his sperm in case the Library traced their transmission and did its worst to their planet before he could return. She still had options but the next few hours would be a lonely vigil. Wendy sensed her fear and promised to remain with her until Zholtair returned.
Verrringah's worries proved unfounded. After five hours a new Morse transmission came through requesting the previously offered Portal Unit and several Sonic Generators. They were duly dispatched and less than an hour later another surprise arrived. A micro portal opened adjacent to GMI-1 and a normal voice transmission came through. It was Sheila relaying the Cuanta's first voice message. It was brief. The Cuanta had established a portal and tapping directly into their local sun had energized their power grid. Once the connection was stable they activated long dormant defense arrays sited on their artificial moons. Next they had regenerated full planetary shielding to compensate for their lost ozone layer. And finally with the planet protected they powered up their communication arrays confident that no extraneous signals would radiate across the galaxy to reveal their location to the meld. The exchange continued for several

minutes then came a strange message that Sheila took pains to pronounce carefully in the Alien's language. It was to be given directly to Verrringah.
On hearing the words the female alien sighed with relief. 'They are willing to trust you.' She explained, 'They want me to give you our planets location.' She concentrated for a several seconds and reeled off a series of numbers. She repeated them. 'They mean nothing to me. They are in a notation that should make sense to you. Do you recognize it?' she asked expectantly.
'They're galactic co-ordinates.' replied Darkon. 'Offhand I'd estimate it at less than 2 days flight from here. In a Lifeship that is; but it'll take several more days for our heavier starships to reach.'
He gave her the gist of their latest communication. 'Your Administrators have resuscitated a select few of your sleepers. They were filter-ported to your Medi-lab to eliminate the platelets and they've successfully revived two of your females with their ovaries intact. They've also filtered all your colleagues on the "outside" and they'll be arriving here over the next few days to be treated for their ultra violet exposure. Your people want us to restore all of you to full health as soon as possible.
'That is good news but do you know when my Verrringah will be coming back?'
'We're expecting the first group to arrive in a few hours. He'll be with them. After all apart from yourself he's the only Cuanta with any experience with us. We've a meeting scheduled in the GMI-1 wardroom in four hours time. You'll see him then.'
He turned to leave then paused, 'Oh! Yes!' he added, 'They've agreed to your ovary request. Wendy can introduce you to the medical staff when the meeting's over. I imagine you'd like to get the ball rolling as soon as

possible.' He spoke to Wendy, 'Make sure she has whatever she needs. We want our new friends to feel at home in the federation.'
'To get the ball rolling?' she asked perplexed.
'A Human metaphor,' Wendy explained, 'It means to start a task. We have a very colorful language, but it plays havoc with every new culture. I'll try to speak more literally until you get used to our strange ways.' They both smiled.
Jeff was in GMI's galley enjoying a coffee with Darkon and William before the meeting. They were busily reviewing the latest militia reports when as always, once the aroma of a fresh brew began to waft through the ship, Ray Rongo emerged from hiding. He still preferred his own company to a hectic social life. Despite the lack of caffeine, most people would claim he was addicted to the dark brown fluid. He drew a steaming mug, laced it with sim-milk and joined them in the loungers.
The Saucer was maintaining its slow progress outbound from the Milky Way and although the militia was within scanner range they had not been subjected to another attacked. Captain Vaslar, out of courtesy for his crewman's discovery of the original message, had been invited to join the holo-conference. His ensign was instructed to bring him up to speed on the developments of the last hours and pass on Jeff's advise, to defer any action they might have planned until the flotilla could regroup near the Cuanta's hibernation planet. The offer of new data on the Library was music to his ears. If the aliens knew how to protect his ship and crew from the devastating temporal shocks he was ready to listen. If they only had theoretical ideas he was still ready to listen. It was better to have a few low probability chances than be left totally helpless with absolutely no course of action.

Running ***from*** an entity that could jump across time and space made no sense. Running ***to*** a location that offered even limited protection at least gave them a fighting chance of survival. He still wondered why the Library had not pressed home its advantage when it had the opportunity. Its unpredictability was unnerving but had he know the inner conflict his enemy was suffering he would have been more optimistic about their own chances.

Several times, since the Humans returned to the hunt, the Library Minds merged with the Meld. Turmoil was increasing. Within the Meld splinter groups were forming. Some divisions were ready to make an all out attack against the Humans to prevent any future primates from evolving into tool-wielding cultures. Others wanted to remain true to their existing plans, to wipe out this species and patiently wait for the next evolutionary cycle. A third group was ready to abandon the Milky Way forever and search for life in other galaxies. Yet another feared since this was the only galaxy ever to seed life to abandon it would mean to abandon forever their quest for symbiotic coexistence.

The portion of the Meld that was the Milky Way Library remained undecided. It wanted to keep options open and that meant protecting the vital bio-matter in what remained of the Saucer until a decision was made. Here it ran up against the multifarious morals of tens of thousands of individual minds to which it owed its existence. While they all valued the sanctity of life, when the Humans had deliberately put their irreplaceable bio-matter at risk they had struck out in anger and rage, and their emotional response had caused the deaths of two sentient beings. Surprisingly their collective conscious was not disturbed and consensus was slowly shifting in favor of a direct attack. The majority was still reluctant to

relinquish long held values towards life but the balance was precarious and it would take very little Human pressure to upset it with dire consequences. That the Library would act was not in dispute, it had already decided how to cause maximum damage to the armada and the infestation of primates throughout their galaxy but consensus ruled and until the majority in the Meld concurred there could be no attack.
As it waited, the Library extended its mind to touch other galaxies where bio-matter was stored. There were several ships orbiting stars the Meld had once ruled but outside the Milky Way no cultures survived to assistance them. Their distant ships could still morph into activity and indulge in interstellar travel converting bio-matter into thrust energy, but in reality intergalactic travel had become impractical. When they had hundreds of humanoid races enslaved and could create new supplies of biomass wherever they were needed they had become cavalier about its use. Now with only a single primate group that was resisting their influence they realized how precarious their grip on the physical world had become. Purified bio-matter was the catalyst that empowered their mental energy enabling activation of the platelets. Without it they could not morph physical matter. They would lose their leverage in the physical realm and become as ineffective as a red dwarf on an event horizon. For the first time since the mass novas the Library Mind felt the embrace of the ice-cold fingers of fear. It snapped back from its wanderings through space returning to the reality of its own Saucer but in its terror emerged dangerously close to its own vessel.
On the bridge of every Militia ship warning lights alarmed. Space hardened officers watched in dismay as the saucer gyrated violently under the impact of temporal

shock waves ripping at the fabric of space within a mile of their enemy. Even at this distance the disturbance was powerful enough to activate their ship stabilizers. The Humans would not realize the significance of this event until much later. The library had reacted emotionally. It had become a frightened animal with immense power and frightened animals will turn to ***FLIGHT*** or ***FIGHT***. It would not be long before the choice was made.

Captain Vaslar was making a routine report to GMI when his ship began to shake. Unceremoniously he terminated the connection half expecting to find the armada under attack. He was relieved to learn the Saucer was suffering and a few minutes later he refocused back into the wardroom holo-suite with the disturbing news. By now he was impatient to learn what the Cuanta knew about the weapon and was equally desperate for some method of defense. The last volley may have been directed away from them but it was many orders of magnitude stronger than the first attack. The energy output was far higher than any antimatter annihilation he'd witnessed. Was it an accidental discharge? Had their weapon overloaded and destroyed itself? Was it a test? The Library was not alone in its fear and two frightened opponents make a dangerous mix. Before long Megan's training and self-discipline would be tested to the full.

## Alien History

Close to the command center the glowing orifice returned but only long enough to eject six gilded pods. This time they were larger and arrived under their own power. They hailed GMI-1 before flying single file into its open docking bay. After entering they took position within reach of the sonic clamps waiting patiently to be relocated to the landing bay floor. As soon as the bay pressurized the pods melted to release their live cargoes. From the pod residue emerged three Humans looking somewhat relieved to be back in familiar territory. Accompanying them was Zholtair and fourteen Cuanta Administrators. Immediately they were ushered to the conference room where the committee, a holographic Megan, and several militia officers were waiting.

Jeff chaired the meeting and after brief introductions the first agenda item was the recent events surrounding the Saucer. Uagair, the Cuanta's Chief Administrator declared his technical qualifications and went on to explained what they knew about the phenomenon. Although in their experience it had never been used it as a weapon they had documented many similar events. In contrast to the Human experience, Morphs frequently accompanied the Cuanta as advisors when exploring the outer reaches of the galaxy. Their best-documented incident occurred during an expedition to a remote star system. While excavating an asteroid orbiting the fourth planet several apparently sentient artifacts were discovered. At their suggestion the morphs contacted the Meld for more information but when their communication was completed the asteroid and all traces of the artifacts inexplicably disintegrated beneath them. Fortunately their craft suffered minimal damage. The morph explained: the

asteroid gravity was too low to absorb all the "temporal stress" between two points in space/time within an expanding universe. However, the Cuanta suspected this was not the complete truth, and this was confirmed a few hours later when they discovered every scan and recording of the artifacts was irreparably damaged. The only common threads among the remaining incidents were the relatively low mass of the affected items and the more severe damage to materials with high tensile strength. The very feature that gives a compound its greatest strength appeared to work against it under temporal stress. The Library appeared uncooperative when questioned and finally declared the phenomenon off limits for discussion. It was clearly a sensitive area, or was it an area of weakness?
'The only clue we have comes from the Morph's own words: "the Asteroid had insufficient mass to absorb the temporal stress." But we have no idea how much mass is needed to provide protection.' Uagair suggested that entering a planetary gravity field might offer limited protection should a threat occur.
He introduced members of his team who were developing nano-technology, and explained how they were underhandedly disenfranchised by the Library's hidden agenda. Shortly after its discovery, research subsidies began to disappear. Private funding became increasingly difficult to obtain with sympathetic sources being tempted away by more lucrative avenues of research engendered by the Library. A few years earlier Nano-tech had been a promising field. It was in use for general production and had made strong inroads into medicine. Hospitals used nanos to diagnostics disease with great success and designs for super nanos to augment the auto immune system were approaching completion. It was estimated

that within twenty-five years they could extend life expectancy almost indefinitely; Cuantas would live until their mental capacity failed and life support nanos were deactivated. Animal trials were successful and they were waiting authorization to begin Cuanta trials when their university was suddenly under boycott. Powerful lobbies arose to challenge the ethics and morals involved. Legal battles evolved into financially crippling confrontations forcing the hospitals to distance themselves from all forms of nano research.

To the university it was clear the situation was being orchestrated to suppress any form of nano development. The Pro-Nano counter lobby was just beginning to make headway when a new priority swamped their civilization. Throughout the central hub their population was decreasing, there was an epidemic of sterility. The university was optimistic nano-probes could discover the cause of the disease and reverse the trend. They sent twenty shipments of their most advanced nanos to the Central Hub, but every starship failed to arrive - "missing in space" was the official designation from the authorities. By then, the faculty was convinced the Library was sourcing the movement against them. They were certain it would do everything possible to prevent nano-technology from being used.

When a thesis was published suggesting the Library planet as the most probability source of contamination, none of the medical authorities would give them credence despite the reproducibility of their experimental data. They dispatched a primary research team: a senior professor and two students, to meet with the federal health authority on Cuanti-2. That starship also "disappeared". It was located several years later orbiting a lifeless moon in an uninhabitable solar system. Unbelievably, all five of

the ships life support systems had failed. It was then the university realized it was on its own and if it was to survive it must do so in isolation from the Library and mainstream Cuantakind.
During the last century of decline they monitored the genocide of their own culture and began to plan for the great hibernation. Secretly, illegally they developed and tested nano-mites that would protect both their bodies and their machines. Without attention they could not expect their hyber-units to survive a single century much less the hundreds of thousands of years needed to keep them isolated them from the Meld until a new civilization could emerge. They needed sponsors and in return bartered hibernation rights for each ship they were given. Ten years before the great sleep they had selected three suitable planets with stable stars and began to colonize.
Despite their best attempts at secrecy as their culture collapsed two of the planets were discovered. The first was attacked by marauding pirates who plundered and destroyed the energy piles releasing deadly radiation, sentencing themselves and their victims to a slow drawn out death.
The second was discovered by a fleet of escapees already contaminated by the Library platelets. When they realized the planets purpose but were refused access to the hyber-pods civil war erupted. What the newcomers couldn’t share they destroyed. Essential, irreplaceable equipment was melted down. Nano databases purged, design equipment cannibalized and key scientists ruthlessly murdered. If the escapees were not going to survive - then no one else would either. When the last of the newcomers died, their escape ships were in disarray.
A month later, for it took that long for the Meld to morph the repairs, ten simultaneous launches heralded the

Library's success. It took another thirteen in High Orbit for their structures to be re-grouped and morph into the single, now familiar, Saucer shaped starship. The vessel powered up and set forth on a voyage of discovery. Its purpose: To find a new world with water and oxygen from which it could evolve another deadly trap. After a millennium it produced the planet that humans would call Alexandria-3. Another millennium and it was deemed ready for 'occupation'.

The third colony had been unable to render any assistance. Its own fleet had been reconfigured into energy converters for the hyber-units and in any case a rescue attempt would have revealed its own location and jeopardized what little chance of success they still had. They could only passively monitor the disaster and watch the Morph Ship leave solar orbit steering a course inbound towards the galactic hub. They were relieved when it safely bypassed their own star system. Their planetary shielding had worked; at least, it had passed a first cursory inspection.

Against all odds they had survived and were now ready for the next stage: the longest night Cuantakind would ever know. The sponsors were the first to sleep or more accurately the sponsors' children since only a handful of their benefactors choose to save themselves. Most having raised families, 'bequeathed' their children the chance of a full life. Gradually the more learned and knowledgably volunteers settled down to the deep sleep leaving only technicians and Administrators to monitor the system's first critical years.

Two tasks remained: to protect their nano maintenance facilities, and to test the cyclic re-wakening system.

The first was straightforward and ensured their most advanced technology would be available for the final recovery. Proudly they announced their success and informed the Humans that full nano production could be achieved within months of the Awakening. The second task took decades and several elderly professors spent their last years on the long duration trials. Only five percent of the hyber-units were designed for multiple re-use. They were vastly more complicated than the one-shot models but they were necessary to allow Cuanta intervention. At regular intervals, initially set at two months, a ten-Cuanta team of administrator/technicians would awake. For a several days they could check the smooth running of the system and passively scan the Milky Way for signs of a new culture emerging. If necessary they could awaken specialist technicians for major repairs and nanomite upgrades.

It took thirty-five years before the system was declared viable. The professors monitored the final test cycle and when the next team awoke the recycle duration was extended to nine thousand years. The surviving senior staff entered the remaining single-cycle hyber-pods to be sealed in 'for the duration'.

Eight days later, and for the first time, a team of Administrators and technician sealed ***themselves*** into hibernation and wondered if their replacement crew would ever wake up.

**Nine thousand years later - they did!**
**The system was working!**

The current team was on their hundred sixty third cycle. For all appearances they were only four years older than when auto-hibernation kicked in. On their previous cycle as they watched the early signs of Human technology they noted the re-wakening period had been dramatically shortened. On this cycle the departing shift had remaining active for their maximum two years period and had woken them manual. They took over as news of the Human's "Ordeal" was breaking and it was clear the fate of the Cuanta would be determined during this cycle. Pod failures had accelerated and nanomite repair activity was peaking in the overload zone. The ensuing months were spent studying their Human database as they monitored the changing events with apprehension. Against protocol, they advised the Outsiders that a first contact was imminent.

The next alien introduced himself. 'I am Dweumna,' he announced. 'During the administration periods part of my task was ongoing research into the Library's Nano technology. As an original member of the thesis team I worked on the early studies. I am conversant with data accumulated by the Admin teams during my hyber-periods. There was always extensive new information at each re-wakening. Without being overly detailed, we've established the Library's Platelets are not true nano machines. Although they act in a similar manner they are essentially microscopic muscles that work at a molecular level. They are controlled by static charges which appear literally from "nowhere". In isolation tests when we endanger the bio-matter the platelets activity increases as does the total sum of the matter/energy balance. That seems to defy basic scientific principal: Conservation of Energy/Matter. We suspect the Meld, which appears to exist outside the normal space-time continuum, introduces energy when it controls the platelets to interact with our physical world.'

Jeff wanted to know more, 'Have you discovered ways to control the platelets yourself, or at least to interfere with the Library's control?'

'In the lab we attached probes to the platelets and controlled them individually, but in practice we can not direct static charges onto them or co-ordinate multiple units. There are no feedback circuits so however the Meld controls them they must use remote sensing at the quantum level.'

'What about shielding them with force fields?'

'Neither matter nor energy barriers have any effect. The only inhibiting factor we discovered is when the energy level of the bio-matter is reduced. By reducing the temperature close to absolute zero, or "killing" the bio-mater we can suspend platelet activity. But as soon as the temperature recovers, or new healthy bio-matter infuses to the platelet location, the activity resumes. '

'You've presumably tried saturating the area with positive or negative static to block the control signals?'

'Yes we did; but the control charges materialize directly on the platelets avoiding any barriers we erect. Our own nano-machines use heat energy from the surroundings as a power source and become inactive at higher temperatures than the platelets, so by the time we freeze the Library platelets our own nanos are already immobile. The Meld platelets utilize any form of bio-matter so the patient's own body can be used as fuel. We do not know how or why they need the bio-matter. In our Lab experiments the isolated platelets functioned perfectly even under vacuum conditions. We hypothesize the bio-matter may be a catalyst for focusing static charges directly onto the platelets.'

Mark turned the conversation to their immediate problem: the escaping Saucer. 'What information do you have on how their starships use morphing technology? We've monitored significant beta radiation whenever the platelets are active, and when the Saucer restructured itself the energy output was tremendous.'

Neuama answered that question. 'That was ***our*** technology.' Was she was angry, agitated? 'It represented the pinnacle of our nano achievement. We could reconfigure a starship in flight without endangering vessel integrity using just the structure of the ship itself and energy from a local star. With repair nanos on permanent standby even damage from a meteor shower was easily repaired. The Library banned the development along with all Nano research so when the ban was announced we deliberately withheld all the data not already published. It is that same technology that allows us to track the Saucer so easily.'

'Do you still have the starship technology, or just the information about it?' Ray was thinking ahead. For long haul passenger ships the ability to effect repairs "on the fly" or in an emergency to reconstruct the ship into escape pods would be a great asset to any transportation company.

'We have the data on file, but we lack the necessary raw materials to build the nanos.' She was unhappy. 'If Atnera had been rich in minerals we could not have colonized it safely without being discovery. We had to select a healthy but less than optimum world to distance ourselves from the mainstream escape routes. Most ore rich planets were plundered by marauders when our culture collapsed. We made a choice that was necessary at the time but now we are deficient in raw materials vital for our recovery.'

'That's just a supply problem. GMI can obtain the minerals for you one way or another,' Jeff was confident of his company's resources. 'Just let us know what you need. Of course they'll expect something in return, some sharing of the technology.'

Jeff was studying the faces the alien of group. They were clearly uncomfortable with his last words. Ray too

noticed the change.
'You look puzzled!' he exclaimed, 'But you're so far advanced in the nano field - if you released just the basics of your technology your planet could live of the royalties for the next thousand years!'
'Royalties?' inquired Uagair and Dweumna almost at the same time.
'Patent Royalties' Jeff added eagerly, 'Copyright Royalties! It's how inventors get rewarded for sharing their secrets.'
The alien expressions remained unchanged. Ownership of knowledge, that was not a concept the Cuanta understood.
'I think we're taking too much for granted.'
The ever-practical Ray realized their knowledge of Human culture was far from complete. He turned to the Chief Administrator choosing his words carefully to avoid embarrassment.
'If I've got it right,' he began, addressing Uagair directly, 'when you monitored us over the last few centuries you've had to be wary of the Meld - to prevent them locating your planet. Did you limit your observation to passive scans? Presumably you couldn't send active probes to collect data?'
'That is true. We could not let the Library learn of our survival. Our automatics monitored all your long range, sub-space communications and advised us when your pursuit approached our star. That is why we were waiting when you came within range of our local transmitters.'
'But without probes you would have difficulty tapping into our long range comms?'
'That too is true. Probes would transmit directional signals since we do not have the power reserves for global transmission. The Library would have traced us and destroyed our colony very easily. For the same reason we

could not have the probes returning to Atnera. It would be suicide.'

'So,' continued Ray, 'Your knowledge of our cultural and financial institutions is not yet complete.'

'That is correct. The knowledge we acquired is predominantly from your new colonies, those relatively close to our star and from the comms between them and their closer trading planets. We realized that as migrants from your mainstream culture they would not fully represent your species.'

'No wonder you're feeling uncomfortable.' Ray candidly acknowledged their concerns. 'In your position we wouldn't want to give away our best bargaining chips either. Your knowledge of Nano Technology, that's your major asset.'

Jeff began to realizing where the Cuanta's reluctance was coming from. Briefly he outlined the Federation's concept of patent rights.

'At the planetary, star-cluster level local laws apply but, for the federation, the principals of "Democracy" rule. That means equality for all sentient beings and we need consensus to make new laws. We fervently protect individual rights and that includes protecting a person's inventions. It's all part of the Federal Constitution from way back in early history.'

'We call the system: Patenting. It allows inventors to register their discoveries and designs, and then they're protected from other people using them to make a profit - unless or course they have a formal arrangement with the inventor.'

'If you decided to patent your Nano Technology,' added Ray, 'you could license other companies to use it and they would have to pay you for that privilege. What you charge them or whatever other arrangements you make is entirely up to you. Once you formalize an agreement it becomes legally binding.'

'But what if they refuse to co-operate? We clearly do not have resources to challenge a large inter-galactic company and force them honor their agreement?' Not surprisingly, Dweumna was suspicious. 'And if we use the limited force at our disposal - it could alienate others in your federation.'

'That's the best part of the system.' Jeff was on home territory now, 'You don't have to enforce those rights yourself. The Federal Commission, that's who you registered your patients with, the Federal Commission is bound by our laws to take action on your behalf and to resolve any disputes. You'll find they've far greater power than any company. Even planets outside the federation keep on good terms with their Patents Office because we also protect *their* inventions.

'That and from fear of having the Federation impose a trading embargo against them.' interjected Ray. 'Even the fringe planets value out markets.'

'We can get you linked to our legislative databases so you can learn more about our culture.' Jeff continued, 'GMI will give you all the help you need in that department.'

The meeting had run on longer than expected. They agreed to adjourn for the day and start afresh in the morning. A break would give the Cuanta time to digest the new ideas and they both knew that tomorrow the agenda needed to focus on the common enemy.

## Attack Attack Attack

Several hours later Jeff was called by Megan Vaslar from the militia fleet. They were monitoring the Library Saucer and now, like the GMI ships, it was vectoring towards Atnera-1. Their crews were still wary following the last temporal shock incident and their agitation only increased when, two days out from the Cuanta home planet, the Saucer suddenly changed course and was vectoring towards them.

As they raced to achieve the safety of planet fall they considered the few options open to them. If they pooled resources they could create a mega-portal large enough for their ships; all but one could escape. The last however would not be able to maintain integrity of the orifice and pass through at the same time and if it was captured by the Saucer the bio-matter, namely the crew and food supplies, would give an enormous advantage to the enemy. Even unmanned Human starships had considerable 'live' units in their automated systems, but the greater danger would be if a hijacked and compromised starship infiltrated an unsuspecting part of the galaxy.

Here, close to the Outer Rim there were only a few stars and fewer planets which could offer protection but if they ran to them for sheltered the fleet would be divided. Its combat capability would be reduced. Everyone on board knew the Saucer could lay siege over a time span that would leave the crews crumbling to dust.

There was one long shot. If they opened portals close enough to their ships that linked them directly to the local stars the fleet would be protected by powerful solar gravity wells. However there was an equally dramatic down side.

If for any reason the ship-deflectors failed, they would be instantly fried by the same, intense solar furnace.
Of more concern were the thrust portals powering their ships. They would be in continuous drag and drift as the solar gravity overwhelmed the starships mass. Their speed would be seriously degraded.
However, if the portals held up and with short range protection from the ships' sonic disrupters the Library would be powerless to attack them. But the Meld had absorbed the human's knowledge and technology during the occupation of the Library. If it discovered a way to destroy or disrupt portals then the Humans and Cuanta would helpless and at their mercy.
They pondered the down side. Extended exposure to the powerful gravity wells that could protect them would exceed every starship's design parameters. Ships are not meant to fly and fight an ongoing battle against gravity at the same time. At the very least, the trade-off would be a speed reduction of seventy percent. At worst hull integrity would be lost leaving them vulnerable to the most basic dangers of superluminary flight; dangers that had destroyed the lives of many early pioneers. The decision was about to be made for them.
The Library Meld was getting more fearful by the hour. At first it felt comfort when the armada ceased their pursuit. Dissention in its ranks eased as the need to take immediate action against the Humans was deferred. But when both task force fleets began to converge on a insignificant minor star it was curious. A thousand minds split from the Meld to investigate and for the first time in a billion years they felt the surge of surprise as they encountered survivors of the fifth guardianship. They infiltrated the Administrators' minds almost immediately and were devastated by the strength of their disciplined

mental resistance. The Cuanta bodies were riddled with platelets but even the most skilled meldlings were unable to coerce significant activity from them. Before they could regroup to make a second attempt hundreds of sonic disrupters burst into life throughout the complex. The platelets remnants disintegrated within the host bodies as they watched.

Unable to affect the physical world, unable to influence the thinking what should have been puny Cuanta lifeforms the Library minds once again felt ice cold tentacles creeping through the substratum of their disembodied existence. They felt discord. In human terms they were afraid. The unbelievable had happened. An inferior species had survived without detection. Not only had this primitive species evolved sufficient mental discipline to thwart their mind control but by disintegrating their irreplaceable platelets it was defeating their only interface with the corporeal world.

Every entity in the Meld shared the fear, and the fear turned to anger, and the anger was directed uncontrollably towards the Grey-Skins who had dared to survive. It was irrational. It was unjust. But despite its inappropriate nature, it swamped the Library Meld extending beyond the Saucer to the Great Oneness. It swamped the totality of the Meld.

Less than five percent of the Meldlings retained their self-control, and that five percent was helpless against the intense panic of the majority. They withdrew realizing the energy about to be unleashed was beyond control. They could only close ranks and await the repercussions. Maybe, if they were fortunate, there would be something worth salvaging after the raging anger had burned itself out. For the first time in its existence a small disciplined component of the Meld faced an awful reality. What would happen if the Great Oneness went insane! For the first time in its existence this subset considered the unthinkable. Could the saner elements separate from the whole?

Fear and panic avalanched instantly, leastwise - instantly by the Meld's timescale. In a humanoid timescale it took several hours and another several hours passed before consensus was reached. But once reached the attack was immediate. But this time it would not be the coordinated attack of a rational combatant but the frenzied assault of a terrified animal.

The first temporal shocks struck the trailing ship in the armada convoy. The result should have been devastating. The militia was taken completely by surprise, lulled into a false sense of security by the Saucer's inactivity since they broke off the chase. Now without warning and without immediate threat the Library had decided to attack. But where the earlier attack had been precision strikes this assault had neither strength nor direction. Although FS-S3F-14 suffered only minor damage, less than would occur during combat maneuvers, it was disconcerting. Only a week earlier they had suffered more disruption when the Saucer itself was affected.

The Saucer was maintaining its trajectory inward along the spiral arm towards the Cuanta star system, towards Atnera. It was gradually closing in on the armada. Even at maximum velocity the fleet they would be overtaken several hours before they could reach the safety of the planet's gravity and a disabled star-ship anywhere en-route would be disastrous.

They knew nothing of the turmoil that was gripping the Meld. It suffered confusion and paralysis as two competing mindsets fought for control. The Meld was divided against itself in a gargantuan civil war.

Megan Vaslar's voice thundered over the.
'Fleet!'
'Make Formation Line-Abreast'
'Activate Gravity Portals - Strength 2-G - Above and Below Vector Line.'
'Execute!'
'Next Shock Wave: ETA Nine minutes.'
Within seconds the militia ships had slowed and slid into Line-Abreast formation. Portals opened and adjusted to flood the fleet with light from the local stars and the gravity that might protect them from temporal shocks.
'Activate sonics!'
They waited tensely amid the irritating buzz of the sonic disruptors... … … …
'Next Shock Wave: ETA Eight… … … ' Vaslar didn't have time to completed the message.
Simultaneously a thousand temporal shocks rippled throughout the fleet. Thousands more followed over the next twenty minutes at irregular intervals. They struck singularly, in groups, sometimes close to the ships, sometimes on board. The term "Exploded" was perhaps an exaggeration. The first barrage had almost no power, no energy, and as the assault continued the only discernable effects were light flashes at the instant of impact. There was negligible physical trauma, just mild puffs of breeze collapsing almost instantly. Either the Library was trying a new tactic, or the solar defense system was working. Comms buzzed furiously throughout the armada but from each ship the feedback was the same. Internal scans failed to detect any foreign matter penetration.

**No damage, no infiltration, no comprehension.**

After a brief respite the eruptions resumed. This time they were more regular with barrages of several hundred impacts every few seconds. Again the lingering effect was little more than a static discharge. What was the Library planning? Would there be an accumulative effect? Was it just a diversion tactic?

Back on Megan's starship Fransis Hitchin, his Chief Engineer, finished issuing the fleet with prototype short range sonic torpedoes. They would only be used as a defense of last resort. She explained their design.

'The sonic resonators activate at launch so when the probe penetrates the saucer and clamps onto a viable super-structure the vibrations radiate throughout the ship. We estimate 90 seconds is long enough to shatter the majority of platelets in the immediate vicinity. That will reduce the ships auto-repair capability after the armaments explode.'

'There're a variety of standard warheads to give your Weapons Officer's considerable tactical choice and in addition there are simple sonic-only models. These will disrupt the saucers morphing functions and hopefully allow safe access if it becomes necessary to board the saucer. And the development team's working on Dweumna's hypothesis: investigating Bio-Destructive warheads that can irradiate the saucer's bio-matter to incapacitate the platelet's catalyst.'

For two months they had been powerless against the library now, with Cuanta help, they were slowly developing both defensive and offensive weaponry.

On the bridge the duty officer Aaron Pann and his comms guru Lisaas Cashmine were dealing with a new danger. They struggled to make sense of intermittent power surges occurring inside the fleet's protecting gravity wells.

'We're still detecting sporadic peaks in gravity flux sir. But I can't get a fix on the location. Their pulse rate and

distortion curves ***DON'T*** match our portals. They must be coming from outside the shields.'
'Could it be a side effect from the solar field interactions, ensign?'
'I don't think so, sir. If it was, I'd expect more consistency. The gravity fields are stable but the fluxes are occurring randomly all around the southern sector - none to the north. That by itself suggests the phenomenon ***isn't*** natural. It could be the Library probing for weaknesses or an attempting to vector in a probe of its own.'
'Lann's our weapons expert. Get him on the bridge so we'll be ready if anything develops. And keep scanning for irregularities. If it isn't natural, another attack could start any time.' Aaron turned to the fleet comms and upgraded their alert status to Level-2. It wouldn't be his lethargy that jeopardized their mission.
On GMI-1 the conference returned to the issue of the saucer.

- How best could they attack it,
- How would they use the illegal anti-matter,
- How to plan for the unbelievably long term follow up they needed.

The militia agreed: the immense time scale of the Meld existence forced the issue. Unless they totally eliminated the platelets from physical space the future for both Humans and Cuanta would be in jeopardy. They would need to contain the saucer and reduce it to sub-atomic particles. Even porting the saucer to the depths of a black hole was a risk. If the hole became rotational it could spew the corruption back into some remote quadrant the universe. The rotational effects might only be mathematical theory but it was a risk they preferred not to take. Already one large segment of the original saucer and its bio-matter were imploding, not far away, in a lifeless region of the spiral arm.

The discussion continued, with both cultures pooling their knowledge. What secrets had the fifth generation uncovered about their adversary that could be used against it? What new innovations might spring from a mixing of technologies and release both of them from the threat of double genocide?

Dweumna was interested in the fleet's portal defense flooding the ships with solar gravity and radiation. How effectively could it port infrared radiation? During hyber-resuscitation their best nanomites were helpless as the morph overran the host bodies. In the low cryogenic temperatures they forfeit the advantage to the Library. In space the same cold principal applied. But if they could access unlimited solar heat energy there would be a different scenario.

'If ported heat energy can raise the saucer above 280° Kelvin our nanos can make a viable attack. We have many designs that can be modified to de-construct the platelets at the molecular level and disintegrate their bio-matter.'

'But you haven't been able to use them yet?'

'The units were fully operational before the Library banned our research. We were using them intensively to process most elements in the Periodic Table. They do destroy the platelets later during resuscitation, but only after the hyber-bodies gain heat. You saw the results when you examined our emissaries. The problem is activation in space where the Library ships operates at extremely low temperatures. Our nanos will be ineffective unless we can raise its temperature.'

'What's the significance of 280°K?' Ray was curious, 'Why does it have to be that high?'

'It's not necessary in the low gravity of space, but we know the saucer can generate at least 1G: standard gravity. The nanos create copious quantities of water and if it freezes, even though the change of state is exothermic, the nanos are forced to work in a dense, solid environment. That significantly reduces efficiency. They were not designed to be weapons.

## Weak Point

Ray was sitting in on the meeting but he was having difficulty focusing. Somewhere in the back of his mind thoughts were assimilating from earlier conversations and something didn't add up. He was uncomfortable. He was not one to disrupt an important conference by nit-picking petty inconsistencies but there was one glaring contradiction he just could ***not*** ignore so when Jeff and Mark broke for coffee he grabbed the opportunity to speak with them.

He approached Jeff first.

'I thought the Meld presence was needed to control the platelets.'

'That's what they told us.' He turned to Mark,

'Wasn't that one of the first tit-bits they shared?'

'Yes! Dweumna was proud of their success analyzing the static controls.'

'And,' continued Ray, 'when they resuscitate their females the dormant platelets become active. They overrun the bodies and kill off the eggs!'

'Yes they explained that Ray. The low temperature squeezes their nanos out of the game. So what're you getting at?'

'Well, if the platelets were active during resuscitation - then the Meld must have ***been*** on Atnera-1 to make that happen. And that means they ***know*** about the Cuanta base. So, how come the whole planet hasn't been annihilated?' He paused watching their expressions change as the significance slowly sank in… … … then he continued… … …

'The Library's had ample time. It's got plenty of resources when it's not spread all over the galaxy sterilizing everyone. So what's it waiting for? It doesn't

make sense for it to hold back and let us find the Cuanta, and all the secrets they've uncovered.'
'That's an interesting point, Ray. It ***is*** contradictory.'
It was Jeff's turn to take the initiative, 'We need to follow this up. Mark, talk with Dweumna without making him too suspicious and try to get some more details. If they're on the level, they may genuinely have missed this. It may be we've stumbled onto a new player in the game.'
As they returned to the table he remembered the Cuanta's schedule.
'Mark. How do you feel about a few days on terra-firma?'
Mark grinned. It would be a useful experience working with the Cuanta and it would certainly look good in his resume.
'They're resuscitating the senior techs right now. If you can get planetside you may be able to monitor the process yourself and use our equipment to coax out some additional data.'
So, a few hours later Mark and Neuama ported planetside with an array of Human technology.
The aliens were taken aback when they realized they had overlooked such a critical factor. After living alongside the platelet threat for so long they were concentrating too much at the microscopic level. They had failed to step back and view the larger picture.
But, when they did, their train of thought astounded the humans with its logic and simplicity.
**Premises:**
- Platelets were embedded in a catalytic bio-matter: (i.e. the hibernation host bodies.)
- Platelets were actively pursuing their destructive objective.
- The Meld will not permit the 5$^{th}$ Guardians to survive.

- The Meld had not attacked.

**Conclusions:**

- If the Meld has not attacked, then the platelets were not being controlled by the Meld.
- If the platelets were not being controlled by the Meld, then the platelets were acting independently.
- If the platelets were actively pursuing their prior objective and the platelets are not being controlled externally, then their prior and continuing objective must be locally encoded.
- The encoding must be in a form readily available to the platelets and/or their Bio-matter.

**Speculation:**

- Bio-matter has been shown to exhibit cellular memory.
- Persisting bio-matter memory may be capable of initiating platelet activity.
- To act independently the bio-matter/platelets needs to be achieving 'life' at a very rudimentary level.
- Bio-matter/platelets achieving 'life' may interfere with or inhibit effective Meld control.
- If living bio-matter/platelets can act independently of Meld control the OOZE in Alexandria-3 base-camp morgue may have been an example of the phenomenon.
- There may be common factors between the Morgue Stasis Chamber and the Hiber-Resuscitation environment.

Dweumna and Neuama were as eager as Jeff and Mark to put their resuscitation under the microscope, and under any other apparatus they could beg, borrow or steal.

An hour later as they exited the Admin-Center portal it was clear the aliens were also impatient to learn more.

They had a suitable Hyber-pod isolated and under surveillance. Mark supervised installation of the Human equipment while the locals arranged an interface to the Cuanta systems. After two more hours and they were ready to initiate the "Wake-Up".

'The female is unsuitable for a normal pregnancy.' Neuama explained, 'She is elderly and has genetic disorders which under normal conditions would have necessitated donor eggs and an incubator. She has the full compliment of medi-nanos and when we revive her we expect the platelets to activate first and attack her ovaries before our own nanos can respond. If the situation becomes life threatening we will use your sonic disrupters and terminate the experiment.'

They waited, apprehensively, until all the monitoring systems signaled a ready status. Then, carefully, Neuama opened the control panel and triggered "Deactivate". Three minutes later, the subject's brain activity reached detectable levels and a dozen monitors began buzzing, recording the infinitesimal energy signatures. As the process continued platelets were detected snaking their way towards the one healthy ovary. But two monitors remained unexpectedly quiet. They could detect neither beta radiation nor the energy infusion that inevitably results during Meld control of the platelets.

Dweumna directed an extraction probe into patient's abdomen.

'The platelets are active but we cannot sense any outside influence. I will biopsy the fallopian tube and isolate it in a magnetic sphere where it can be observed and monitored more accurately.'

He took a sample, expelled it into the iso-chamber and immediately relocated it to a cubical a safe distance away.

For safety, the extractor was sterilized and exposed to intense sonics.
Several sets of alien eyes stared intently into their monitors. In turn they each confirmed the platelet activity.
'The sample is viable.' It was Jegrega the group leader confirming the results. He turned to the resuscitation crew, 'There is sufficient mass in this sample for a complete diagnosis. When you are ready, revert to normal resuscitation procedures.'
Under closer scrutiny, at the molecular level, it was clear the bio-matter was in control. Several organic cells surrounded each platelet and with coordinated choreography were 'riding' their charges like a cavalry of medieval armored horse. When the bio-matter was attacked by defensive lymphocytes it retaliated using the platelets as shields and weapons. At other times it used them as tools to lacerate openings in body tissue to forge new pathways. Their progress was always upstream towards the ovary. Their static charge remained neutral.
Meanwhile, deep in space the fleet was on high alert and vectoring towards Atnera when battle alarms blasted into life. For a blistering half second an intense energy source erupted in their midst. Slightly divergent energy radiated inbound tearing a path towards battle cruiser FS-S3F-14 a few nano light-seconds away. Within the defensive portals every starship had deflectors set to maximum. None-the-less the impact tested the limits of their shields. They barely withstood the assault and were immediately the target to a barrage of temporal shocks. This time the shocks were well coordinated and close to their target but thankfully the Cuanta predictions proved true. The solar gravity wells successfully dampened the deadly energy and onboard the crew barely felt the disturbance.

# Space Zero The Meld

When Captain Ragoon radioed in the Damage Report, Megan felt relief for the first time since they began the pursuit. After weeks living on a knife edge, the tensions began to ease. He ***was*** concerned about the energy source. Had it endured longer it could have been disastrous, nevertheless, this was a weapon he understood. More importantly, he trusted the shields. They might fail under the onslaught but the fail point could be calculated and he knew exactly what their design parameters would allow.

But back in the Meld, intense disappointment and disbelief prevailed. It had sacrificed valuable resources to initiate the portal attack. Careful analysis had determined the energy needed to drain the cruiser's shields and the solar source could provide sufficient power in less than four point six seconds. Yet it had failed. The Library was unable to maintain integrity of its morphed teleport generators. Feedback had irradiated its bio-matter causing total lost of control. The portal collapsed before the target's shields were sufficiently weakened and rendered the temporal shock follow-up completely ineffective. Worse still, a significant portion of bio-matter had been destroyed by the radiation.

The facts had to be faced! Their attacks had failed and would continue to fail unless the saner elements made an agonizing decision. Most of the meldling minds were so disorientated and ineffective that they made consensus and co-ordination almost impossible. If it wanted to survive, the rational segment of the Meld must sever itself from the disruptive elements. In short, it had to amputate itself from the infected meldlings.

The dominant more assertive minds gathered together. Slowly, painfully, they began to detach, began to form an independent entity. Gradually, reluctantly, the remaining minds that were still capable of coherent thought made

their choice. Some, even though they could not accept the goal of active genocide, tried to join the New Oneness. They were forcefully held back, forced to remain within the unstable mass, abandoned possibly for all eternity within the psychotic insanity that remained.
Finally the New Oneness broke free. Finally it could view the Humans as a virulent pathogen, resistant to treatment that must be eradication for ever. This time, there was no discourse from weakly meldlings too feeble to save them selves. This time, there were no dissenting voices.
It searched for new stratagem a "Final Solution," that would rid it of the Sixth Guardian Culture for ever. Already the New Oneness was thinking with greater clarity, experiencing intense exhilaration it had not felt since the ancient beginnings. Consensus was in harmony with the whole. Soon it would be ready to attack. It looked in on itself, pleased that almost every mind from the Saucer had chosen to remain. Their common purpose had seeded its new consciousness.
'It is mutating!' Jegrega shouted the urgent warning to the investigation team. 'The bio-matter is replicating!' He picked up a hand resonator aiming it carefully at the center of the iso-chamber. His finger resting lightly on the firing icon, 'Standby with the disrupters in case the isolator fails.'
Every eye, Human and Cuanta, was once again glued to the displays. They scrutinized the alien conglomerate's activity. It had paused on its journey to the ovary. Instead it was interacting with the bio-matter from the biopsy, the living cells of the fallopian tube. Something had happened. It had a new purpose. The original target appeared forgotten. Instead all its energy was being expended on replication, reproduction.

‘Where’s it getting the energy from?’ Mark had been studying the instruments, but the values didn’t agree. ‘It seems to be using more energy than should be available?’

‘I am looking at the cellular activity.’ answered Jegrega, ‘There is significant exothermic chemical activity. But they are reactions that should not be happening. I can not determine what is initiating them.’

‘Could our monitoring equipment be having any effect?’

‘That can be checked.’ He turned to Dweumna. ‘Switch off the equipment in sequence and watch for effects. If that produces no results, rotate through the combinations in order.’ For ten minuets the mass continued absorbing the living tissue and growing. Then it paused. Then it began again.

‘We may have a solution.’ the excited cry came from Dweumna.

‘ I am deactivating monitors three and seven again.’

A minute passed, then another, then a third.

‘Re-Activating three and seven’

After only twenty seconds, to their great delight, the replication began again. Dweumna repeated his actions three more times to confirm the results: they were the consistent. With a sigh of relief he disconnected the remote sensors that were responsible for the effect and assigned his two best technicians to continue the observation.

Jegrega led the team into a side office to discus the results. A short comms call to GMI-1 and data from the Morgue Ooze on Alexandria-3 was downloaded. When the information was compared, no one was surprised to find similar energy signatures generating from both the morgue monitors and autopsy tools.

Thirty minutes into their meeting the senior tech monitoring their experiment came hastily into the room.

'I apologize for the interruption.' She seemed unsure who was in charge. Finally her eyes rested on Jegrega. 'The replication has re-started. The metabolism is seven percent of the original rate and we are using only one passive shielded monitor. The only energy is from its own thermal store. What action shall we take?'

'Do we have destruction capability if it escapes the first level containment?'

'Yes, all the standard safeguards are ready, and the Humans disrupters are focused on the entity.'

'And,' added Jeff, 'since we're in range of the Life-Ship our starguns can port it directly into the sun if it proves reluctant to leave!' The Cuanta squirmed visibly at Jeff's abuse of his native language. They preferred the literal use of words. It was more efficient and miscommunication was eliminated. Talking with humans would take time to perfect.

'Kill or Cure!' interjected Mark. 'Do we kill it now? Or do we grow it. Do we cultivate it, learn how it works and maybe turn it against its inventors. It's the only thing we know of, other than the Library, which can handle the platelets.'

Jegrega turned to the technician to instruct her, 'Attempt to divide it in two. If you are successful, attempt to destroy one part while it is still inside the isolation chamber. Once we know the organism can be terminated begin feeding the residue with matter and energy and monitor the effects. Apply all our defensive techniques and if the growth rate becomes excessive you are authorized to destroy it at your discretion. We can repeat the experiment with another hibernation subject if necessary. This is primarily a data gathering task and having a viable organism after the experiment is a secondary consideration.' The tech left but when discussion resumed it veered to an entirely new direction. ***Could*** the Library's own weapon be turned against it?

## Prisoners of Hell

The New Oneness was thinking clearly once more, it was the epitome of original thought. If it could no longer manipulate immense quantities of energy and matter in the corporal universe it could go to the opposite extreme. With eons of expertise using nano technology pillaged from the fifth guardians it could easily overwhelm the Humans. It knew of quirks and idiosyncrasies they had yet to uncover, it understood the flaws inherent in the systems and how to exploit them. It lacked only the opportunity to initiate a new mode of attack and that opportunity would present itself when the militia reached Atnera-1. Meanwhile it maintained the current, ineffective, temporal attacks to lull the Humans into a false sense of security. Then without warning it would unleashing a new and terrible weapon on an unsuspecting foe.

Fransis Hitchin, Megan's Chief Engineer, was organizing support teams to port down to Atnera and assist construction of the growing Cuanta home base. The militia work parties would release the alien specialists to concentrate on the nano-manufacturing plants desperately needed to develop "Saucer Eating" nano-bots. Some thirty-five percent of the militia personnel were allocated to the task, in all twenty ten-man teams. Five teams were assigned to mine for raw materials and the remainder to fabricate living quarters and develop the infrastructure. With dawn braking over the Cuanta Hiber-base twenty portals opened planetside ready for the assembled teams and equipment to disembark. As soon as base camps were established and supplies checked they called in to establish fixed comms links. One by one the first eighteen reported in. Fransis waited for the last two, and waited, and waited … … … and waited. After fifteen minutes she initiated the calls herself but got no response. Opening viewing portals to the delivery points she made 360 degree sweeps around the locations. But all she could see were a few inches of disturbed soil where the teams had exited the portals. Beyond that: nothing. No comms chatter, no bio-readings, no energy signatures. She hit the alarms. One team might suffer a catastrophe; it might even disappear without a trace, but TWO teams? That was way outside statistical probability.

In minutes the room was swarming with the best techs on the ship. A blanket ban on portal use was imposed as a dozen experts poured over the portal logs. All were clean, no malfunction, every system was operating well within its design parameters. Internal onboard scanners showed the two teams clearly marching through the portals onto the planet. Both teams appeared stable when the portals closed behind them.

'I want a thorough examination of both recordings, manual and computer enhanced. And I want it ten minutes ago! Jump to it, we have twenty lives at stake.' When Fransis barked the order even the senior officers flinched. They knew the seriousness of the issue and knew when not to make flippant remarks.

'I want full surface scans of the planet and I want every life form larger than a mouse identified and located.' Then remembering "The Ordeal", 'Get me subsurface scans down to five hundred feet for a mile around the delivery zones, and scan for any abnormal energy readings particularly temporal irregularities. If we don't have a serious malfunction the Library may be involved. And remember, we're in a race against the clock. If they're still alive we don't know how long the missing teams can survive.'

She leaned back in the chair exhausted. But despite the adrenalin flooding her body she was thinking clearly. Her mind rapidly scanned a hundred theoretical possibilities, but with the same affect striking two portals working independently from different classes of starships, almost all potential portals malfunctions could be eliminated. An old saying goes: "When you eliminate the impossible, whatever you have left must be true however strange it may seem."

If the portals could be eliminated, and the teams were delivered planetside, as indicated by the scans, then either they were still on the planet or they had been scooped up, hijacked, before they realized what was happening.

Did the Cuanta have that capability she pondered, or was the Library trying to "Divide and Conquer" At the moment she preferred to believe the latter, but made a conscious note not to close her eyes to the less favorable possibility.

She put a comms call through to Sheila Fayamore, the resident First Contact specialist. Sheila would have the best insight into the Cuanta and Library thinking. A shuttle was dispatched to bring her from LS48 to the Command Ship. They would need to work closely for the next few days and comms links were neither safe nor reliable. She knew Darkon would be furious, but a couple of night sleeping alone would do him no harm. After reading the initial reports on Cuanta interaction Fransis needed further insight into their mind set. Would they help or hinder the search?

By the time Sheila arrived Eheledana had contacted the ship from the Hiber-Center. A satellite engineer by profession she was monitoring the high-orbit defense system when the teams ported down. For the few minutes of transport the lower planetary shields were interrupted to allow entry. That was when the echoes appeared. At the time she paid them little attention to them, occurring as they did with the same pulse rate and distortion curves as the Human's portals. She flagged the entries in the log as 'non-standard' for no better reasons than to break the monotony and prove she was doing her job. It was only later when Captain Vaslar contacted the center ordering a portal lockdown that she looked more closely into the records. Both had occurred within seconds of the original portals opening, and collapsed within seconds of their shutdown. As far as she could determine the only difference was slight beta radiation emissions just noticeable at the limit of sensor range that lasted for the duration the Echo. All other parameters appeared identical. She expected her information to be dismissed as unimportant, but this was her first chance to speak with the Humans and it was an exiting opportunity she was not going to miss.

The hint of Beta radiation was a bombshell to Fransis. It pointed suspicion and away from the Cuanta and directly at the Library Saucer. The satellite logs confirmed no other unexplained portal activity had occurred planetside so when the satellite and starship scans failed to locate either the missing two teams or degrading signs of temporal disturbance there was only one conclusion. Their enemy had intercepted their transport and either killed or abducted the teams, there was no way of telling which. If the teams were alive the only location which offered any chance of rescue was the saucer itself, but at present any attempt would be suicide. They could only wait and watch as the situation developed. Both cultures focused on the Saucer monitoring it with all available resources.

In the depths of an obscure, shapeless, colorless room devoid of the slightest frame of reference nineteen astro-soldiers huddled together to conserve body heat. There had been twenty in the original two teams. They vaguely remembered stepping through their starship portal and walking onto the planets surface. Sergeant Sharif recalled his immediate reaction: It hadn't looked quite real. It was more like a Tri-Di theater where parallax and perspective were not quite accurate around the edges of the scene and monocular clues were subtly "Out of Sync". But before he could react he was clamped by invisible energy fields and forcefully pulled skyward. He was sucked into a whirlwind tunnel and dragged breathlessly through a seemingly endless series of portals. He lost count of the impacts his body endured bouncing across the badly aligned openings. Bruised, numb, aching: he was deposited hapless into this featureless void. Eighteen more battered and bleeding survivors were unceremoniously extruded from the 'walls' and 'floor' to join him. When their last team mate arrived, the sergeant recognized him as Private Joe Yoman the youngest, newest rookie from his ship - he was dumped alive and screaming in two separate pieces. One leg with and a quarter of his abdomen still attached had been sliced off with surgical precision. But before they could reach him the floor oozed up and engulfed the bloody mess, muffling his cries for help. Within the floor his silhouettes remained visible, heightening their terror, impenetrable mounds undulating like two metamorphic chrysalis. Everyone realized the significance of what was happening. Only the Library could morph like that, and they were its prisoners!

They could hear the victim's screams - they could hear him begging for death. Sharif looked at the soldiers around him, they all nodded in agreement. He raised his laser piston aiming at the head area of the larger mound and fired. The beam was absorbed but the screams continued. Together those still strong enough to do so drew their weapons and fired in unison. But the screaming refused to stop.

It was difficult to breath. The atmosphere inside the 'room' was low in oxygen content, the air was thin, the temperature cold, and a high pitched frequency played havoc on their auditory nerves. They assessed their injuries. Several broken bones - they jury-rugged the necessary splints, a few dislocations - painfully but successfully relocated, but the most of the two crews though battered and bruised were still viable for combat if, that is, they could find an enemy to fight. Only two of the troops were in an uncertain state, both had head wounds and suspect concussions. One was delirious; the other had not regained consciousness since arrival. Rations were assessed but the greatest danger was the lack of water. True to their training they had all ingested copious quantities before dispersal and should be viable for up to thirty-six hours. But after that dehydration would set in, unless hyperthermia struck first.

Relief came several hours later when the screaming finally ended. By then the void had been completely examined. No visible apertures, just a seamless corner-less sphere slightly flattened at the base where they were gathered.

The New Oneness within the Saucer was satisfied with its success. Overlaying Portal Transporters of it's own in a stacked series several hundred deep it had stolen almost four thousand pounds of healthy Human bio-matter. Even now it was digesting the first five percent of the mass that lay decomposing within the twin mounds. Soon it would start on the remainder of its prey, but first it wanted to tap their minds to extract whatever knowledge they had of the Human's plans.

It began with the unconscious creature. Carefully, out of sight of the main group, it morphed thought sensors from the floor. They oozed around the man's head - not engulfing it - but fanning out like fine lace tentacles. The Oneness began to probe the man's thoughts. But the specimen was vastly different in nature to the professors and students it had studied at the Library Complex on Alexandria. Those minds had been clear and organized; the patterning throughout their brains had been for the most part consistent. Here something was dramatically awry. This mind was jumbled and disorganized with contradictions at almost every level. What should be simple thoughts about his next meal were contradictory and complex. He intended to eat foods that were not available to him. He knew they were unavailable but still intended to eat them for his next meal. That was absurd, that was - is, impossible.

The Oneness changed its approach. It sought out ideas regarding the Human's mission on Atnera-1. At first they came through clearly. This unit would be constructing habitation quarters. The Oneness probed for the reasons. But found none. This Human did not appear to know why it was building. When the Oneness probed deeper it was swamped by cascading thoughts with very little in common. What was the connection between a theoretical view from a habitation window and the view from a shuttle ferry's porthole of a moon silhouetted against its sun? This brain was inefficient and confusing. The Oneness stimulated other areas in the human's neo-cortex attempting to trigger more meaningful thought patterns, but all it could find were more of the same random

connections. It questioned itself: had the Human been damaged during capture? If so it should be absorbed and processed for its bio-matter immediately. Then it paused. Though the probability was low, this unit might be the most viable it had captured. It would retain the life form until a more suitable sample was identified. Adjusting the atmospheric balance within the void it forced the Humans to lose consciousness. Then the mass probing began, with the same dismal results. None of the creatures had optimized minds. It did not make sense. They were all the same sentient Human species yet even within the group their minds appeared to be structured in vastly differing ways. Watching them interact might reveal more than probing so again the life support system was adjusted; this time to match the Humans own preferences. Within an hour they had all recovered including the two concussed units. One was still delirious but the other: Rhomasta began to make sense although he was speaking oddly. His words sounded more like poetry.
Sergeant Sharif was the first to realize what he was up to. Military training dictates that prisoners assume their captors are monitoring their every word and action. This was his attempt to hide his real meaning from the enemy. He encouraged Rhomasta to continue. Using street slang the junior NCO's story unfolded. As one of the shuttle pilots he'd been issued with the new stargun and since it had never been recalled it was nestling safely in his backpack amongst the food rations. Slowly he explained the settings. Setting-5 for Water might go unnoticed at first, then, they could switch to Setting-6 and attempt an escape. It would be touch and go as to how many could jump through the doorway before the Saucer retaliated and an explosive decompression would thwart their plans completely. But if even one of them escaped the militia

would know where they were and that meant hope, no matter how slight, for a rescue.
Carefully Sharif instructed his troops. He too spoke with a forced dialect mimicking the Starship Captain of a popular Tri-Di series. The captives realized he was up to something and played along. He had them layout their food rations in a line and hold out their mugs for a water handout. Rhomasta walked along the line with the hidden stargun spouting water in a steady stream. The fact that it worked meant they were close enough to the Lifeship stable portals, and the Saucer wasn't jamming their signals… … … not yet. He reached the head of the line and filled the Sergeants mug. 'Ready?' he asked quietly.'
'Whenever you are soldier'
Rhomasta nodded.
'Squad! Standby! - 5 - 4 - 3 - 2 - 1 - GO!'
Rhomasta swung the backpack towards the sergeant and flipped to Setting-6. The portal opened immediately to his right, 'GO! - GO! - GO!' yelled Sharif gesturing his men towards the opening. Their training paid off. Instantly the three nearest men turned and leapt through the exit. The remainder rushed the opening dragging the injured with them. Fifteen made it before the Saucer retaliated. The sixteenth was only inches away when Twenty-Gs of artificial gravity yanked the poor man away from the portal hurling him towards the far side of their prison. The stargun almost ripped from Rhomasta's grip. He struggled to hang on, managing to reactivate a portal between them and the gravity source just in time to save two more lives. The stargun was torn from his broken hand and followed them into the portal triggering its collapse. Seconds later he and the sergeant crashed fatally wounded into the cell wall. They barely had time to grasp hands in a victory salute before the wall morphed to engulfing them. They

felt millions of microscopic tentacles burrowing deep into their bodies. The pain was intense and they realized the hours of agony that the Library had planned for them. It didn't need them alive as it drained their bodies - it was only be doing so for its own sadistic pleasure, it wanted to enjoying their suffering.

The sergeant forced a smile. The Saucer was too late. He had already taken action as the walls began to engulf him. His left hand like the rest of his body was now completely immobilized but its task was complete. He felt the pressure of cold plastic on his index finger as it pressed against the base plate of his laser pistol, as it pressed against the fingerprint sensitive auto-destruct icon. He could picture the circuitry checking, rechecking, confirming his identity, then with relief, he felt the icon become warm, then hot, then burning. He felt the blood in his finger begin to boil. Peacefully he said goodbye to his family, to his friends, to his shipmates. Three seconds later the pistol reached overload. It exploding, vaporizing their screaming remains. They died with honor - they died true to the military creed - their last thoughts were of the comrades they had saved.

The three GMI ships were close docked when the first warning alarm penetrated the ship. Tom was delighted. He recognized it instantly as activation of the Stargun Supply System and raced to the control room in the Hospital Ship: SH03. It was a disappointment. The monitor showed the water tank as the only sector active. He was about to leave when the emergency sirens roared into life. For a moment, caught off guard, he stared in disbelief at the implausible display. Two, three, four, five, the reception count was climbing at a questionable rate. By the time it paused in the mid teens he was outside the isolation chamber looking incredulously into the viewer.

It was a war zone. The room was crowded with troops in bloody tattered uniforms, several with what looked like emergency first-aid dressings over serious wounds. As he watched two more bodies slammed through the portal at neck-break speed colliding with the walking wounded.

He hit the manual alert then disregarding his own safety he punched the door release to the isolation air lock and stepped inside. The outer seal closed immediately but it seemed an eternity waiting for the portal to collapse before the inner door was allowed to open. Once inside he raced over to the two crumpled bodies that had literally dropped in. Though seriously injured they were still alive. He called for full medical backup and began triage. While two senior NCOs commandeered the comms station to reporting back to Fransis and Vaslar, the remainder did what they could to assist the wounded and attempted in a dozen different voices to explain their miraculous escape. The medical personnel arrived within minutes but proceeded with great caution. Methodically they checked internal scanners for contaminants and radiation, activated sonic disrupters for a full five minutes, selected and re-assigned a replacement Isolation Ward, interrogated Tom and three of the survivors to ensure they were lucid with a minimum of self control, and only then authorized the 'All Clear' for entry.

Finally the ward normalized and the airlock activated allowing the hospital team access. Five minutes later all four operating rooms were manned, surgical teams were in place and the most serious patients were being prepped. By the time the security teams arrived for debriefing ten minutes later the emergency center was running at full load.

# Space Zero The Meld

## Nano Invasion

With portals offline Megan moved his starship adjacent to the GMI trio. The ships loose-docked so he could disengage instantly if the need arose. Loose-docking comprised of a two hundred meter umbilical corridor magnetically locked to both ship hulls. The ships airlocks were only opened long enough for personnel to enter or leave the ships. In an emergency the self-sealing umbilical could be jettisoned and would provide limited life support for anyone trapped inside. There was a manually operated air lock at the midpoint point with both doors magnetically held open. It housed a backup oxygen supply, four full capability EVA suits, and docking thrusters. All militia personnel were trained in its use. Sheila on the other hand was not. Although familiar with zero-gravity she had never trespassed outside before. As Fransis led her out of the ship she was awestruck by the monochromic vista. They were not quite "In Space" but it was close enough to feel the overpowering agoraphobia that grips every planet-lubber facing the ice cold universe for the first time.

The hospital ship shaded them from Atnera's sun and in every direction the sky was filled with a billion stars. Each shone clearly, bright and stark against the inky blackness of space. Not for them the twinkling a planet's atmosphere provides; instead these points of light were rigidly fixed, constant and unmoving in space, the cold reality of light thousands of years old. And the sheer numbers! None were lost to contamination of a night sky. She found a constellation she could recognize. But out there between familiar patterns were hundreds of stars she never knew existed. It was like removing infra-red goggles and suddenly seeing the galaxy in the full light

spectrum. With her naked eye alone she could detect the subtle differences in their color. What would her home planet look like from a viewpoint such as this? She wondered how much beauty was missing from the tourist holograms so widely dispersed back home. A tug on her arm, then another, she snapped back to reality. Fransis did not want to remain too long in the corridor, just in case! As they floated across the meandering link Sheila soaked in the spectacular view and wondered, was this was the reason Darkon was so at home in space.
Her joy was short lived. Once onboard the Hospital Ship business became serious; they listened in on the hostage debriefings. Not knowing their enemy was now a different creature from the one they glimpsed at Alexandria, the sudden change of tactics to a truly malevolent and malicious entity was difficult to understand. But to Megan's military mind the change was easily accepted: for whatever reason someone new was at the helm. Whatever internal politics had taken place, a new commander was calling the tune and once again the enemy had the upper hand. Megan wanted to launch a counter attack, take the initiative and put the Library on the defensive. But what tactics could he use. Conventional energy weapons would only be absorbed by the Saucer and used against them. They couldn't 'Blow it up.' It had survived a nuclear onslaught and reformed in the middle of the cesspool of radiation. Their only mode of attack appeared to be at the cellular level and in that area he was way out of his depth. He needed input from the specialists and that input was nearer than he had dared to hope.
Mark shuttled up from the planet and found him in his quarters. The news from Atnera was encouraging. Following discoveries from the biopsy, Jegrega's team was busy growing a self sustaining organism that could

contaminate the Saucer's bio-matter destroying its ability to morph. A second research team had redesigned their platelet 'eating' nano-probes and already begun mass production. A third was almost ready with a new strain that would deconstruct the platelet debris at the atomic level preventing the Library from ever using them again. All they needed was a means of dispersal and a heat source to increase the saucer's temperature and that was what he was here to discuss.
On the Saucer the New Oneness waited patiently for the next stage of its attack. True, it was disappointed after losing ninety-five percent of the bio-matter it abducted. But the quantity already processed was more than sufficient for the task at hand and it was considerably better quality than the material it acquired from Human waste on Alexandria-3. Vegetarian cultures do not produce the best dung. It was especially pleased with the quality of the brain. Its original owner may not have used it very efficiently but the organic material was in excellent condition and would prove an ideal platelet catalyst. It waited. It was patient. A few days later the Humans began testing remodeled portal/teleporters. It waited. It was in no hurry. While the Humans and Cuanta were monitoring the tests with every available technology the Library would not interfere. An espionage cell does not draw attention to itself during a security purge.
For five days only inanimate objects were transported. Then the trials switched to bio-samples, insects, small rodents, large mammals, and finally a Human. At each stage, energy levels were analyzed from both sides of the portal. They were compared for consistency. Expected variations were programmed into the portals control system and when they were exceeded it would suck-back and auto-collapse protecting portal integrity. Inside the

starships finely tuned sensors monitored for the slightest hint of Beta radiation. Sonic disrupters saturated the portals to destroy any morphed platelets that might gain ingress. Any mass greater than a speck of dust floating on the breeze was identified and analyzed. The humans expected further attempts to kidnap their personnel or forcefully gain access to their ships but they were not prepared for the insidious infiltration the New Oneness had planned. They were not prepared for a complete paradigm shift of stratagem.

The Saucer knew all the human history and literature. It noted how the wooden "Trojan Horse" had tricked the fortified City of Troy. Its current enemy would never fall for such a ploy. But it extrapolated, how about the sawdust left over after carving the horse. True, it could morph sawdust using the platelets, but they would easily be spotted and destroyed. Now with the energy available from new bio-matter and a local sun it could use the hi-tech skills developed by the fifth species to create its own nano-devastation. For three days a thousand minds working together evolved a unique design. Once complete and tested the New Oneness began replicating its targeting nanos at lightning speed.

Eventually, twenty billion were stockpiled awaiting release. Then during a three hour orbit over the Hyber-Center they were teleported a mile above the upper Cuanta Defense screens. Gravity would draw them down to the planet passing unnoticed through the defenses. They were too small to reach high velocity and burn up on entry. Instead, with simple hard wired programming they slipstreamed, billions of invisible gliders, homing in to a predetermined location just outside the Cuanta Complex's main entrance. After ten days half a ton of the contamination had mingled with surface soil burying

itself within the particles of mud and debris. It was for all practical purposes invisible. Content with its plot the saucer powered down and allowed itself to drift aimlessly along the magno-gravimetric tides between the stars. To observers it appeared to be out of control drifting slowly away from the Atnera System.
Although suspicious the Humans were relieved when the Library attacks ceased. Still they were alert, monitoring all portal transports and had successfully ensured no further loss of personnel. The Cuanta residential district was rapidly filling with newly awakened natives, some already working in the Nano factories, others rebuilding the social Infrastructure. Defense nanos at the Center's periphery had engaged and defeated a variety of suspect entities attempting to infiltrate the Admin Center, but after several sporadic encounters the attention faded. With no evidence linking them to the Library the Administrators wrote off the encounters as local sub-surface organisms that were disturbed by construction at the surface.
The library would have been pleased with their verdict. It expected the center to be heavily defended by nanos, so had sent in only a dozen independent units staggered over three days to probe the defenses. That none returned confirmed its suspicions. So to remain concealed, it withdrew the body of its nano force ninety meters beyond the last known contact point. It was determined to infiltrate into the Human armada before revealing itself. After three weeks it was satisfied with its progress. For a brief microsecond while the Cuanta Hyber-Base was in nightfall, the Saucer radiated an intense directional beam at the half acre in front of the center. It was detected immediately sending the center to high alert. But when during the next ten hours nothing happened and no

damage had resulted it was again written off as a 'Near Miss'. Whatever the Library was trying to do as it floated on the tides of space a few billion miles away, they were sure it had been unsuccessful.
But ten hours is the blink of the eye to the Library. This attack was working on a two-solar-day trigger. For the next two daylight periods the nanomites buried in the soil soaked up the solar energy storing it for the next phase. On the third sunlight period they were ready for portal transport. As soon as people, Humans or Cuanta, began to cross the contaminated area towards the Human portal stations then, like tropical leeches, they attached themselves to footware and lower clothing as the lifeforms passed. The micro-nanos were hitching a ride into the Starships. Burrowing through clothing they clung to the skin of their host careful not to irritate the delicate flesh and warn their adversary. They were not designed to attack lifeforms, their task was more deadly. For several hours they rode their hosts as they moved about the starships all the time sensing the radiation levels. After several cycles they had determined the area of greatest intensity and disembarked their hosts the next time that area was passed.
They found themselves surrounded by many still dormant nanomites that had been casually brought onboard earlier that week on the mud and soil of normal footware. These units, not yet primed for destruction, were activated. Here on the floor and walls of the Starship Corridors looking no worse than a faint stain they slid just below the surface heading towards the radioactive source. When they reached a point where the intensity exceeded their trigger level they begin their task. Closing in on their target they soaked up radiation becoming more energetic. They were not sentient and could not know, but they were hunting

down the ships prime energy source, the Power Core. Once close enough they would fan out on their 'Search and Destroy Mission,' looking for any computer assembly, chemical or biological, that crossed their path. The Library knew nano-technology was in its infancy for this species so to keep the nanos small and undetectable it hadn't wasted resources programming them for resistance or self defense. It doubted that even with the Cuanta assistance the Humans were capable of reacting in time and building effective countermeasures. The Saucer was confident, by the time Humans from the inhabited sectors of the Milky Way reached their decimated militia fleet this last outpost of the Cuanta would have joined the rest of their species in extinction. By then the Human Starships would be loaded with enough self-replicating nanos to incapacitate any rescue force.

Given time, and it had plenty of time on it side, the Library would reduce the Human species to planet-bound primitives. From there, it would destroy their civilization star system by start system. Nano-technology was more difficult to initiate than controlling platelets but once started it needed very little maintenance and in the end the results would be the same.

As it pondered which branch of the evolutionary tree would spawn the Seventh Guardians it contemplated Atnera. The planet would make a good location for the next Library. It was a little further out from the Central Hub than previous sites, but it had a plentiful supply of bio-matter and would soon have a useful nanomite production industry. Its own failure to genocide the fifth guardians completely may yet be a cloud with a silver lining. For the moment it was content to listen in on the Human Comms and await the cries of distress it knew would soon be coming.

Group by group the nano trigger-points were reached. Group by group units disbursed slithering aimlessly until they stumbled across a current carrying circuit. Then they followed the electron flow back to a vulnerable component. Some nanos were burned out on unexpectedly high voltages carbonizing to create potential short circuits. The majority survived and began 'organizing' the components. Their task had a simple program. Dismantle the molecules and stack similar atoms together. The 'Modus Operandi' sounds like a recipe for organization and order. But instead it results in carefully constructed micro units of immense complexity rapidly being reduced to useless clumps of raw material. The nanos then move on heading deeper into the high intensity radiation until another target is found. If more than one nano zeroed in on the same component they worked alongside but oblivious of each other. Their simple programming was efficient and deadly.

The Groups moved slowly but within hours of boarding system failures began to occur. At first it appeared just a bad day for the maintenance engineers. But when all the ships started signaling problems and the rate of failure accelerated they knew the situation was serious. Battle plan Beta was initiated radiating sonics for a full hour with no effect. The lack of Beta Radiation left the militia blindly looking for the wrong saboteurs. Failed component after failed component was replaced only to be destroyed again within hours. The only discernable pattern was a gradual shifting of the failures towards the Power Core. It was the Cuanta who first realized how their ally's ships had been compromised. They recognized the library's approach the gradual decomposition of critical components which would inevitable be followed by decomposition of the ship's structure. But clearly the

Library was not using its traditional bio-mater/platelet techniques.
They suspected nano-technology as the only medium that could pass unnoticed through the portals. But before designing countermeasures they had to obtain samples and examine them in detail. There was no obvious method of entry for the invaders and Eheledana was able to confirm no mysterious echoes had occurred since the abductions. At this stage all they could offer were investigative nano-bots to examine the infected ships and upload their findings for analysis. Working in Human starships would be a simpler task than defending their own equipment as the Humans had no native nano-bots to segregate. Any nano-activity would be of enemy origin. All but two starships: GM-1 and Megan's FS-S3M-122 powered down their nuclear facilities reducing the radiation in an attempt to slowdown the onslaught. It had a small effect but would gain them only a few hours respite. Once Life Support was compromised they would have no choice but to port down to Atneral-1 where they would be at the mercy of the Saucer. If it still had ability to intercept transports they could lose everyone who tried to escape. Uagair made it clear that while they were contaminated the Starships would not be allowed to make landfall, nor would their shuttles. It was a reasonable ban but made a difficult situation worse.
Meanwhile in the Hyber-Center activity was intense. With the Library switching tactics the Cuanta hastened to strengthen their own defenses. Nano-probes were quickly designed and distributed in a pincer movement to surround and protect the newly developed housing and manufacturing zone. The sphere of containment then split into three factions. The first maintained the perimeter defense while a second like a tightening trawler net closed

in to the central focus scanning for infiltration. The third: the Attack-Nanos, followed behind for support if and when resistance was encountered. However, when they did locate an area of infestation there was no initial response. They were ignored. They didn't know it yet but the alien's simple programming had no response to discovery. It had not been expected. The leading attack-nanos closed in on the first enemy unit. It remained motionless. Cautiously mindful of their own defensive programming they began to dismantling the invader feeding data microsecond by microsecond back to their nanomite brothers. Still the intruder offered no resistance. When the disassembly was complete and the data uploaded they moved to an adjacent unit. This unit also remained motionless allowing itself to be dismantled. They dismantled ten more without the slightest sign of resistance. When they targeted the thirteenth unit Zholtair suspended their activity. He reprogrammed several attack nanos for capture mode. When the next target unit was surrounded he opened a micro portal to transfer the nano-probe to the iso-chamber. To their surprise the unit immediately sprung to 'life' as did a hundred more units in the immediate vicinity. They migrated to the soil surface and began scanning the local area, but made no further movement. More units in the surrounding soil became alert and started scanning their immediate location but these made no attempt to surface. Slowly Zholtair manipulated the portal opening towards the target and while this agitated the unit it made no attempt to avoid capture. Once it was safely inside the iso-chamber he collapsed the portals and suddenly activity within the soils stopped as quickly as it began. It was puzzling. They scooped in another dozen units - each time with the same strange effect. Whenever a micro-portal opened the

Library nanos came to life. When it closed - they went dormant again.
It took several hours before Jegrega's team had schematics of the Library invaders and their programming. A few more hours and the nanos' tactics were understood. But these were not tactics designed to decimate their ground base. Indeed without defensive capability these nano enemies could never mount a successful attack against the Cuanta. Their target was obvious. He contacted Captain Vaslar and advised him to resume using Morse code but without the automatic translators. Once again Joanah Quahn became a most valuable commodity. The signals bleeped out from the comms station at an interminably slow pace as Megan waited impatiently for his junior comms officer to interpret the message. He did so carefully.
'They think they've found the problem, sir. They've located nanomites all over the base that react to our portals. They don't know exactly how but they become active whenever the portals are open. They're apparently programmed to seek out our A. I. components and dismantle them. They're almost certain they're the ones that are attacking our ships.' He went on to expand the Cuanta findings.
'Ask them what we need to do ensign. We'll be lucky to last another ten hours.'
'They're working on a solution, sir. But they don't expect to have enough counter measures for thirty-six hours.'
'We'll be overrun. It'll be all over long before then. Tell them we need a solution within the next six hours or they might as well forget it.'
'Yes Sir, I'm telling them.' He tapped out the urgent message and waited for a reply. Several minutes passed. 'They're responding sir.' He listened intently.

They have a suggestion Sir. But they say it's very risky.'
'What have they got? We've not in any position to bargain.'
'We've got to go on full energy shutdown, sir. They say the nanos are programmed to home in on electrical current and we have to terminate absolutely every circuit including our portable tools to stop them. They say we can port any of our personnel planetside if we want to risk it but they must remain outside the Hyber-Center. Oh! they're offering to extend their defense shields to protect our ships if we drop to geo-stationary orbit.'
Megan did a few mental calculations. They had sufficient insulation suits and rations. He knew the emergency procedures and if they could minimize activity and reduce air consumption they could survive at least twenty four hours. Survival beyond that depended on the stamina of the troops to keep the mechanically air scrubbers working. Heat, or rather the lack of it, would be the biggest problem. Without power they would have no control over the ships orientation. They would be baking on the sunward side of the ship and freezing on the opposite. As a last resort they could reactivate life support and use portable portals to escape planetside. It might just gain them the time needed for the Cuanta to make their counter measures available.
Megan ordered the fleet join him in low orbit. When they arrived he sent messengers shuttles to every ship to orally deliver his instructions. Their ally had been careful to avoid tipping off the library and he appreciated the precaution. The Library would have a field day if it knew what was about to transpire. He made it clear - No-one was to port unless their survival was in immediate jeopardy. If the Library detected the ships were being abandoned it might launch an immediate attack.

On the GMI ships the reaction was the same, with one special difference. The Hospital Ship still had one working isolation ward. It was designed to be jettisoned for recovery by a HAZMAT ship with full containment facilities. After jettison it had an internal power supply complete with its own life support system and an extra day's oxygen supply. It could be detached with a two-man team assigned to wait out the disaster.

In the current predicament, when they were halfway through the last day's air - which would mean the Cuanta had failed to solve the crisis and the rest of the armada was doomed - they would jettison from HS03, activate the emergency comms to the MFI Home Base and relay all available information. They would be the last ones to abandon ship and port planetside - if their portals were still functioning and the Library didn't intercept.

Geney and Ray volunteered with Darkon to man LS48, as skeleton crew. William and Trudel were transferred to the safety of HS03. Sheila, after a heated argument made it clear if she was going to die in the frozen hell of space it wasn't going to be among with strangers in the Hospital. She insisted since the Lifeships emergency air was being shared with the other GMI ships it wouldn't mater where she chose to die. Darkon couldn't argue with her logic, and he didn't want to. Rations for two days were handed out surplus air shunted between the docked ships then the trio separated to safe distances with the Isolation Ward primed and ready for manual jettison. The remaining lifeship crew enjoyed a last coffee in the galley before retiring to the limited comfort of the cabins and powering down.

With even the standby systems offline the silence was intense. Creaks and groans radiated along the ship's superstructure as thermal differenced balanced themselves in a never ending musical serenade. Sounds usually hidden by the ship's background noise now echoed like a ghost endlessly dragging chains around its castle towers. Every few minutes a sickening crack announced another capacitor short circuiting, reminding them that the Library Nanos, however slowly, were still going about their deadly task.

## Invasion Repelled

Planetside the best Cuanta technicians were busy designing an armada of new nano-devices. Some needed to be small to track down the saucer's units in the tiniest of crevasses. Others required more complexity with full remote sensing and capable of locating the 'disease' in the most heavily shielded areas of the ships. They also needed comms functionality to "call in the troops". The troops in this case were full attack nanos with enough A.I. to recognize their own teammates and not attack them. And all the units by long established protocol had to have finite life spans with the ability to self destruct on command. Despite the Humans' urgency the Cuanta would not cut corners to save time. Centuries of experience had taught them the cost of long term rectification always outweighed short term benefit. They had seen too many promising planets abandoned because amateur nano-makers disregarding safety protocols allowed self replicating disasters to swarm out of control. Now with Atnera their only planet they would not take that risk. As Jegrega and Zholtair oversaw the project, Neuama and Jeff poured over a dozen starship schematics painstakingly locating optimum areas for release of the new nanos. Megan had grudgingly released the highly sensitive data, much of it still classified and on the secrets list. By his reckoning, if the Cuanta proved unsuccessful, he would fall prey to the Saucer long before any Courts Martial could be convened and should they succeed he'd get the credit for saving the whole damn fleet. He reminded himself with pride it was for decisions like this that he was the senior officer of this taskforce, and of the three Battle Station Commanders in this militia, he had decades more experience than the two contenders.

The hours rolled on.
Redesign - Build –Test,    Redesign - Build - Test,
Redesign - Build –Test.
Jeff monitored the time. He couldn't contact his ships and would dearly like to know how they were faring. It was the first time in his life he had been out of contact with everything familiar. Uncertainty was new to him and he didn't like it. No longer in control, he was totally dependant on the aliens he had known for only a few weeks. It was a situation they never taught at Officer Training. Like those in orbit he could only sit and wait. He comforted himself with the thought that at least ***he*** was waiting in relative safety.
Darkon turned to Sheila. Despite their thermal protection they were cold. The cold radiated from every surface of the ship. In the darkness they could taste the moisture in the air. It was still liquid but before long it would crystallize. He began pumping the mechanical $CO_2$ scrubber. Better to do it now while he still had energy. In the darkness he remembered their first night together, remembered watching her sleep silhouetted against the moonlight. He pictured her again, recalling how even then the Library was changing their lives. How would their life have been if the Library had been just a library? It was ironic. Without its threat they would never have met. He would never have known the pleasure of missing someone so much. He felt her shiver, and wished there had been time to teach her the ancient Tibetan skills. He focused his mind, raising his core temperature a couple of degrees. It would help a little without depleting his resources too much. After all, in forty hours it would all be over one way or another. His hand was resting lightly on her face and he could feel her eyelids began to twitch. She had

been sleeping for several hours and was entering another period of REM sleep.
For a few minutes she was back home near her first learning center sitting quietly on a park bench. She realized Bianca, her best friend from school days, was with her but they were both much older now both adults. It must be summer she thought realizing she wore a bright lemon silken blouse with matching pantaloons. Her garments soaked up the sun's energy sending pulsing rainbow colors in zigzag patterns dancing across the diagonals at irregular intervals. Gazing down at the light show she realized she was FAT! Startled, even horrified, she dropped both hands to her swollen abdomen feeling the mounds of unfamiliar flesh. She was puzzled. When had her figure disappeared? When had she put on so much weight? When had… … … "Ouch" she felt it KICK! Then again! Startled, she looked at Bianca. She was FAT too! Bianca was smiling and rubbing her own tummy.
"It always catches me off guard." She smiled, "It's my first!"
Parents and Nannies with their charges were milling around a fountain amidst the squeals of joyful children. One small girl caught Sheila's eye. "Mommy" cried the beautiful red-headed rushing towards her with outstretched arms, "Mommy". Sheila's eyes opened wide; she awoke with a sudden intake of air.
'Are you alright my love?' Darkon asked.
'I was having such a strange dream.' she answered still half asleep. 'I was back in my hometown. Everything was so peaceful. Everyone was so happy. Now I'm back here and it's freezing!' Snuggling closer she began to shiver again. 'Do we have any thing hot to drink?'
He reached into the ration case and felt around for two pre-packs crushing their igniters to initiate cooking.

They'd have hot drinks in about three minutes. Carefully he lowered the drinks under the thermal covers to contain any escaping heat and after a short wait he felt the thermocouples pop to signal the drinks were ready. 'I'm not sure what we've got,' he said passing one to Sheila, 'We can swap if you don't like this one.'
'As long as it's hot and wet I won't complain.' She chuckled. 'It's like camping out in the back garden for the first time with my sister, and hoping our parents would forget we were still outside. How long was I asleep?' She ran her fingers over the mechanical brail chronograph bumping into his hand as it approaching from the opposite direction. 'Almost seven hours she exclaimed! You should have woken me. I don't want to spend our last few hours together just sleeping.'
'You seemed so peaceful,' he lied, knowing full well the true answer would make her angry. In her present state of mind she would use sixty percent less oxygen sleeping and he could drop into deep meditation and reduce his air consumption by at least half. He knew Ray and Geney with similar training would be doing the same.
The warm drinks provided respite for a few minutes.
'It's so difficult just laying here, having nothing to do. What do find to think about Darkon?'
Again he found himself lying. In truth he would normally stop thinking, just let his mind wander aimlessly where it would. He'd passively watch the thoughts pass by and occasionally linger on the forgotten memories they invoked. He knew to do more and actively pay attention to those thoughts would consume considerably more oxygen as his mind would be ushered into full consciousness. It was necessary to 'switch off' the intellect and surrender to the more primitive parts of his mind. Just as in the oceans back home a Free-Diver would

train her body and mind to stay submerged for upwards of eight minutes he understood the need for the total physical and mental discipline that could keep them alive for the necessary two days.

'I think of pleasant things' he answered, 'like stretching out on the beach on a hot summer evening with a cool onshore breeze wafting salty air currents all over my body. Hearing the seagull cries as they circle lazily over the coast line searching for the night's roost. I imagine the chorus of the softly lapping sea as it breaks over rocky outposts reaching far out into the ocean waves, the deep roasted aroma of fresh coffee drifting on the breeze from the last of the fishing smacks as it chugs by in the fading light heading for the safety of the harbor and the welcoming arms of the stony harbor walls.'

He would have continued, but Sheila was asleep again. Taking the half-finished pre-pack drink from her hand, he sealed it stowed it between them where it would stay warm. He was content. He let his mind drift with just a small part in the background listening for the arrival of their Cuanta lifesavers. As the endless hours ran on he began to feel the strain. Sensory deprivation was playing tricks with his mind. They were tricks he was expecting, but they demanded mental resources to combat them and that entailed consumption of their limited oxygen. The greatest delusion was a compelling need to check on Ray and Geney in the adjacent cabin. He knew they had an emergency alarm, a mechanical gong. They could strike it at any time and it would reverberate clearly throughout the ship. The exertion needed to visit to their cabin and the oxygen he would consume getting there was totally unnecessary but the urge to do so dominated his mind where already a dozen deadly scenarios were playing out. Some were plausible - others completely insane. He let

then amuse him; laughing inwardly at the funny side of their themes.
His favorite, and it kept recurring, was a sentient Black Hole dressed up as a twentieth century businessman. It came complete in a dowdy pinstripe suit, white shirt and crimson bow-tie with incongruous bare feet sporting toenails painted jet black. The entity kept yelling through the cabin door trying to persuade Ray to open up and give it access so it could suck the unwary pair into its inky black depths. One part of Darkon's mind knew a real black hole in the corridor would be close enough to ingest them all, door, corridor, cabins, the whole ship, and probably the whole star system too. Another part was begging Roy not to fall for the trick and to keep his door tightly shut. In a moment of weakness he felt his hand sliding to the holstered stargun ready to port the black hole into the sun, or a local black hole. Then reality jumped back and he realized the incomprehensibility of sending a black hole into itself. Eventually he drifted into a long, deep sleep.
Ringing in his head woke him five hours later. Actually it was the alarm of the mechanical clock just inches above him. It signaled the start of the next work period. The sounds of cursing from the adjacent cabin suggested Ray's timepiece was running to the same schedule. It was now twenty six hours into the shutdown. Darkon spent thirty minutes pumping the mechanical scrubbers partly to warm his body partly to shake the cobwebs and delirium out mind. It did him good. The influx of oxygen to his depleted body was exhilarating. His thinking recovered to a healthier state. He woke Sheila and encouraged her to have ten minutes exercise on the scrubbers too. With another day of inactivity and limited air it would be the only opportunity to breath deeply for many hours. The

Excess $CO_2$ pulled from the air would make breathing a little easier for a while. They heated breakfast and ate heartily, still in the dark. Darkon desperately wanted to know how Jeff and the Cuanta teams were progressing. Did they have any chance of purging the ships of the lethal plague? He could only wait, and hope.

Planetside in the Admin center there had been no sleep since the infestation was suspected. This was not as much a problem for the Cuanta as it was for the Human. Their alien metabolism was much slower and their mental capacity more developed. It was common place for them to remain active for three to four days after which they would deep sleep a full day to stabilize their sleep cycles. That ability was being used to the full to help their Human friends and the teams were mildly amused by Jeff's need for sleep after a mere twenty hours. They let him rest for four hours, until they needed his advice.

He was still groggy but after a strong coffee, or whatever passed as coffee on Atnera, he was alert once more. They would be ready soon but with limited shuttles it would take several trips to seed all the starships. Together they scheduled the delivery routes sending at least one batch of Anti-Nanos to each stricken vessel on the first launch. More importantly the Shuttles were loaded with maximum oxygen to refurbish basic onboard-supplies. Each shuttle was already being saturated with the counter measures it needed to render immunity from the Library nanos. It would not be long before they could lift off.

Jeff was relieved when within the hour and at peak take off weight five shuttles roared into life, streaking upward into low orbit. As each reached its first target the heavy clunk of docking clamps resonated throughout the ship. A first batch of nanos was unleashed and spent several minutes purging contamination from the airlock and its support circuitry. Those batches would remain in and outside the lock to prevent re-infestation and maintain a safety zone between ships. Next, laser guard barriers were energized to zap any airborne contaminants. When the 'All Clear' was given Cuanta teams raced into the sickened vessel. Pressurized feeds hooked into the emergency oxygen inlets and desperately needed supplies were replenished. Next the primary nano release points were located and the main nano force unleashed. Finally Nano-Control relays linking the ship to the Atnera Base were activated. Medical teams with several sealed nano cages remained onboard while the shuttle undocked to target the next starship on its schedule. After attending to the crew's immediate need, their prime task was to decontaminate additional shuttles to support the nano-dispersal program, hence the additional nano cages. As soon as their shuttles were purged they would be cleared to land and collect the main nano consignments from the planet. The Cuanta did not want to port the anti-nanos to the starships. If the Library intercepted delivery it could develop a new strain to augment the current plague.

Darkon and Sheila awoke to the thunder of a shuttle docking with LS48. They were both painfully cold with hypothermia beginning to set in. Darkon checked Sheila's vital signs, weak but steady then went to check Ray and Geney. They too were awake and in slightly better shape. The two men headed towards the bridge and met the rescue team releasing the counter measure nanos directly into the engine room ducting. Theirs was the last of the three GMI ships to be treated. Already HS03 and GMI-1 had dispatched their four remaining shuttles planetside and were awaiting their return. One had been assigned to dock with and service LS48. The Cuanta medics wrapped the crew in heated blankets and assisted them onto the bridge. Fifteen minutes after the nanos release Darkon initiated the startup sequence but was not surprised when it failed. The recovery team recommended waiting for the shuttle to arrive and deploy the main nano supply before attempting another restart. Then they left, undocking and freeing up the airlock for the returning shuttle.

An hour later another thunderous crash as a returning shuttle docked. Within minutes nanos were being distributed to critical assemblies throughout the ship. After they had been active for thirty minutes Darkon tried again to reboot the primary computer. There was no response. He tried the first backup unit, then the second, then the third and finally on the fourth there was feedback. It identified the first defective unit, Geney rushed to replace it. Another dead unit was located, then another, then another. Slowly one by one the defective assemblies were renewed. Before an hour had passed Life Support came back online to a chorus of cheers as the overhead heating radiators began to glow. A few minutes later their Comms was up and running. He checked in with HS03 and GMI-1, both were proceeding smoothly similar results. With the full crew back onboard and working hard they were exhausted by the time the Nano Controllers declared ten minutes since the last Library Nano was detected. It didn't mean the scourge was purged but it did mean they had begun the final mopping up process. Ninety percent of the Cuanta Nanos were programmed to self destruct after forty days. The remainder would go dormant after one hundred but remain on standby for twelve months in case the plague returned. When all three ships passed the ten-minute threshold and the isolation ward had been re-initialized to computer control the starship trio re-docked. The crews assembled in the Hospital Ship's dinning room for a

celebratory meal. They were joined by the Cuanta shuttle crews who remained aboard monitoring the decontamination. Onboard the Militia ships the junior rank mess halls were once again back to the boisterous normal and in the wardrooms the best wines in the Milky Way were being opened without regard to cost. The only casualties had been a few cases of frostbite, and one bad case of alcohol poisoning by a terrified rooky. The military was counting its blessings when the GMI Trio of ships began to shake violently.
'Bridge! What's happening?' the three captains had grabbed their comms and were urgently calling their own duty flight crews.
'LS48: It's not our ship Darkon. We're being affected through the docking port.'
'GMI-1: Jeff, the disturbance is from the Hospital Ship, we may have to initiate an Emergency Dock Release if it gets worse. We've still got leeway on structural integrity but the stress is peeking at almost sixty percent.'
'HS03: I think it's the orbital stabilizers sir. We're having trouble taking them off line. We've sent a tech to pull the circuit board it should be… … …' the shaking stopped, 'he's done it. We'll get a maintenance team on it immediately sir.'
'Patch me through to the tech; I want to speak with him now.
'One moment sir,' she flipped the controls, 'Mike - the big boss want to talk with you, He's on channel-7 - he sounds upset, be careful.'
'Thanks Jamie, I'll see you on the bridge in a few minutes.'
He switched channels, 'Engineer Mike Bowman Sir.'
'Relax Mike I'm not going to bite your head off. What's your impression of the damage?

And why wouldn't the system shut down. I need to know if we still have a serious problem.'
'I'm just putting the panel under the scanner sir.' He inspected the unit for less than a minute. 'I can't be certain sir, but it looks like the nanos had just started on this unit. They may have been zapped before they got beyond the outer power supply circuit.' He checked the restart log. 'Looks like it passed several diagnostic checks in the last four hours, one only twenty five minutes ago.' He continued examining the board. 'There's a grayish powder all over the feedback circuits and there's some more on the comms receiver too. I don't recognize it. It is magnetic though, it's clinging to the tip of the screwdriver so it could easily have caused several short circuits. That's about all I can tell from here sir. I need to get it to the lab for a full diagnosis.'
'Thank you Mike. Copy me in on the full report and let me know immediately if you find anything to suggest we still have an ongoing problem. Keep our Cuanta friends in the loop too they may have some input on the powder.'
'Yes Sir, thank you Sir.'
'And thank you Engineer.' He closed the channel.
'Mike flipped back to the bridge, 'Jamie, I'm going to be at least another hour. They've dumped me with some extra work and I've got to do a full analysis on this piece of junk. Can you wait that long before we go for lunch?'
'For you Mike, I'd wait 'til midnight.' she smiled at him even though he couldn't see her. 'But don't you dare forget I'm up here waiting!' she teased.
In the hospital ship emergency room life was back to routine, a variety of minor injuries walked in after the disturbance subsided. A few sprains and several lacerations requiring no more than disinfecting and skin cell regeneration to close the wounds. Then a new patient

was ushered in, one who would tax the center to its limits. Ulaneea the Senior Nano-Control Supervisor helped his assistant Porataxeee to the reception area. The receptionist was visibly taken aback.
'Err, yes,' she uttered tentively, 'I'm Nurse Parmond, what seems to be the problem?'
The older male Cuanta looked at his partner, then back at the Human. 'This may be difficult.' He said in a quiet tone, the epitome of understatement.
'My partner is… … …,' he paused searching for suitable words in the Human vocabulary, there were none. He tried to explain.
'Before hibernation she was pregnant. We could not assess the damage to her fetus during resuscitation so instead of continuing the pregnancy she is reabsorbing the fetus.'
The receptionist looked dazed, she was clearly feeling out of her depth.
'It is similar to the way your own Hydra - the phylum: Cnidaria - reabsorb their buds if the environment becomes unsuitable for breeding.'
He tried another approach.
'During the disruption Porataxeee was thrown heavily against furniture and has sustained internal damage. She can sense her placenta is badly torn and urgently needs medication we have on Atnera. Until then she must be sedated and monitored closely. This type of trauma during re-absorption has a high risk of sepsis and complications if it is not treated immediately. How can you help?'
At last, Lois Parmond had something she could deal with. She put through two calls, One to Julian McNess; he was the senior medic, the Hospital Ships Captain, and the one with the best contacts with the Cuanta. She briefed him on the female's condition and asked him to join them as soon

as possible. The second call via the bridge hooked up to the Cuanta Hyber Center and within minutes Ulaneea was warbling with the medical team planetside. Lois listened in amazement to the conversation not understanding one word of it. It was like a two birds cooing to each other across the valley back home. The tones were gentle and clear, the Cuanta language was a delight to the ear.

The Cuanta dispensary had ported the urgently needed medication directly to the hospital ship.

It failed to arrive. Three times they tried. Three times the portal was intercepted and the medicine snatched away by the Saucer. Finally they launched a trauma med-team and supplies in the smallest available shuttle. Life was becoming extremely inefficient without portals or teleporters but the Library still had a monopoly on their use.

When the Cuanta extended their planetary force field to surround the militia ships the New Oneness had mixed feelings. Although it could no longer monitor its nano attack it remained confident of the outcome. It knew the nanos were powering down every last electrical circuit and would soon be dismantling the nuclear cores. Glistening piles of uranium would be organized in the engine rooms of a dozen starships and would slowly approach critical mass. Then they would erupt in an atomic inferno, a firework display of unimaginable power, a glorious display of death and destruction. Every ship and everything inside a twenty mile radius would be obliterated in the blink of an eye. The humans would get a taste of their own medicine and the Cuanta would endure the deadly fallout. The meld stood ready to intercept every portal attempt to desert the floundering ships, to ingesting every escapee into its digestive interior, to feed its insatiable hunger for fresh living Bio-matter. The

pathetic hydro-carbon life forms were so fragile they did not deserve to live.
But now, even through the Atnera's shields, it caught glimpses of individual ships aglow with energy at levels strong enough to radiate through the protective bubble. That was wrong. By now they should be almost helpless. They should be cold dying ships. Instead they looked almost ready for combat. The New Oneness became angry, it became furious. These pitiful Humans and the last dregs of the Cuanta were yet again daring to challenge the ONE! They could NOT be allowed to succeed.

# Space Zero The Meld

## Back from the Black Hole

Deep inside the distant black hole, remnants of the Saucer's earlier debacle were about to emerge. After the meldlings forsook their sinking ship, leaving it shrouded in unnatural negative gravity, it had continued on a downward plunge into the void. But like a soapy air bubble ninety-nine-point-nine percent full of water its descent had gradually slowed until acceleration and inertia finally exhausted. By then intense gravitational pressure had compressed its bulk to microscopic proportions but the internal sphere remained intact. There were side effects. The molecules comprising the grav-generators had fused under the tremendous forces. Though still intact and maintaining slight negative-G their controls were destined never to operate again. The function it exhibited now was locked in for eternity. And that function, defying gravity, was slowly easing it upward and outward at an ever increasing pace. A pace that would soon be hurling it to freedom across the event horizon even faster than it had entered.

The New Oneness, in the original Saucer at Atnera, was oblivious to the event but several scattered meldling minds, astronomers, voluntary outcasts from the original Meld, had returned to their lifetime studies. They were stunned to see ejecta from a black hole. Once the New Oneness became aware of the incident it immediately dispatched emissaries to investigate and could hardly believe the report they brought back.

The saucer segment was intact, a solidified sphere of mild anti gravity bouncing on an erratic path away between the stars, shying away from gravity wells instead of racing toward them. The New Oneness contemplated the invaluable refined bio-matter and platelets hidden within its depths. Although the vessel was vectoring away from the galactic plane it was within a thirty degree arc from their present location. Recovery was a viable option. But how much of the Saucer's own resources could be spared? Outwitted again by the Guardian Alliance it was desperate for additional supplies. Carefully it calculated the requirements for an intercept and morphed releasing a single grav-thruster and seven percent of its mass to pursue the mission.

The alliance observed the split but was oblivious to its motive. Its off-plane trajectory made no sense, there were no energy signatures anywhere along the projected route, there appeared no reason for the separation. They monitored the event hoping they would recognize any danger before it was too late. The last attack had been unnerving and the local Saucer was still their immediate worry. By now it must know its nano attack had failed and would already be planning another assault. But what if the detachment returned with reinforcements? They didn't want to think about that just yet. If the alliance was to attack the saucer it must be soon but still they lacked a method of delivery. Several militia scientists shuttled down to Atnera in an attempt to evolve a solution.

The following dawn saw the best minds from both sides sitting together to brainstorm. By then radiation generators to animate the catalytic bio-matter were tested and under production, new-generation platelet destroying nanomites were being stockpiled and newer portable sonic disrupters were readily available for inclusion within the warheads.

First the meeting examined problems with conventional delivery systems.

# Space Zero The Meld

What was already known:

- The saucer is resilient to normal forms of matter or energy attack.
- It can morph its structure allowing conventional torpedoes to pass through in empty space.
- If the bulk of the ship remains intact any minor damaged can be repair in minutes.
- Normal target areas such as the main thrusters do not maintain fixed positions. With dynamic morphing the components are continuously being relocated.
- Aware of their Sonic-disrupter technology the Saucer will have counter measures to target sound sources and dampen internal resonance.
- The alliance cannot rely on portals delivery systems since the Library has proven supremacy in that area, with an interception capability.

The brainstorming began.

Julian McNess started the ball rolling and posited the idea of contaminating the Saucer's infrastructure, or interfering with its internal comms.

Zholtair threw in a suggestion for a 'fishnet' of force fields to drag the bombs into close contact with the ship.

Tom was in favor of spolling a dozen lifelike humanoid bombs planetside and letting the Library abduct them into its interior.

Mark Quison suggested finding stars with suitable radiation levels to match the bio-activation frequencies and spolling the radiation from a dozen points all around the saucer.

The Cuanta began to understand the concept of brainstorming and added their thoughts.

Neuama would like use the portals as scalpels to dissect the saucer into more manageable parts.

Jegrega saw them using low-AI, high gravity homing bombs scattered all around the ship to be drawn inescapably onto it.

Dweumna wondered how much of a star could be ported into the heart of the ship to disorient it while conventional torpedoes were used.

The session was going very well.

Jumping in on “the heart-of-a-star” idea Ray suggested a less dramatic approach.

‘Why don’t we port in a few kilo-tones from the heart of Atnera’s molten core?’ he elaborated, ‘Its not enough energy to be used against us, but even if the molten platelets don’t disintegrate they’ll be very difficult to control and to morph into anything usable - cooling them down will be a lot harder job for the saucer than heating them up.’

‘Then tighten Zholtair’s net and pull Jegrega’s torpedoes down on top of them.’ added Uagair triggering an eruption of laughter from the Human side of the table that lasted several minutes…

- until someone realized the idea was a very viable tactic.

‘Is that possible?’ the query came from Uagair.

‘It should be,’ answered Jeff, ‘a portal pair could be pre-programmed for the task.’ He pitched the problem back to the Cuanta,

‘How seriously would the loss affect your planets stability?’

‘Less than a hundred tons will not have a noticeable effect if it is taken evenly from points around the equator. The effect would be negligible on the surface.’ Uagair pondered the concept for a few minutes. ‘It would overcome the Libraries thermal advantage. Our probes would be waiting for the mass to cool down and could attack the outer surfaces as soon as its temperature dropped to a manageable level.'

'And if we irradiate the Saucer as it cools,' interjected Jegrega, 'any bio-matter that survives the inferno will be corrupted as a catalyst. The Saucer will have difficulty morphing'

'But how do we get the Saucer to co-operate? It's not going to just sit there and wait for us to punch it in the face!'

'Diversion - of course' Ray was back in his element. 'We start shuttling equipment down to one of the empty factories. Genuine stuff - the Library won't be fooled. Maybe a few escape pods and the equipment to convert them into high speed torpedo craft. We actually build them, just in case it is observing. Then on an open comms line we ask for a dozen volunteer pilots and bombers for a suicide mission. We arrange for them to be ported down directly into the ships. The library will want to intercept the transport as soon as we attempt to portal. When Eheledana confirms the echoes have appeared and the library's working its guts out to capture its next meal we can throw a dozen meat carcasses through the portals riddled with our version of the ooze. At the same time we project holograms of real pilots to mislead them. For the few seconds it's focused on capturing them and using all its resources to link together its intercepts, we open up our preprogrammed portals to maximum dilation and drop the molten dessert right into its throat. While it's recovering, or trying to, the fleet swings into action porting every available bomb to surround the Saucer. And that includes launching the new shuttles and their contaminated meat "Pilots" to join them. If the Saucer recovers enough to intercept a few, who cares? It'll have too much of a belly ache to do anything once it's got them. The bombs can auto link their defense shields and turn Zholtair's 'fishnet' into an inescapable cocoon. If they're primed for contact detonation, all the force-net has to do is keep itself just outside the thermal threshold as the Saucer cools down then tighten in for the kill. Kazapp! And it's all over. The nanos will be warm enough to beat the pants off the Library platelets.'

'You make it sound too easy.' Jeff was suspicious, 'There's a lot that could go wrong.'

'As long as we distract it long enough to drop in the molten core, everything else is minor detail. Sure we need to iron out a few details but it follows the STAW & STAC principal. Throw curry down its throat and while it's choking pick it to pieces.' Ray smiled. He wondered how the militia would try to make it more complicated.

'What happens if we can't generate portals on the inside of the saucer?'

'Then we open them immediately outside the ship; a dozen pentagonal portals interlocked at the edges in a regular dodecahedron formation. We'll completely encase the Saucer then drown it in tons of superheated molten lava. For all meaningful purposes it'll be in the middle of the planets core. If their shields don't collapse they'll be so weakened it'll take most of their power just to resist the pressure. And if they succeed in grabbing our "pilots" the ooze will be degrading them from the inside too.'

'How,' inquired Neuama, 'do we handle the missing portion of the Saucer if or when it returns? The same tactic may not work a second time.'

'At less than a third of the mass we may be up against an easier target unless it picked up some additional resources. Either way the task will be a lot simpler if we eliminate its big brother before it gets back.'

The meeting continued long into the evening with both sides elaborating on tools they could add to the war chest. Eventually they thrashed out a potent stratagem. By the time the meeting drew to a close the Cuanta, remembering the Human need for sleep, had prepared overnight quarters for their guests in an adjacent hall and a lavish meal was awaiting them. They could return to their ships in the morning but for a few hours they were free to relax and unwind.

Since the Meld split apart, it had stabilized remarkably quickly. The pace surprised even its own meldling minds. Turmoil and conflict common in earlier conflict evaporated within days of separation. It was clear earlier disruption had been due to a 'vocal' minority and most of those minds had been protecting the Library data banks for several cycles. These were the minds that repeatedly interfaced with the Guardian species. Was it possible that over time this interaction had destabilized their thinking? Could those minds have been influenced by the primitive, aggressive nature of the five earlier species? Were they responsible for their personality change, or was it an illness? The old Meld was at a crossroads. Should it disregard the New Oneness and go about its own independent existence trusting the Oneness would leave it in peace after the Humans had been eradicated? Or would its new aggression turn against them when all other scapegoats were gone? Did the old Meld have a duty to protect the emerging species? And did justice demand it intervene to save the Humans even if that meant confronting the Oneness and risking its own existence? There were too many questions to answer. It would require careful introspection before consensus could be achieved.

Away from the central plane two projectiles were converging. The first, the ejected Saucer fragment, was out of control reacting only to the laws of pure physics and maintaining a slowly curving locus. The second, the active fragment from the Saucer was narrowing the gap. Knowing its own gravity would soon affect the target it reconfigured its grav-thrust engine. Its minds knew with inverted polarity the capture would be easy. As the only two negatively charged gravity masses in an almost empty sector of space they would inexorably be drawn together, the exact opposite effect to magnet poles, and once in contact forces stronger than gravity would constrain the assembly while it was analyzed. Gradually their loci converged until a gentle jolt signified contact. The recovery saucer immediately morphed sending streaming tentacles to engulf its cohort within a gleaming fishnet prison. The inanimate hostage offered no resistance as the fishnet congealed around it. All available resources, platelets and spare mass, poured over its structure to form a sturdy new ship for the return journey. Rather than wasting momentum the assembly thrust sideways engendering a new trajectory to interplay with local stars and slingshot itself on a vector for Atnera. Once the first star-throw was complete the investigation began. The New Oneness probed the protective surface of its prize. Morphing platelets struggled in vain attempting to cut through the hardened surface. But the platelet material was so densely compressed the amalgam remained stubbornly resistant, the sphere remained sealed. Every point on the surface was tested with the same frustrating outcome. The saucerlet would have to wait for more resources before teleporting inside the sphere to salvage the Bio-Matter and any viable uncompressed platelets. It would have to wait until it reached Atnera and, without recovering any useful fuel from the merger, the return trip would take longer than planned. That made it angry - it wanted to take the sphere and smash it into the ground like a tantrum stricken child, to stomp all over it - to break it open and it knew the anger and frustration were unwarranted.

During the last few weeks the New Oneness had become more aware of its aggressive and belligerent feelings, and they seemed to be occurring without any real cause. It looked into itself. Without the passive influence of the original Meld it was difficult to constrain its stronger impulses. That had not happened before. It contemplated the minds which comprised it. Most had military backgrounds with "Action Oriented" behavior, the remainder came from a mixture of occupations but all were successful and dominant citizens, influential leaders in their own fields. Here there was no hierarchy; all minds were in principal at least equal. Here the most timid and suggestible mind had equal sway with the most educated, learned and rational mind. Some minds were more capable of good decision making, but in the Meld they were continually overruled by the masses whose thinking lay centered in the middle of the standard distribution curve. Were they elitist to think their minds could make better leadership decisions than others? Were they wrong to think that the masses were either under-educated or too lazy to learn good judgment? Was that the even greater "sin" of arrogance? Should the Meld have forsaken pure egalitarian management for representative democracy or would that just replace mediocrity by selection of the most popular (but maybe incompetent) citizens as leaders?

## Escape from the Meltdown

The alliance was ready, the Militia and GMI primed, and ten new Assault Shuttles stood at Launch-Alert outside Atnera's massive hangers. As mid-day arrived the Hyber-Center prepped the trap. Opening comms to the Central Hub's Support Ship FS-CH-107 it requested portal dispatch for the ten volunteer shuttle pilots. The reply came thirty seconds later as the starship launched the first diversionary, superluminar torpedo towards the Saucer. It was followed by a barrage from every fighting ship in the armada. Within seconds two hundred missiles were hurtling towards the common enemy. As the leading armament reached the saucer the latter morphed an opening allowing the missile to pass harmlessly through.

Then began: 'The Dance of the Swiss Cheese'. All through the structure Multiple openings were created and collapsed allowing unhindered passage for the missiles. But before the Oneness had time to gloat the barrage did an about turn. The broadside slowed dramatically as the missiles swung around in unison to return for a second pass. As the drama began the GMI ships initiated their holograms and ported all ten ooze infested carcasses planetside, directly into the Atnera assault craft. Eheledana alerted Mark and Jeff when only seven arrived. She detected five echoes but two were unstable and apparently failed in their abduction attempt. It was regrettable but even three contaminants onboard the saucer were a valuable asset. Her message was also a coded signal to prepare to port the magna. Jeff manipulated the portals to open deep inside the planet where they would not be detected from orbit. They were fully operational but would have no effect until their matching pairs opened within the Saucer.

The new oneness was getting annoyed. The humans could not expect to damage it with their puny weapons but this persistent need to morph openings and avoid impact was irritating, and consumed valuable resources. The missiles were running in predictable patterns and avoidance was just an exercise in trajectory logic; even their algorithms were ridiculously simple.

The ‘game’ continued for almost eleven minutes then the unbelievable happened. As it morphed yet another opening, the center of the tunnel failed to develop in time and the missile locked on. Clamps shot out like spikes from a wheel hub gripping the sides of the tunnel radiating their resonance through the target ship. The Saucer continued morphing to isolate the resonance but it was having difficulty. The last four missiles failed to exit and they too clamped onto the ship. And this time they all exploded. Two contained anti-platelet nanos the third and fourth, trapped close to the surface vaporized large holes on the outward surface. The Saucer began morphing the wounds closed but it could not complete the process and when the barrage made its next pass only the first two missiles passed ineffectively through. The Meld could feel its control weakening. Several times it tried re-morphing the openings, but every attempt failed. It watched helplessly as the remainder of the armaments struck with decimating results. The oneness struggled desperately with its platelet control but was fighting a losing battle against the artificially created ooze. The gelatinous mass was gorging itself on the heat from the torpedoes and tapping into the Saucer’s energy reserves. Even on surfaces exposed to space the ooze was moving with visible gaseous bubbles circulating just below its shimmering skin. Two last missiles swung back to on their final pass. Together they struck the ship dead center

spraying plasma through the entirety of the ship, piercing out from the opposite hull before spewing into space.
Suddenly ten laser beams lit up the crippled Saucer. They originated just outside the Atnera atmosphere. The ten new assault craft were homing in on their target. Megan, seeing the extent of the destruction already in progress, recalled the three "unmanned" ships. He aborted their part of the mission leaving seven ooze contaminated drones to target the already crippled Saucer. With minor adjustment a balanced seven prong final strike was programmed to evenly distribute the living death throughout the ship. The New Oneness was struggling. For the first time in eons it was out of control. It infused its old home, searching for platelets and bio-matter in a failing attempt to recover control. In a few limited areas it began to make repairs. Slowly like a human recovering from a stroke its platelet body began to erect defenses against the intruding ooze. Confidence increased as the harassed minds worked together to completed more of their morphing tasks. The Meld was regaining control and rebuilding from the center outwards when the attack shuttles struck. Plasma beams vaporized entry channels inward from the saucer's outer hull. Once inside the seven nose cones synchronized ejecting their contaminated carcasses forward to fuse in a pulpy mess at the heart of the enemy ship. Immediately the area was saturating with intense radiation at the frequencies needed to regenerate the ooze while powerful sonic resonators burst into life shattering the surrounding platelets. Beta emission from the remnants of the Saucer began to drop. The Saucer was dying.
Planetside, Jegrega and Jeff monitored the decrease. Their stratagem turned upside-down when initial contamination by the high jacked ooze 'pilots' worked more dramatically than anyone expected. The Saucer was in

disarray burdened by its deadly ooze passenger. It was dead in space with no viable means of propulsion. All that remained was "Waste Disposal" and that was in the capable hands of Megan and the militia.

The commander waited a full hour after the last Beta radiation was detected. By then the ooze, the nanomites and the sonic resonance would surely have completed their task. The platelets and bio-matter would be finished. A dozen portals were opened connecting innards of the Saucer's carcass to Atnera's magna core. Megan and his crew watched in awe as differential pressure across the portals did its worst. Twenty tonnes of superheated lava began extruding into the ship. Slowly the void originally occupied by the ooze flooded with fiery heat. Free from the immense pressures within Atnera the unrestrained magma expanded outwards engulfing the ship. In its path lighter elements vaporized, venting as gas and plasma, blasting their paths into the all welcoming emptiness of space. Denser matter liquefied on contact only to be 'sucked' into solution by the magma. The only escapee, creeping ahead of the intense heat and destruction, and apparently comfortable in the vacuum of space, was the Ooze. With the saucer succumbing to the molten red liquid the much enlarged organism pushed free of the ship to drift on the undulating tides of space. Megan dispatched a drone to erect a containment field and meeting no resistance tractored the mass of living death to a safe distance, isolating it for later use. By the time the Hyber-Center rotated into the shadows of nightfall spectral analysis showed the Cuanta nanomites success; no trace of the platelets' chemical signature could be found. The nano-bots by transmuting the Meld's platelets had severed its connection with the physical world.

Megan collapsed the magma portals and scanned the local quadrant for a planetless star in which to dump the debris. He found one, a relatively cool red dwarf, with a single burned out planetoid in uninhabitable orbit. Carefully he re-opened the mega-portal between the star and their molten nemesis, launched three monitor drones, and stood back to enjoy the view as solar gravity dragged their enemy inward through the portal. Already passed 'The Point of No Return', the Library Saucer's carcass was in free fall, face-to-face with the ultimate crematorium.

In the fleet every set of eyes, Human and Cuanta, watched its death throws. One moment the molten blob appeared to hover, silhouetted against the backdrop of the red dwarf, shrinking as it plummeted ever downward. In the next, streams of vivid orange plasma burst forth spewing outward to entwine and enmeshed within the violent magnetic flux of the star's corona. The kaleidoscopic spectacle expanded obscuring almost a quarter of the solar surface. Then slowly, it began to fade, began to blend into the dimming background light until all that remained were recordings in data banks of the observer drones and the memories of a few hundreds relieved, sentient lifeforms.

Given a choice, Megan would have thrown the oozing organism into the same merciless pit - but detached remnants of the Saucer were still at large and heading towards Atnera. That threat would arrive soon and the ooze was their best ally, it was their only ally.

The New Oneness was alone again and this time without its connection to the real universe. In the time it took Atnera to make a single rotation it had slipped from dominating the war to becoming the defending force. It was devoid of even a single weapon to revenge itself against these two simpleton species. This was humiliation at its worst. In the vastness of the Milky Way the only physical matter that remaining even partially under its control was the small recovery section it had dispatched earlier with just a single grav-thruster. And that remnant was the only sanctuary the minds of the New Oneness would find.

It reexamined memories of the bio-attack that had vanquished its corporeal resources. From Human reports and its own investigation it knew and understood the episode in Alexandria-3's morgue. Indeed it had been amused they considered it a deliberate attack. In truth the Library had been more worried than its enemy. Had the Humans not eradicate the Ooze, the library would have been forced to extricate itself from the planet. Centuries would have been lost before the Humans would trust it again. It paused. The New Oneness realized it was thinking like a simple sentient. It could not waste time with the ramifications of its losses. It must take immediate steps to optimize its remaining resources.

Pondering the precarious situation, it watching helplessly as its adversaries with uninterrupted portal capability pulled vast quantities of Sea Water into onboard purification tanks. It watched fresh foods being transferred into their stores. It ached to scream out loud, to rush headlong into a combat yelling, 'You're not allowed to do that you moronic lifeforms!' In the Oneness where consensus had been so easy a mere one day earlier, there were more factions than before the split. Business minds were ready to concede defeat, to accept they had been beaten by two lesser species that fought for their survival with the tenacity of demons and had won the war. Their own military minds were divided. Hard core professionals wanted to fight until the last platelet was lost, while the better educated, higher ranking commanders preferred to regroup and appraise whatever short and long term options were still be available. The remaining few, a very small minority, wanted to re-merge into the Original Meld but their unpopular pleas were quickly drowned out by a cacophony of hostile responses. The only consensus was: Regroup with their remaining resources and prepare a strategy for defense. The minds of the New Oneness continued procrastinating until the Human/Cuanta forces broke orbit and were vectoring unmistakably towards their returning Saucerlet. Defensively they relocated and joined the recovery team.

The armada now in long haul formation had re-established their solar gravity defense shields. It was tracking the Saucerlet not knowing the large segment from within the black hole had been reacquired and would complicate their task. From every starship twin manipulator beams were locked down onto the probe that towed their lethal cargo of ooze. There was no way the contaminant would be lost in transit or allowed to ingress their ships. And each ship was ready to port a deadly portion of that ooze into every missile exiting their launch bays. In their favor, the Saucerlet had neither portal not teleport capability and could no longer intercept their deliveries. But that was something the militia would not realize until later.

Meanwhile long range sensors were detecting an explicably high density for their quarry. The cause was disturbing and further acerbated when readouts showed an unprecedented eighteen percent mass variation as the craft underwent incomprehensible maneuvers. The armada would spend several unproductive days analyzing the data before they were in range of their target, a fact that was not missed by the Saucerlet.

With only one grav-thruster it was hardly in a position to outrun its pursuers. It needed an alternative option. It needed somewhere to shelter, somewhere to hide and recover until it could figure out a solution. The minds of the New Oneness spread out to examining every star and planet within range. They were seeking a landmass that would obscure their position. The armada would trace them to any star they chose so the planetary system must afford protection. A large mass planet with magnetic poles and a violent climate to jam aerial searches would be ideal. It would be an added bonus if the atmosphere was toxic to both Humans and Cuanta and too corrosive for their starships. One by one star systems were analyzed and rejected.

Then after three days a probing mind hit the jackpot! The mind named the star Lasthope (AKA: Last Hope) and its two planets Hide and Seek. Seek, on the inner orbit was comparable to Alexandria or Atnera in earlier stages of their planetary evolution. The land masses were still in the violent volcanic stage with a solid crust just beginning to form. Most of the water still in gaseous form resided within the atmosphere. Torrential storms ravaged the surface with most of the acidic downpour evaporating on contact with the ground. It was not yet ready to supported life. The outer planet: Hide, was a gas giant almost a hundred fifty thousand miles in diameter four hundred and sixty times the mass of Seek. Several minds had penetrated its toxic atmosphere. Their compressed sphere could survive the torturous storms and caustic, abrasive environment but the armada would be shredded within minutes. Their only concern was the intensity of the ever present electrical storms. Fortunately since the platelets were magnetic even direct strikes would simply skirt around the outside of the Saucerlet under boundary effect and leave the inner sphere and its contents safe and intact. The greatest danger would be during entry and exit from

the atmosphere and that though difficult could be controlled by varying the outer gravitational charge.
With the armada less than two days behind and this solar system only one day's travel ahead, the Meld would have nearly a full day to penetrate the atmosphere and locate a suitable holding site. By the time the militia arrived they would be unable to track beyond the first few miles of upper rarified gasses. Once again the New Oneness would be setting the rules. Their adversary would have to wait until they were disposed to continue the attack and that gave the Saucerlet the upper hand. It would remain within Hide's protection until it was combat-ready and then choose where and when to engage in battle. In the worse case scenario it could outwait the humans. If necessary it could remain hidden below the clouds until human memories faded or the siege drifted into unreliable folk law. A hundred, a thousand, ten-thousand years - Time was on the side of the New Oneness. The Saucerlet changed course again - and this time it had a purpose.
The armada realizing its intentions fired a dozen superluminary torpedoes with explosive nanomite warheads. They would take several hours to reach the target but they would intercept the long before it reached the safety of the planets. The New Oneness had plenty of time to retaliate. The majority of its minds immediately relocated close to the old Meld. They waited patiently as tension in the space/time fabric peaked then the first subgroup dropped into the center of the lead missile. The temporal shock ripped the warhead apart triggering its explosive charge and scattering the nano cargo across a thousand cubic miles of open space. During the next hour each warhead in turn suffered the same fate as the mind groups staggered their return. It sent a stern warning to

the fleet to remain within its protective gravimetric shields.
It was pointless to waste more missiles - the Saucerlet had too much time to retaliate and more probes would only suffer the same fate. The alliance anticipated the need track their foe once it entered the atmosphere and the gas giant was too massive to destroy the way they had obliterated Alexandria. Megan opened a comms link to Atnera. Once again Cuanta expertise was needed.
For several days tranquility had reigned over the home planet. The Meld might return but for a few days at least they were relieved from an eternity of fear. The GMI personnel and eighteen military construction units were working and living among the natives in relative comfort and after the cramped conditions of their starships to be free to wander through the farm areas surrounding the Hyber-Center was a pleasure few could resist. And for the geeks intent on enjoying the hi-tech aspect of every situation, the Cuanta were happy to introduce their new technologies. They would soon be mingling with billions of Humans inhabiting the Milky Way and the enthusiasm of this small band of allies, to mix and socialize with the newly awakened Cuanta, gave them hope that their re-emergence into the galaxy although difficult would not be impossible. But they were returning to their old territory as a replaced species, as foreigners, as aliens in their own home. They knew that would be the price when Great Sleep began. But now the reality of what it meant was beginning to have tangible meaning.
Language was difficult. The flowery Human speech needed complex programming and extensive AI before their translators could eliminate confusing, contradictory implications and hidden half-meanings. Then add more AI to detect voice patterns and emotional undertones, in

an attempt to compensate for human concepts such as: sarcasm. For the Humans it was much simpler. Their only adaptation was to constantly remember the Cuanta "habit" of saying what they actually meant. To human ears their ally's language was distant, unemotional and monotonous, but at the same time extremely accurate. A technique was spreading through the grapevine which gave the perfect solution: "Whenever you became uncomfortable listening to a Cuanta's speech, just close your eyes and imagine you're talking with a computer". The technique worked well, apart from having to close ones eyes.

With Sheila's training communication was not a problem but her professional interest in Cuanta history exhausted the patience of several Administrative staff. They were on tight schedules to expedite the mass resuscitation and her continual questioning was a distraction. They insisted she restrict inquiries to the outsiders who, with only menial chores, could afford the time. And thus began a strong friendship with Verrringah. Before hibernation the young Cuanta female had been a mediocre student at a minor learning academy and lacked academic skills. Only the success of her father's mining company and his faith in the Hyber-Project led to her inclusion in the Long Sleep but regrettably her partner had not survived resuscitation. The Cuanta unlike Human culture valued Science over the Arts. Verrringah's skills with music and writing were only considered suitable as a hobby or pastime. They were not recognized as professional skills. She was pleasantly surprised to hear the Human value system was so different, pleased that they had evolved a complex infrastructure to share and disseminate art throughout their society. But pictures, paintings, carvings, statues, that was a difficult arena. These were concepts she was

unfamiliar with. Why would someone spend several weeks manually reproducing a scene or image when a technically perfect copy could be created in a few microseconds? Had the Humans perhaps extended "Art" a little too far?
Sheila would got the chance to experience Cuanta "recreation" a few days later when the two ladies dragged their partners to a 'social evening' Cuanta style. For the natives it was a Tri-D documentary of their early beginnings, with a short history of their last few years before hibernation. Located in the largest hanger the display zone occupied the full center third of the building. Floating seater-platforms surrounded the 'stage' at both ends of the huge hall and were controlled by complex management algorithms that ensured everyone had an uninterrupted view. As the scenes changed the seaters floated gently to better locations optimizing their customers viewing pleasure. The seater's control console allowed a choice of viewing preference. Vertigo sufferers could restrict their ascent to only a few feet above the ground while the more daring could open up full inversion. In this mode the seaters would activate artificial gravity before suspending the guests almost upside-down over the center of the stage. Zholtair explained the proceedings to his guests in extreme detail, before admitting his team had designed and built the new Hyber-Center. After about an hour there was a break in the show. The seats retreated to ground level docking points allowing the customers take a break. This break was a social custom and there would be two more during the show. The purpose Verrringah explained was to allow socialization. Strangers would have the shared theme of the show to discuss even if they had little else in common. However since many Cuanta did not bring translators they

spoke only briefly before returning to their seating unit to order refreshments. Verrringah and Zholtair selected the local beverages. There were many official drinks plus a few specially brewed by the outsiders. The latter not surprisingly tended to have a genuine alcoholic base. Sheila tried a flower based wine with a low alcohol level. Darkon, recalling his student life, selected a much stronger brew resembling the double distilled spirits he and his co-conspirators had concocted before their rule-loving dormitory master confiscated the still.

'Hi Darkon' He turned to see his crew from LS48 approaching on their seater. 'These chairs are fantastic!' shouted Geney as they slid alongside. 'I just punched in your name and it flew straight over here.' She had clearly been imbibing the brew all through the first session.

'You'll have to excuse her Boss', pleaded William in a similar state of intoxication, 'It's our first weekend pass in months.' Trudel and Ray also showed signs of wear. It was unlikely they would last to see the end of the show.

'Weeeee'll catch up with you later!' cried Geney as the seater whisked them away for the start of the second part of the evening's entertainment. 'Call me if you have trouble getting the hotel room door to open again!'

'What's that all about?' Sheila asked seeing a mischievous grin spread across Geney's face.

'Galaxy knows.' answered Darkon, straining to keep a straight face. He was almost certain nothing had happened all those years ago, almost certain - but not quite a hundred percent sure. He'd know one way or another once the alcohol was purged from his system and his mind cleared. He was enjoying being 'on holiday' and noone knew when the next safe day would be.

The evening unfolded, the show went on, and eons of history were compressed into a few short hours. With his usually razor sharp concentration slightly blurred around the edges, (along with his vision,) Darkon was at peace for the first time in weeks. With the woman he loved snuggling against him and new friends cooing in their strange language just a few feet away he was happy and content. He wasn't sure but he may have dropped off to sleep several times during the show.

## Cuanta Relief

He finally woke up thinking he was back on the bridge of his Lifeship. Immediately in his field of vision was the hulk of the Saucer and for a moment he thought the nightmare had returned. Instinctively he turned to his first mate demanding a status update.
'Update to what?' Sheila replied also in a dreamy state, 'what in galaxy's name are you talking about?'
He looked around realizing where he was, not in his ship, not in any ship, he was in a planet-bound theater. Slowly he brought his body and mind back under control. Looking into the display he was in time to watch the attack shuttles bury them selves deeply inside the dying Saucer, he watched the vessel shudder as internal explosions ripped at its innards. Then the glow began. The essence of Hephaestus: the god of fire, the inferno from hell, the magnificent glow of deadly molten magma, the tortuous heat welled up from deep within the ship. The audience went silent as the glow spread ever wider and when finally the last visible vestiges of the Saucer dissolved into a blood red ball of death the Cuanta audience erupted into terrifying roars. It was clear the fear and hatred bottled up during the Long Sleep had finally found an escape.
'DAK ACODEA! DAK ACODEA! DAK! DAK! DAK!'
The chorus echoed through the hanger.
'DAK ACODEA! DAK ACODEA! DAK! DAK! DAK!'
It was repeated a hundred or more times getting louder with every chant, begging for extermination of every ruthless member of the Acodea species responsible for the death and destruction of their civilization, begging revenge for the trillions of Cuanta left childless and alone to die heartbroken and unfulfilled in the crumbling

remnants of their once glorious empire. They watched the portal array open, relentlessly dragging the loathsome aberration into the nuclear fireball of the sun. Tenor jumped to fever pitch with citizens of Atnera screaming their hatred in their shrill chirping voices. In a flash of pure orange plasma the fiery ball, the vestige of evil for so many species disintegrated. As the orange hue faded from existence a gargantuan roar reverberated through the hanger theater threatening to collapse the whole building. Then it went quiet.

Every Cuanta in the audience was breathing heavily - recovering from their explosive experience. All but two seater-units had re-docked. Only the human occupied seaters remaining airborne. Darkon surveyed the scene below. Exhausted bodies lay collapsed at every dock. Their friends Verrringah and Zholtair were likewise indisposed. Apprehensively he looked for the docking icon on the seater's consol. He pressed it. Geney, on the second airborne seater was doing the same. Instead of returning to the normal docks both the seaters drifted to a manned staging area to the side of the hanger. As soon as they landed a medic stepped aboard and ran a scanner over their two friends.

He turned towards Darkon, 'Your companions will recover in a few minutes.'

'What happened?' William and Ray asked the same question. 'Is it another attack from the Saucer?'

'It is not an attack. There is no danger, we are in full control. This was essential treatment.' The medic thought for several seconds before continuing. 'In your language the closest description would be: stress relief therapy.'

He went on to explain,

'That is why we scheduled this display. Every necessary person was required to attend.'

'Necessary for what?' demanded Sheila.

'We monitor everyone after resuscitated. Less than one in twenty had coped successfully with the stress. Throughout hibernation we were subliminally thinking and were in fear of the Acodea that is our name for the Meld. On revival we had to acknowledge they were still intent on our extermination. Most of us only heard spoken reports of the Saucer's destruction. It was insufficient. The display tonight was to make those reports a reality. It was to show at a visceral level that the Acodea threat, although not terminated, is under control.' He looked at console readout, then at the dozens of medics checking the seated audience. 'So far almost everyone has released their tensions successfully. These results are significantly higher than we expected.'

'Higher?' asked Sheila, 'In what way "significantly higher"?'

'We anticipated between two and four percent of our population would require additional therapy.' He checked the consol screens again. 'The results so far extrapolate to only twenty seven patients.'

'That's quite a difference.' Sheila added, 'Are your doctors usually so conservative with their estimates?'

'The estimates were based on initial tests with our own recorded show. Yesterday Jegrega watched your edited version of the Saucer offensive, the film you will be sending to your NEWS dissemination groups for your own culture to view. He was surprised by the difference in the emotional response. It was more profound. Verrringah explained your use of Tri-D for entertainment and that you have developed techniques to maximize visceral arousal.'

'That's true,' Geney intervened, 'I've been a Tri-D addict since school days. But what they put together here just for the NEWS is nothing to some of the "Tear Jerker" films we can view back at the Hub.'

'Jeff gave us copies to add to our show.' the medic continued, 'We tested the effect on nine of our patients with extremely beneficial results so we replaced the five last segments with your show. I belief it was the quality of your imagery, particularly the final sequence, that allowed our people to feel they were participating in the Acodea's defeat. Tonight they *EXPERIENCED* the death of their enemy. It allowed them to feel they have regained control of their lives.' He turned to Darkon, 'Knowing a fact and feeling the truth of that fact can sometimes be different realities. Tonight, for most of our people, those realities have merged.' He repeated the scans, 'Your friends are recovering.'

Zholtair stood up cautiously. He appeared to understand, and feel, what he had just experienced.

'That was,' he paused, 'an unusual show. Our displays do not often elicit such reactions,' he admitted, 'but we expected something different when we were instructed to attend. This is the best I have felt since re-wakening.' He sat with Verrringah stroking her hand until her eyes opened.

She smiled. 'What just happened, Zholtair? I feel so alive again. I feel the way I did when we first arrived on Atnera, seven years ago.' She paused thoughtfully then corrected herself, 'Seven "Awake" years ago.' She became exited, 'Can we bring Sheila and Darkon to our dwelling as our guests until tomorrow? No one is expected to be at work tomorrow - they told us that on the Display invite.' She tuned to Sheila, her eyes almost begging, 'Please Sheila, Please; stay with us'

Sheila looked at Darkon with the same begging eyes. He smiled and nodded back, 'We'd love to visit. We can collect our overnight bags on the way passed our quarters. Unless you have something else lined up Sheila?' he teased.

Verrringah had always wanted to entertain. Her parents had many friends and colleagues who were constantly visiting for dinner, evenings out, for the weekend. But she had barely begun studying when the college was closed and from there she and her mate were shipped directly to Atnera on one of the last escape ships. Life had been difficult without a solid education, without skills she was valuable primarily for her fertility. Because of that she and Terry had been assigned to the first batch of Hibernation pods. After their pod failure, facing just a few years life expectancy, she became part of the outsider group. The village was a closed community living closely together. Administrators never visited and certainly would not remain in the open overnight. She accepted the situation. She accepted she would never be able to entertain the way her family had done. She accepted that she would never share the skills she had learned from her mother. She accepted it all, and it made her very sad.

Now, today, she would have her first guest, she would have two guests. As she strolled back from the Admin-Center oblivious to her surroundings her mind raced over their food supplies. What could she spare? How should she prepare the meal? What would they talk about over the final late night drinks? When should she wake them for breakfast? And what should that be. This was going to be the happiest day of her life. Before she realized it they had reached the village. 'We are the last building on the right.' She explained excitedly, 'It is functional and hygienic.' She led them into the dwelling. 'Zholtair built it himself, with a little help from the other villagers erecting the roof.' She was proud of her partner's

achievement. 'It took him months to create the windows he wanted to make them the old way.' She took Sheila into the kitchen to keep her company while preparing the meal.
'Doesn't Zholtair help with the cooking?' Sheila asked.
'Only when I let him,' she replied, 'you would be surprised at how much he works on the house. We have the driest dwelling in the village.' The small talk continued as Verrringah began to cook the meal. Sheila watched closely, amazed at the way natural crops were prepared without hi-tech appliances.
'This is one of only three concessions we get from the Center,' she reached up to grasp a pressurized infuser. 'One spray over each dish protects us from the local parasites and fungi. It is all we need beyond our crops.'
'And what are the other Two?' Sheila asked.
'We have routine medical checks and treatment, and they process our bodies when we die.'
'Nothing else?' Sheila was surprised.
'When the Center was open, and they had someone to supervise us, we were allowed to use the computers to find information for surviving on the outside. Zholtair wasted weeks when we were first resuscitated trying to find a way to protect us from the solar radiation. That's why he spent so much time on the roof, and why our walls are so much thicker than the rest of the homes. They all laughed at him working after dark for so many weeks. But when our pod-mates died last year from the sun's effects they all began to make their walls and roofs more solid too. It may be just a coincidence - but here on the outside we take coincidence very seriously.
Darkon and Zholtair were relaxing in the living area. Zholtair prepared the table for the meal then poured two cups of home brewed wine. 'Do not fly after drinking

this,' he advised, 'we outsiders are not restricted by the old laws and this bottle is the most potent I have made.' Darkon took the wine and tasted it.
'WOW!' he exclaimed, 'This has a kick like a horned rucktan!' He sat down to drink it in the safety of a large chair and wondered if it carried the penalty of a hangover. He was snoring long before dinner arrived.
'DARKON!' Sheila screamed, 'Wake up!'
'You can't go sleeping when we're visiting our friends.'
'Do not blame your mate Sheila.' Zholtair rose to his defense, 'I gave him my best wine. I did not realize how susceptible you humans are to fermented drinks.' He gently shook Darkon's outstretched arm to wake him. 'Treat him with care.' he advised Sheila, 'he may be - *what is your closest phrase*? - "a small part fragile."'
'"A little fragile", is the way we say it,' laughed Sheila, 'and it's very appropriate to someone who's been drinking too much alcohol.'
Darkon hauled himself through tightly bound layers of slumber, each one taking a noticeable toll on his resources. Finally he was awake.
'I think the rucktan won that round.' He advised his host, then smiling broadly. 'I wish we'd had that brew for our graduation party.'
As he was led to the dinner table, he struggled to get his eyes working again.
Apart from fighting with Verrringah to keep her food offerings down to manageable proportions the meal went well. Their host was in her element entertaining her first ever guests. And although Darkon and Sheila were unsure of the nature of many ingredients their taste buds were in Valhalla. Whereas the Cuanta were delighted by the multitude of divergent tastes at their first meal on HS03, this time it was the penetrating strength and clarity of

freshly grown food with the tang of newly cut herbs and spices that satisfied the Humans. These were flavors that never survive even the best hi-tech storage. Through the alcoholic haze Darkon was savoring every byte.

He began reminiscing. The closest he'd been to food this good, he claimed, was during military training. He rambled on barely noticing how enthralled his audience had become. A two week survival exercise halfway up a mountainside on some remote uninhabited world had been extended when their 'Lift Home' failed power up. They had to wait for a replacement thruster to be sent from stores. Unfortunately for them during the delay a scheming young officer, desperate to be noticed, decided this was the perfect time to make a challenge for the Survivalist Duration record. He persuaded their Sector Commander to authorization the attempt. For another ninety-three days they sweltered under tropical heat and monsoon rains being forced to live off the land. With only a primitive wood burning oven they jury-rigged from salvaged scrap metal they ate well living on fruit, buries, insects and a few small furry animals. After they'd shattered the longstanding record by four days their recovery shuttle was allowed to pick them up.

'But by then the damage was done,' complained Darkon rubbed his belly. 'I'd piled on twenty-three pounds in those three months, and I've never been able to get rid of it. He smiled at Verrringah then rubbing his belly a second time adding, 'I may have put on another ten pounds tonight.' He feigned getting up from his chair then collapsed from the effort.

'Stop that!' snapped Sheila with a grin, slapping a backhander across his chest, 'they can't understand your humor.'

Then to their hosts, 'He's O.K. he's just playing around.'

He smiled and he straightened up in the chair.
'I really enjoyed that Verrringah. It was a great meal, thank you.' Then as an aside to Sheila, 'Give me a reminder when we get back onboard. I need to update the wardrobe with my new measurements.'
She slapped him again then gave him a long hug. They both burst out laughing.
With the meal finished and the table cleared the women once again retired to the kitchen where Verrringah demanded an explanation for: "*those confusing speech patterns and mannerisms*." 'My translator could not make sense of the words you used,' she confessed, 'and it has the latest AI programming.'
'I'll let you into a secret,' confided Sheila, 'We humans are always confusing ourselves. Your language is much easier to use.'
'Can I give you another wine Darkon?' Zholtair was being a good host, but he was not surprised when the offer was declined. They talked on and on about the Cuanta's thoughts for expanding to a second more favorable planet, and what plans they were making for their personal future together after the war. The talking was difficult since both men found it hard to think clearly after their heavy meal and too many drinks.
Sheila's laughter had been echoing from the kitchen for about an hour. They did not notice it stop. Had they done so, then like parents whose children had suddenly gone quiet, they would have been suspicious. The men had paid little attention as their women went back to the kitchen and hardly noticing as Sheila paused to pick up her overnight bag. Suddenly Zholtair became alert. 'This is not normal.' He sniffed the air. 'I think they have overcooked something.'
Darkon sniffed the air but without the keen nose of a

Cuanta it was a while before the aroma was strong enough for human detection. Then his nostrils flared as the familiar aroma revived long forgotten memories.
'I don't believe it!' he murmured in disbelief, 'Not here! Not so far from home.'
'You are only a mile from your quarters.'
'No Zholtair, from my home planet, from Earth, the Human planet of origin. It's in the database somewhere under Sol-3.'
He sucked in another lungful of the aroma. 'It's coffee! They've got trees on Earth that produce small berries. We roast them until they go hard then crush them and infuse them with heated water. We strain the liquid, and drink it while it's still hot. It's called: **COFFEE!**' he yelled the last word out loud at the top of his voice, and was rewarded by giggles and laughter from the kitchen.
'That is a lot of effort to make one drink.' Zholtair commented.
'Ah! But we can get a pre-processed powder form of the stuff. It's nowhere near as good, but you only have to pour boiling water over it. Or you could use cold water and a half second burst from a hand laser.' He joked.
'This smells like its being brewed the old fashioned way, s-l-o-w-l-y.'
He caught another whiff escaping from the kitchen.
'It's not as potent as your wine Zholtair, but if we drink too much it makes us humans very agitated, something to do with its caffeine content.'
'Damn!' he yelled, 'It won't be ready for at least another fifteen minutes, and the aroma's already got me feeling thirsty.'
'Did you bring your hand laser?' queried Zholtair.
'That's not for real coffee.' He explained his joke, 'I'll just have to sit here and suffer a while longer. Sheila

knows exactly when it will be ready. Wake me up when it arrives please, your wine is making me so sleepy again.'

Twenty infuriating minutes later the girls burst into the room with a jug of the steaming brown liquid. Verrringah moved a small table and two low chairs to the seating area and poured the drinks.

'You'll have to drink it black,' Sheila told them, 'we don't have any sim-milk.'

'But we do have these.' Her host added opening a small storage jar. 'I made them a few weeks ago, and they can last for several months.' Inside were dozens of flat round biscuits. 'Sheila says you can dip them in the coffee to give them an extra flavor.'

Over the next hour the pot of coffee and a large proportion of the biscuits slowly disappeared. By then Darkon had taught Zholtair the art of "dunking". Like the coffee pot the conversation gradually ran dry and the women folk went about preparing the sleeping arrangements.

Tonight with just a thin layer of organic material between themselves and the stars Sheila and Darkon would share a straw mattress overlaid with home woven blankets. 'Don't worry about the bed bugs,' Sheila whispered, 'I packed an emergency liner from the hospital ship. It will keep them all out and,' she added mischievously flashing him a seductive look, 'it will keep everything else safely inside.' But she would be disappointed. Within seconds of his head hitting the pillow Darkon was fast asleep. It was the deepest sleep he had enjoyed for several months. Just over two hours later as his first sleep cycle completed he was awake. It was a "***Call** of Nature*", or to be precise considering the amount of Zholtair's wine he had consumed that evening, it was a "***Screaming at the Top of Your Voice** of Nature*". He was glad he remembered where the primitive toilet was located, and where the outdoor washing facilities could be found. Relieved, he returned to the living area and gazed out into the clear night sky. Just discernable to the human eye he could detect the faint haze emanating from the planetary shields and beyond that the hanging lanterns of the night, billions of stars twinkling through an unpolluted atmosphere.

Two arms grabbed him from behind, but just before retaliating he caught the delicate aroma of Sheila's favorite perfume: 'Allure of the Dark Side'. He tried to turn but she held him securely. 'And just who are you daydreaming about at this time of the night?' she taunted, nibbling his ear. 'Don't think you're going to fall asleep on me as easily a second time.' She continued to caress him, her fingers sliding tenderly over the sides of his body, up and down as far as she could reach stroking him with the lightest of touch, a butterfly hovering just out of reach.

'No!' she ordered defiantly as again he tried to turn to face her. 'Stay still!' she commanded, her hands sliding gently under his garment climbing like giant spiders from his waist to his neck then down again, then up, then down, a sea of waves teasing the beach with tantalizing rhythmic cycles. Moist lips surrounding playful teeth nipped and danced along his spine in tormenting harmony. He reached backward to touch her and felt the cool nakedness of her soft flesh, but still she would not let him turn. She brushed her body lightly against his gliding effortlessly, sensuously, on a thin glaze of fresh moist perspiration. He felt her nipples harden as they pressed into him, felt them slide gently across his back as she swayed her body sideways tantalizing him with her every move. She sensed his agony straining for release. Then before he could take control she swung him around engulfing his manhood to take him deep inside her. This was her night and she was in control. He would be drained long before she'd let him fall asleep again. For an hour she played him, a fisherwoman reeling in a giant Barracuda, holding him back with the peak of ecstasy just beyond his reach, she exited him almost to the limit. Time after time she thrilled him just short of the pinnacle, until she herself was finally ready. Again she drew him to the brink of untold rapture, held him hostage at the very threshold of the carnal pleasure his aching body craved, held him helpless for what seemed an eternity. Then finally in the ultimate demonstration of femininity she launched them together across Lust's steamy threshold to drown in the turmoil of unbridled ecstasy. When their convulsions subsided she was complete. They lay as one in each others arms saturated in the sweaty juices of love, waiting for the world to beneath them to stop spinning. Within minutes the two humans were deeply asleep. Within ten minutes the bed liner from the hospital ship began absorbing their secretions, venting the aroma of freshly fallen pine leaves throughout the room.

## To Search a Giant

By the time Verrringah and Zholtair awoke the following morning, their rest day, the sun had already climbed halfway to the zenith. For their farming lifestyle this was unprecedented. And it happened today of all days, while they had guests. As her partner dressed Verrringah still in her nightgown rushed to the main room expecting to find her disappointed guests already departed. She opened the door. To the side of the room the two humans lay on the makeshift bed, Sheila's head nestling on Darkon's shoulder. She could just make out their slow shallow breathing and realized, with relief, that they too were sound asleep. There was time to make breakfast. She rushed to the kitchen. Zholtair joined her a few minutes later and took over the chores while she dressed.

Sheila was the first to notice an aroma of fresh bread wafting through the room. Quickly she woke Darkon. He felt guilty about sleeping so late in their hosts' home. 'But,' he joked defiantly, 'If you recall - I have a very good reason for over-sleeping this morning.' He stroked her cheek, and received a playful bite to his thumb for the effort.'

'I feel like eating *you* for breakfast,' she replied.

They were dressed when Verrringah passed through the room heading for the kitchen.

'We will eat outside today.' she told them,' 'Now the Center has activated the solar filters we can enjoy the sun. It is pleasing to feel its warmth without worrying about the radiation.'

Darkon paused in the kitchen to chat with Zholtair. 'I wondered why you're still living as outsiders.' He was curious. 'I thought the Center would let you join them once the medical checks came back clean?'

'It is the crops, Darkon.' He explained, 'Neither Verrringah nor I have any special training so we are not useful for the rebuilding program. However, although the center has adequate synthesized supplies there is a shortage of fresh food and they value our surplus especially for their enzymes, vitamins and trace elements. The crops were already planted so if we tend them until the harvest the Center will exchange them for credits towards training and accommodation next year. We will use the funds to subsidize our living standards while we retrain.'

'But don't you find this life rather primitive?'

'We were living outside for five years and expected to die before the end of winter. Now you have repaired our bodies, a few months discomfort is not a burden. It will allow us to start our new lives better placed than before the hibernation. And this year we can enjoy the sun. In the old days, before the Library, our younglings would spend all summer under its glow and their flesh would discolor a deep bronze. I have a few databank images of my family before "*the end*".'

They ate breakfast outside enjoying the summer heat, eating the fruit and freshly baked bread. It was washed down with a local hot drink but this time without alcohol. The mild grogginess at the back of his head reminded Darkon just why he no longer consumed the alcohol on a regular basis. 'Once in a while,' he thought, remembering Sheila's late night surprise. He smiled, 'Once in a while it could be quite enjoyable.' He hadn't felt this carefree for many years and more surprisingly, he hadn't once thought of his job, his ship, or the Saucer. He idly wondered if he would still be a bachelor this time next year.

His comms signaled. It was Jeff and it was business. He and Sheila were required at a meeting with the Armada that afternoon. Capt. Vaslar wanted information about the Saucer and when Megan made the call himself everyone knew the situation was serious. They had two hours to make the most of their visit before returning to the Center. Verrringah took Sheila on a tour of their farm while Zholtair introduced Darkon to the rest of the men folk in the Outsider group. That was more than enough mental exercise for Darkon's ailing brain. He was looking forward to catching one of HS03's doctors and getting a detox pill to blow away the remaining alcohol haze.

The conference started promptly at fourteen hundred hours ship time. Megan and his team, a dozen weapons specialists and engineers, slotted into the hologram locations around the table. GMI leaders and senior Cuanta joined them. After brief introductions Megan defined their situation.

The Saucerlet was hiding inside a gas giant protected by an atmosphere their ships could not enter. Continuous electrical storms made conventional scans below six miles impossible but when limited contact was made the Saucerlet exhibited an exceptionally high specific gravity and extreme, inexplicable gravity fluctuations - both positive and negative.

'That's not a lot of information. We've been scanning the planet for six hours now, but as expected our instruments can only penetrate the surface of the atmosphere and when the signals do reflect back most of them are too scrambled to interpret. The same goes for passive surveillance, the only readings of any use are the spectrographs and they just give a general picture. As I see it there are only two choices. We either go with Hunt and Destroy, or wait for the Saucerlet to "Cut and Run" then go for the kill. If we go hunting we desperately need some new tools. And if we wait for a prison break, my grandchildren could die of old age before anything emerges.' He addressed Jeff and Jegrega, 'You should have received all the data we've collected so far. At this stage we're open to any ideas you can throw our way.'

'Thanks Megan,' Jeff answered, 'we've got your data. Our teams are dissecting it right now trying to find anything we can use. How are your teams doing Jegrega?'

'One area we are investigating is the gravity flux. We suspect the Saucer uses grav-propulsion and that implies they have negative G capability. Gravity and electrical energy are sufficiently dissimilar it may be possible to create a gravimetric imaging system.'

'But won't the sheer size of the planet drown out a ship as small as the Saucerlet?'

'It will. The gas giant in the background will obscure the signal completely. That occurs when you observe what is directly in front of you, the ship is almost impossible to see. We have to detect the changes not the scene.'

She tried to explain it in terms a soldier would understand.

'In ground combat, when your enemy is camouflaged you have difficulty seeing him. But when a soldier moves too quickly you can perceive the movement with ease even though you may not have time to determine exactly what it is that is moving. You target the movement not the entity. The gravimetric image of the planet is relatively stable and unmoving. We must design a system to work like a predator's brain, to perceive the subtle changes in flux and intensify, then highlight the movement on the viewer. It can be held as an after images when the movement stops. In theory you will be able to locate the target while is still inside the cloud layer.'

'But surely the Saucerlet will be stationary. It must know movement will give its position away.'

‘If it’s using the violent magnetic storms as camouflage those clouds are almost a hundred miles deep with violent internal dynamics. The Saucerlet will not be able to maintain a fixed position and that translates into detectable motion.’

‘So! How soon before you’ll have a prototype up and running.’

‘We are still at the theoretical stage. It will take several days to build the devise but we cannot test it in this solar system, there are no suitable planets. The imager may not work in real-world conditions.’

They were being offered a carrot, but it was held just out of reach. ‘What else can you suggest?’

‘I am Oomaran,’ a young female research analyst identified herself to the meeting, ‘before hibernation my specialty was quantum physics. I am told you have access to antimatter weapons. What is your current stock?’

‘We have seventy three five-kiloquad-units (5KU) onboard and just over a thousand 1KU missiles on standby for portal delivery. But that’s barely enough to make a dent in a gas giant let alone annihilate it.’

‘Can they be dispersed just to affect the atmosphere?’ She added?

‘I can answer that one Megan,’ it was Valery Marsler. She paused waiting the go ahead from her fleet commander, then continued…

‘Capt. Valery Marsler of the FS-S2M-46. Before the Library’s ban I conducted field trials with the Class III Anti-Matter Deployment System. We normally configure the containment field collapse so it will dispense the A.M. as either a fast moving directional arc or a slowly self expanding sphere. Once it’s released it reacts to gravity the same way as normal matter so in the gas giant it would simply sink annihilating the gas it passed through and doing the same to any of the surrounding gas that pressed in on it from all directions. At best we'd get a thousand vertical tunnels sinking to the ground and they'd be filled in within seconds.'

'What about wind dispersal within the storms?'

'No effect. Any gas particles that come in contact will the A.M. are annihilated immediately along with their kinetic energy. The bulk of the A.M. simply falls under gravity using itself up as it cuts through the atmosphere. We determined a direct strike was needed with dispersal inside the target to achieve any results.'

'What about the "slowly expanding sphere" idea?'

'The same applies. It's ideal for clearing buildings but I wouldn't recommend it for destroying an atmosphere. I don't believe the A.M. can help us with the present situation. But once we have the Saucerlet grounded we can use them to eliminate its mass.'

'Grounded! Why? Can't we use our A.M. in space? That's the promise the munitions companies gave when they were grabbing trillions of credits for development it.'

'I wouldn't want to travel through a war zone that had used Anti-Matter Capt. Vaslar. It is totally undetectable and if your starship runs through it neither shields or plating will protect you. Planetside the A.M. particles will fall under gravity and use themselves up annihilating the air and the ground. In space they could float for millennia as a worse hazard than meteor dust.'

'Totally undetectable, Valery? Surely not?'

'For all practical purposes, yes. The dispersed A.M. annihilates any active scan radiation so there's no feedback signal and there's enough distance between the A.M. molecules for the scan to pass through and return from a normal echo. We don't even get the absence of signal as you would with a black hole. After our first and only in-space test, two of the monitoring drones were written off during the fourth hour as they closed in to inspect the damage. The recovery shuttle collecting the target remnants was punctured and we lost three of the crew to asphyxia. When they examined it back in space dock sixty percent of the hull had micro perforations. The atmosphere just leaked out. It was as air tight as a sieve.'

'So why wasn't that released to the military? Why was it kept secret?'

'It became a moot point after the Library banned the research. The government didn't want to tip off any terrorist groups there was a new 'Dirty Bomb' available with a long after life. We spent three weeks with twenty starships portal-scrubbing that sector of space trying to gravitate any left-over A.M. into the local sun. Of course we had no way of telling how successful we were so the federation reclassified the whole star system as a Class-five Bio-Hazard.'

'Where does that leave us?' demanded Megan, 'No Go with detection and No Go with the Anti-Matter. What's left?' He was disappointed. 'Does anyone have any new ideas?'

'How much radiation is needed to animate the bio-matter?' Eheledana proffered a suggestion.

'Our tests indicate at sixty micro watts on both frequencies at a distance of one meter for one minute is sufficient. That has consistently produced animation.' This was Jegrega's home ground. 'But it only occurs with bio-mater the Library has already used. We had no animation after a full day of radiation using normal bio-matter. However, once animation has occurred, it will feed on any form of Bio-Matter and spread the contamination.'

'With portal powered generators a satellite ring around the planet could saturate the upper atmosphere with the activating frequencies. It might even achieve total penetration. Could that activate the Bio-Matter within the Saucerlet?'

'Is that possible,' Megan was getting interested, 'or will the signals be distorted by the storms? And how will we know how far the signal penetrates?'

'You may not need perfect penetration. With portal power you will have ample overkill capacity and loss or distortion as high as fifty percent will still leave sufficient energy to achieve activation. A micro portal near the surface of the gas giant can listen out for signals and confirm penetration. Once the planet is saturated it will not matter where the Saucerlet is located, it will be irradiated. If it remains in the atmosphere the contamination will eat it away from the inside, and if it jumps to orbit to evacuate the new ooze you will be waiting to attack.'

It was a plausible idea. The specialists thrashed out the fine details while the armada personnel retired to discuss tactics. After three hours the meeting resumed. The Cuanta were ready to begin manufacturing the satellite transmitters and the armada could start to modify their more powerful comms arrays for the new frequencies. They could be ready to configure the network within ten days. At the same time the imaging team would push ahead to prototype the gravimetric scanner. If either theory proved successful the war might soon be over.

The New Oneness within the Saucerlet was concerned. Yet again the Cuanta and Humans were working together and getting results. Hiding in the storms of this enormous planet had been an excellent choice at the time but now it was becoming a prison. After several days it had little success cracking open the gravity fused sphere to salvage the platelets. The only noticeable effect was a thin corrosive film covering the outer shell resulting from the acidic nature of the clouds. Platelets within the corrosion were being recovered and made morphable, and with them it could begin to make repairs. The New Oneness had tried temporal shocks against the pursuing starships now in low orbit around Lasthope-2 but the gas giant's mass worked against them. Temporal stress was totally ineffective this close to the planets powerful gravity well. Alternate weaponry was needed. The meldling minds circumnavigated the planet analyzing the contents of their surrounding clouds. There were a variety of chemicals it could refine to augment its depleted arsenal and it knew the humans were especially dependant on the purity of their breathing gases. What could it create to turn their air toxic? It morphed a production plant and began to compress and store both the gasses and the solid particles suspended within them. There were many chemist minds within the New Oneness and they were hatching a plan.

Day five arrived. Eleven portal powered transmitters were already built with three more under construction and the armada had finished modifying their starship comm. arrays. Every unit was tested and in full working order. They were ready to link up. But first they needed to create a portal chain between Atnera and Lasthope. Two armada ships were dispatched to act as relay posts at the militia end of the supply route. Darkon's crew on LS48 departed Atnera to do the same for the opposite end of the route, but this time Sheila was forced to remain behind. LS48 was limited to carrying only two satellites and the prototype gravimetric imager. For two long days the ships crawled across space with limited protection from their reduced solar shields. Finally they were in position.

Atnera opened the first portal to HS03 in high orbit. HS03 opened their portal to forward to a midway point between themselves and LS48. When it was stable they transmitted the coordinates to the Lifeship. Geney opened their portals to match the feed and establish an exit portal midway en-route the armada. The process continued with the final delivery portal in close proximity to Megan's command center. The portal chain was tested with an empty escape pod and after minor adjustments was working perfectly. Atnera dispatched the first satellite. It emerged three seconds later from the portal adjacent to FS-S3M-122 and was manually ported onboard. The ship's engineers immediately ran full diagnostics with positive results. One by one the remaining units were despatched through the chain and distributed among the orbiting starships. No single ship would house all the devises and make itself a target for the library. Geney reconfigured the lifeship portals to pick up the two onboard units and they too were transmitted safely.

Darkon signaled Megan to receive the next delivery directly onto his bridge and ported the Grav-Imager right into his lap. 'We have another package he advised, your new operator for the scanner. He's coming directly from the Atnera.' A short call to the Cuanta home base and a glowing orifice opened off Megan's starboard bow. He barely had time to recognize it from their earlier descriptions when a lone EVA suit exited. The glow blinked out.

'Captain Vaslar.' The voice came across the comms link in perfect galactic speak, again with a central hub accent, 'Request permission to come aboard, Authority LS48/GIO-1.'

It matched the security code Megan had received from Darkon. 'Permission Granted,' he replied automatically,

'We're opening a portal to our airlock'. The portal formed slightly to the right of the visitor who piloted the EVA suit through into the airlock and descended to the floor. As the portal collapsed artificial gravity re-established at a standard 1G and the airlock pressurized. Two junior ranks went to assist the newcomer and escort him to the bridge. They were amused at the pilot's small stature until he removed the reflective faceplate. Their mouths dropped open. It was the first time either had seen a Cuanta. The alien was used to the response. He waited for the Humans to recover. 'I am expected on the bridge,' he spoke quietly, 'Please escorting me to that location.'
It was Megan's turn to be amused when the two escorts entered the bridge. They were still shaken by their sudden exposure to the alien. 'At Ease, soldiers,' he snapped, 'Our guest only eats meat on Fridays.' He referred to an ancient Human religious practice. 'You're quite safe until then!' As the bridge crew burst into laughter the escort detail visibly relaxed.

## Cat and Mouse Games

Megan greeted the alien. 'I'm Captain Vaslar it's an honor to have you aboard. Without your help we'd be joining the rest of the guardians on the extinction pile.'
'I am Gruucaar, a member of the design team for this project. Oomaran was my student for several years before changing to another field of research' He looked about the bridge scanning the Humans equipment. 'Your own designers have been efficient with this room.'
'We put a lot of effort in to our warships, but this class of starship probably had the best designers the federation could afford. Our domestic styles are less rigid. Oomaran, the imager was her idea wasn't it?'
'It was. She has a powerful mind but she prefers to work with theoretical science. The practicality of applied science does not interest her. Where is the equipment, I will need assistance interfacing with your systems.'
Megan nodded to his comms officer, 'Send them in Lisaas.' She paged Joanah Quahn and Fransis Hitchin to the bridge. 'What can you tell me about this device? How accurate is it?'
'I assessed your vessel from the outside. We should detect movement of mass as low as thirty percent of your ship. Below that we are uncertain. Further tests are required.'
'Ah, this is Fransis, she is my Chief Engineer. And this is Joanah on Comms. He's the genius who detected your original Morse code signal.' He took Joanah aside, 'I want you to stay with Gruucaar, I think that's how he pronounces his name. Treat this as diplomatic security. Apart from keeping him in comms contact with anything and everyone he needs I expect you to make sure his personal needs are satisfied. He is unfamiliar with our ship and our culture so I'm holding you responsible for

his well being. Contact anyone you need but don't call *me* unless it's a dire emergency - do you understand?'
'Yes Sir! Have arrangements been made for his accommodation, Sir?'
'Not yet. I'll assign him the quarters we reserve for the visiting top brass. You will use the adjacent batman's cabin. And one other thing, if it comes to an emergency evacuation, his safety and the safety of his equipment is second only to mine. Without that machine and someone who can operate it we may lose this war.' He turned to leave, 'And try not to bore him with stories about your grandpa!'
Two hours later the imager was installed and ready testing. Fransis programmed an observation probe for auto recovery and released it into free fall. The imager followed the probe for two miles into the clouds then the image was lost.
'That's not far.' commented Joanah linking the ships own scanners to the adjacent screen. Their own image was slightly clearer with the probe still just visible.'
'We are eighty-five percent static and only fifteen percent motion detection,' stated Gruucaar, 'the baseline is at set to the same ratio that your human minds normally use. I am adjusting the ratio to 50-50 now.' The image jumped at them. The gas giant faded into the background with slowly rotating shadows indicating the powerful circulatory storm patterns. Just off center screen a clear pulsing light indicated the last known position of the probe.'
'Ten seconds to go.' Called Fransis, 'then the probe should start maneuvering, if it survived the storms… … … Five seconds… … … any time now!' on cue the probe's image burst into brightness repeating a slow figure of eight pattern as it continued to descend. The

ship's scanner couldn't compete. 'What depth are we at now?' enquired Fransis.

'Twelve decimal four miles and accelerating vertically.' the Cuanta replied. 'At what depth is it programmed to return to orbit?'

'It'll attempt that at the twenty five miles mark, if the control module is still intact.' They waited in silence watching the two screens.

'Twenty miles… … … Twenty-three miles... ... ... adjusting ratio to 25:75.' The image was becoming blurred but the probes position was easily visible as a bright point. Crosshairs on the screen pinpointed the location of the strongest signal, and were augmented by positional parameters in both Human and Cuanta notation.

'Twenty-five miles and still descending - acceleration is decreasing - twenty-six miles.'

'Twenty-seven decimal eight miles - no vertical momentum'

'Twenty-six miles, it is rising… … …'

'Twenty-five miles… … … Twenty-four miles… … …Twenty-three miles'

They waited as the image increased in size.

'It's on our own scanner again.' cried Joanah, and we're getting its telemetry.

'It's not going to break orbit. It's not reached escape velocity and it's using full thruster power. It's barely maintaining altitude.'

Fransis switched her station to portal control and fed in the parameters from the imaging screen. After forty seconds of frenzied activity her excited cry punctured the atmosphere on the bridge, 'Got it!' she exclaimed; and immediately apologized to the Duty Bridge Officer. She must remember to keep her excitement under control. After all she told herself, "I am the Chief Engineer of a military ship and we are on active duty". In a quieter voice she added, 'I'm sending a recovery detail to bring it in.'

A few minutes examination confirmed their fears. Twenty minutes exposure to the atmosphere had eaten away almost all the probe's superstructure. Its fuel cells, too unstable to recover, were jettisoned and exploded from a safe distance. Their additional protection around the control module had dissolved totally and in another minute the module itself would have been exposed and destroyed. That confirmed it: there was no way their ships could fly into the clouds to hunt the Saucerlet.

The results were good: the grav-imager passed the short range test. Its data was consistent with the probe's nav-logs to within zero point five percent. It was a better than expected. The next test would be live. First they would scan the planet from high orbit. This would push the imager to its limits and probably beyond. As they dropped to lower orbits the chances of the saucer avoiding their scan increased as they would need to follow conventional search patterns. The Imager used passive techniques so the Saucerlet could not detect them, but they did not know what capability the Meld had for monitoring their activity. The next few hours would be intense, so they adjourned for a break and a meal.

Joanah showed Gruucaar his quarters and a few minutes later they entered the mess hall. Every crewman's head turned to watch the alien. Joanah thought quickly, he grabbed an empty glass and a heavy knife and struck them together as a gong several times. 'Your attention please,' he asked knowing full well he already had the attention of everyone in the room. 'Your attention please, I'd like to introduce you to Gruucaar. He's the first of our Cuanta allies to be seconded to the fleet. You'll be seeing him around the ship for several days. Please give a round of applause to welcome him aboard.' He started clapping, and the mess hall followed suit. As the roar died down the soldiers returned to their meal, satisfied their presence had been acknowledged.

'Well handled Quahn,' said Megan as they reached the officer's table. 'Please join us.' He offered an adjacent seat to the Cuanta specialist, leaving Joanah to find a place at the far end of the table.' Over the meal discussion continued to determine a stratagem for the surface scans. Gruucaar explained the limitations of the Grav-Imager, and Megan advised the ships capability. Fransis Hitchin his chief engineer listened in knowing it was she who would make the final decision and carry the can for the mission's success or failure. She would need to liaise with Megan to arrange backup support in the event the Saucerlet attempted to escape. It would be a busy shift.

An hour later they assembled on the bridge. Plans had been thrashed out. The satellites were launched and active. Three starships escorted the leader. They would be ready to defend or attack depending upon what fate had in store.

'Ready when you are captain,' advised Fransis.

'Attention all ships. Attention all ships.' Capt. Vaslar's voice penetrated the air waves. 'Commencing Search pattern Alpha. I say again, Commencing Search pattern Alpha.' He nodded to Fransis.

She checked the ship's scanner and indicated to Gruucaar to start the Grav-Imager for grid block one. Five minutes later he confirmed "Nothing Detected".

They continued for two hours until every grid block had been checked.'

'Search pattern Alpha complete sir. No contacts. Ready to initiate Search pattern Beta,'

'Attention all ships. Attention all ships.' Vaslar's voice chilled the air waves a second time. 'Commencing Search pattern Beta. I say again, Commencing Search pattern Beta.'

He was not disappointed. His career had taught him patience. When searching for survivors after a battle, adherence to the search algorithm brought the best results. Hunches, emotions, they only wasted time and worked against the repetitive slog of Block by Block scanning. Eight hours later he was not surprised to hear Fransis' voice again. She was clearly disappointed with the results.

'Search pattern Beta complete sir. No contacts. Ready to initiate Search pattern Charley,'

'Attention all ships. Attention all ships.' Vaslar's voice resonated for the third time. 'Commencing Search pattern Charley. I say again, Commencing Search pattern Charley.'

This, the third and final search, would take a full day. He handed over to the First Mate and went for his scheduled break. After dinner before returning to the bridge he put a comms link through to Jegrega to keep his allies up to date with developments. He confirmed the Bio-Transmitter grid was working after nine hours continuous operation and significant animation signals were penetrating to ground level. They discussed the lack of Grav-Imaging on the first two scans and Jegrega admitted there was a less than twenty percent expectation of success. He was more optimistic for the longer low orbit scan and confided there was a slight risk that the Saucerlet had already disintegrated. Megan preferred to ignore that possibility. He wanted positive indication, whether it was good or bad.

He'd been back on the bridge for three hours when there was a flurry of activity around the imager. They were detecting something. 'It's gone again'.

'I have noted the Grid position. We will execute a lower orbit scan after we complete the current search pattern.' Gruucaar was not going to be led astray by the first sporadic signal. 'Continue scanning the grid block.'

Ten minutes later they had another hit. And this time, although faint, the image was steady. Whatever the target was it was jumping around a within a four mile radius and its depth varying between twenty-two and twenty-three decimal six miles. Every few minutes the image leapt several miles outside its normal range then pulled back within seconds. 'If that's the Saucerlet, I'd hate to be inside without inertial dampers.' She looked at the Grav-Imager, 'Is there any indication of its mass, Gruucaar?'

'It must be at least the minimum size, thirty percent of this ships mass, or the signal would not be this strong. It could be considerably larger.'

'Captain, we have a target.'

Megan examined the imaging screen. The signal was steady and strong. It was his call. They knew of no other ship in the area and it was unlikely any other ship could survive the atmosphere. No natural phenomenon could have such dense mass unless a volcano was erupting and he could rule that out since there was no infra red signature. 'Monitor it for another twenty minutes and see if it remains stable, but keep our ship running the same search pattern. If it is our Saucer we don't need to show it we've got its position.' He returned to the bridge and dialed in the coordinates from imager. 'Attention all ships. Attention all ships. I'm transmitted targeting coordinates. Commence transmitting carrier waves on both predefined frequencies at full power until further orders. All ships trim for battle.' Battle Alerts sounded throughout the fleet.

'Capt. Marsler, break formation and vector twenty miles aft of my position. Prime three A.M.s for downward directional dispersal to release zero decimal five miles above target. Link targeting to Imaging System.'

There was a short pause, 'Missiles primed and locked.'

Gruucaar waited for the next lateral shunt. As soon as it occurred he called out, 'Strike!'

Megan ordered, 'Fire when Ready!'

Valery flipped the safety and fired. 'Missiles hot and running' she advised. Three torpedoes tore into the atmosphere angling downwards towards their detonation point. When the control signals faded they switched to inertial guidance to complete their task. Nine seconds later with their position confirmed the trio of torpedoes, dropped power collapsing their secondary containment fields. Anti-matter poured out annihilating the protective domes and falling downward within the walls of the Primary containment cone. A split second later the secondary containment field regenerated, ballooning above the A.M., propelling it down the inverting cone at incredible speed. Gasses in their path disappeared into nothingness the deadly particles giving no hint of their approach as they fanned out. Half a mile deeper as they passed through their target altitude they comprised three quarter-mile overlapping disks of annihilation. The Saucerlet had been the source of the signal but its location at the moment the destructive wave swept past was barely within the containment zone. Only a portion of the sphere came in contact with the Anti-Matter but that was sufficient to annihilate almost eight percent of its mass. Instantly the ship morphed to seal the breach before the corrosive gasses could begin their work. Quickly it salvaged the now exposed bio-matter and began to decompress accessible platelets from around the edges of the slice. The recovered grav-thruster was now accessible, it was dismantled and rebuilt.

The New Oneness realized it was in danger. Anti-matter weapons made it unsafe to remain within the clouds. Twice more the armada released A. M. and twice more it sustained significant damage. Whatever tracking system the Humans were using it was too effective. The Saucerlet must escape or gradually be eroded away. It computed an evasion pattern at the extremity of its safe depth and worked quickly to restructure itself in preparation for flight. Carefully it guarded the weaponry newly created from Hide's atmosphere as it tracked towards the northern magnetic pole. Soon it would be ready to break cover. The fleet trailed behind, releasing anti-matter at irregular intervals. Five more releases, four partial hits.

As it approached the pole the Saucerlet amassed tremendous static charge within it shell. It was almost ready. Positioning itself directly above the magnetic pole it transmitted the charge to its outer surface and was instantly repelled with immense acceleration along the gas giant's magnetic flux. As it shot through the upper atmosphere trailing threads extending dissipating the static charge, freeing itself from the grip of Hide's powerful magnetosphere. Its Grav-Thrusters turned negative augmenting the departure and affording directional control to the Saucerlet. At near superluminary speed the Saucerlet escaped Hide's immense gravity and headed away from Lasthope. The chase was on and in close pursuit were seven of the best armed starship in the federation. Jujag Jugarn captained FS-S1M-37 the latest and fastest Battle Station starship. It led the pack and was closing in on Saucerlet. Then it made a fatal mistake. It opened a portal between the ships and began transmitting the Bio-activation Signals at full strength. The Saucerlet retaliated immediately opening a valve to a pressurized compartment and discharged a stream of contaminated magma through the miniature portals directly into the path of the lead ship. At the same time it generated a command signal to lower the ship's defensive shields. The minds of the New Oneness had infiltrated the armada spying from within the ship bridges. It took only one unguarded moment for the new access code to be observed and stolen. Now it would cost the ship it life.

## Kill or be Killed

As the shields dropped Jugarn's starship ran headlong and unprotected into the molten stream. It sliced through the lightweight alloys taking out critical systems and structures before exiting the tail end of the ship. Instantly, on first impact, FS-S1M-37 fell silent - their comms capability melted. Air vented from the ship as safety bolts sealed the cabins preventing access to the central core of the ship. Half the crew died in the first barrage. From the twin engine rooms automated distress calls were initiated but never completed. The armada picked up the beginning of their two automated signals. The first an Space-Zero emergency call, the second a data stream from the Black-box in reverse time sequence. The Saucerlet came to an abrupt halt in space for a mere half second, just long enough to disgorge a blanket of granulated rock in the flight path of the stricken starship. It returned to full power to make good its escape. When the pursuit ship, without its shields and still running at full power, ploughed into the rock the effect was the same as being ravaged by a barrage of meteor fragments. The crew had no time to reach the escape pods before the ship and everyone inside were peppered by the deadly impacts. In the blink of an eye the pride of the federation was transformed to mass of useless space junk. Seventy two souls perished.

Captain Smitte, on the support ship FS-CH-107, immediately ported an inspection/recovery droid onto the bridge. With the speed differential between the starships it was jettisoned through the ship into space with its rear scanners transmitting the first images of the carcass. The portals were quickly repositioned capturing the droid and returning it to the ship's bridge. It began the inspection but within minutes it became clear the damage was irreparable. Two automated Tug shuttles were ported ahead of the ship to bring it under control. They would extend their shields to preserve the ship's remains for later human examination.

By the time the fleet caught up with them the Black-box transmissions had been analyzed. What had happened was clear. How it had happened, that was a different matter. Jugarn's penchant for security was well known and it was fortunate that no Cuanta had visited the ship since decontamination. Even the Bio-transmitter satellites had been held inside containment fields while they were onboard. Only the captain and three senior officers had personal security codes to access critical ship's systems and Jugarn insisted the bridge officers change their code at each shift handover. The black box record identified the code used to lower shields. It belonged to the on duty bridge officer and he had updated it less than an hour before the attack. What confounded them was their total comms blackout had only been broken for only three status update signals none of which contained the code change and in any case all the transmissions were short range directional and encrypted. There was no way for a saboteur or spy, Human or Cuanta, to intercept the information. Yet, the Library had acquired the code and used it against them with staggering success.

The armada was in a dilemma. If they deactivated control of their critical systems via remote comms they would be seriously handicapped if internal comms were disrupted. The bridge would be unable to control engineering in the event of a hull breach in that section, a high risk during battle. If they kept remote control intact, they would be vulnerable to the Saucerlet repeating the attack. Captain Smitte completed recovery of the disabled ship and had it secured internally within its maintenance dry-dock when the second attack struck. The two starships from the Sagittarius-Carina arm of the Milky Way were the target. Simultaneously their shields failed and outboard docking thrusters fired sending them on a collision course. Without shields their combined momentum would be catastrophic. Several starships engaged manipulator beams across the two vessels to hold them apart. Vaslar watched in horror as one by one the beams collapsed and the haze around each of the starships vanished. That haze represented the outer edge of the ships' shields. They were unprotected from the impending detonation. With seconds to spare Smitte released docking clamps on his two automated Tugs and ported them between the endangered starships. With their onboard AI systems online they immediately recognized the colliding ships as a threat and triggered protective protocols. Their shields activated instantly, expanding and interlocking to cushion the impact. Manipulator beams locked on their wards restrain them attempting to absorb their momentum. It gained the precious seconds needed for the fleet to re-establish control of their systems. Starship shields were reactivated and powerful manipulators augmented the tugs while teams of engineers raced to the manual overrides to cut off the docking thrusters.

As soon as order was restored Megan ported over to Vargan Smitte on the Support ship,

'What happened, Vargan? What's special with your ship and how come your systems weren't disrupted?'

'They were and we lost all our automated systems too, but we ***are*** a Support ship,' he replied. 'We've got a dozen additional levels of redundancy and considerably higher safety factors all around.'

'You're portals were still working though! How come? Whatever you've got we need it and we need it fast.' Megan was deadly serious.
'That's the easy part Megan.' he explained giving a crash course on Support Ship design, 'Only the ship's *normal* portals link into the remote comms. The ones we use around the dry dock are all hard wired to individual control stations. It keeps comms interference to a minimum and prevents accidents. It's the same for the tug's systems. We can't control any of it from outside, not even in an emergency. We'd have to port someone directly into the tug's cockpit, and he'd need to know all about the AI and how to override it.'
'So we just need to pull the comms plugs, right? It's that easy?'
'Can't be done, Megan, comms are an integral part of the system. Most of the safeguards and failsafe features are interlinked through the comms. The dry dock systems were specially designed without the safeties. That's why it costs a small fortune to train our operators. Some of them earn more than me!'
'Can't we just disable the comms circuits?'
'Not in practice. Look at it this way, without the comms safeguards there's nothing to make safety adjustments when you port aboard. Nine times out of ten when a portal opens it could slice through critical cables and components - that's where the safety Protocols come in. When we open the dry dock portals it's always done at least a hundred meters clear of every structure. The trick I just pulled with the tugs, that's the first time in fifteen years I've used a dock-portals without being able to see both openings clearly. If the ships had crashed … well … I'd rather not think about that … but we'd nothing to lose so I took the risk trusting my coordinates were right …

I've never been so scared in my life. Normally when we port Shuttle Tugs we try to use the ship's primary system.'

'How much duplication does your Support ship have?'

'There's plenty of spare capacity. With portal generators, we have the usual four for the drive thrusters, another four for general purpose, and one heavy duty long range model. Oh yes, and there's a GP model in each of the escape shuttles.'

'And Shields?'

'That's a problem. All three shield systems, weapons control, and short range sensors are fully integrated. I doubt the designers could uncouple them.' He thought for a few minutes, 'How portable are your independent shields? How many do you have?'

'Just double redundancy. We need five to protect the dry dock when we're fully operational, and a sixth as backup for the main ship. They're all anchored into Impact Safe housings.' He guessed where Megan's line of questions was leading 'That only leaves four truly portable units. They would need to be carefully preprogrammed for each Ship, and without comms they won't be able to interlink.'

Megan made some fast mental calculations. 'Could one unit extend to protect two of the smaller Battle Cruisers? They're the same class so they can be "Close-Docked", at the fore and aft airlocks, they could function as a single ship.'

It was Vargan's turn with the calculations. He flipped open a hand unit and checked the shielding parameters against the starship specifications. 'It'll give you Ninety-three percent standard strength subluminary, and ninety-one percent above that. But the power drain will be enormous. You won't be able to run it at the same time as your main shields or the power conduit will vaporize.' He

saw a sly grin wrap round his commanders face. 'O. K. Megan, I can have them re-programmed and fitted in about two hours.'
'Good man. No comms chatter about this I'll port to the fleet commanders myself and bring them into the loop. I want to be ready to go after this damn Saucerlet in three hours at the latest. It's personal now.' He left to circumnavigate the armada.
With minutes to spare on his two hour deadline Vargan put a comms call through to Megan confirming the fleet had been upgraded. There were two controls to initiate the backup shields. They could be activated from the bridge or engine room at the touch of an icon/button but to power down it took a keyed switch that had to be held on for five seconds. Even then the ships normal shields would simultaneously re-activate. There were no feedback circuits, no hardware and no software for the Library to tap into to kill the system. There was one big drawback: if a ship died with this type of shielding active there would be no way to get back inside to turn it off. The second startup was linked to the ships Comms system. If the main shields went offline for any reason, it would activate the backup system automatically. Again the system could only be shut down using the manual shutdown procedure. It was the STAW & STAC principal again. Vargan was pleased with the work. The fleet was ready
The armada returned to pursue the Saucerlet. Six ships, two locked together like proverbial Siamese twins, and a shuttle with its cargo of ooze in tow sped after their quarry. Megan understood how Santa Anna felt on the last night at the Alamo. Next time they engaged the enemy no quarter would be given and none expected. Nothing could

be allowed to survive. The battle would go down as the turning point in Human/Cuanta history.

The twinned battle cruisers were leading the pack. Their double thrust capability made them a difficult target to disable and being Close-Docked two meshed sets of shield/deflectors could withstand the heaviest assault. Beside and to their rear in V-formation were Megan and Valery's battle station class starships and at the trailing edges of the "V" hung their third battle cruiser and Vargan's combat ready space dock. This time as they approached the target they opened a single large portal directly ahead of their formation. They started transmitting the Bio-activation frequencies, six focused beams with their point of convergence centered on the Saucer. Within seconds their target began dancing violently in an attempting to escape the beams. It may not know what their affect would be but it knew they were dangerous.

It retaliated against the lead vessels venting another stream of radioactive magna towards the portal. A fraction of a second later in rapid succession the twin lead ships' defense shields collapsed but this time backup system kicked in. The New Oneness watched in dismay as its salvo of molten death splattered on contact with shields that had no right to be there. It retransmitted the shutdown codes several times but the tell tail aura of the shields stubbornly refused to fade. It jettisoned a second volley towards Megan's ship and transmitted their shutdown codes but to no avail the result was the same. The shields flickered once but appeared to remain online. It was bewildering. When the Humans resumed their pursuit the Oneness had dispatched a team of minds to infiltrate each ship. Unseen and undetectable the incorporeal entities hovered around the bridge and

engineering stations of every ship, their sole task was to spy on the duty officers as they routinely updated their codes. The minds could easily sense the keyboard strokes as the Humans entered them, even in the dark. It was impossible to have made mistakes. The New Oneness knew the authorization codes it sent were correct, but the starship shields were still active.
What it didn't know, what it couldn't know, was everyone involved when the new system was installed had been ordered to silence. They crews knew somehow the Library was spying within the ships, visually, audibly, tacitly, maybe advanced nanomite technology had been introduced, they weren't sure - but they couldn't ignore that somehow it ***was*** observing them. They realized the dire need for silence and absolute security. After the installation no one had spoken, written or even dared to joke about the new system. The Library had no clue, no way of to know how much the hardware had changed. And without understanding, it was mystified and was getting angrier by the minute.
It had re-morphed its teleport system but with limited power it would need to get very close to the fleet and maneuver to a more suitable position before its next weapon could be effective. That required careful planning, and would take time to prepare. For protection and to gain valuable thinking time the Saucerlet raced into the corona of an adjacent star. It could take the heat and radiation but the Humans would need to remain at a safe distance. There would be sufficient distance and ample time to avoid their A. M. attacks. It insulated its inner core allowing the outer sphere to soak up the radiation on the sunward side and retransmit some of it outward. The rest was used to irradiate its own armory. Within minutes

it was optically invisible to the armada, and feeling secure.

But that was before Gruucaar switched on the gravimetric imager. The Saucerlet jumped out, highlighted at center screen. The fleet feigned an attack, portals like butterfly nets swept downwards towards the Saucerlet missing it each time by a few hundred yards as their target nimbly sidestepped each pass. It was an easy avoidance but at each pass the humans analyzed the Saucerlet's escape stratagem. Once again the New Oneness became angry. It was too easy to avoid these Humans. A simple side step of a several hundred yards in one of six directions and it could still maintain the same solar altitude with barely an effort, but it was getting irritated and annoyed. Their butterfly net swept down again, and again, and again. It was becoming bored!

That was just what the Humans wanted. Its escape pattern was becoming predictable. Their butterfly net swept down again, and this time as the saucer began to move six sets of portals opened across its predicted escape paths. Before the saucer realized what was happening it was flashing through one of the gaping orifices to emerge twenty percent closer to the sun's core at the deepest point the portal could retain integrity.

Instantly the Saucerlet reversed gravimetric polarity and shot back through the open portal before it collapsed. Had it been Human the New Oneness would have smirked. Its lightning fast reactions had been too fast for their pathetic trick to work.

But, its gloating victory was short lived. As it shot through the exit portal it was no longer in real time/space. This environment was surreal. There were no stars, no radiation, no gravity an emptiness devoid of everything. It tasted the temporal stresses to feel how far it had moved.

It knew Human portals could not possibly propel it beyond the limits of the expanding universe.
But here there was nothing, oblivion. Had it have been shunted through time itself to a period before the "Big Bang"? 'Impossible!' thought the New Oneness. Humans even with Cuanta help could not command the energy needed for such an excursion.
Then realization hit. It was still close to the star it had been basking in moments earlier and if it could not sense those surroundings it meant only one thing. It had ***not*** emerged from the portal, or to be more precise, it had not emerged from a closed circuit of back-to-back portals. The Humans were treating it the way it treated the two hijacked teams from Atnera. It had bounced the soldiers through the same back-to-back portals for a thousand cycles before opening an entry into its prison. Now it was the Library's turn to be trapped inside the void of never ending portal transits.
The minds of the New Oneness attempted to breach the walls of the imprisoning torus and observe from the safety of space. Immediately they were returned through the opposite wall of the tunnel. They tried again, and again. Not even their minds could escape. For the first time in the span of six civilizations their minds and the Saucerlet were ensnared, helplessly trapped. Within the void their immense momentum would coast them effortlessly through this corridor of meaningless nothingness for all eternity holding them incommunicado with the rest of the universe forever. The minds were scared. They were terrified. Until their vessel came to a stop it was impossible to investigate for weaknesses where the portals meshed, for weaknesses where it might be possible to morph between the microscopic gaps.

With no other matter in the torus their grav thrusters were useless. There was only one way to achieve any velocity reduction: primitive jet propulsion. It re-evaluated the chemicals it had stored from Hide's atmosphere, and morphed a potent mixture. Several hours later, like an antique rocket ship, it fired retro rockets in a slow controlled burst that would last almost a day. It had to carefully balance its decelerating locus between the portals. A single impact would impart spin that would take excessive energy to neutralize or worse create unpredictable effects and damage. Once relative speed reached near zero it could begin eating away at the portals. Meanwhile it was trapped, an animal awaiting its own slaughter. But this beast was going down fighting. And once it was free it would extract a slow and terrible vengeance against its captors.

# Space Zero The Meld

## Death Knell

Megan and Vargan were pleased with their success. It was obvious the Saucerlet would eventually break free of the containment circle, portal integrity couldn't be sustained indefinitely. Even portal thrusters collapse occasionally. They would need a more permanent solution before the inevitable happened.

An emergency meeting was called but with portals fully engaged maintaining the torus the senior staff had to shuttle across to Megan's wardroom. Once there the first item on the agenda was to assess their resources. They had Bio-transmitters and the Ooze was still under the tug's control but with all available portal generators committed to the containment ring it was be too risky attempting to introduce it into the circle manually. Darkon's Lifeship was speeding towards them but it might not arrive in time. As an interim measure targeting co-ordinates were locked into every armament to allow conventional torpedoes to respond instantly if the Saucerlet breached containment. If the portal joints failed the need for caution would be over and further incidental damage would be irrelevant. They brainstormed their options with the ooze. It could be ported inside the Saucerlet, or the enemy vessel could be coated with the quivering mass like a layer of icing sugar over a birthday cake. But unless they could limit its morphing and neutralize its grav-thrusters it might still escape.

'Once it breaks out, it will probably make an escape bid immediately.' Captain Rick Larester of the FS-S1F-84, one of the paired battle cruisers, had been studying the Saucerlet's tactics. 'It seems to prefer "Hit and Run" guerrilla tactics rather than open warfare. There may be some options there. It's tried several attacks but I don't think it has many armaments, and certainly no conventional weapons.'

If its thrusters go negative,' hypothesized Valery, 'we could surround the Saucerlet with at four high density masses in pyramid formation. That would lock the saucer tightly at the center. It would be forced to use positive thrust to escape. We'd get a brief window to target it with high velocity gravity torpedoes, with the full range of munitions including the ooze.'

'And,' Vargan added, 'if we install torpedoes on the four large masses then whichever one the Saucerlet attracts itself to, to initiate an escape, it will be in perfect position for a short range strike.' Captain Smitte was familiar with resistance fighting. 'And at slow speeds grav-thrust is not particularly maneuverable.'

Megan wanted to know what would be used to create the four masses. 'The Library may have chosen this star deliberately because of its lack of planets. It's not much use for ambush but at the same time there's nowhere to hide and very little matter to use as ammunition.'

'How much mass can you hold in dry dock, Vargan, assuming its high density?'

'Probably three times as much as you need considering the Saucerlet's current size. What're you thinking Valery? The dock's portals have a very limited range.'

'Darkon's ship must be passing a few star systems on his way here, and the LS48 has long range portal capability. Can he pick up some very dense rocks for us?'

'If he can, we could use the docks portals to position them at critical points around the containment zone. Hey! We could even choose when to let the saucer escape.' Vargan smiled, 'I'll get him on the comms now. We'll need to thrash out the best way deliver them.' He left the meeting to make arrangements.

Darkon was pleased to get back into the fight even if he would only be playing the role of supply officer. A slight detour took him within portal range of a local star's Oort cloud. He ported continuously until his ship passed beyond range, and by then the dry dock was eighty five percent full. It made Vargan's vessel slow to maneuver but that would only be for a short period while his crew manually created the four carefully positioned rock piles. Seven hours later the task was complete. Megan handed over missile control to Fransis Hitchin. As his Chief Engineer she was the person most conversant with their armaments. Secretly she liaised with Valery in case they were able to force the saucer into a gravity well where their anti-matter weapons could safely be used. She was covering all the bases. The ships, except for Vargan's dry dock, took formation juxtaposed the four rock masses checking every onboard system and confirming their status. They were ready for battle.

Megan fired the distress flare, a comms-free signal visible to every vessel. When the flare erupted the armada initiated the Bio-activation transmitters and exactly two second later the six ships in unison collapsed all portals. Instantly the entrapment circle vanished. The saucerlet was free. With portal capability restored the three battle cruisers immediately migrated thirty percent of the ooze directly into the heart of the Saucerlet while the remaining ships ported the residue to surround and cloak its hull. Taken aback by the abruptness of the attack the New Oneness was slow to respond. As expected its thrusters went full negative, but to the dismay of the New Oneness the vessel barely moved. The sheer mass of the rock piles held it firmly at their C-of-G. There was barely detectable movement with each pile outweighing the Saucerlet by two orders of magnitude. Before the ship could reverse polarity it was attacked by the first barrage of missiles. It morphed passageway holes successfully letting the missiles pass safely through, then they reversed direction to try again.

During the precious seconds before they reversed for their next pass the Saucerlet took the initiative. Two teleports opened deep inside its heart and two nuggets of highly radioactive heavy metals just short of critical mass were gripped by magnetic force fields. The Saucerlet waited for the few nanoseconds that the shields would drop as the next ship fired a volley. The unlucky starship was Megan's sister ship the FS-S3F-24 captained by Hosane Ragoon. As the torpedoes launched two masses of uranium 239 materialized inside his ship at the same point in space. Together they exceeded critical mass. Geiger Müller counters responded but for too short a period to be of any use. Within the protective walls of the ship's shields a nuclear furnace erupted creating immense pressure. A split second later the vessel vaporized. Its shields collapsed and like an atomic pressure cooker breaking containment, radiation and plasma burst into space tossing the armada and its hostage around like ears of corn in a squall. Had they been in close formation it would have been the end for the fleet. But separated as they were alongside the four now fused rock piles they withstood the devastation, dented but unbroken.

To his credit, Hosane's final salvo escaped the fury almost intact. His missiles ran hot and true towards their quarry. At five miles out a network of force fields from both salvoes sprung to life enmeshing the Saucerlet just as its grav-polarity went positive. The hog-tied vessel shot forward heading for the largest rock pile and ran full-frontal into a broadside from the pile's own missile bank. It fought back releasing a bombardment of molten rock and shrapnel radiating outward in all directions. Several missiles in the force net detonated but the net held and re-meshed. The Saucerlet still accelerating crashed through the rocks its force field expelling shrapnel in a star burst of its own. The force net tightened and strengthened with every missile transmitting the twin bio-frequencies at extremely close range. Still gaining velocity the Saucerlet was dragging more than five hundred missiles and the ooze along with it. The armada followed close on its heels firing more barrages to reinforce the net, strengthening its deadly hold. The Saucer's force field flickered, then again, and the haze began to dim. The ooze inside it was finally working. As its shields weakened the force net tightened like a boar constrictor squeezing life sustaining air from of its prey. Several torpedoes exploded within the force net reflecting their shock waves back into the Saucerlet. And when its shields finally collapsed the shell of the sphere was assaulted by three hundred hungry warheads. The outer ooze twitched convulsively several times, paused frozen in space for almost a minute. Then the head end jerked sending a ripple of movement through the bloated mass. It jerked again and again as its rhythmic pulsing returned. It appeared to shrink as it soaked into its victim's sphere. An hour later it extruded back to the outside and detached from what was left of the saucerlet.

Quickly containment fields were regenerated and the shuttle once more took control of their repulsive ally. Cautiously probes approached the Saucerlet's remains. Their scans showed only inorganic matter. The ooze had done a thorough job. Two sonics probes were dispatched to dispose of any remaining platelets before Cuanta's nanomites were released to deconstruct whatever debris remained. The five surviving captains were satisfied.

They ported the debris close to the star and utilized a dozen anti-matter bombs with slowly expanding dispersion to annihilate the remains. When they were satisfied nothing remained the shuttle tug gave the 'coup de grace' to their unwilling ally, porting the deadly ooze into the heart of the star.

When Darkon and his crew arrived an hour later it was all over. A service was held for their deceased comrades and, as the "Roll of Honor" was read, their coffins were jettisoned into the same star. In tribute to their sacrifice, the rock piles were refined and fused into the time honored six-bar cross with their names etched deeply into its surface. The cross was released into solar orbit where, for a thousand years, passing starships could download the hero's names and a history of the battles that saved their species from extinction.

# Space Zero The Meld

## The Epilogue

Three day later the armada returned to Atnera to join the celebrations. By then negotiations with the federation were under way. The limit of a thousand sentiments had passed and the Cuanta were welcomed into full membership of the Federation. Two star systems with ideally habitable planets were assigned for their exclusive use and back at the Central Hub transport fleets were assembling to assist their relocation.

Darkon and Sheila visited Zholtair and Verrringah at the Outsider village. They watched the sun slowly setting and recalled First Contact: strangers coming together in hope and trust, united by a common enemy. Against all odds they had survived the Meld's genocidal intent and their cultures had grown strong together. Tomorrow would see the dawn of a new era. Darkon and Sheila looked forward to the next sunrise.

The New Oneness conceded defeat. During the centuries to follow it would rejoin the old Meld where once again the gentler minds would balance its aggression. By its own violation it had abandoned the physical realm and now after Human and Cuanta ingenuity had shattered any hope of returning, its fate was sealed.

Time itself would degrade any value the Meld's immortality once possessed. Already it could feel the universe around it speeding up and isolated in this ethereal void all it could do was think.

And those thoughts were becoming more difficult, more abstract, more meaningless, and more singular.

In the end a solitary thought remained … … …

**"I AM!"**

# Appendices

## Glossary of Terms

| | |
|---|---|
| ACODEA | Name for the Meld and the Library entity in the Cuanta Language |
| AI | Artificial Intelligence |
| AKC | Alexandria Knowledge Center, AKA 'The Library' |
| Cuanta | The fifth Guardian Species |
| FSS | Federation Space Service |
| GMI | Galactic Merchant Insurance |
| Graveyard Fleet | GMI's Solar Scrap Yard for Obsolete/Written-Off Space Vehicles |
| Gravnami | Temporal Shockwave |
| Horned Rucktan | Semi-Domesticated herbivore often used as a Beast of Burden |
| HS | Hospital Starship |
| Library (the...) | A learning faculty created by the Meld |
| LCC | Library Center Complex |
| LS | Lifeboat starship |
| MD | Managing Director |
| Meld (the...) | A civilization of disembodied minds that have abandoned the corporeal form: The Creators of the "Library" |
| Meldlings | Individual Non-Corporeal Minds within the Meld |
| PA | Public Announcement System |
| Planetside | The accessible surface area of a planet |
| Rob-3 | Robot: General-Purpose Mark III, Ore-Freighter - standard issue |
| SL-VR | SuperLuminary Virtual Reality - VR for Starships at Warp Speed |
| Stargun | Space-Hole Teleporter Gun |
| STAW & STAC | "Simple Things Always Work & Simple Things Are Cheap" |
| Saucer (the...) | The Morphing Starship used by the Library mind Subset of the Meld |
| Saucerlet | A detachable segment of a Saucer morphed for a special task. |
| Portal | A 'Doorway' connecting two distant locations in across physical space |
| Superluminary | Velocity Exceeding Light Speed, (i.e. > 186 miles/second) |
| Vanquanda | An aggressive, amphibious, reptilian carnivore length > 3 meters |
| Waiter-bot | Robot: General-Purpose, Programmed for Restaurant Service |

\

# Planets & Moons

| anet | | Names of Orbiting Moons | |
|---|---|---|---|
| **me-&-Position** | **Local Name** | **Moons** | **< - Inner Orbit - - - - - Outer Orbit - >** |
| exandria-3 | The Library | none | |
| nera-1 | Atnera | none | (Hibernation Center for the Cuanta) |
| e-3 | | 1 | Bounty |
| sthope-1 | Seek | None | (Volcanically active) |
| sthope-2 | Hide | None | (Gas giant) |
| adray-1 | | none | |
| adray-2 | | none | |
| adray-3 | | 1 | Woodar |
| -3 | Earth | 1 | Luna |
| loma-2 | | 4 | Aramaic, Bumara, Corinne, Delta |
| gonia | | none | |
| ydom-4 | Troy | 1 | Helena |

# Index to Chapters